HARD
EVIDENCE

PAMELA CLARE

BERKLEY SENSATION, NEW YORK

THE BERKLEY PUBLISHING GROUP
Published by the Penguin Group
Penguin Group (USA) Inc.
375 Hudson Street, New York, New York 10014, USA
Penguin Group (Canada), 90 Eglinton Avenue East, Suite 700, Toronto, Ontario M4P 2Y3, Canada
(a division of Pearson Penguin Canada Inc.)
Penguin Books Ltd., 80 Strand, London WC2R 0RL, England
Penguin Group Ireland, 25 St. Stephen's Green, Dublin 2, Ireland (a division of Penguin Books Ltd.)
Penguin Group (Australia), 250 Camberwell Road, Camberwell, Victoria 3124, Australia
(a division of Pearson Australia Group Pty. Ltd.)
Penguin Books India Pvt. Ltd., 11 Community Centre, Panchsheel Park, New Delhi—110 017, India
Penguin Group (NZ), Cnr. Airborne and Rosedale Roads, Albany, Auckland 1310, New Zealand
(a division of Pearson New Zealand Ltd.)
Penguin Books (South Africa) (Pty.) Ltd., 24 Sturdee Avenue, Rosebank, Johannesburg 2196, South
Africa

Penguin Books Ltd., Registered Offices: 80 Strand, London WC2R 0RL, England

This is a work of fiction. Names, characters, places, and incidents either are the product of the author's
imagination or are used fictitiously, and any resemblance to actual persons, living or dead, business es-
tablishments, events, or locales is entirely coincidental. The publisher does not have any control over
and does not assume any responsibility for author or third-party websites or their content.

HARD EVIDENCE

A Berkley Sensation Book / published by arrangement with the author

PRINTING HISTORY
Berkley Sensation mass-market edition / October 2006

Copyright © 2006 by Pamela White.
Cover design by Rita Frangie.
Interior text design by Stacy Irwin.

ISBN: 0-425-21260-2

BERKLEY SENSATION®
Berkley Sensation Books are published by The Berkley Publishing Group,
a division of Penguin Group (USA) Inc.,
375 Hudson Street, New York, New York 10014.
BERKLEY SENSATION is a registered trademark of Penguin Group (USA) Inc.
The "B" design is a trademark belonging to Penguin Group (USA) Inc.

PRINTED IN THE UNITED STATES OF AMERICA

10 9 8 7 6 5 4 3 2 1

This book is dedicated to Sgt. Gary Arai and Lt. Tim McGraw, who saved my life on the night of August 24, 1987. You are the real heroes.

ACKNOWLEDGMENTS

With deepest thanks to Kenlyn Kolleen and Free A Child for inspiring this story and for fighting the battle against child sex trafficking on the streets of Denver and in the villages of Nepal. To help, go to www.freeachild.org.

Special thanks to Sgt. Gary Arai for his insight on police operations and gear and to Scott Weiser for his gun expertise.

Special thanks also to Vince Darcangelo for letting me borrow his last name—and certain other attributes—for my story.

Muchísimas gracias to Anna de la Peña for the Spanish translations.

Caffeinated thanks to Aimee Culbertson for making my latte dreams come true. You kept me going till the wee hours.

With gratitude to Cindy Hwang and Natasha Kern for your support and guidance.

Personal thanks to: Michelle White, Timalyn O'Neill, Karen Marie Moning, Kelly LaMar, Sara Megibow, Dede Laugesen, Vickie McCloud, Kally Jo Surbeck, Alice Brilmeyer, Alice Duncan, Mimi Riser, Bonnie Vanak, Norah Wilson, and Jan Zimlich. I don't know what I'd do without you!

And with love to my family and to my sons, Alec and Benjamin, whose love and support means more to me than they can possibly know.

CHAPTER 1

COFFEE WAS TESSA Novak's heroin. And right now she craved it with the desperation of a street junkie. What she wanted—what she *needed*—was a triple-shot grande skinny vanilla latte made with organic shade-grown Mexican beans. What she was going to get was toxic gas-station swill.

Serves you right for losing track of time, girl.

The last of the decent coffee shops had closed fifteen minutes ago while she'd been sitting stupidly at her desk reading through files.

She nosed her car into the brightly lit gas-station parking lot, braking for a couple of skateboarders who seemed oblivious to the dangers of both traffic and gravity, and parked next to an SUV that was blasting Eminem. Then she grabbed her handbag out of her briefcase and stepped out of her car into the reek of exhaust and gasoline fumes.

Even though it was October, the air was still warm—one of those strange Colorado Indian summers that dragged on forever. Although most of her friends at the paper were happy with the warm, sunny weather, Tessa wished it would hurry up and snow. She loved the cold, loved the fresh smell of a new snowfall, loved the way the landscape transformed overnight from a dirty, gray city to a world of pure, sparkling white.

She'd grown up in the South and hadn't made her first snowman until she'd moved to Denver three years ago at the age of twenty-five. Though that was the least of what had been wrong with her childhood, it had somehow become symbolic of everything else. The year's first snowstorm had become a kind of ritual for Tessa, an annual celebration of her escape.

This year the snow was late.

She hurried across the parking lot and through the glass doors. The smell of the city was replaced by the odors of stale hot dogs, industrial cleaner—and coffee. Cutting through the short line of people at the register, she followed her nose to the back counter and found a glass pot half full of what looked like dirty motor oil.

She stopped, stared at it, her mind at war with her craving. She looked over at the attendant, an older man with short gray hair and a bulbous nose. "How old is the coffee?"

"How should I know?" He scanned a woman's cigarettes, didn't even look up.

"Oh, I don't know." Tessa lifted the pot, sniffed its contents, kept her voice sweet. "Maybe you work here or something."

"It was there when I came on two hours ago."

Which meant it might have been sitting on the warmer since Jesus was a child.

But a fix was a fix.

Consigned to her fate, she tipped the black liquid into a large foam cup, then grabbed four vanilla-flavored creamer packets and dumped them in one at a time, wishing to God she'd looked at her watch twenty minutes sooner.

She'd been working late again, more because she had nothing better to do than because she truly needed to. Her contribution to tomorrow's newspaper—a short follow-up piece about the police officer from the 321st who'd been killed on a domestic-violence call—had been filed hours ago. She'd taken advantage of her complete lack of a love life to spend her Tuesday night reading through more of the documents she'd requested from the police department's contracts office. She was on a fishing expedition, she knew, but that was how many of the best investigative stories began—with a reporter picking up rocks just to see what lay hidden beneath.

And what had she found so far? Not so much as one wriggling worm.

No lucrative contracts given to relatives. No padding of expenses. No money transferred to companies that didn't exist.

Chief Irving ran a tight ship—not perfect, but tight.

Tessa told herself she should be pleased. After all, she wasn't out to cut the Denver Police Department off at the knees. If the cops weren't crooks, that was a *good* thing. Unfortunately, "Nothing Bad Happening" didn't make for a splashy sixty-point headline.

Tessa had moved to Colorado from Savannah to take a seat on the *Denver Independent*'s elite Investigative Team—the I-Team—as the cop reporter. Relatively new to journalism, she'd been astonished to land the job. She'd worked hard to prove herself to Tom Trent, the paper's demanding editor in chief—okay, so the guy could be a complete jerk—by putting in sweatshop hours, sacrificing sleep, and foregoing any chance at romance to justify her place on the team. But it had been a while now since she'd unearthed anything worth its weight in newsprint. What she needed was a big story.

No, what she *needed* was caffeine.

She lifted the cup to her lips, sipped, grimaced. It tasted far worse than she'd imagined, but it was potent. She took a bigger sip and started toward the counter, grateful to see the line was gone.

She'd just pulled a couple of bucks out of her purse when the door opened with a jingle and a pretty, young Latina ran in, panic in her eyes, tears streaming down her face. Barefoot, wearing cutoffs and a skimpy tank top, she looked strangely out of place for this time of year.

"¡Por favor, señor, ayúdeme! Ayúdeme!" she sobbed. "¡Me van a matar!"

Please, sir! Help me! Help me! They're going to kill me!

Startled, Tessa stopped in her tracks.

The girl ran to the counter. "¡Ayúdeme! ¡Llame a policía!"

Help me! Call the police!

But it was clear the attendant hadn't understood a word she'd said. He stared at the girl in openmouthed confusion, frozen like a statue.

Tessa's mouth reconnected with her brain, and she tore through her purse for her cell phone. *"Quién? Quién te va a matar?"*

Who's going to kill you?

The girl looked at Tessa through pleading brown eyes, her entire body trembling, then glanced back over her shoulder. *"¡Madre de—!"*

Mother of—!

It was over in an instant that seemed to stretch on forever.

A shiny black car, one tinted window sliding down. The girl's terrified scream. An explosion of bullets and shattered glass. A squeal of tires. The stench of burning rubber.

Tessa found herself on the floor on her belly, the rapid hammer of her pulse overwhelming the silence. Before her, the girl lay lifeless in a pool of blood and coffee, her eyes open and empty, tears still sliding down her cheeks.

"DID YOU SEE the weapon?"

Tessa had already gone over her statement twice. The cop, a young detective named Petersen whom she'd seen once or twice before, was just going through his notes, trying to be thorough. They'd brought her to the other side of the store while the scene was photographed and the girl's body was tagged and bagged. EMTs loaded the body bag into an ambulance for transport to the medical examiner. Another ambulance had already taken the attendant to the hospital with a suspected heart attack.

Outside, lights from a dozen squad cars flashed red and blue. Uniformed officers kept the curious at bay. Others questioned bystanders or combed the store and parking lot for evidence. Over the years Tessa had been to hundreds of crime scenes, but this was the first time she'd seen it from a victim's perspective. Somehow it didn't feel real.

"Y-yes, sir, just a glimpse." Why was it so hard to think?

She pulled the blanket the victim's advocate had given her more tightly around her shoulders, tried to stop her shaking, forced herself to concentrate. "The shots came so fast."

"But you couldn't see the shooter. Is that correct?"

"I only saw his arm. He was wearing black gloves and a black leather jacket."

"You didn't get the make of the car or the plates."

"N-no, sir. I saw a shiny, black car, and then . . ." She felt herself moving toward tears, swallowed hard. "And then they started shooting."

A shiny, black car. Silver hubcaps turning. Spinning.

"The hubcaps." She spoke without realizing it. "They had a separate piece in the center, jagged like a buzz saw. It was spinning on its own—or so it seemed."

"So the driver's got himself a fancy set of rims. That might help us out. Did you see any emblem on them—any kind of symbol?"

She tried to remember. "No, sir. I'm sorry."

"I have to say I love your accent. Where are you from?"

Confused by the trivial question, it took Tessa a moment to answer. "Georgia."

It was then she saw him.

He stood outside the police tape just on the edge of the parking lot, half in light and half in shadow. His hair was dark and pulled back in a shoulder-length ponytail, his jaw darkened by a heavy growth of stubble. At least six feet tall, he wore a pair of worn Levi's—and a black leather jacket. And he was watching her.

Tessa met his gaze and felt her heartbeat trip. "There's a man—!"

But he was already gone.

"There was a man standing there—a man in a black leather jacket."

Detective Petersen looked over his shoulder in the direction she was pointing and frowned. "Who can I call to come pick you up, Ms. Novak?"

"Aren't you going to question him?" Tessa's gaze roamed the darkness.

"I'll have one of the officers look around. Right now, I need to get you safely home. Do you have family I can call?"

"No, no family." Even if she'd been on her deathbed and her mother had lived nearby, Tessa wouldn't have called her. She hadn't spoken with her mother for ten years. "I'll just drive myself. My car's over there."

Detective Petersen looked at her through solemn brown eyes. "Sorry, but I can't let you drive. If there's someone I can call—a friend or coworker?"

And she realized he was right. She shouldn't be behind the wheel. She could barely keep her knees from knocking. And suddenly she wanted to talk to Kara. "I'll do it."

A former member of the I-Team, Kara McMillan was perhaps the best journalist Tessa knew and one of her closest friends. Kara had broken one of the biggest stories ever to hit Denver—and had come close to being murdered in the process. If anyone would understand how Tessa felt right now, it was Kara.

Tessa fumbled for her cell phone, scrolled down until she came to Kara's name, and pressed auto-dial. It wasn't Kara who answered, but Reece, Kara's senator husband.

"Kara's putting Connor and Caitlyn to bed," he said. "Can I have her call you back?"

Somehow the warm sound of his voice made it harder for Tessa to keep it together. She felt tears prick her eyes, and her voice quavered. "I-I'm sorry to bother you, but I need a favor. I-I was getting coffee, and this car drove up, and . . . They shot her, Reece. She's dead."

"Who's dead? Tessa, are you all right? Where are you? Are the police there?"

"I-I'm fine—just shaken up, I guess." She forced her mind to focus. "I'm at the gas station at Colfax and York. And, yes, the police are here."

"Find an armed officer, and stay close to him. I'll be right there."

JULIAN DARCANGELO WATCHED the pretty blonde climb into the Jeep of the man who'd come to pick her up—probably her husband or live-in lover. Her young face reflected both shock and horror, the reactions of the healthy mind to the fucked-up reality of murder.

How long had it been since Julian had felt those emotions? He didn't even bother trying to remember.

He watched the Jeep turn and head back down Colfax, memorized the license plate number out of habit, careful to keep to the shadows. He hadn't meant for her to see him, had wondered at the reaction on her face. She'd seemed to recognize him, but that was impossible. He'd only been in Denver for a few months and had spent most of his time in places no woman would choose to go. Besides, he knew without a doubt that he'd never seen her before. With long, curly blond hair and big eyes, she wasn't the kind of woman a man could easily forget.

The killer wouldn't forget her either and might well come back to finish the job. Burien hated sloppy work. He wouldn't want a witness, particularly not one who might have spoken with the victim. It wouldn't surprise Julian if the shooter showed up dead in an alley in a week or so, riddled with bullets from his own weapon. Burien had a nasty temper, even for an old Russian mafioso.

Julian had been pursuing Burien for what seemed like a lifetime. He'd started tracking Burien and his partners—Rafael Clemente García and Jarrett Pembroke—in the late nineties, eventually infiltrating García's operation. He'd sent García and Pembroke to prison and had called it justice when they'd died behind bars, García by suicide, Pembroke beaten to death by a fellow inmate who hadn't appreciated his choice of career. But Burien had slipped away.

Julian had taken full responsibility. He'd let the job get to him, and his lapse in judgment had cost him his relationship with Margaux, left two good agents dead, and given Burien the chance he needed to slip away. Julian had resigned the next day, but he'd never stopped looking for Burien.

When Ed Dyson had called from HQ in D.C. and asked him to come back to help flush Burien out of hiding, he'd agreed, even though it meant having to work again with Margaux, who was handling computer ops. Ridding the world of Burien would be more than worth whatever personal price he might have to pay. For four months now, he'd served as FBI liaison to the Denver Police Department's vice unit. It wasn't the deep-cover work he was used to, but the position allowed him to work independently, to utilize police resources at will, and to spend plenty of time on the streets, sniffing out Burien's trail.

And Julian was close, so close. He could feel it.

He'd had the basement apartment down the street under surveillance for a week, had known it was one of Burien's cribs. He'd chosen not to move quite yet, sure he'd spook Burien and drive him further underground. He'd never imagined one of the girls would run. They never ran. They were too afraid, too drugged, too broken to run.

Goddamn it!

The plainclothes officer who'd been watching the place tonight claimed he hadn't known the girl had bolted until Burien's men jumped in the car to follow her. He'd called it in, unsure how to intervene, uncertain whether his orders permitted him to intervene. Julian had been on the other side of town and had heard the call go out over his police radio. By the time he'd arrived, the girl was dead.

Now Burien was responsible for another murder, and the weight of it settled on Julian's shoulders. He'd gotten used to that weight, to the burden of knowing he'd enabled a killer to keep killing. Both of them would pay—Julian by dragging that burden with him for the rest of his life and Burien when he landed behind bars or someone put a bullet through his skull.

Julian watched the taillights of the Jeep disappear, hoped the man driving it had the smarts to protect the woman beside him, then glanced at his watch. First, he'd lead a team through the apartment to collect whatever evidence had been left behind. Then he'd head to the station and make certain the witnesses' names weren't in the police report where Burien could too easily find them. He turned and walked down the dark street, an image of the pretty blonde's stricken face in his mind.

* * *

"I<small>F ONLY</small> I hadn't frozen!" Tessa dabbed the tears from her eyes. She hated crying in front of people, even friends. "If only I'd dialed nine-one-one right away or pulled her into the aisle!"

She'd already had a shower to wash the girl's blood away and was wearing one of Kara's nightgowns and bathrobes while her own clothes ran through the washer and dryer.

"It's not your fault." Kara sat beside her in sweatpants and a denim shirt that obviously belonged to Reece, her long dark hair pulled back in a sleek braid. She looked remarkably unruffled for a mother of two. "There's nothing you could have done in those few seconds that would have made any difference."

"Drink." Reece thrust a tumbler into her hands. "Kara's right. There's no way the police could have made it in time, and a display of potato chips isn't going to stop automatic weapons fire. It's a damned miracle you weren't killed, too."

Tessa tried not to think about that. She knew it had been close. She'd been standing perhaps three feet from the girl when the shooting had started. "I guess it's lucky for me the guy could aim."

Lucky for me. Not so lucky for her.

She took a deep swallow of whatever Reece had handed her, unaware until she felt the burn that it was scotch. She coughed, then took another drink.

"Oh, Tess, I am so sorry!" Kara rested a comforting arm around her shoulders. "And quit trying to act tough. You've just survived a nightmare. No one is supposed to be okay after witnessing a murder."

Her sympathy cut through Tessa and unleashed new tears. "Did you blubber like this after that bastard at the cement plant tried to kill you?"

"I had nightmares for months and cried a lot. Ask him."

Reece nodded, his face grave. "If you weren't shaken up by this, you'd be weird."

Tessa laughed. "Well, it's good to know I'm not weird."

"I didn't realize you spoke fluent Spanish." Reece poured more scotch into her glass. "Did you study it in college?"

Tessa shook her head, spoke without thinking. "I learned growing up."

"In Georgia?" Kara looked surprised.

But Tessa hadn't grown up in Georgia. She'd never told her friends where she'd been born or just how she'd come into the world. That life was behind her.

She changed the subject. "I saw a man after the shooting. He was watching me while I was talking with the cops. He had on a black leather jacket just like the killer. When I spotted him, he vanished. I told the officer, but he didn't seem interested. Someone needs to find him."

"I'm sure the police know what they're doing." Reece sat down on the ottoman in front of her and rested a reassuring hand on her knee. "You'd best leave that up to them."

Both Tessa and Kara glared at him.

He stood, pushed a hand through his blond hair. "Oh, wait. That's right. You're a reporter, and that means trying to catch killers, doesn't it?"

"Reece!" Kara frowned.

But Tessa needed to explain. "She was young. She was so young and afraid, and they killed her, just shot her down. I saw it happen. I watched her die. She pleaded with me to help her, and instead of helping, I watched her die. I have to do something."

Reece crossed his arms over his chest, looking stern and senatorial. "Not tonight you don't. Finish that drink, then it's off to bed."

"Thanks. You two are the greatest."

A wail came from upstairs.

"Caitlyn! I'm trying to wean her." Kara shook her head, then looked up at Reece. "Will you check her, hon? If she sees me, she'll just—"

"—want breast. I have the same problem." Reece winked at his wife, a smile on his face, then headed up the stairs.

Tessa found herself smiling, too. "You are so lucky, Kara."

Kara gave her a reassuring squeeze. "You'll find a man of your own one day, Tess. Now let's get you settled."

Tessa soon found herself lying between soft sheets that smelled of fabric softener, the roughest edge of her nerves smoothed by soap, scotch, and friendship. There was something comforting about a home with a mother, a father, and small children. She didn't know exactly what it was, but she liked it, perhaps because she'd never had it herself.

You'll find a man of your own one day, Tess.

How Tessa hoped that was true. She longed to have what Kara had—a career, babies, a happy marriage, a man who cherished her. Still, she wouldn't hold her breath. The women in her family had never had much luck with men. As she drifted off to sleep, it wasn't thoughts of her ideal man that filled her mind, but the image of the man in the black leather jacket.

CHAPTER  2

THEY FOUND EXACTLY what Julian had known they'd find at the abandoned apartment. The cops, new to this sort of thing, didn't know what to make of it, and Julian, wanting to prevent leaks, wasn't going to fill them in.

The front room was a mess of junk-food wrappers, half-empty liquor bottles, and other trash. A stained beige couch faced a television that sat on an overturned crate. Beside the crate sat dozens of videos, almost certainly porn, most of it homemade.

The kitchen reeked of garbage gone bad, the trash piled high with used paper plates, beer cans, and food cartons. The dimly lit bathroom smelled strongly of urine and mildew, orange piss stains on the floor, grime and hair in the sink.

"The maid's year off," Julian said to Petersen, who was still young and green enough to look shocked.

Across from the bathroom, the smaller bedroom had held two unmade double beds crammed into opposite corners. An electric cord was tied around one of the bedposts—a crude and painful way to restrain someone. Apart from a handful of scattered videotapes, the closet was empty.

But it was the master bedroom that told the story. Four mattresses on the floor, their sheets stained with semen and old blood. A small plastic trash can filled with dozens of used condoms. Black and gold condom wrappers scattered across the filthy tan carpet. A set of leather restraints—the kind used to tie a woman spread-eagle to a bed—in a heap in the corner. Used syringes, half-empty packets of birth-control pills, antibiotics, maxi pads, and boxes of unused condoms.

"Holy fucking shit." Petersen gazed around him, clearly stunned. "She must've been a hooker."

"Don't make assumptions, Petersen." Julian kept his tone neutral, glanced at his watch. It would be oh-four-hundred before they finished here.

"Look at all those syringes! Shouldn't we get DEA in here?"

"This is a vice operation until I say it isn't. Got it?"

"Yes, sir."

Julian thought of the girl whose blood he'd seen spilled on cold tiles tonight. She'd run for freedom, had gotten death instead. Someone had silenced her, but this evidence, if handled correctly, would speak for her. Julian would make damned sure of it.

TESSA GOT LITTLE sleep, her dreams turning to nightmares after the scotch wore off. Each time, it was the same—the girl ran through the door, begged for help, and was riddled with bullets while Tessa watched, frozen in place, unable to breathe or scream or move. And each time, Tessa woke up, gasping for breath and covered in cold sweat.

She finally gave up trying to sleep at about four and watched CNN on mute until Kara and Reece got up. Then, while Kara got Connor ready for school, Reece gave Tessa a ride to the gas station to fetch her car.

"You're welcome to stay with us for as long as you like," he said. "We're heading up to the cabin this weekend. We'd love it if you'd come with us. I hear it's supposed to snow in the high country."

"Thanks. I might take you up on that." She gave him a hug and a kiss on the cheek, then stepped out of his Jeep and turned to face the scene that had haunted her all night.

It looked different in the morning light—small, dingy, desolate. The shattered doors and windows of the little store were boarded up. The building was cordoned off with yellow police tape. The interior was dark apart from one flickering fluorescent light.

How many times had she driven past this place? How many times had she stopped in to gas up or get coffee? Now she wondered if she'd ever be able to walk through its doors again.

It struck her as strange that if she'd made it to her favorite coffee shop on time, she wouldn't have witnessed the killing. It would have been just another press release, just another news brief—girl killed in drive-by, investigation ongoing.

But she *had* witnessed it. She'd seen a young woman live out the last moments of her life in terror before being cruelly murdered. She knew she would never forget it.

A red SUV pulled into the parking lot and stopped at a pump, and a man in a suit stepped out, yammering on his cell phone. It took him three swipes of his credit card to realize the place was closed. He drove off in a huff.

Tessa fished her car keys out of her purse, unlocked her car, and slipped behind the wheel, determined to pull herself together. She drove home, tried to revive herself with a hot shower, and did her best to hide the dark circles under her eyes with makeup.

"You look like hell, girl," she told her reflection.

Her reflection stared back through eyes that were red and puffy and full of shadows.

A part of her wanted to call in sick and crawl into bed, but she was done crying. She knew she wouldn't be able to help anyone—most especially the girl who'd been murdered last night—by hiding. Besides, she probably wouldn't be able to sleep anyway. It was best to stick with her routine and face the day head on.

Seeking the comfort of the familiar, she dressed in her favorite black silk suit—the color seemed fitting—and headed first to the local coffeehouse for a cup of salvation and then to the paper. By the time she'd had a few sips and made it to her desk, she felt almost human.

She checked her phone messages and e-mails and then rummaged through the stack of press releases she'd grabbed from her in-box. Ketamine stolen from another vet clinic. An alleged sexual assault. A fatal crash on I-70.

Surprised not to find any mention of the shooting, she picked up her phone and dialed.

"We're not releasing the police report." Larry from Sheriff's Records was grumpier than usual. "The incident is still under investigation. You know the drill."

Across the newsroom, Sophie Alton pointed at her watch and held up three fingers. They had an I-Team meeting in three minutes.

Tessa nodded, gathered her notes for the meeting, and reached for a sharpened pencil. "Is Chief Irving going to issue some kind of statement?"

"You'll have to call the press office for that."

She forced sugar into her voice. The least she could do was try to make him feel guilty. "Thank you, Larry. You've been so helpful. I know your time is very valuable. You have a good morning, and I'll be in touch."

She hung up. "Bless his heart."

"Larry being a dick again?" Matt Harker, the city reporter, stood and smoothed his hopelessly rumpled tie—the tie he put on every morning and threw on his desk every afternoon. "Someone ought to investigate why city employees are so obnoxious. Does the city train them to act that way? Did someone steal their Prozac? Do they drink too much coffee?"

"Don't knock coffee, Harker." Tessa picked up her latte and followed her coworkers toward the conference room. "It's not right to insult other people's religions."

Sophie, her straight, strawberry-blond hair done in a sleek French braid, held back for her, notepad and water bottle in hand. "Are you all right? You look tired and upset."

"Thanks." Tessa willed herself to smile as if she'd just been given a big compliment. "Tired and upset was exactly the look I was going for this morning."

Sophie frowned. "Okay, *don't* tell me what's going on,"

Tessa saw the concern in her friend's eyes and wanted to

tell her. Sophie was perhaps her closest friend. They'd shared the travails of working for Tom Trent, being perpetually single, and working in the male-dominated field of investigative journalism. But Tessa didn't think she could tell Sophie about last night—not without crying again.

She would rather face a firing squad than cry in the newsroom.

Tom was waiting for them by the time they reached the conference room, tapping his pencil impatiently on his notepad. He was a big man—over six feet and probably close to three hundred pounds. With a mop of gray curls on his head, he'd always looked to Tessa like a cross between a sheepdog and a linebacker, but his personality was pure pit bull.

On his left sat Syd Wilson, the managing editor. It was her job to make the news fit, and doing so under Tom's direction had turned much of her spiky black hair white. Joaquin Ramirez, the sexy photographer who reminded the women at the paper of a young Antonio Banderas, was talking over photo possibilities with Syd, while Katherine James, the newest member of the team, read through her notes. Handpicked by Tom to take Kara's place, Kat had come to Denver from her hometown newspaper in Window Rock, Arizona, on the Navajo reservation, where she'd broken a big story about toxic uranium mining. Petite with waist-length dark hair and hazel-green eyes that revealed her mixed heritage, she kept mostly to herself.

Tessa took her seat, jotted down some notes, and tried to tell herself this was just another Wednesday morning, just another I-Team meeting.

Tom never bothered with small talk. "Alton, what's the latest?"

Sophie had barely taken her seat. "I got a tip yesterday about a woman who filed a federal lawsuit against the Department of Corrections. The suit claims she went into premature labor in lockdown, asked for help, and was ridiculed by the guards, who didn't believe she was having problems. She labored overnight in her cell alone, and her baby was stillborn the next morning."

Tessa met Sophie's gaze, shared the disgust and anger she saw there. But this was what investigative journalism was all about—shining light into the dark corners so that wrongdoers could have no place to hide.

Tom didn't react at all, but after a lifetime in journalism, he'd probably seen and heard everything. "What can you pull together by deadline?"

"I can write up an overview of the lawsuit—probably fifteen inches. I'd like to follow up on the medical angle later in the week—how many doctors per inmate, how well equipped the facility is to deal with women's medical emergencies and such. I've put in an open-records request and am getting the usual runaround."

Syd nodded, scribbled, did the math. "Photos?"

"The plaintiff's mug shot."

Tessa's thoughts drifted back to last night. She didn't hear Matt talk about his story on city council members holding illegal secret meetings via a previously unknown e-mail loop. She didn't hear Katherine discuss the latest on Rocky Flats, the site of a former nuclear weapons plant now open to the public as a recreation area where people could picnic in the plutonium.

¡Por favor, señor, ayúdeme! Ayúdeme! ¡Me van a matar!

"Tessa!" Sophie leaned forward and touched her hand to Tessa's forearm.

"Not enough coffee yet?" Joaquin grinned.

Embarrassed, Tessa sat upright, looked down at her notes. "There's been another ketamine theft from a vet clinic. It's the third this month. I could contact the drug task force and see if we're looking at a new K craze. But there's something else . . ."

She paused for a moment, steeled herself. "I witnessed a murder last night—a drive-by."

A murmur of shock passed through the conference room.

Tom said nothing.

Tessa took a deep breath, forced aside her emotion. "I stopped off at the gas station on Colfax and York and saw a teenage girl get gunned down. I was standing maybe three feet away from her when they opened fire. The cops haven't released the report yet or issued a statement, but I'd like to run with it anyway."

"God, Tessa!" Sophie stared at her through wide blue eyes. "You could've been shot!"

True to form, Tom wasted no time on sympathy. "What did you have in mind?"

As soon as he asked, Tessa knew. "I'd like to write a first-person, eyewitness account. I'd like to follow the case as it moves through the justice system. I can use my knowledge of cops and courts to fill in the personal experience of witnessing the crime."

Tom's bushy eyebrows came together in a frown, and he opened his mouth to speak.

Sure he was going to reject her idea, Tessa interrupted. "I know it's unusual, but I can't be objective on this story anyway, so I shouldn't pretend. I think a first-person account will bring the idea of murder home to people in a way an ordinary news story can't."

"I think it's a great idea," Syd offered. "It's sure to draw readership—a murder mystery being played out on the front page of the paper."

Sophie, Matt, and Joaquin offered their support, as well.

"There's something you ought to consider." Kat tucked a strand of long, dark hair behind her ear. "You'll be letting the killer in on everything you know. Are you ready for that?"

Tessa remembered the terror in the girl's eyes.

¡Por favor, señor, ayúdeme!

Screams. Bullets. Blood.

The man in the black leather jacket.

Instead of fear, she felt anger. "Yes, I think I am."

There was silence for a moment.

Then Tom tossed his pencil down onto his notepad. "All right, Novak. You're on. Just don't write anything sappy. We aren't goddamned Hallmark."

GYM BAG SLUNG over his shoulder, Julian walked down the hallway of the shabby hotel over threadbare blue-and-orange carpet that looked like it hadn't been cleaned since the seventies. He'd been in hundreds of places like this—roach-infested, pay-by-the-hour dumps that squatted in every city's darkest corners. One thing kept them in business—the buying, selling, and trading of sex. Cheap, clandestine, and staffed by people too poor and too street-smart to ask questions, they made the perfect place for working girls to take their johns, for married men who wanted a bit of tail on the side—and for scum like Lonnie Zoryo.

Julian had been cultivating Zoryo, one of Burien's lackeys, for a few months now, playing the part of a repeat customer with a taste for the forbidden. He had enough on Zoryo to put him behind bars for several lifetimes, though he knew Zoryo wouldn't live to serve his entire sentence. Inmates had a strange intolerance for men who raped kids.

Julian hadn't filled Dyson in on this little deep-cover job but was working under the radar, sharing bits and pieces with Chief Irving on a need-to-know basis. What he'd been doing wasn't strictly legal in that it wasn't a sanctioned police or FBI action. But he didn't care. He wasn't officially on the FBI payroll, and he wasn't officially a cop. Subsequently he wasn't following anyone's official rule book. He had his reasons.

He walked to the end of the corridor and turned left, barely noticing the moans coming out of one of the rooms on the right. When it came to sex, nothing shocked him anymore. Then again, he'd grown up on the lam with his father, thinking it was normal to get out of bed in the morning and find half-naked whores passed out next to his father on the couch. If Dyson hadn't pulled him out of that Mexican prison all those years ago, kicked his teenage ass, and given him a new start, Julian would probably be spending a lot of time in places like this one.

No, he'd still be in prison—or dead.

Ed Dyson had come to visit him behind bars and had offered him a deal: put your fluent Spanish and Mexican street smarts to use for us, or rot in your cell. Sentenced to thirty years for manslaughter at the age of seventeen for accidentally killing a man in a fistfight, Julian hadn't needed to think hard about his answer. The man he'd killed had had lots of friends on the inside, and every one of them had wanted a piece of Julian. He'd never have survived the year.

He owed Dyson his life.

He knocked on the door to room 69—Zoryo's idea of a joke—and waited. He felt the impact of Zoryo's heavy footfalls, saw a shadow pass over the peephole in the door. Locks tumbled, and the door opened to reveal Zoryo standing shirtless in a pair of khaki slacks. The tiger tattoo on his chest proclaimed his pedigree as a former Red Mafia enforcer, while his big, hairy belly spoke of his love for steak and booze. He stank of cigarettes, alcohol, and old sweat. In his hand was a 9mm Taurus.

"Eh, Dominic, my friend. Good to see you," he said in his heavy Russian accent, motioning for Julian to enter, a big smile on his unshaven face. "Come in."

Julian stepped into the room, taking it in all at once: the unmade bed littered with CDs and DVDs; the open suitcase; the roll of duct tape and box of ammo on the dresser; the drapes concealing a single window; the half-empty bottle of vodka on the nightstand; the bathroom with the toilet seat up; the television showing Zoryo's twisted idea of a home movie.

But that's what Julian had come to discuss. He was, after all, an eager customer.

He slipped into the repulsive persona of Dominic Conti and a Philly accent. "Hey, Zoryo. What you got playing? Is it up my alley?"

Zoryo shut and locked the door behind him. "You like girls, yes?"

Julian dropped the gym bag on the bed, let it fall open to reveal the cash—a stack of hundreds—and turned to face the television screen. He fought back his rage and revulsion, pretended to like what he saw. "Ooh, she's nice—young and firm."

On the screen, a naked Zoryo was committing rape. Together with a laundry list of other felonies, it would get him life. The son of a bitch was going to pay. Starting today: Julian would take him, and he would do all he legally could to break him. Then he would use the information Zoryo gave him to close in on Burien.

Julian forced himself to concentrate on that fact and not what he was watching. If he wanted to help the young woman on the screen and the millions like her, he could not make the mistake he'd made last time. He could not let himself feel.

"She was." Zoryo turned his gaze to the screen, a look of predatory lust on his face. Then he glanced over at the money. "You ready to buy?"

"Of course." Julian reached into the gym bag, picked up the stack of hundreds, dropped it on the bed, knowing it would whet Zoryo's other appetite. "What else you got?"

Zoryo took the bundle, flipped through the bills. "Where you get this kind of money? You come every week, pay with cash money."

Julian knew Zoryo had already been digging on Dominic and had found the information he'd planted. "I work a few deals on the side—a couple sites on the 'Net, a bit of Colombian agriculture."

"Websites? Drugs?" Zoryo dropped the bills back into the bag and did something completely unexpected.

He raised the Taurus and pressed the barrel to Julian's temple. He moved his face close to Julian's, his breath stinking of vodka and cigarettes, his blue eyes flat and liquid. "It's all bullshit, Dominic. You do shit work—small time. You are small fish. You think you can compete with me, swim in my ocean?"

Julian felt his pulse slow and his mind clear as it always did before violence. Itchy from lack of sleep, he would enjoy this. He met Zoryo's gaze, grinned.

In fewer moves than it took to brush his teeth, he had Zoryo facedown on the floor, arm wrenched behind his back, his broken nose bleeding onto the carpet, the 9 mm lying harmlessly nearby. Zoryo gasped and groaned, too winded for words—probably the result of Julian's knee driving into his solar plexus.

Julian pressed his .357 SIG Sauer against the base of Zoryo's skull. "I may be a small fish, old man, but I'm also a federal agent. You're under arrest for being a fucking sick pervert. You have the right to remain silent. Everything you say can and will be used against you in a court of law—if you live long enough."

Zoryo groaned.

TESSA SPLASHED COLD water on her face, the chill helping to stop her tears. She'd finished the article, knew it was some of her best writing ever. But when she'd gotten to the end, she'd lost it. Matt had seen. So had Kat. Sophie had offered her a box of tissues.

Where were firing squads when you needed one?

Mortified, Tessa had taken the only dignified course of action. She'd turned the article in to Syd and had hurried to the sanctuary of the women's room, where she'd finally given in to the tears she'd been fighting all day.

Behind her the door opened.

"I thought I'd find you here." It was Sophie.

"Lucky guess." Tessa reached for a paper towel, blotted her face, and opened her eyes to find herself surrounded. Sophie had brought reinforcements.

Lissy, the fashion editor, stood with her hand on the curve of her four-months-pregnant tummy looking worried and glamorous in Vera Wang maternity. Holly, who wrote for the entertainment section and was Tessa's most annoying friend, stared past Tessa to the mirror and adjusted her short, platinum-blond hair.

"You're the only woman I know who thinks she has to hide when she cries," Sophie said.

"And your solution is not to let me hide?" Tessa tossed the paper towel into the trash. "Bless your heart! How thoughtful."

Lissy reached out and gave Tessa's hand a reassuring squeeze, her green eyes filled with concern. "Sophie told us what happened. We just wanted to make sure you're all right."

"I'm fine."

Holly looked away from her own reflection, fixed Tessa with a glare. "Like hell you are! You've got mascara down to your chin, and your skin is all blotchy. Here."

Holly held out a little bag inside which Tessa found sample-sized tubes of mascara, moisturizer, and concealer, together with samples of blush, eye shadow, and lipstick.

"I always carry one with me. You never know when you're going to start bawling or end up at some guy's apartment overnight. You can keep that one. There ought to be enough to cover up a couple of crying jags."

Tessa might have laughed off Holly's gesture as superficial—many of Holly's actions were—but more than anything she wanted to feel like herself again. "Thanks, Holly."

While her friends tried to persuade her that crying in public was no reason to feel embarrassed, Tessa washed her face and put on fresh makeup.

"You're human, Tessa." Lissy assured her. "Quit trying to be Superwoman. You make the rest of us look bad."

Tessa finished applying mascara and tried to explain. "I don't know why I feel the way I do about crying. I guess to me it's a sign of weakness."

As she spoke those last words, the bathroom door opened and Kat stepped inside. "We Navajo believe a woman's tears purify. We think of tears as a sign of strength, not weakness."

Tessa lowered the mascara wand. "Then I must be one heck of a strong woman."

"I just came to let you know your article made both Syd and the copy editor cry, so you're not alone." Kat looked straight into Tessa's eyes, something she rarely did. "Your words will make people feel the anguish of that girl's death. You'll make her real to them. You think you've done nothing for her, Tessa, but you have."

Then Kat turned and walked out of the bathroom, leaving Tessa and the others staring after her in silence.

CHAPTER 3

IT WAS JUST after dawn when Julian left the Denver County Jail and headed back to his house. Sunlight stretched warm and golden through the city, beating back the night, spilling its glow against the ragged wall of snowcapped Rockies to the west. He'd promised himself some time in those mountains when this job was done—provided he was still alive, of course.

He sped south on Speer in his battered blue pickup. The window was down, cold morning air blasting him in the face. He wanted a shower. Zoryo's cloying stench covered his skin like a greasy film, and his mouth was slick with the putrid taste that came from talking to sick fucks like him.

Aware he had only days, perhaps a week, before Burien discovered that Zoryo had been arrested and moved to cover his ass, he'd spent the night in a secluded part of the jail hammering Zoryo with questions about his filmmaking habits, about Burien, about the girl's murder. He'd pushed Zoryo hard, denying him sleep, water, and food, watching him inch closer to breaking.

There was no way the bastard was getting out, and Zoryo knew it. No criminal defense attorney would touch his case, and the public defender was no match for the kind of evidence

Julian had collected. No one even knew Zoryo had been arrested—not yet. Julian had all the relevant warrants under seal and in his own safe. There were too many leaks for Julian to take chances. For the moment, Zoryo was alone in the world—and under Julian's control. The bastard's only hope lay in divulging what he knew about Burien and spending the rest of his life in solitary confinement where the other inmates couldn't rip him apart.

Already Julian's interrogation had yielded a few decent leads, including a strip club on Colorado Boulevard called Pasha's. Zoryo had offered up the name in exchange for the luxury of time on a steel toilet. He'd led Julian to believe Pasha's might be some kind of drop-off site. Even if the club was only used to launder money, it was another piece of the puzzle and, hopefully, another nail in Burien's coffin. Of course, that's assuming Zoryo wasn't making stuff up or leading him into a trap.

"If you lie to me about what's out there," Julian had whispered, his face inches from Zoryo's, "there will be consequences in here."

Then he'd left Zoryo under suicide watch in solitary lockdown, more to keep him alive than to intimidate him.

Julian would check the club out later. First, he needed some sleep.

He turned into the neighborhood where Dyson had placed him—the kind of working-class neighborhood where people kept to themselves and checked to make sure their doors were locked at night. He pushed the remote to open the garage, turned into the driveway of the bungalow that pretended to be his home, and slipped quietly inside. By the time the garage door closed behind him, he had already keyed in his password and was inside.

The house belonged to the FBI. With fireproofing, bullet-proof windows, and a state-of-the-art surveillance system, it was intended to withstand snipers and drive-bys and to alert him to anyone who came snooping around. It wasn't a home; it was a lair.

Used to moving from place to place, Julian had furnished it

with only the basics—his weapons, ammo, his computer system, his workout gear, a couch, a TV, his clothes, a few dishes, and a bed. He couldn't think of anywhere in his thirty-two years that he'd truly thought of as home. His life was a montage of dark streets, seedy hotels, prison cells, bare apartments, and nearly empty houses like this one.

And if he sometimes wanted more?

Well, that was just too damned bad. A man like him wasn't meant to live behind a white picket fence with a wife and kids.

He slipped out of his leather jacket, tossed it onto the couch. Then he removed his shoulder harness and Kevlar, slipped the Sauer from its holster and carried it with him to the bathroom. Placing it on the counter within easy reach, he stripped and turned the water on as hot as he could stand it. He was about to step under the spray when his encrypted cell phone rang.

Only three people had that number. He had no choice but to answer it.

He turned off the water, walked naked into the bedroom, picked up the phone. "Yeah."

"You have a problem." It was Margaux. She spat the words, the bitchy tone in her voice making it personal.

Julian wasn't going to be baited. "Go ahead."

"You see the front page of the *Denver Independent* this morning?"

"No. I'm just getting in."

"Well, how's this for a headline? 'Eyewitness to Murder.' "

Then Margaux read a first-person, exacting account of the shooting at the gas station. A description of the victim. The girl's plea for help—first in Spanish and then translated precisely into English. A description of the shooter's arm and the driver's car with its rims.

As Margaux read, Julian realized the details could only have come from one person—the pretty blonde. He'd read her account of the shooting in the police report and had removed her name in what was now a wasted effort to protect her. Then he'd asked Irving not to release the report to the media. He hadn't known Tessa Novak *was* the damned media.

Frustration and anger chased through him. Did she realize

what she was doing? Was she that desperate to make headlines? Did she want to end up dead or worse?

Just another damned journalist out to build her career on other people's misery.

Margaux kept talking, her voice a syrupy poison in his ear.

"Here's the best part: 'Then on the edge of the parking lot, I see him. Tall and surrounded by an air of menace, he's wearing a black leather jacket, just like the killer. His long hair is pulled back in a ponytail, and stubble covers his jaw. He watches me for a moment, half concealed by darkness, and I find it hard to breathe. Am I looking into the eyes of a cold-blooded killer? I point him out to police, but he's already gone.'"

The words hit Julian like a fist, made his brain buzz. He was a federal agent, someone used to moving in the shadows, and he'd just been described on the front page of the fucking newspaper. "Jesus Christ! Damn it!"

"'An air of menace'—wow! Compelling stuff, Julian, though I think she's giving you too much credit." Margaux laughed, a cold, glassy sound. "Burien's men will be reading this. So will he. Do you think they'll make you from the description?"

"I doubt I'm the only man with long dark hair and a black leather jacket in Denver." Still, it was a possibility he couldn't ignore. He would have to be prepared.

At least now he knew why the blonde had seemed to recognize him—she'd seen his leather jacket and assumed he was the killer. The woman had good instincts. He was *a* killer, just not *the* killer.

"You're getting sloppy, Julian. If you blow this case—"

Rage flared in his gut, but he kept his voice calm. He was not going to let her throw what had happened three years ago in his face every goddamned time they talked. "You stick to your Internet ops, and let me take care of the street."

"And the reporter?"

"I'll handle her." Chief Irving wouldn't be happy to see this either—the details of an ongoing investigation spilled to the public.

"If you don't, Burien surely will. And you know what he likes to do with women."

TESSA ARRIVED AT the paper after what was almost a restful night's sleep, latte in hand, to find the I-Team meeting postponed and Tom waiting for her in his office.

"Chief Irving is in there with him, and they've been shouting," Sophie warned her.

"Oh, good! I just love to start the day with a bit of yelling." Tessa dropped her briefcase by her desk and walked to Tom's office, fairly certain she knew what this was about. "You two wanted to see me?"

"Sit down, Novak." Tom gestured toward a chair, clearly angry. "Chief Irving was just explaining the limitations of the First Amendment."

Tessa looked over at Chief Irving and saw he was angry. He was a big, beefy man with a with a round belly and white bristles for hair. He looked out at her through pale blue eyes that told her he'd already had his fill of bullshit for the day— not surprising since he'd been conversing with Tom. He wore a tan trench coat over an awkward blue suit, his black shoes long since having lost their polish.

"First, Ms. Novak, let me say how sorry I am that you witnessed such a terrible and violent crime. These past two days can't have been easy for you." His eyes and the warmth in his voice told her he meant what he said. It was certainly more than she'd gotten from Tom.

Tessa swallowed the lump in her throat, looked at her feet. "Thank you, sir."

"We'd like to catch these guys and throw them behind bars for the rest of their lives, but the story on the front of today's paper is going to make it harder for us to do that."

That had her head snapping up. "How can that be? I would think making this information public might prompt people to call in leads."

"That's because you're thinking like a journalist and not

a government pen pusher." Tom's interruption set Tessa's nerves on edge.

Chief Irving pretended not to hear him. "It might bring us a few leads. But what it's really going to do is tell whoever is behind this murder exactly what we know."

"How does that hurt anything? The killer already knows there are witnesses."

"There were certain details—what the girl said to you, for example, or the spinning rims—that only someone who was at the scene would know. Those details might have proved helpful to us when interrogating suspects. That's why we opted not to release the police report. But you've just shared it with the entire Denver metro area."

Tessa felt her temper kick in. "People have a right to know what's happening in their neighborhoods."

Chief Irving nodded, then frowned. "Sure, they do. But they've asked us to do a job for them, and sometimes doing that job means temporarily controlling the flow of information."

Tom gave a snort. "Spoken like a true bureaucrat."

Tessa held up her hand to shut Tom up. "I know you and your officers have a job to do, Chief Irving, and I don't mean to make that more difficult. But I have a job to do, as well, and this time it's not just about journalistic idealism."

Tom's frown deepened.

"It's about a teenage girl who was shot down right before my eyes. She was a living, breathing person, and someone murdered her when she wanted desperately to live. I have to do whatever I can to see that she gets justice, to make sure she isn't forgotten." Tessa felt a surge of hot emotion, felt tears prick behind her eyes. She willed them back.

Not in front of Tom!

Chief Irving nodded. "I understand that. I respect that. But it's not only the case I'm worried about, Ms. Novak—it's you. By announcing to the world that you're an eyewitness, you've made yourself a target. These guys aren't exactly shy about killing. I'd hate to see them come after you."

Tessa had thought long and hard about this last night when

she should have been sleeping. "What do they stand to gain by killing me now? Everything I know is now part of the public record. If they kill me, they'll just draw more attention to what I wrote. Surely they're not that stupid."

"You're assuming they'd want to kill you to silence you. But what if they had an even more basic reason for coming after you?"

Chills skittered up her spine. "Like what?"

"Revenge. Pride." Chief Irving's lips curved in a grim smile. "Pleasure."

TESSA WALKED THROUGH the main entrance to the hospital, feeling uneasy, her conversation with Chief Irving still playing through her mind.

"If I were you, Ms. Novak, I'd take a long vacation," he'd said. "Failing that, I'd buy a gun and learn how to use it."

"I already own one—a twenty-two."

"Good. Pack it. I've already ordered extra patrols for your street."

Tessa told herself Chief Irving was just being cautious. There was no evidence to suggest her life was in danger. Kara had been getting death threats for a while before they came after her. Tessa hadn't even gotten so much as an impolite e-mail. She had nothing to worry about.

Then why are you carrying a handgun, girl?

Like Chief Irving, she was just being cautious.

Tom had all but gone apoplectic when Chief Irving promised to give her an exclusive when the killers were caught, provided she dropped the story now. He'd launched into the thousandth rendition of his "Watchdogs of Freedom" speech, bringing a look of bored resignation to Chief Irving's face. Obviously, Irving had heard this speech before, too.

"This is outrageous! No journalist at this paper has ever caved to pressure from the city, and I can assure you Novak won't be the first!"

Chief Irving hadn't been pleased. "We'll be as helpful as we can be, Ms. Novak, but we're playing this one close to the vest. And don't go on a charm offensive against my men with that sweet southern accent of yours because I've warned them all not to discuss this case with you. If you want information, you come to me."

Tessa had agreed to that much.

She stopped at the hospital's front desk and asked one of the volunteers for Bruce Simms's room number. She'd spent the morning working on a routine story about the recent ketamine robberies and had planned to start researching Denver's gang history, as most drive-bys in Denver were gang related. But when she'd learned the gas-station attendant had been moved out of intensive care, she'd known she had to speak with him.

"Room three-thirty-two, miss."

"Thanks."

Tessa found Mr. Simms sitting up in bed, watching a soap opera in a blue-and-white hospital gown. He was pale but alert, an oxygen tube beneath his nose, deep reddish bruises on the backs of his hands from multiple IVs. He glanced over, saw her, and his eyes widened.

Clearly he recognized her.

"Mr. Simms? I'm Tessa Novak. I hope you don't mind my stopping by."

"You like *Days of our Lives*?"

"I don't watch much television." She took that as an invitation and sat in the chair next to his bed. "I work during the day."

"It's all crap anyway." He clicked off the television. "You're that reporter. You came in for coffee. I read your piece. You come here to interview me? I got nothing to say."

"I'm here for personal reasons, Mr. Simms. You and I watched someone die. I thought—"

"I didn't see nothing." His mouth was clamped shut, but his eyes—hazel eyes more gray than green—told a different story.

"Oh, well, I imagine you were fighting your own battle for survival, weren't you?" She gave his arm a sympathetic squeeze. "I'm terribly sorry that you became ill as a result of the shooting. I must say the whole thing nearly frightened me to death."

Charm offensive? How dare Chief Irving reduce years spent studying deportment and communication to mere manipulation!

Even though Mr. Simms had read the article, Tessa went through the story again, told him what she'd seen. The car. The rims. The blood. The man in the leather jacket.

"She was so young, Mr. Simms. We were the last two people to see her alive. That matters to me."

For a moment there was no sound but hospital noises from out in the hallway.

"She used to come by most every Sunday afternoon with the others." Mr. Simms looked up at the dark television screen. "There were four of them, girls about the same age. They'd come in, buy gum, candy, maybe shampoo or lip gloss, then they'd go again. Never smiled. Never said a word till that night."

It was the first real information Tessa had gotten about the girl. "Did you know her name? Do you think she lived nearby?"

"I told you they never said a word, didn't I?" He glanced sharply at Tessa. "No, I didn't know her name. But, yeah, I think she must have lived nearby. They always walked to the store together. Never saw her by herself. It was always the four of them, and they were always dressed kind of shabby."

Curious, Tessa couldn't resist asking. "Did you ever see her with anyone else—a man, someone who looked like a gang member? A man in a black leather jacket perhaps?"

His eyes narrowed. "You're fishing for an article. I don't want to be in no newspaper."

She met his gaze, held it. "No, sir. I'm trying to find some peace of mind. Besides, I would never quote you without making it clear you were being interviewed."

He seemed to measure her.

"There was an older woman who sometimes came with them, but she never entered the store. I always figured her for one of their mothers. But . . ." He paused for a moment. "I always thought it was strange the way she watched them—like a hawk. I figured maybe she wanted to make sure they didn't steal nothing."

"Did they ever try to steal anything?"

"Nope."

"How about the black car? Did you see it or its driver before?"

"Can't recall. The place is a damned gas station—cars coming and going all goddamned day and night." He picked up the remote, clicked the television back on.

Tessa stood, took a business card out of her purse, and scribbled her home phone number on the back, knowing her time with Mr. Simms had ended. "I hope you're feeling better soon, Mr. Simms. If you think of anything else, or even if you just want to talk, you can reach me at this number."

He took the card, glanced at it, then looked up at her. "I'm leaving town as soon as I get out of here. Going to stay with my brother in Omaha, maybe move there."

And Tessa knew he was being cautious, too. "Good luck. And thank you."

She walked out of his room and down the hallway, running what he'd told her through her mind. Four girls about the same age, always together, most of the time under the watchful eye of an older woman. Never spoke. Never smiled. Walked to the store to buy candy dressed in shabby clothes.

Perhaps they were sisters or best friends, and the older woman was someone's mother. It wasn't surprising that they didn't talk to anyone else, given that they probably spoke little or no English, but it was a little odd that they didn't chatter with each other. Teenage girls were not exactly known for being quiet. It was strange, too, that they never smiled. Whoever heard of teenagers on a somber candy binge?

The shabby clothes pointed to a life of poverty. Perhaps the girls were wearing hand-me-downs or Salvation Army castoffs, cobbling together a wardrobe out of bits and pieces no one else wanted, seeing scorn and pity in other people's eyes, feeling ashamed just to be seen. Maybe that's why they kept to themselves.

Tessa knew only too well what that felt like.

¡Por favor, señor, ayúdeme!

The girl hadn't been wearing shoes—a dangerous thing on city streets. That tended to support Mr. Simms's belief that she lived nearby. So perhaps that's where Tessa should start.

She glanced at her watch, saw that it was nearly three. That gave her a good hour and a half before dark to walk the streets, knock on doors, look around for signs of gang activity. The victim was a teenager and poor, both of which fit a gang theory.

Tessa lifted her gaze and saw *him* come around the corner. He was wearing a dark blue cable-knit sweater instead of a black leather jacket, but she would have recognized him anywhere. And she could tell from his scowl that he recognized her, too.

The breath left her lungs in a rush. She took one step backward on unsteady legs, then another, her heart slamming in her chest, her lungs too empty to scream. Then beside her, she saw the fire alarm.

She lunged for it, but found herself hauled up against a rock-hard chest, a steel hand clamped over her mouth, her feet lifted off the ground.

CHAPTER 4

JULIAN SAW SHE was about to pull the fire alarm and did the only thing he could—clamped a hand over her mouth and pulled her out of the hallway and into the nearest room, a large closet full of linens. He kicked the door shut behind him and worked to subdue 120 pounds of desperate, terrified female that kicked, twisted, and struggled in his arms.

He turned her to face him, held her fast. "I'm not going to hurt you, Tessa."

At the sound of her name, she froze, and Julian found himself looking into the biggest, bluest eyes he'd ever seen. Framed by long, sooty lashes, they stared up at him in unblinking horror. Her face was pale, her skin creamy and translucent apart from a few tiny freckles on her nose. She felt small in his arms, fragile and soft. Holding her this close, he could feel her heart pound, smell her fear, taste her panic.

"If I wanted to kill you, you'd already be dead." He'd said it to calm her, realized when her pupils dilated that his words had somehow had the opposite effect. "I'm going to release you, and you're going to stand here and listen to me, got it?"

She nodded.

He lowered her to her feet, let her go—and found himself

staring at the working end of a sweet little .22 revolver. Where the hell had that come from?

Smooth, Darcangelo. What's your day job again? Special agent, you say?

"S-stay away from me!" She was trembling—not a good thing when her finger rested on the trigger of a gun pointed at his chest. It hurt to get shot, even wearing Kevlar. "I-I saw you that night! I know you were there!"

"Put it down, Ms. Novak. I told you—I'm not going to hurt you."

"Why should I believe that? I know you're carrying a gun. I felt it beneath your sweater!" Her voice quavered, hovering somewhere between rage and terror. She gripped the handle of the gun with two hands, steadied it.

He weighed his options. He could tell her he was a federal agent—except that she was a reporter. How could he be sure she wouldn't splash his name all over the damned paper? He could disarm her, but there was a chance he'd hurt her or she'd pull the trigger either accidentally or on purpose. Neither option was ideal.

He took one slow step toward her. "Put down the gun."

"Not a chance! You came here to kill him, didn't you? You came here to kill Mr. Simms so he couldn't talk to the police!"

He'd come to question the old guy, but he didn't want to tell her that. "If that's what you think, shoot me. Here, I'll even make it easy for you." He took another step forward, stretched his arms out to his sides. "Aim just to the left of my breastbone. A little twenty-two round will ricochet inside my rib cage, shred my lungs and heart, and I'll be dead before I hit the floor."

She gaped at him in surprise, and her gaze dropped to his chest.

It was the break Julian needed.

He pivoted out of the line of fire, grabbed her wrist, wrenched the .22 from her grasp. It took less force than he'd imagined, and he heard her gasp—whether in surprise or pain, he couldn't tell. He turned to face her, found her rubbing her wrist and watching him fearfully through those blue eyes.

"I told you to put it down. You should have listened." He

popped out the cylinder, tapped the bullets into his hand, and pocketed the rounds. Then he snapped the cylinder into place and handed the gun back to her.

The damned thing had been fully loaded and ready to fire.

She dropped the little pistol into her purse, her wary gaze never leaving him. "H-how do you know my name?"

"I know almost everything about you." He recited what he'd learned after doing a little digging on her this morning. "Born in Rosebud, Texas, on March 9, 1979, to Linda Lou Bates, age fourteen. Father unknown. Grew up on welfare and food stamps with your mother and maternal grandfather. Graduated Rosebud-Lott High School in 1997 with a GPA of three-nine-eight and left Rosebud behind the next day."

No longer pale, her cheeks had flushed red with what Julian supposed was anger or embarrassment. He continued.

"You earned an associate's degree in English from Austin Community College in 1999—the year you changed your last name to Novak. Moved to Athens to study journalism at the University of Georgia and graduated Phi Beta Kappa. Then you took your first reporting job at the *Savannah Morning News*. You moved to Denver three years ago to take a seat on—"

"I-I don't know who you are, but I'm getting security!" Quick on her dressy little feet, she darted past him toward the door.

He caught her easily, turned her about, and hauled her against him—just as the door opened and two middle-aged women wearing blue cleaning uniforms walked in. Unsure what she might say and wanting to avoid a scene and get rid of the women, Julian ducked down and silenced her with his mouth.

Tessa heard the door open behind her, felt the hot shock of his lips on hers, and in dazed disbelief realized what he was doing. He was trying to shush her, trying to control her. It was nothing less than assault, and it both stunned and enraged her. She pushed against his chest to no avail, tried to scream, but when she opened her mouth, his tongue invaded, turning her scream to a stifled squeak.

A bolt of heat, unexpected and unwanted, shot through

her, and her insides seemed to melt as he attacked her senses, his tongue teasing hers with stolen strokes, his lips pressing hot and unyielding against hers. She couldn't stop herself from noticing how hard his body felt, couldn't stop the minty taste of his toothpaste from flooding her mouth, couldn't help taking in the scent of him—spice with just a hint of leather.

He's a stranger, Tess—maybe even a murderer.

Tessa's mind knew it, but her body didn't seem to care. The adrenaline in her blood warmed to pheromone, icy rage to steam. And before she realized it, she had quit fighting him, quit fearing him, quit breathing. Worse, she'd begun to kiss him back, her tongue curling with his, her bones going liquid as his hand slid slowly up her spine.

Behind her, the women gasped, giggled.

Tessa had forgotten all about them.

"¡Perdónenos!" Pardon us!

The door closed, and Tessa realized dimly that the women had gone.

But he didn't quit kissing her, not all at once. He nipped her tongue, drew her lower lip into his mouth, sucked it. Then, abruptly, he grasped her shoulders and held her out before him.

"I hope you listen closely, Ms. Novak, because I'd hate to see you on an autopsy slab." His eyes were darkest blue. His dark brows were bent together in a frown, his square jaw clean shaven, his lips unusually full for a man's. "I know you get paid to sensationalize other people's suffering, but this is one crime you'd better leave to the cops. You've already stirred up enough trouble with today's article. It would be best for both of us if you don't write another."

"Sensationalize—? You—! Oh!" She was so furious she could barely speak. "I watched that girl die! She begged me to help her, and I couldn't! But I'm going to do my best to help her now. I'm going to find out who killed—"

He gave her a little shake. "What you're going to do is get yourself killed! Let the cops do their job. Go chase an ambulance or something."

"Let go of me!" She jerked away from him, wiped a hand

across her mouth, tried to erase the lingering evidence of his kiss. "You drag me in here, assault me, insult me, and then try to tell me how to do my job? Who *are* you?"

"Are we on or off the record?"

"On."

"You don't need to know who I am."

"Off the record, then."

He seemed to hesitate. "I'm Julian Darcangelo, and I'm one of the good guys."

"That's a scary thought." Tessa thought he looked like one of the bad guys—a shadowy, criminal type. She didn't realize she'd spoken those last words aloud until the corner of his mouth turned up in a sardonic grin.

"You know better than to judge people by appearances, Ms. Bates. Oh, I'm sorry—it's Novak, isn't it? And next time you hold a gun on someone, don't let him get so close. Never take your eyes off his."

Then he brushed past her, opened the door, and strode out into the hallway.

By the time her legs were steady enough for her to follow him, he was gone.

TESSA SAT IN the cooling water of her bath, sipping a glass of pinot grigio and trying to soak the day's tension away. She'd intended to leave the hospital and canvas the neighborhood around the gas station to see if anyone else remembered seeing the four girls or knew where they lived, but she'd been too shaken, too angry, too confused for that.

Instead, she'd sat in her car in the hospital parking lot and called Chief Irving, demanding to speak with him immediately.

"Who is Julian Darcangelo?" Chief Irving had repeated her question, as if he couldn't believe it. "Why the hell are you asking me that?"

"I just ran into a man claiming to be Julian Darcangelo at University Hospital," she'd explained. "He says he's one of the good guys. I thought you might know if that's true."

"Damn it! Tell me what happened."

And so she'd told him, well aware Chief Irving hadn't yet answered her questions.

"Let me get this straight. You tried to pull the fire alarm. He grabbed you and dragged you into a closet, where you pointed a loaded gun at him. He disarmed you, and then"—Chief Irving had coughed or choked—"and then he *kissed* you?"

"*Assaulted* me."

"Christ! That's just great." Even through the spotty cellular connection she'd been able to hear Chief Irving swearing. "What I'm about to tell you is not to be repeated, recorded, or reported in any way, do you understand, Ms. Novak?"

"Yes, sir."

"I'm only telling you this because I really see no other choice. But if I read his name in your paper, you're going to become a persona non fucking grata at the station. You'll get a parking ticket every day of your life—and two on Christmas!"

"Is that a threat?"

"You bet it is."

"Okay, then. Glad we got that cleared up."

"Julian Darcangelo *is* one of the good guys, and that little description of him you ran in your article might put his life at risk. That's all you're getting." And with that, Chief Irving had hung up on her.

She'd put Julian Darcangelo's life at risk?

You've already stirred up enough trouble with today's article. It would be best for both of us if you don't write another.

She'd realized that could mean only one thing: Mr. Darcangelo was some kind of undercover cop. That's why he'd known so much about her. He'd done a background check, digging into her private past. Then he'd thrown her secrets in her face.

God, what if she'd shot him? What if she'd killed an innocent man?

She didn't want to think about that.

Then again, Mr. Darcangelo was anything but innocent.

Certainly, she was relieved to know he was a cop and not a killer. She would have been appalled to think she'd responded like that to the kiss of a cold-blooded murderer.

God, the man could kiss!

Had she ever been kissed like that before? No, she hadn't. Not in her life. She'd never found kissing to be that pleasurable, perhaps because she'd always been afraid of what might follow. She'd vowed not to make the mistakes her mother had made and had kept men at arm's length, waiting for the one man she knew she could trust and love.

She thought she'd met him during her junior year in college. A theater major with a poet's face, Scott Chambers had seemed to fall as desperately in love with her as she was with him. It was only after she'd slept with him that he'd confessed he'd always wanted to have sex with a true blonde. Not long after, he'd taken up with a dance major, leaving Tessa to wonder how she could have misjudged him so completely.

That was seven years ago, and she hadn't been near a man since. The last man she'd seen naked was Lissy's husband, Will, and that had been an accident, though not an unwelcome one from Tessa's point of view. Will was a former college football star and had the body of a god.

It wasn't that Tessa didn't want sex. She fantasized about it. Wished for it. Yearned for it. But never again did she want to find herself lying on some man's sheets feeling used and empty and alone. Besides, her fantasies of sex had been much more satisfying than the act itself. Except for one kiss this afternoon.

Was she truly so sex starved that she'd responded?

Like a plucked string.

Not only did she know it. *He* knew it, too. He must know it.

Tessa closed her eyes and tried to remember every detail—the pressure of his lips, the probing heat of his tongue, the hardness of his muscles. She felt a flutter in her belly, felt her nipples tighten, and found herself touching her lips as if to bring back the sensation.

But it hadn't really been a kiss, had it?

It was nothing more than a way to shut you up, girl.

At least he hadn't used a sock or duct tape.

Of course, she didn't like the fact he'd dug into her private past. He knew things about her that she'd never shared with anyone. Whenever her friends asked about her family, she evaded, letting them assume she was from Georgia. She'd worked hard to lose her Texas accent and adopt the more genteel tones of Georgia. She'd struggled to pay her way through college, putting in sleepless nights at the school paper. Then she'd fought her way up the ladder at the *Morning News*. Along the way, she'd stopped being Tessa Bates—the poor little white-trash girl with no daddy—and had become Tessa Novak.

Never once had she looked back.

She didn't want to look back, didn't want to remember the poverty, the shame, the isolation. Trying to sleep while Grandpa and Mama fought all night and the police came. Going to school in clothes that her neighbors had given to the Salvation Army. Coming home to find Grandpa passed out on the floor after spending the day with Jack Daniel's. Getting caught stealing books from school because she wanted so much to read. Wondering if what the other kids told her was true—that Grandpa was also her daddy.

Tessa's mama is her sister—and her mama. That's what my mama says.

The rumors hadn't been true. Her mother had assured her of that. But Tessa no longer gave a damn who her father was. She didn't need to steal books to read, nor did she wear castoffs. She bought what she needed with money she'd earned through hard work. She wasn't running from her past, as Mr. Darcangelo had seemed to imply, taunting her with her former last name. No, she'd worked her way free of it.

Outside her apartment in the street, a police siren wailed, making her jump. The sound of it sent chills down her spine. The victim's advocate had told her she might be on edge for a while. Unfortunately, the victim's advocate had been right.

Feeling strangely vulnerable in the bathtub, Tessa released the drain with her toes, then stood, wrapped herself with a towel, and finished getting ready for bed. Drowsy from the wine, she checked to make sure her door was locked, then she slipped beneath her down comforter. But it was a long time before she fell asleep.

* * *

JULIAN WORKED THROUGH his aikido routine in the dim light of his basement, sweat running down his face and bare chest. Instincts were his first line of defense. His body was his second. He trained it, kept it in fighting shape, just as he did any other weapon.

Aikido also cleared his head, helped him think. He ought to be sleeping; apart from a catnap this morning, he'd been awake for more than forty-eight hours. But he was too tense for that, his thoughts tangled in long blond hair. He needed to stop thinking about Tessa Novak. He had a job to do, and it didn't include doing her.

Too damned bad, really.

He shifted his mind to Burien—again.

Zoryo'd had little to add to what he'd already told them, claiming not to have seen Burien in years. But the old man at the hospital had been more helpful than Julian had expected. He'd been able to describe the girls—and the middle-aged woman who'd acted as their guard dog—in some detail. Simms had guessed the girls lived nearby, and the details he'd shared had fit what Julian already knew about Burien's operations: he kept the girls in small groups and dominated them through terror, using a mixture of brutal punishments and small rewards—like candy.

The bastard was clearly using Denver as his home base now, but where was he? He'd been the brains of the operation before, calling the shots from Los Angeles, while García had handled the supply problem in Mexico and Pembroke had overseen transportation. They'd had some cribs in the Denver area but never any major interests, keeping mainly to border states. Although Operation Liberate had brought down both García and Pembroke, Julian had lost control of his emotions and moved early, enabling Burien to escape.

Julian had come close to losing control of the situation today, too. One minute he'd been on top of things, the next he'd been staring down the barrel of a .22. He had to give the woman credit. It had taken a lot of courage for her to pull a weapon on him. He outweighed her by a good eighty pounds and stood almost a foot taller, and still she'd tried to defend herself.

That wasn't the only way she'd surprised him. He'd clamped his mouth over hers to silence her, had thrust his tongue between her lips to stifle her scream—and she'd melted. That was the only word for it. Her entire body had softened in his arms, her resistance gone.

And then she'd kissed him back, her response sweetly sensual and so arousing that he'd forgotten the kiss was just a tactical maneuver and had found himself enjoying it. He'd kept kissing her even after it was no longer necessary, savoring the feminine feel of her, inhaling her scent, feeling satisfaction at her little gasp when he'd sucked on her lip.

Damn it, Darcangelo! Stay on task!

He stopped, crossed the room to his water bottle, and drank deeply. Then he went back to the center of the room and started his routine again.

The trick was finding Burien, getting to him without him knowing anyone was coming. It seemed no matter how close Julian got, the son of a bitch was one step ahead. He was as hard to grab hold of as smoke, but he wasn't a master at disguises or a linguistic genius. He was an arrogant thug with an obvious Russian accent. Wherever he was, he would stick out. He knew this and lived a reclusive life, using his minions to deal with the outside world. Utterly without pity, he controlled his sordid empire through fear.

S-stay away from me! I-I saw you that night! I know you were there!

Julian knew Tessa had been terrified of him, certain he was a killer come to kill again. No doubt that explained her reaction to his kiss. Danger was an aphrodisiac for some women. God knows, it had been for Margaux. She'd loved to fuck after a bust and had liked it rough. There'd never been tenderness between them, nothing sweet, nothing soft. She'd been drawn to him because of his dark past—and because her father, an FBI legend, hadn't approved of him.

The thrill of danger—surely, that's all it had been. Tessa

had felt his .357, had thought he meant to use it, and when he'd kissed her, her fear had transformed into lust.

That's fine for her, but what's your excuse?

His next kick found him off balance. He stopped, swore.

Did he need an excuse to enjoy kissing a pretty woman?

Yeah, he did—if it caused him to lose focus. He was here to stop Burien, not to diddle some headline-chasing journalist, no matter how soft and sexy she was.

I watched that girl die! She begged me to help her, and I couldn't! But I'm going to do my best to help her now.

Her eyes had misted with tears when she'd spoken those words, as if she'd really meant them. Julian found himself remembering the stricken look on her face the night of the murder. Something stirred in his gut. Understanding? Sympathy? Protectiveness?

He took another deep drink of water, washed the feeling away.

Ms. Novak was single—he knew that now. The man who'd picked her up that night was the husband of a friend—a state senator who'd been exonerated of murder some time back. But even if Julian hadn't been on a case, he wouldn't have tried to get her into bed. He could tell she placed complicated expectations on sex. She wasn't the kind of woman who would come—and then go. She'd want love and commitment. She'd want the white picket fence.

Not that Julian hadn't wanted those things, too, once upon a time. He'd fallen head over heels in love with the young Mexican prostitute his father had paid to fuck him for his fifteenth birthday—a romance that had lasted until he'd walked in and found her screwing his father. Then, many years later, he'd thought himself in love with Margaux, but in retrospect, their time together seemed more like a triple-X flick than a real relationship. He'd been an idiot to mistake it for anything other than what it had been—sexual obsession.

Since then, Julian had limited himself to women who knew what they wanted and took as much as they gave. No commitments, no attachments.

No tenderness. Nothing soft. Nothing sweet.

No, he had no business even thinking about Tessa Novak. The kind of life he lived wasn't meant to be shared.

He set the water aside, walked across the center of the room to start his routine again, and was almost relieved when his phone rang.

It was Chief Irving.

"It's Zoryo," he said. "Get to the jail now."

Julian grabbed his shirt and ran for the stairs.

CHAPTER 5

"SONOFABITCH!" JULIAN SLAMMED his fist against the steel railing of the gurney, his head throbbing with rage. "Well, Zoryo, you bastard, you found a way."

Zoryo didn't respond. He lay on a triage bed, staring at the ceiling, dead. His face was blue and engorged, his throat bruised. His fleshy chest and belly were bare, the tiger tattoo on his chest pale against his blue skin. Red marks on his skin showed where the paddles of the defibrillator had singed him.

"He must've really wanted to die to pull it off like he did." The crew-cut jail captain, a paper pusher by the name of Willis, stood next to the gurney, arms crossed defensively across his chest. "It took determination."

"Determination? You sound like you admire him. The man was a stone-cold killer and a baby raper—and you let him escape justice." Julian slipped clenched fists into his pockets, turned his back on the captain—a better option than slamming them into the idiot's face.

Chief Irving cleared his throat. "You need to understand that Special Agent Darcangelo put in months of hard-core undercover work catching this scum. Zoryo was his best lead on a top-priority case."

Now that lead was gone. Months of risk and countless

hours of pretending to be turned on by the same abominable filth Zoryo enjoyed amounted to nothing but wasted time. Julian's only consolation was that Zoryo's death had been slow.

The bastard had strangled himself, hanged himself from a height of only three feet. A guard on rounds had found him in his cell, already dead, dangling from a garrote he'd fashioned from his bedsheet and had wrapped around his sink, his knuckles dragging on the floor.

"I've already spoken with both guards and determined they weren't at fault. They followed standard operating procedure for—"

"Standard operating procedure?" Julian gave a snort of disgust, turned to face Willis. "How can you fucking talk about 'procedure' when one of your inmates is dead? Isn't a corpse proof that your procedures were insufficient?"

Willis's spine grew stiffer. "When someone is that set on killing himself—"

"You watch him like a hawk, for Christ's sake! Why do you think I had him put on suicide watch?" Julian had no use for bureaucrats.

"There will be a full investigation into this, believe me, and when it's done—"

"I don't give a damn about your investigation!" Julian pointed toward Zoryo's corpse. "What I need is the information locked in his brain so that I can stop a killer!"

Then Julian turned and strode out of the infirmary, through the various checkpoints, and out the back door into the well-lit parking lot, his blood at the boiling point. He should have stayed. He should have spent more time questioning Zoryo and less time at the hospital. He should have ordered Zoryo placed in restraints.

Goddamn it!

"Darcangelo!" Chief Irving's voice followed him.

Julian stopped, turned, and saw Irving hurrying after him as fast as his girth permitted. Too furious and restless to stand still, he paced the empty parking space between two cars, jamming his fists back into his pockets.

"For what it's worth, I'm sorry. I know how much you put on the line to bring Zoryo in. I know what he meant to you."

Teeth clenched, Julian met Irving's gaze. "Do you?"

"Yeah, I do." The old cop gave a stubborn nod. "And I know something else. Beating up on yourself for not preventing this won't change what happened three years ago."

Julian gave a snort of disgust. "If I'd have done my job three years ago—"

"Zoryo would still have been out there doing what he liked to do!" Irving's voice carried across the parking lot, got the attention of a couple cops who stood talking beside their cruisers in the yellow glow of a streetlight. "At least you got him off the streets. If he really was as important to Burien as you think he was, you've dealt Burien a serious blow. How long do you think before Burien realizes Zoryo is missing?"

"A few days, a week at best."

"How will he react?"

"He'll close ranks, alter his routine, replace Zoryo with someone else."

There was always someone else. No matter how many sick bastards Julian put away there always seemed to be another.

"When you bring Burien down, you'll bring the rest with him. Now go home and get some sleep—and that's an order. You've been pushing it too damned hard." Irving clapped a hand on his shoulder. "Tomorrow we've got something else to discuss."

Feeling a weariness that went beyond lack of sleep, Julian turned toward his truck. "What's that?"

"Tessa Novak."

TESSA GOT UP after an almost sleepless night, showered, and drove to the nearest coffee shop, wondering if it would seem extreme if she asked for five shots of espresso. She settled on her usual three and nudged her way through traffic to the paper, trying not to think about the shooting—or Julian Darcangelo and his devastating mouth.

Once at the paper, she sipped her way back to life while

reading through press releases and e-mails at her desk. Safety tips for Halloween. Twelve arrests at a prairie dog protest in Boulder. Cops donating time to a local battered women's shelter. The arrest of a parole officer who . . .

Tessa read through the press release in disgust. "God, I've heard a lot of weird stuff, but this beats it all. A parole officer was arrested on suspicion of stalking. Do you want to know what he was doing?"

Sophie looked up from her own notes. "Will we still be friends if I say no?"

"The guy was ejaculating into black pumps—you know, women's shoes—and leaving them in the bedrooms of his female parolees."

For a moment there was silence in the newsroom. Then it exploded with a chorus of female moans. "Ewww!"

Matt adjusted his pathetic wrinkled tie. "Can you imagine that first phone call to a lawyer. 'Hi, can you help me? I'm in the pokey.' 'What's the charge?' 'Jerking off into shoes and leaving them in women's bedrooms.' "

"You think that's strange? There was this man on the Rez who . . . well . . ." Kat paused. "One word: sheep."

Thank God it was Friday.

But the day only got weirder.

Tom was in a bad mood because he'd argued with his girlfriend, who, much to everyone's amusement, was Kara's freespirited mother, Lily McMillan. He bit off everyone's heads during the meeting, until finally Syd asked him to snap out of it. The two of them got into a shouting match that ended when Kat got up and walked out of the room.

"This isn't productive," she said simply before the door swung shut behind her.

And the meeting was over.

Tessa made a few phone calls about the parole officer, then she wrote up a quick six-inch story, finishing in time to have lunch with Sophie.

They chose salads—really just piles of wilted leaves with cucumber slices and cherry tomatoes thrown on top—and sat in their favorite corner of the cafeteria.

"Do you think Kara knows how vital her mother is to the smooth functioning of the newsroom?" Sophie asked, dousing her leaves with a packet of Italian dressing. "Maybe we should call her and beg her to ask her mother to make up with Tom, start the Lily McMillan Fund, or something."

Tessa drizzled ranch on hers. "I think Kara spends most of her time trying not to think about it. How would you feel if your mother were sleeping with Tom Trent?"

"I'd say she deserved hazard pay." Sophie picked up her fork and jabbed a tomato.

They talked over their news stories while they ate and were soon joined by Holly, who also had a salad, and Lissy, who had a thick, juicy cheeseburger that looked like sin and smelled like heaven.

"Pregnancy is the only time in a woman's life when it's all right for her to be fat, and I'm making the most of it," Lissy said, when they all eyed her lunch with envy. "Besides, I didn't eat for the first three months because I was too nauseated."

For a while they talked about Lissy's pregnancy—how she was feeling, how Will was pampering her, what her plans were for the birth. Then Lissy and Holly told them about some new designer line that was being manufactured out of Denver and the upcoming show that the designer, Anton, was hosting at the Adam's Mark Hotel.

"High fashion has finally come to Denver." Lissy dabbed the corners of her mouth with a napkin. "Last year, Anton did incredible things with grommets and peasant patterns."

Sophie and Tessa looked at each other.

"Grommets?" they said, almost in unison.

But as Tessa listened to her friends' cheerful conversation, she found herself feeling disconnected, as if she weren't really there. She smiled. She laughed. But inside she felt wooden.

It was Sophie who finally said something. "How are you holding up, Tess—and don't say 'fine,' because I can see for myself that's not true."

"I'm just tired." At first Tessa meant to steer the conversation away from her problems. But then she realized she wanted to tell them. "I've had a hard time sleeping. Every time I hear a noise, I wake up, and yesterday I ran into the man in the black leather jacket."

They gaped at her.

"Oh, my God, Tessa! Did you call the police?"

"Funny you should ask."

Tessa wrestled for a moment with what she could tell them. She hadn't told Tom anything, knowing the information wouldn't be safe with him. Swearing them to secrecy and keeping her voice to a whisper, she told them how she'd gone to see Mr. Simms and had ended up in a linen closet kissing a tall, dark-haired man she'd thought was a murderer who'd turned out instead to be some kind of undercover police officer. She told them everything—except for Julian's name and the details he'd uncovered about her past.

"You actually held a gun on him?" Lissy stared at her. "A gun with bullets in it?"

"Oh, who cares about that?" Holly smiled. "Go back to the part where he had his tongue in your mouth."

"He only did that to shush me up. It wasn't a real kiss."

"It sure sounds like it turned into a real kiss. I'll bet he's attracted to you." Holly gave her a self-satisfied smirk. "He *did* keep kissing you."

Tessa's stomach did a little flip. She didn't know what to say.

"You know, Tessa," Lissy said, "I think this tall, dark, and deadly guy went out of his way not to hurt you. He could have arrested you—maybe even shot you."

"And if he's an undercover cop and Chief Irving is worried that *his* life is in danger, then I'm worried about you." Sophie paused, took a sip of her mineral water. "Whoever is behind the shooting—they sound really dangerous. Could be you've stumbled onto a big story—or had it stumble onto you."

Tessa had lain awake last night thinking the same thing. "Most drive-by shootings are gang related, so that's where I'm going to start. This afternoon I'm going to check out the neighborhood around the gas station and see what I find."

* * *

TESSA PARKED HER car on the side street across from the gas station, which was once again open for business, then walked south. She wasn't sure why she chose this street, except that it seemed to her the girl had come from this direction. Having nothing else to go on, she was willing to trust instinct.

It was an older neighborhood with mature trees. Aging apartment buildings competed with even older houses for space. The sidewalk was crumbling in some places, sloped in others where tree roots had pushed it up. Most of the yards were maintained, their lawns brown from the dry fall and scattered with orange leaves. A few of the houses had tricycles on their porches and Halloween decorations on their doors and windows—families with small children. Parked cars lined the street on both sides—small economy cars, old junkers, newer SUVs, even a sports car or two. Clearly, people visiting the theaters and businesses on Colfax felt safe enough to use this neighborhood to park.

It wasn't the kind of neighborhood she'd associate with gang activity. She knew what poverty was, and this wasn't it. The folks who lived here were not desperately poor; they simply weren't wealthy enough for a new coat of paint every year. Perhaps some gang claimed this street as part of their territory but rarely came through.

She saw her first bit of gang graffiti on the side of an apartment building. At first it seemed a jumble of blue letters made to look three-dimensional, crowded together and piled on top of one another. She walked up to it, tried to break it down.

The biggest word was "CUZZ," a slang term for Crips.

Then the words "Syko" and "Flaco" emerged—probably the names of the gang members who'd painted it, one clearly Hispanic.

Beneath that was "O.G."—original gangster—and "SLOB" with the "B" covered by a black "X" to indicate "Blood killer."

Beside that was scrawled "Trey-8," street slang for a .38.

Syko and Flaco were trying to take credit for killing a member of the Bloods with a .38.

She wrote the words down in her notepad, then took out her camera, stepped back from the wall, and snapped a picture.

She knew the Crips were the biggest gang in Denver and, like their rivals, the Bloods, were under the direction of gang leaders in Los Angeles. Both gangs sold crack and other drugs, fighting each other and the city's numerous Chicano and Mexican Nationalist gangs for supremacy on the streets. Yet, compared to the gang scene in New York City and Los Angeles, Denver was Eden—few shootings, little fatal violence.

Tessa tucked her camera back into her purse and walked the length of the alley, finding a few more examples of graffiti, some from harmless taggers, the rest from the eloquent spray can of Syko and Flaco. She headed back to the sidewalk and continued down the street.

It was a bright, sunny day, the sky wide and blue as only a Colorado sky could be, and she realized with a sense of relief that she'd gone at least an hour without thinking of Julian Darcangelo and his lethal lips. She'd no doubt overreacted, imagined more heat and finesse in his kiss than there actually had been. She'd been afraid for her life, after all, adrenaline surging through her system and heightening her senses. He probably kissed like a fish.

Her spirits lifted a notch, and she decided to knock on a few doors.

No one answered at the first three houses on the block. The fourth was home to an elderly African-American couple who wanted to talk about their grandchildren but knew nothing about gang activity or the shooting.

"We don't read the papers," the husband told her. "Too much bad news."

The fifth house was inhabited by several college students, one of whom was home—an Anglo kid with spiky brown hair.

"Whoa, yeah," he said when she told him about the shooting. "Yeah, I read about it in the *Indy.* Are you the chick who wrote that? I've seen that car around—the one with the hot rims. Hot car."

But he couldn't tell her who drove the hot car, nor did he recognize her description of the victim. And though he'd seen boys he thought were gang members hanging out on Colfax, he'd never seen them come this far into the neighborhood.

Four houses farther down, she spoke with a young Asian-American mother while her two toddlers ran laps around her ankles. The woman said she'd read about the shooting but had seen neither the car nor anyone who looked like a gang member. But when Tessa described the victim and asked her if she'd ever seen four young women walking together down the sidewalk, the look of surprise on the woman's face was unmistakable.

"Oh, gosh! Yes, I think I saw them once or twice. Tyler, stop it!" She reached down, separated one child from the other. "I think I saw them a few times this summer while I was working in the garden—four Hispanic teenage girls and an older woman. I can only garden on the weekends when my husband, Terry, is home. Were they gang members?"

"I don't know, but I'm trying to learn all I can."

"Tyler!" The woman gave an exasperated moan. "I guess that explains why the police were at their house that night. They probably came to tell her family she was dead, didn't they?"

"I imagine so." Tessa felt her pulse quicken. "You know where her family lives? Can you show me which house it is?"

One of the little angels let out a piercing wail.

"Tyler and Sasha, I'm going to put you both in time-out! You're not going to print my name, are you? I don't want my name in the paper, especially not if there's a killer out there."

"I understand. I won't use your name if that's what you'd prefer."

The woman picked up her crying daughter and led Tessa out onto her porch. "Third house down and across the street. A lot of people come and go from there, mostly men. It's been pretty quiet since the police were there."

Tessa counted the houses, saw a dilapidated white bungalow with a black roof. "Thanks so much. You've been a huge help, Ms.—"

"Aito—Wendy Aito. Good luck." Then the woman vanished indoors, balancing her daughter on her hip, her son in tow.

Tessa crossed the street, thinking of all the things she'd like to tell the victim's family.

I wish I had been able to help her, but I froze. I'm sorry.

It happened so quickly, I didn't have time to react.

I'm so, so sorry.

Tessa approached the house, felt a strange sense of misgiving, thrust it aside. Ms. Aito had said this was where the girl's family lived. It wasn't the killer's hideout. She walked up the cracked sidewalk, up the front steps, and knocked on the door.

No one answered.

She knocked again.

Still no one came.

She knocked a third time and had just fished a business card out of her purse when the door opened to reveal a little old woman with bowed shoulders, tight white curls, and thick glasses. She was using a walker.

"I don't want any!" the woman said in a thin, trembling voice.

Tessa held out her card. "I'm not selling anything, ma'am. I was wondering if you had a moment to talk."

"Speak up!" The old woman tapped her ear, pointing out her hearing aids. "Can't hear a thing. Needs a new battery, but I don't get out much. Come in."

Tessa walked inside.

JULIAN WATCHED TESSA enter the old lady's house, watched her come out twenty minutes later, saw the old lady point to the rear of her home.

"Oh, for God's sake!"

Chief Irving was right—she was persistent.

Irving had ripped Julian's head off this morning for the kissing stunt at the hospital.

"Tessa Novak is not just a reporter, Darcangelo. She's a member of the *Denver Indy*'s elite Investigative Team and the best cop reporter I've known. Half of my men are scared shitless of her. The other half think they're in love with her. And I'll tell you something else—I respect the hell out of her! I've spent the better part of three years trying to convince her we're not crooks. Now do you want to tell me why you dragged her into a linen closet and kissed her yesterday? She's calling it assault, and I'm just damned grateful it's not on the front page this morning together with your goddamned name!"

Assault? Julian supposed it *had* been involuntary. Then again, he hadn't wanted to kiss her, either—at first. Besides, her tongue had found its way into *his* mouth, too.

But he hadn't told Irving this. Instead, he'd taken responsibility for his actions and made it clear that he'd had few options that didn't include making a scene or leaving bruises on Ms. Novak's pretty skin. Then he'd gone to the morgue to watch the ME dissect Zoryo. Though the lab results weren't in yet, the cause of death looked like suicide by asphyxiation.

Still angry as hell about losing Zoryo, Julian had spent the afternoon brooding and sitting in his truck down the street from the basement apartment, writing down the license plate numbers of all the men who'd driven up, parked their nice cars, and walked around back expecting a little forbidden action, only to hurry away when they saw the police tape. He would send officers to question each and every one of them. Once he told them about the dozens of DNA samples the cops had acquired from the victim's body, the sheets, and used condoms, they would crack like eggshells and tell him anything he wanted to know.

He'd spotted Tessa several houses down the street, the sight of her both pissing him off and causing a chemical reaction that had his blood heating by a few degrees.

It's called "lust," Darcangelo.

He'd watched her progress as she went door to door, enjoying the sway of her hips in her navy blue skirt, the bounce of her golden curls against her tailored jacket, the feminine shape of her legs. And he'd wondered what in the hell he was going to do with her.

She walked to the back of the house, saw the police tape, and stood there, staring at it. Then she ducked beneath it.

And then Julian knew.

CHAPTER 6

Julian made a call on his radio. Then he grabbed a pair of cuffs, slipped them into the pocket of his jacket, climbed out of his truck, and walked round to the back of the house. He knew the DA would drop the charges, but at least he could teach her a lesson.

She was at the bottom of the back stairs, peering through the door's little window, so preoccupied with her prying that she didn't hear him approach.

"Be damned glad the three bears aren't home, Goldilocks. You're under arrest."

She gasped, whirled about, looked up at him. Then her big, blue eyes narrowed. "You!"

He lifted the yellow tape, motioned for her to come up and out. "Crossing police lines is a municipal offense, but obstructing government operations is a felony."

"What government operations?" She climbed the stairs, her heels clicking on the concrete, then ducked under the tape.

"Hands behind your head. Fingers laced, feet apart. You know the drill."

"You can't be serious!" She stared up at him as if he'd gone insane.

"I've never been more serious." He rested his hand on the

small of her back, propelled her away from the hazard of the stairs, the silky softness of her curls beneath his palm.

She knocked his hand away. "Don't touch me!"

"Assaulting a police officer, resisting arrest, failure to follow a lawful order." He looked at her over the top of his sunglasses, entertained by the look of astonishment on her face. "You're building quite the rap sheet, Ms. Novak."

She gave a little feminine cry of rage, dropped her purse onto the ground, and assumed the position, fury on her pretty face. "Chief Irving is going to have your head!"

She was probably right. Still, he couldn't help but smile. Compared to the hardened killers he usually dealt with, this was going to be like arresting Barbie. "I think he might demand to know why you were snooping around on a case he's asked you to drop."

"I don't answer to Chief Irving! You do!" She turned her head and glared at him. "Besides, I wasn't 'snooping around'! I thought the girl's family lived here. I wanted to offer my condolences."

"You should have sent flowers." He walked up close behind her to search her, saw her stiffen. She really *didn't* want him to touch her. Or did she?

He reached around to feel between her breasts with the edges of his hands. "You have the right to remain—"

The moment he touched her, she gasped and jerked her arms down to her sides, tottering on her heels and falling back against him.

Had an adult male done that in the middle of a bust, Julian would have assumed the suspect was gearing up for violence and would have subdued him. But Tessa wasn't the murderer-rapist he was used to frisking, and he found her skittishness both amusing and strangely appealing.

He steadied her, placed her back on her fancy feet. Then he grasped her wrists and forced them back to her head. "Easy, Tessa, I'm not going to molest you."

He worked quickly, his hands finding their way over her narrow rib cage and her gently rounded belly, down her slender waist and the flare of her hips, up the sleek length of her calves and thighs. "You have the right to remain silent. Anything you say can and will be used against you in a court of law."

The words came automatically—and it was a good thing, because the thinking part of his brain had shut down. It didn't help that everywhere he touched her, she tensed—her shoulders, her belly, her thighs. As an agent, it was second nature for him to be aware of even the subtlest motions of those he took into custody; it was a skill that had kept him alive. But this was something different.

It was physical. It was chemical. It was damned distracting.

And it told him something he didn't necessarily want to know: Tessa Novak might look cool and aloof, but inside she was fire.

Down, boy.

"You have the right to speak to an attorney and to have an attorney present during any questioning. If you cannot afford a lawyer, one will be provided for you at government expense. Do you fully understand these rights as I have explained them to you?"

"Go to hell!" Her voice had lost some of its defiance.

"Use of fighting words." He took her wrists, bent her arms behind her back, and slipped the cuffs onto her wrists, leaving them looser than he would otherwise. "I hope you've got a good lawyer. A cozy stay at Club Fed is looking more likely by the minute."

A black-and-white slid up to the curb, its lights flashing.

Right on time.

"Maybe while I'm in booking I should file charges against you. How about kidnapping, false imprisonment, sexual assault, and false arrest for starters? That might make an interesting news brief, don't you think?"

He jerked her about to face him, leaned down close, and lowered his voice to the tone that frightened grown men with guns. "This isn't a game, Ms. Novak. I know things about kidnapping and sexual assault that are beyond your worst nightmares. If I see my name in your paper, heads will roll, starting with yours."

Her eyes grew wide, and her breath caught, but her chin came up.

Julian felt an absurd impulse to kiss her.

He thrust the impulse aside, reached down, picked up her purse, and searched it, while Petersen escorted her to the cruiser. Wallet. Sunglasses. Lipstick. More lipstick. Nail file. Tampons. Keys. Half a dozen pencils. Loaded .22. Notepad. Digital camera.

He scrutinized the last two and saw she was looking into a gang angle—a fact that bothered him. He didn't like the idea of her on the streets tangling with gangbangers.

"Sorry to see you under these circumstances, Ms. Novak," Petersen said, his hand on the top of her head to guide her inside the vehicle. "We'll get you down to the station and get you processed."

Julian placed her purse in the front seat. "She's got a loaded double-deuce in her purse, Petersen, though I'm not sure she knows how to use it. And be sure to book her on one count of falsifying information on a driver's license while you're at it."

"What?" she cried. "You're just making stuff up!"

He pulled off his shades, met her gaze, saw the outrage and disbelief in her eyes. "It says you weigh one-fifteen, but I know for a fact you're not a pound under one-twenty."

Her cheeks flushed crimson. "Oooh!"

Hungry and thirsty, Tessa sat in booking on a molded chair of orange plastic that was bolted to the floor—and which desperately needed to be scrubbed—her legs and feet bare and freezing. A few chairs down, a filthy man with a scraggly red beard and tangled blond hair sat in dirty jeans and an even dirtier plaid shirt, his gaze sliding over her body as if she were naked.

"What you in for, baby?"

"Castrating some guy because he annoyed me."

He stared at her for a moment, the lust vanishing from his eyes, then crossed his legs and looked away. "Bitch," he whispered.

Tessa still couldn't believe she was here. In booking. In the Denver jail. Under arrest for multiple felonies. She kept expecting someone to tell her it was all a joke or a terrible mistake and release her. But nobody was telling her anything. They hadn't even let her make her single phone call.

Officer Petersen had driven her downtown and escorted her to a controlled checkpoint. "Welcome to the Denver Hilton," he'd said.

He'd uncuffed her and asked her to remove first her shoes, which were passed through a little window one by one, and then her pantyhose. Next, a female guard had given her a thorough pat down, touching the few body parts Julian hadn't. After groping her, the guard had escorted her through the checkpoint to the waiting area, where, one by one, new arrests were called back to be fingerprinted and photographed.

Tessa felt humiliated—and furious. She knew it was against the law to cross police lines, but journalists did it all the time, usually with the cops' tacit approval. Never had Tessa heard of a journalist being busted for ducking under the yellow tape. And the rest of it—he was just making it up.

Obstructing government operations? It would never stick. Neither would assaulting a police officer. How could she possibly assault a man who was so much bigger and stronger than she was? Julian was probably some kind of black belt on top of everything else, but even if he'd been a ballerina in a pink tutu, he'd have been able to take her down without breaking a sweat.

He'd nearly frightened her to death, sneaking up behind her like that. Then he'd put her through a humiliating pat down—

Oh, God, she couldn't think about that. She couldn't.

She couldn't help *but* think about it.

She'd tried to play it cool, to act like getting frisked by six foot three of dark-haired, potent male was nothing more than an irritation—like getting stuck in traffic. But the moment he'd touched her, she'd lost her resolve, jerking her arms down, losing her balance, falling backward into the hard wall of his chest.

Easy, Tessa, I'm not going to molest you.

What in the hell had been wrong with her? She'd watched dozens of arrests during her career, had researched Koga arrest-control techniques. She'd known what he was going to do.

Sure, but you didn't know how it would feel, *did you?*

He'd stood so close behind her, his presence overwhelming. She'd felt his breath against her hair, heard the tight creaking of his leather jacket, smelled his spicy aftershave. She'd even sensed his body heat. His big hands had seemed to burn through her clothes, scorching her skin as he'd worked his way over her. And when his hands had slid over her pantyhose and up her thighs, she'd actually felt herself grow wet.

How could her body respond like that when she hated the man?

Okay, so maybe she didn't hate him, but she certainly didn't like him. Twice now he'd used force to intimidate her. And he'd found it amusing. She'd seen the humor in his eyes when he'd looked at her over the top of his sunglasses.

You're building quite the rap sheet, Ms. Novak.

Well, she'd be the one laughing when Chief Irving busted him down to dogcatcher.

Then again, something told her Chief Irving didn't have much control over Julian. Maybe it was the fact that Julian looked nothing like her idea of a undercover cop, plain and invisible. Or maybe it was his cockiness, an air about him that said he took orders from no one.

What had he been doing there? Obviously he'd been watching the place. Did he expect whoever had rented the apartment to return?

Be damned glad the three bears aren't home, Goldilocks.

What had he meant by that? Perhaps he'd been referring to the three surviving sisters. But why would they pose any threat to her? Or maybe he was referring to the killer, to whomever had been in the car that night. But that made no sense, either. Wendy Aito seemed certain the girls lived in the house, and Mrs. Davis, the little old lady who rented the upstairs, said they lived there, as well.

"They had a lot of male visitors," she'd said, in a tone that made it clear she disapproved.

Why would the girl have been running away from her home? Domestic violence? A boyfriend turned violent? Some kind of gang raid? Whatever the case, no one lived in the basement apartment now. From what Tessa'd been able to see, the apartment was empty.

"Tessa Marie Novak!"

Tessa cringed inwardly at the sound of her name shouted through the booking area. She was the only woman in the room. Couldn't they have just motioned for her?

A short cop with cropped dark hair and a mole on his narrow chin fingerprinted her, took her mug shot, then motioned for her to stand on a scale. The red digital number raced up to stick at 124.

It says you weigh one-fifteen, but I know for a fact you're not a pound under one-twenty.

Bastard!

"This way." The cop spoke to her in a bored voice, motioning her to follow him toward one of a half dozen holding cells.

Small rooms with thick glass windows, they looked something like fishbowls for people. She'd seen them before, but she'd never noticed their finer points—steel bunk, steel sink, visible steel toilet. No privacy. No comfort.

"If I might ask, sir, when do I get to make my phone call? And is there any way I can have a blanket or get my shoes back? My feet are freezing."

He ushered her into a vacant cell. "The chief is on his way to see you."

Finally! "Do you know when—?"

The thick steel door shut with a heavy click.

Tessa paced in her cage for what seemed forever, then, stomach growling, she sat on the steel bunk, pulled off her suit jacket, and draped it over her chilled legs and feet. She'd counted the tiles on the floor twice by the time Chief Irving appeared on the other side of the glass.

She stood, slipped back into her jacket.

A key in the lock. A metallic click. The door swung outward.

"Chief Irving, I am so glad to see you!"

She took one look at his face and knew the feeling wasn't mutual.

JULIAN WATCHED ON the monitor from the booking control room as Tessa followed Irving out of the holding cell. She looked pale and shaken as she walked up to the front counter, signed for her personal belongings, and walked on her still-bare feet toward a dressing room. He turned the dial, followed her with the camera, and saw her wipe her eyes. Was she crying?

Something twisted in his chest. He ignored it.

Crying was better than dead.

A door opened behind him.

"What did you say to her, Chief? She looks upset."

"I don't know whose ass to kick—yours or hers. But right now I feel like kicking yours."

Julian watched as Tessa walked into a dressing room and shut the door, blocking out the camera. Then he turned to face Irving, crossed his arms over his chest. "Fair enough."

Irving sat his girth in a rolling office chair. "She reminds me of my oldest daughter—tough on the outside, not so tough on the inside. I hate having to be hard on her."

"Don't tell me you've fallen for her fragile Southern belle act, too, Chief." Julian gave a snort of disgust, even as he acknowledged to himself that what Irving said about her was true. "She's got the entire DPD wrapped around her pretty pinky finger."

"Don't pretend you're not attracted to her, Darcangelo. I've worked with men my entire life. I can smell it when a cop gets a hard-on for a woman involved in one of his cases."

Julian hid his surprise. "Okay, I won't deny she's attractive." *An understatement.* "But *I* didn't just let her walk out of here without so much as a citation. She's interfering with my investigation, and I can't let her do that. There's too much at stake—including her life!"

"All true." Irving nodded. "But we poor city cops can't throw our weight around and bend the rules like you federal boys do, and I can't have you compromising my department's relationship with the media."

Feeling pissed off now, Julian stood. "What would you have had me do? Sit there while she scared off potential suspects?"

"I'm not sure what I would have done, but it's pretty clear that her stumbling over the crime scene was an accident. She was looking for information on gangs and got lucky."

"Yeah, lucky. How lucky would she have been had they come home?"

"They're not coming back, and we both know it. But I get your point, and so does she."

"What did you tell her?"

"Only that she'd be floating in the Platte River tonight if the occupant of the apartment had found her instead of you."

"That's why she was upset?"

Irving nodded. "And the fact that she's still traumatized by the shooting—can't sleep, has nightmares, keeps remembering the girl's last words. Survivor guilt."

Julian knew all about survivor guilt.

"I told her I'd make this up to her by having one of my men offer her some practice using that twenty-two of hers after work on Tuesday. That's you, Darcangelo."

Julian sat, gave a snort. "No way! Sorry, Chief, but I've got more important things to do than teach—"

"You'll do it, because I'm asking you to do it. I've done more than a few favors for you these past months—letting you call the shots, keeping my own men in the dark, concealing certain activities from your real boss. How much longer do you think I can sit on the murdered girl's autopsy report or deflect attention off Zoryo's arrest and suicide?"

Irving had him by the balls.

"Okay, I'll do it—once. But Tessa Novak is not my responsibility. I have a job to do, and it doesn't include babysitting a reporter."

"Keep her alive, Darcangelo. How you work out the conflict is up to you. In the meantime, just remember what the good book says."

Julian had never read the Bible. "What's that?"

Irving stepped into the hallway, looked back at him. "Never pick a fight with someone who buys ink by the barrel."

TESSA ACCEPTED A ride back to her car from Chief Irving, then drove home. She'd have some explaining to do on Monday, but she didn't feel like dealing with Tom tonight. Right now, all she wanted was to devour a pint of chocolate chip ice cream and watch mindless television.

She pulled into her assigned parking space, let herself in through the front entrance, and checked her mail. Nothing but junk.

She took the elevator to the seventh floor, let herself into her apartment, flicked on the lights, and locked the door tight behind her. All was as she'd left it. She dropped her briefcase by the door, let out a sigh of relief.

What had she been expecting? Fifteen armed gang members?

She went about her after-work routine, trying to shake the sense of foreboding she'd felt ever since Chief Irving had told her—off the record, of course—that it was the killer who'd lived in the basement apartment, not the girl's family.

"You'd be dead by now—or you'd wish you were," he'd said. "We'd eventually find you floating down the Platte."

She'd seen in his eyes that he was trying to scare her, but she'd also seen he was telling her the truth. And she'd done the most unprofessional thing she'd ever done—she'd confided in a source. She'd told Chief Irving how much trouble she'd had sleeping. She'd told him how every little noise made her jump. She'd told him about her nightmares.

She'd been certain he'd think she was a big wimp, and she'd said as much, only to have him lay a fatherly hand on her shoulder.

"Witnessing cold-blooded murder is no small thing, Ms. Novak. I've seen grown men who were bigger wimps than you—men with badges. Take some time off. Go visit your folks. Get out of town for a while. You'll feel better for it."

Then he'd offered to have one of his men guide her through a bit of practice shooting at the police shooting range.

She'd been reluctant at first, not wanting to make this any more real than it was. Besides, how hard could it be to point a gun at someone and pull the trigger? But then she'd remembered how quickly Julian had disarmed her, and she'd accepted. It wouldn't hurt to become more comfortable with the gun, to take a few practice shots. She'd studied the owner's manual, but she'd never once pulled the—

Down the hallway a door slammed, made Tessa jump.

And abruptly she knew what she wanted to do. She hurried to her phone and dialed Kara's cell phone, hoping it wasn't too late. Kara answered on the third ring.

"Oh, thank God I caught you! Can I please, please, please take you up on that invitation and come up to the cabin with you? I need to get out of town for a while."

THERE WERE SO many ways to savor women, so many ways to control them, to own them. Alexi had mastered them all— and become a very wealthy and powerful man because of it. He'd lifted himself from the frigid, gray streets of Moscow to a life of luxury in America. Few men could comprehend the control he had over the lives of others—or the great burden he felt when something went wrong.

He'd come close to losing everything three years ago. Julian Darcangelo had infiltrated his organization like a virus. But Alexi had turned the tables, manipulating Darcangelo to rid himself of two tiresome partners, using him to ferret out the weaknesses of his organization. It was a risky but symbiotic relationship—Darcangelo kept Alexi on his toes, and Alexi gave Darcangelo a life purpose. Alexi knew more about Darcangelo than the bastard knew about himself, and Alexi used it to his advantage. One day Darcangelo would have to die, but for now Alexi found him a useful, if formidable, opponent.

Still, he could not afford for any of his employees to make stupid mistakes.

He lowered the .44, watched the idiot he'd just shot slump to the floor. Then he shifted his gaze to the others, enjoying the scent of fear that permeated the warehouse. "One of my girls is dead, and I think this is good. She should be dead. But I wonder—how did she get away? She runs three blocks to a gas station, and no one stops her until witnesses are thick like flies on shit. Do you have an explanation for this?"

He lifted the pistol again, smiled when his target sank in a puddle of piss to his knees, hands raised in supplication.

"I-I don't know how she got out! Oh, God! Jesus! I was asleep, I fucking swear it! It was Toby's turn to watch the door!"

Alexi considered shooting this one, too. His business was only as strong as its weakest link, and this fool had crumpled so easily. What would he do if the police got hold of him—or, worse, Darcangelo. "You are nothing! Look at you—groveling in your own urine. Can you not even look death in the face?"

The imbecile slowly lifted his pale, sweaty face, his entire body trembling, his breath coming in sobs.

"Ah, see?" Alexi smiled. "You are not a complete coward. What will you do for me if I let you live?"

"Anything you ask! Anything you want! Oh, Christ!"

Alexi lowered the weapon. "There are two witnesses to this sloppy shooting, yes?"

A frantic nod.

"One of them is a journalist. See, she has written about the shooting for her paper." He held up a copy of the *Denver Independent*. "Very nice article."

"I-I'll pop her for you. I'll pop them both!"

"That is a kind offer—but very stupid. One does not simply shoot a reporter. It makes the other reporters ask questions."

"Wh-what should I do?"

"The old man—he has a bad heart, one leg already in the grave. You won't even need a gun. But the journalist . . ." Alexi considered the situation, weighed the pros and cons. "I want you to watch her. I want to know everything about her— where she goes, who she sees, what she eats for dinner. Then we shall see."

CHAPTER 7

THERE WAS NOTHING as therapeutic as a good snowball fight, and Tessa got into several on Saturday. She and Connor vanquished Reece twice, making up for their bad aim with sheer quantity of snow. Then she and Kara lost in a valiant struggle against the men. They were forced to award top snowball honors to Connor, who, at the age of six, was fearless.

When she wasn't outside playing like a kid in the snow—who'd have known making snow angels could be so fun?—she was inside the warm cabin, lending a hand in the kitchen, entertaining fourteen-month-old Caitlyn, or sitting in front of the fire and talking with her friends. Kara and Reece didn't push, and for a time Tessa said nothing about her investigation, wanting more than anything to put the shooting out of her mind.

But cradled by snowcapped 14,000-foot peaks, sheltered by groves of fragrant ponderosa pine and bare, white aspen and surrounded by the warmth of friendship, she felt the tension she'd been carrying all week melt away. And for the first time in days, she slept deeply.

Of course, it didn't hurt to know that Reece was armed. Tessa had caught sight of the holster that was clipped to his belt when he'd taken off his snow-soaked sweater. It wasn't just for her sake, she knew. He'd been carrying a concealed

weapon ever since the TexaMent ordeal that had almost gotten
both him and Kara killed.

By Sunday afternoon, Tessa found she wanted to get their
thoughts on the investigation. Over glasses of hot apple cider,
she told Reece and Kara what had happened since she'd last
seen them, leaving out anything that might compromise national security—Julian's name, her background, and the fact
that she seemed to turn to warm Jell-O every time Julian
touched her. When she finished she found herself looking at
two sets of somber eyes.

Kara broke the silence. "This is serious, Tessa. During the
TexaMent nightmare, Chief Irving told me he hoped I didn't
end up getting killed. He never said the kinds of things he's
saying to you. Floating in the Platte? Good lord!"

"Kara's right." Reece stood and added more wood to the fire.
"I trust Irving completely. If he thinks these guys are *that* dangerous, you need to do everything you can to protect yourself—
starting with staying away from that undercover cop."

"It's not like I've been trying to run into him, you know."
Tessa took a sip of her cider. "How would you handle this,
Kara?"

"I'd do what you've done—follow the gang angle and see
where it led."

"What if it led to the Platte?" Reece stoked the blaze, his
face toward the fire. Then he shut the glass door and went for
his coat. "I'm going to grab more wood."

He seemed angry.

"He's just worried about you, Tess."

Tessa nodded, feeling a warmth that had nothing to do with
the fire. She wasn't used to having people care this much
about her. "I know."

Then Kara glanced toward the door, as if to make certain
Reece couldn't hear them, her lips curving into a smile. "I
want to hear more about this undercover cop. You don't have
to tell me his name. Just tell me what it was like when he
kissed you!"

Tessa felt herself blush to the roots of her hair. "You're as
bad as Holly!"

* * *

JULIAN SAT AT the bar, pretending to be mesmerized by the topless blonde as she wrapped herself around a steel pole to the sterile rhythm of techno. She squatted down, offered a glimpse of her barely concealed crotch, then rose and reversed the view. A fake blonde with equally fake breasts, she had a smile painted on her young face. If she was eighteen, he was eighty.

He'd had the place under surveillance hours after Zoryo mentioned it. Three video cameras in the window of a fifth-floor hotel room down the street recorded everyone who came and went, catching every vehicle that entered the big parking lot. But there was only one way to find out what went on inside the club, and that was to be there.

Sunday night clearly wasn't the big moneymaker at Pasha's. The place was nearly empty. Last night it had been packed, with horny college boys mixing with bikers, CEOs, and geeks to indulge in their one common interest—tits and ass. None of them cared how the girls came to work there or what kind of conditions they endured. They came to satisfy a craving, some content merely to stare, others trying to cop a feel, a few hoping to arrange for more.

Julian had spent last night in the shadows, taking advantage of the crowd to look around. He'd located the cameras and the exits and watched who came and went through the guarded door to the right of the stage. Unless he was very much mistaken, there was more than accounting going on back there.

Tonight he was pretending to drink heavily and tipping big, hoping to catch someone's attention. Money was the only thing men like Burien lusted after more than women. Flashing lots of jack might be enough to get him behind that guarded door. It might also get him rolled.

The girl finished her dance routine with her breasts thrust out and her hands on her narrow hips in a sad attempt at seductiveness. The handful of hard-core patrons applauded, and one or two tossed cash. Julian pulled a fifty from the wad in his pocket and held it out to her, hoping to draw her nearer. It worked like a magnet.

She took the money, gave him the first genuine smile he'd seen all night. "Thank you."

She spoke with an accent—Russia, maybe Ukraine.

"My name's Tony—Tony Corelli." He leaned closer but didn't touch her. "What's your name, sweetheart?"

"Irena." A garden-variety Russian name and probably no more real than her breasts. She smiled but didn't make eye contact. "Would you buy me a drink?"

He knew damn good and well she wasn't old enough, but he pulled out another fifty. "Anything you want, baby."

They made small talk while she sipped her watered-down drink. Julian learned she was from Ukraine and had come to America after a talent scout had promised her a modeling job with a top New York agency. It went without saying that she should have known better. She was too short, her face too plain for the pages of *Vogue,* but when combined, poverty, ambition, and naiveté made powerful blinders. She wouldn't say why she was working as a stripper, but he already knew. Like millions of other girls, she'd arrived to find the promises false and the job quite different from the one she'd been offered.

"So, Irena," Julian leaned closer and lowered his voice to a husky drawl, "is there someplace we can be alone?"

"That is not allowed." For a moment she met his gaze, and he saw himself through her eyes—just another old man who wanted to get between her legs.

He was used to that look. He'd seen it too many times in too many places from too many girls just like her. But he didn't really want her at all. He wanted the man who had betrayed her, the man who was using her, the man who held her leash.

ON MONDAY MORNING, Tessa hit the newsroom feeling rested and refocused. She'd put the shooting into perspective, gotten Julian Darcangelo out of her mind, and put together a clear plan of action. She checked her messages, made an appointment for tomorrow morning with Chief Irving and the leader of the gang taskforce, then headed to the I-Team meeting.

"I had a productive afternoon on Friday," she said, omitting the fact that she'd spent a good part of it in jail. She hadn't yet figured out how she was going to tell Tom. "I found evidence of gang activity in the neighborhood—both witnesses and graffiti. I also found neighbors who claimed to have seen the car and the victim at one point or another. I've asked for a year's worth of gang-related police reports, as well as all correspondence between Denver's gang taskforce and the Los Angeles police. I'd like to have a news feature by Wednesday."

Tom nodded, then picked up a piece of paper and slid it across the conference table. "Care to explain this? A source in sheriff's records faxed it to me this morning."

Her arrest mug shot.

Tessa's pulse tripped. She met Tom's gaze, smiled. "I found what one witness thought was the victim's home and was arrested for going under the yellow tape. Chief Irving personally tossed the charges and apologized."

"He damned well better have." Tom leaned back, watched her coolly. "Any reason you didn't tell me?"

"If they hadn't let me out, you'd have been the first person I called."

Joaquin picked up the piece of paper, a grin tugging at his lips. "Nice shot."

Tom moved on. "James, what's the latest on Rocky Flats?"

But Tessa knew she hadn't heard the last of it.

"HER NAME WAS María Conchita Ruiz, age sixteen." Dyson sounded tired. He was in his late sixties now, beyond retirement age and deserving of some rest. Still, he kept going. Julian admired the hell out of him. "We got a positive ID from the Mexican consulate ten minutes ago. Mexican authorities say she disappeared on her way home from her *maquiladora* job in Ciudad Juárez."

Julian read through the report Dyson had just faxed over.

"That fits his pattern. His coyotes bring them across near El Paso, then divvy them up along the way, using truck stops, cheap hotels, and rest stops as transit points."

Human contraband was the easiest to conceal. Once controlled through threats, drugs, and violence, it could be hidden in plain sight.

"I sent Margaux up to Longmont to check out reports of underage girls working in a massage parlor there. The town has a large Hispanic population with a lot of undocumented agricultural labor. Could be Burien's taking advantage of that. She doesn't think so, and she knows him better than anyone except you. But the U.S. attorney's office has gotten several tips, so it seemed worth a look-see. Anything to report on your end?"

"I'm up to forty-seven suspected johns. We start questioning them today."

Julian didn't mention Lonnie Zoryo or his extracurricular activities at Pasha's. He hated keeping Dyson in the dark, but he'd suspected for some time that Burien had a mole at HQ. It was the only way to explain how the bastard had managed to remain one step ahead of him for so many years. He couldn't imagine it was Dyson—the very idea was unthinkable—but rather someone who worked in the same office. Until he knew who it was, he would keep some of his cards hidden.

"Heard you had a bit of trouble with a journalist."

Margaux's big mouth.

"One of the witnesses happened to be a journalist. I handled it."

Yeah, you handled it, all right, Darcangelo. You handled her, and now you can't get her off your mind.

"Good. I want this guy, Julian. I want his balls stuffed and hanging on my wall by Christmas. Let's get him and go home."

"I'm with you."

Julian hung up, read through the report again. He'd gotten the results of toxicology yesterday. Forensics had done all they could, giving Julian as complete a picture as he'd ever have of the victim's last hours. Combined with the evidence they'd taken from the basement apartment, it would lead him to the men who had imprisoned her—and hopefully to Burien.

Cause of death had been nine fatal shots to the torso—that much had been obvious. What hadn't been obvious was the heroin in her system and the track marks on her arms. Or the array of bruises on her body. Or the semen inside her that had come from seven distinct sources of DNA. Or the restraint marks around her wrists where she'd recently been bound.

María Conchita Ruiz had been born free and had died a slave.

You could have saved her.

It was the truth. Julian might have raided the place, put an end to what he knew was going on there, freed María and the other three girls. But he'd done his job—and waited. And while he'd been waiting for one of Burien's higher-ups to visit the girls and lead him back to his boss, María had found the strength to run.

Julian had made the opposite choice last time, busting down the door and charging in, guns blazing, to save a carload of kidnapped teenage girls from a similar hell. They had survived and gone home to their families, but Burien had escaped, his thugs wounding Margaux and killing two agents in the process.

Julian still struggled to live with that choice. Now he would have to live with this one.

He set the report down on his desk, then walked toward the shower, still sweating from his workout—aikido and weights. He'd slept late, having stayed at Pasha's until two a.m., talking with Irena and making headway with the bartender, an idiot named Chet who liked to brag about the number of strippers who'd danced on his dick. Julian had pretended to envy him while tossing back shots. Then he'd staggered out the door in a feigned drunk and headed off down the street to his truck, making certain he wasn't being followed.

He hadn't cracked the place, but he was making progress.

Tomorrow, he'd take his first look at what the surveillance cameras had picked up. But today he was going to pay a few upstanding members of the community a visit—and confront them about the way they spent their free time and their extra cash. Then he would check on Tessa and make certain she was keeping out of trouble.

Keep her alive, Darcangelo.

How the hell had she become his problem?

He stripped off his sweatpants, turned on the water, and stepped under the spray.

TESSA SAT ON the median in the middle of Speer Boulevard and watched a homeless beggar who said his name was Arthur work the line of cars stuck at the red light. Most of the drivers, on their way to lucrative jobs downtown, ignored him. Others rolled down their windows, passed dollar bills to him, and were rewarded with one of his nearly toothless grins and the words "God bless!"

She'd been interviewing him for about half an hour, the rhythm of their conversation dictated by the color of the traffic light. He smelled strongly of alcohol and had the restless edge of someone who'd lived most of his life on the street. Dressed in a dirty green army coat and tattered jeans, he held a cardboard sign that read, "Vietnam vet. Anything helps."

But Arthur wasn't really a war vet. He was an escaped felon who'd thumbed his way to Colorado from Louisiana, or so he claimed. When that announcement hadn't scared Tessa off—and after she'd laid a five-dollar bill in his hand—he'd started talking. He told her how gang members picked on the weaker homeless people, stealing their money, their booze, and their drugs, beating them up if they resisted—or just for fun. He told her how most of the time, those who'd been beaten chose not to seek medical help for fear the police would get involved.

"It's the rules of the street," he'd said.

The light turned green, and the queue of cars accelerated and moved down the street.

Arthur came over and stood beside her, his gaze on traffic. "It's too damned warm," he said. "I make better money when it's cold. People feel bad for me."

Tessa went back to her questions. "Have you heard any rumors about a turf war, any talk about a teenage girl being killed in a drive-by?"

Arthur glanced down at her as if she'd asked something really stupid. "There's always a turf war goin' on. And, yeah, I heard about the shootin', but I ain't heard no one say who done it. Was she wearin' colors?"

¡Ayúdeme! ¡Me van a matar!

"No, not that I could see. She wasn't wearing much of anything, actually."

Arthur nodded. "Coulda been anyone who done it. Maybe gangs. Maybe her pimp. Maybe she was workin' as a mule."

Her pimp? A mule?

Tessa hadn't considered those possibilities. "She seemed too young to be working as a prostitute."

Arthur laughed. "You ain't spent much time on the streets. A lot of homeless kids end up turnin' tricks, bein' pimped. Some trade sex or do porno for food. They gotta survive somehow. Hell, some join gangs to keep away from the pimps and the dealers."

The light turned yellow, then red.

A new queue of cars drew up beside them. Arthur went off to beg, while Tessa digested what he'd told her.

Was it possible that the girl had been a homeless teen who'd gotten mixed up with a pimp? Had she been trying to escape and been killed in retribution? Were the three other girls family and friends, as she'd assumed, or were they part of some pimp's stable? She remembered what Mr. Simms told her about the older woman.

I always thought it was strange the way she watched them—like a hawk. I figured maybe she wanted to make sure they didn't steal nothing.

A window rolled down, and a middle-aged woman with short brown hair and a round face waved a white flyer out the window, interrupting Tessa's thoughts.

"First Baptist Church is offering a soup kitchen this Sunday," she shouted over the sound of idling motors, thrusting the piece of paper into Arthur's hand. "Lots of good food and warm winter clothes. Be sure to come, and bring your lady friend."

Arthur turned to Tessa and handed her the flyer, his lips curving in a smile. "She thinks you're my woman."

Tessa glanced down at her denim jacket, black turtleneck, jeans, and the Merrells on her feet. Did she look homeless?

Arthur laughed at her reaction. "You want to talk with the gangs, you gotta hit Crack Park in Five Points or head into Aurora."

"Crack Park?"

He grinned, then turned back toward waiting dollar bills. "Curtis Park. But you'd best watch out, darlin'. Them boys'll eat a tidbit like you for lunch."

MORE THAN ANY other street, Colfax told the story of Denver. It carved its way east to west, from the projects of Aurora past the golden dome of the state capitol to the skyscrapers of downtown, passing from poverty to ostentatious wealth, from adult bookstores to art galleries, from pawnshops to museums, until it turned into Highway 6 and disappeared into the mountains beyond. Its sidewalks were walked by hippies and housewives, prostitutes and politicians, students and senior citizens, businessmen and bag ladies alike.

Tessa parked her car in front of a Muslim grocery at Colfax and Yosemite and walked east into Aurora. She'd spent a few hours in Curtis Park, interviewing more homeless people and hearing similar stories from them. Everywhere she'd looked there was gang graffiti, most of it street advertisements for crack dealers. But she hadn't seen anyone who looked like a gang member or a dealer. She'd have to come back at night.

Now it was nearing evening, and the streets bustled in the waning daylight. A young man dressed in jeans and a gray hooded sweatshirt sold homemade CDs out of the trunk of his car, his speakers throbbing with bass. An elderly grocer adjusted the display in his window. A gaggle of young Latinas stood by the front door, sipping soft drinks and giggling.

They stopped giggling when she walked up to them.

She switched into Spanish, introduced herself, and showed them her press card. The girls watched her through mistrustful eyes as she told them about the shooting and described the victim. But before she could ask them whether they'd heard anything, they hurried away, shaking their heads.

"No sabemos nada," said one. *We don't know anything.*

She got the same reaction from an elderly African-American couple, a group of young men playing a game of three-on-three, and the cashier at the nearby liquor store.

No one wanted to talk with her.

She couldn't blame them. She knew what it was to grow up poor, to trust no one, to fear outsiders. And that's what she was here—an outsider.

She had just passed what was obviously a housing project when a group of five boys—all around the age of ten—walked up to her. Most wore Oakland Raiders caps turned to the side, and a few had blue bandanas tucked in their jeans pockets or tied around their necks.

Mini-Crips?

"You want somethin'?" one of them asked, crossing his arms over his chest.

He looked pretty tough for a kid still small enough for Tessa to turn over her knee. She felt a stab of sadness that anyone so young should have to be so hard. Had she been this way?

"I'm Tessa Novak with the *Denver Independent* newspaper. I'm looking for someone who can tell me what's happening on the streets." She showed them her press card, thought of the graffiti she'd seen near the site of the shooting. It was taking a big risk, she knew, but if she didn't do something, she wasn't going to get anywhere. "Syko or Flaco around?"

And what are you going to do if they *are the killers, girl?*

The boy who'd spoken to her shrugged, and the kids walked off.

"Short conversation," Tessa murmured to herself, inwardly grateful they hadn't seemed to have heard of the two.

She'd be lying if she said she wasn't nervous. More than once she'd felt a strange prickling on her neck and had gotten the feeling she was being followed. She knew there was violence on these streets; she'd written news articles about it. But she also knew most of the people living here weren't dangerous. Like everyone else, they were just trying to make it through another day. People passing through from wealthier parts of the city saw the graffiti, the poverty, the decay—and they felt afraid. What they didn't see was the sense of community, the loyalty, the flower beds, the hardworking parents trying to give their kids a better life.

She continued on her way, crossing the intersection at Sable, aware it was almost dark. She needed to hop on the bus and catch a ride back to her car, but she'd realized a block or two back that she wasn't seeing only Crips graffiti now. She'd crossed into a part of town claimed by both Crips and Bloods. She'd stopped to document the graffiti down a side alley when that strange prickling ran down her neck again.

Then she heard voices approaching from behind.

She turned—and found a dozen young men headed straight for her. It was too dark for her to see their colors, but she had no doubt they were gang members. Her heartbeat ratcheted up a few notches.

Teenagers, Tess. They're teenagers.

The teenagers were taller than she was. They stopped a few feet away from her, glared down at her. More than one held a gun.

Tessa swallowed, willed herself not to show fear.

"I'm Syko. That's Flaco. Word is you're lookin' for us."

"Gentlemen," she said. "I'm so glad you're here."

CHAPTER 8

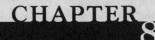

SYKO AND FLACO weren't happy to see her. That much Tessa knew for certain.

Adrenaline spiking, she showed them her press card and handed them each a business card. Then she told them about the shooting, described the victim, gave them the address of the house where the girls had been seen.

"I saw your graffiti down at Colfax and York, and I thought if anyone knew what was happening on that end of town it would be you two."

The kid closest to her, the tallest one of the bunch, laughed. "Hey, Flaco, you hear this shit? You put in some work down at Colfax and York?"

The youth beside him shook his head, his gaze fixed on Tessa. "Hell, no, man."

"Lots of people get lit up on the streets. Don't mean we know who done it."

"Have you heard anything, any rumors about who did? Another gang maybe?"

"Why should I tell you?" Syko shrugged, took a step toward her, crowding her.

She stood fast, lifted her chin, heart thrumming. "Because

I'm the only one stupid enough to stand by myself in a dark alley and ask."

Sniggers passed through the group, and Syko gave a snort.

Flaco shook his head, a smile on his face. "You're loco, lady."

"Could be we heard something." Syko eased off, gave her space. "Could be we're too smart to talk about it, even with a sweet *chula* like you."

"Is there a turf war going on?"

"Hell, Blondie, you mean more than usual? No."

"Have you ever taken in kids living on the street?"

"Take 'em in, give 'em food, a home, family. It happens."

"What do you do if they try to leave the gang?"

Syko crossed his arms over his chest. "Depends. Sometimes we give 'em a courting out. Sometimes we kick the shit out of 'em. Could be she was leavin' some other gang, but I doubt it. There's worse things than gangbangers on these streets."

The other kids laughed and nodded.

"I've heard pimps prey on homeless teens, force them to work—" She felt the attention of the group shift, heard the safeties on several handguns click off.

She wondered for a moment if she should pull her gun, too, and she felt an impulse to laugh at the thought of her standing in an alley drawing her gun with a bunch of gang members. But then she remembered how quickly Julian had taken the revolver from her. She didn't want to give the bad guys another weapon to use against her.

"Dark Angel," Syko said, looking beyond her down the darkened alley. "Fuck!"

Then he and Flaco murmured something to the group in words she didn't catch. Heads craned. A few younger members of the group took several steps backward, but Syko and Flaco held their ground.

Heart in her throat, Tessa turned toward the crunch of boots on gravel.

A man walked in long strides through the darkness toward them. Nothing but a dark silhouette, shadow against shadow, he walked down the alley with the grace of a predator. She didn't need to see his face to know who he was.

Julian.

He walked up to stand beside her, acknowledged Syko and Flaco with a nod of his head, and rested his hand in the small of Tessa's back, the heat of his touch burning through her denim jacket. The intensity of his presence seemed to make the air vibrate, the signal unmistakably one of suppressed violence, menace, dominance.

"Yo, Dark Angel, we just kickin' it. Is Blondie here with you?"

Dark Angel?

Tessa almost laughed. Then she heard Julian's answer.

"Do me a favor. Keep an eye out for her, and spread word that she's under my protection. She has a bad habit of getting herself into trouble."

Furious, Tessa started to object, but Syko cut her off.

"You got it, man." Then he looked down at her. "Why didn't you say you was Dark Angel's woman?"

"Because I'm not!"

But no one was listening to her.

"We gotta jet. See you, Blondie. Dark Angel, man." Then Syko gave a jerk of his head and the group turned on their heels and strode back down the alley.

Tessa whirled to face Julian. "You just scared off the only interview I've gotten all day!"

He took her arm, his gaze on the alley behind her. "Time go to, Goldilocks. I'll give you a ride back to your car."

She jerked her arm free. "Forget it. I'll take the bus."

"No, you won't." His gaze seemed to scan the street.

"Who the hell do you think you are?"

"Your best chance of getting home in one pretty piece."

She gave a disgusted snort and stomped off ahead of him. "Oh, please! I was doing just fine without your help. I didn't need to be rescued!"

"They're killers, Tessa." He overtook her in one step, fell in beside her, each of his strides easily two of hers. "They got to be gang leaders by pulling the trigger."

"They weren't going to pull the trigger on me!"

From the distance came the wail of a police siren.

"Maybe not, but I didn't feel like taking that chance just so you could grab a headline."

"Headlines?" For a moment, she couldn't believe what he'd just said. "You think I'm doing this for the glory?"

He glanced down at her. "Aren't you?"

"No! I'd much rather be at home sitting in a hot bath reading a book than slinking down some stupid alley scared to death. I'm just doing my job."

"You're not just a reporter, Tessa. You're a murder witness. Or had you forgotten?"

"Of course I haven't forgotten!" She felt tears of anger sting her eyes, blinked them back. "*She's* why I'm here! I can't let my fear keep me from doing right by her."

"Either you're brave, or you're stupid." He pointed to the left toward a beat-up pickup truck that might once have been blue. "My truck is over there."

Whatever she was, she wasn't brave. Confronting Syko and Flaco had taken more from Tessa than she'd realized, and as the adrenaline wore off, she found herself wanting desperately to be home behind locked doors. Disappointed with herself for being so easily shaken, she let herself be herded toward his truck.

"You drive that? I was expecting the Batmobile."

He opened the passenger-side door. "You're sweet. Get in."

She climbed into the front seat, still seething. She'd gone through a lot of effort to find Syko and Flaco, and she'd actually been making progress when Julian had driven them off. He was interfering in her ability to do her job. His misleading message about their relationship might make the streets safer for her, but it might also make it more difficult for her to connect with people. Syko and Flaco had seemed anxious to get far away from Julian.

And then it hit her. Why would a dozen armed gangbangers fear one man? They'd outnumbered him in every way—fists, feet, bullets. And yet they'd been afraid.

Julian slid into the driver's seat, slipped his key into the ignition, and glanced over at the woman beside him. He had to admire her courage. There weren't many women who'd have dared to do what she'd just done. She was pissed off, and he couldn't blame her. He'd blown her interview flat out. If he were in her very fine shoes, he'd feel just as angry.

He'd spent the past three hours cruising the streets, looking for her, his sense of urgency growing stronger as the sun set. He'd known she was following a gang angle, had felt certain she'd head into Five Points or Aurora. He'd spotted her little black Thunderbird with its press plates at Colfax and Yosemite and had regretted that he hadn't put a tail on her.

When he'd finally caught sight of her, she'd been standing in that alley surrounded by Syko's gang, one small, soft woman against a dozen men with steel, and he'd felt something he hadn't felt since he was a kid—fear. His heart had kicked him in the ribs, and honest-to-God adrenaline had shot through his veins. He'd walked into that alley loaded for bear, only to discover she didn't need his help. Somehow she'd wrapped a group of hardened street thugs around her itty-bitty pinky finger.

He started the engine, slipped into traffic, turned west on Colfax.

"I'm parked at Colfax and Yosemite."

He didn't tell her he already knew that.

Then she gave a laugh. " 'Dark Angel'? More like 'Fallen Angel.' "

"You're right about that, honey."

"What is 'Dark Angel' anyway? Your gangsta-rap name?"

"Just a name."

"Why are they so afraid of you?"

"Recent experience."

For a while, neither of them spoke. Julian glanced over to find her glowering out her window, looking like a furious kitten. It was the first time he'd seen her in blue jeans, and he couldn't help but like what he saw—soft curves that seemed all the more feminine because they were sheathed in pants. Still, he was amused.

This was her barrio look?

Although she was clearly angry with him, her body language told him rage wasn't the only thing she was feeling. Her legs were pressed tightly together, her hands clutched around her notepad and held fast in her lap. She was nervous, afraid to be with him.

So she felt the connection, too.

What you're feeling is chemical, he wanted to say. *We can work it off at your place.*

"I'm not your enemy, you know," he said instead.

She glanced warily at him. "You could've fooled me."

"I think we got off on the wrong foot." He drew up to the light at Yosemite and braked. "I'll make it up to you over dinner."

What the hell are you thinking, Darcangelo?

Clearly he *wasn't* thinking—not with his brain. The last thing he needed was to spend any real time with her. They'd end up having animal sex on the floor, and afterward she'd look at him with hurt in those big blue eyes when he told her there'd be no white picket fence.

Her eyes flew wide for a moment. "Oh, no! No, no. That would be a major conflict of interest. No, I couldn't do that."

"Sure you could."

She gave him a sideways glance. "What do you mean by that?"

"Come on, Tessa. We're both adults. It's called sexual attraction." He could almost see the color rising in her cheeks.

"I-I don't know what you're talking about."

"Don't you?"

"You are far too sure of yourself, Darcangelo."

"Mmm-hmm."

"If you want the truth, I really despise you, especially now that you've cost me a night's work. You're cocky and arrogant, and you've interfered with my job!" The words seemed to gush out of her. "In fact, I'm so angry I want to hit you, except that would be bad manners. I don't hit people."

"I understand." He had to hide his smile. "And you're right, you know."

"I am?"

"It would be a conflict of interest and a bad idea for us to have sex."

Are you listening to yourself, Darcangelo?

"Just drop me off at . . . My car! No, no, no!"

Julian looked to the spot where her little T-bird had been parked—and saw a skeleton. In the hour and a half since he'd seen it, the car had been stripped, hubcaps, tires, mirrors, engine components, and presumably most of its interior stolen.

"Oh, my God!" She started to open the door. "Oh, God!"

Julian reached across her and held the door shut. "Stay in the truck! You don't need to go anywhere near it. I'll call it in, have DPD take care of it."

"But it's my car!"

"It was."

The light turned green. He accelerated.

He reached for his radio, made the call, arranged for a tow to the impound yard. When he was done, he looked over to see Tessa staring out the window, wide-eyed and clearly stunned.

"Now you know why I leave the Batmobile in the garage. I'll take you home."

"Fine." She looked over at him, arms crossed, obviously still angry. "But don't think this makes up for arresting me or ruining my interview. I live at—"

"I know where you live."

TESSA TURNED HER rental car into the underground parking garage and had to drive down two levels before she found a spot. Not only had she lost her car—the first new car she'd ever owned—but her parking karma sucked. She turned off the ignition, grabbed her briefcase, glanced at her watch.

"Damn!"

She was late for her interview with Chief Irving and the head of the gang taskforce. Did Christiane Amanpour or Barbara Walters or Jane Pauley have problems like this? Somehow she didn't think so.

They don't have Tom Trent for a boss either, girl.

She'd arrived at the paper this morning to find photocopies

of her mug shot stuck on bulletin boards throughout the building with the word "WANTED" typed above it. She might have found it funny if she hadn't lost so much sleep last night, first arguing with Julian in her imagination and then fighting nightmares. Even a triple-shot latte hadn't been able to restore her sense of humor. She'd vented to Sophie about the arrest and the interrupted interview—taking care to keep Julian's name secret—and was astonished when Sophie smiled.

"I think Holly's right," Sophie said. "He likes you."

"Oh, well, lucky me! I suppose if he loved me I'd be in federal prison."

Then, to make matters worse, Tom had spent forty-five minutes after the I-Team meeting grilling her for every detail of her arrest, clearly gearing up to bellow in Chief Irving's ear. It had taken every evasive trick she knew to keep from giving him the arresting officer's name. In the end, she'd had to resort to the truth.

"I can't give you his name. He's an undercover officer." *And I want to punch him right in his sickeningly handsome face.*

Tom hadn't been pleased, but, as a staunch advocate of reporter-source confidentiality, he hadn't been able to object.

Now she was a full twenty minutes late. She could only hope Chief Irving hadn't given up on her. She hopped out of the car, locked it, and hurried to the nearest stairwell, rehearsing her questions as she ran up the steps, the staccato click of her heels reverberating off the concrete walls.

If there was so much violence between gangs and the city's homeless, why was so little being done to combat it? How many reports of attacks against the homeless had they received over the past five years and how many had they investigated? What was being done to protect homeless youth from gangs and other street predators?

It wasn't the news story she was looking for. It didn't answer the question of who'd killed the girl. But it was a worthy issue on its own, and she felt sure there was at least some connection between all of this and the shooting.

¡Por favor, señor, ayúdeme! ¡Me van a matar!
Please, sir! Help me! They're going to kill me.

The girl's terrified screams echoed in Tessa's mind, made her stomach knot.

Gunshots. Shattered glass.

So much blood.

Lost in her thoughts, Tessa ran headlong into a wall of chest and found herself staring up into a pair of dark blue eyes.

Julian.

Startled, she jerked back from him, lost her balance.

Strong arms grabbed her, steadied her, held her fast. "We just keep running into each other, don't we, Tessa?"

He was dressed as he'd been the first night she'd seen him—dark hair tied back in a ponytail, black leather jacket, jeans. His jaw was clean shaven, his eyebrows dark slashes on olive skin, his lashes long. And those lips . . .

She remembered only too well what it felt like to be kissed by those lips, the shock of it, her body's response. She wished he'd been bald or toothless or had a vicious scar on his face—anything to make him less handsome. Somehow just the sight of him was enough to make her mouth water and her brain go blank. Then she remembered how much she disliked him.

"What are you doing here?"

Clever, Tessa! He's some kind of cop. What do you think he's doing here?

"I'm the 'shadowy criminal type,' remember? Criminal types belong at the police station." He bit his lower lip, measured her through narrowed eyes. "But if I didn't know better, I'd say you're following me."

The opposite was closer to the truth, and they both knew it. He hadn't run into her by accident last night. He'd tracked her down.

She laughed. "Why on earth would I want to follow you? It's not as if you're going to get all chatty and tell me what angle you're working on this shooting."

"Not likely." Then his mouth turned up in a slow, sexy smile that made her insides skitter. "Maybe you're hoping I'll kiss you again."

Heat rushed into her cheeks, and she gaped at him. "You're delusional, Darcangelo!"

He grinned a self-satisfied, smug grin that told her he knew exactly what that kiss had done to her. "Am I?"

She forced her expression to go ice cold and pulled herself out of his grasp. "I hate to wound your male pride, but I haven't given that little peck on the lips a single thought. Besides, that wasn't really a kiss."

Head high and shoulders back, she stepped around him.

Julian was tempted to laugh. She might pretend to have sleet for blood, but he'd never known a woman to melt down quite like she had over a single kiss, pretend or otherwise. He could *feel* her arousal. But why argue with her about it when he could prove it?

In one move, he had her up against the wall, her wrists shackled by his hands, her arms stretched out on either side of her head. "You're right. That wasn't a kiss, but this is."

"Wh-what the—?"

"Shut up." He ducked down, brushed his lips down the curve of her cheek, ran the tip of his tongue over the whorl of her ear. She smelled good enough to eat, her perfume subtle and sexy and so female. Hungry for her, he sucked her earlobe into his mouth, pearl earring and all.

He heard her quick intake of breath, felt her body tense.

"You . . . are sooo . . . arrogant!"

"I said shut up." He released her right wrist, cupped her chin, tilted her head upward.

Then he kissed her deep and hard.

And she melted.

Her body seemed to go liquid, every soft, feminine inch of her pressing against him. The contact sent a bolt of lust blazing through his gut, made him painfully hard, his erection straining to be someplace more welcoming than his jeans.

In a heartbeat, the kiss turned rough. Teeth scraped skin, bit, nipped. Tongues invaded, clashed, plundered. He felt her hips move, betraying her need. Then her arms wrapped around the back of his neck, and she whimpered.

The sound was like gasoline on the fire already raging in Julian's veins. He groaned, felt his control slip. He hadn't meant for it to be like this. He'd kissed her to wipe that conceited look off her face, to prove to her that she wanted him despite her words last night—not to get caught up in wanting her.

But he wanted her. Right now. Right here.

Trailing little bites down the satin skin of her throat, he slid his hand up her soft nylon-covered thigh and under her skirt to cup her through her panties. They were silk. And they were already damp.

Tessa was lost. She was lost in his scent, in the hard feel of him, the heat of his lips on her skin. If there were some reason she shouldn't be doing this, she couldn't remember what it was. God, she hated him, wanted him, needed him.

She felt the pressure of his hand against her, and her knees went weak. Rather than hitting his hand away, she found herself pushing against the pressure, parting her legs for him. "Oh, Julian!"

Heat spread in a liquid rush through her belly. And when he flicked his thumb over the hard bead of her nipple, she moaned, the sound reverberating up and down the stairwell.

A door opened.

Footsteps.

He growled deep in his throat, cupped her hard, pressed his erection against her belly. Then he whispered. "If you try to tell me next time I see you that you haven't been thinking about fucking me, I'm going to call you a liar."

With that, he released her and was gone.

Shaking, her body on fire, Tessa struggled to compose herself. She straightened her skirt, picked her briefcase up off the floor where it had fallen, and smoothed her hair. How had she let this happen? My God, she'd practically been having sex with him in the stairwell! And she'd enjoyed it!

A police officer passed her on his way down the stairs, gave her a nod.

And then she remembered.

Chief Irving!

She glanced at her watch—*damn, damn, damn!*—and ran the rest of the way up the stairs.

CHAPTER 9

TESSA TOOK A sip of her latte and tried to read through what she'd written so far. She was aiming for fifteen inches—a news feature about the conflicts between Denver's homeless population and its street gangs. It ought to have been a relatively easy article to write, but she couldn't seem to focus.

She couldn't get the feel of Julian off her lips or the taste of him out of her mouth. Where his skin had touched her, she smelled of his aftershave—spice and leather. Her nipples still tingled, the feel of her silk bra almost unbearable against their stiff tips. The ache he'd caused between her legs refused to go away, leaving her so frustrated she found herself unconsciously crossing her legs in an attempt to make the sensation stop.

Focus, focus, focus, Novak!

What was she going to tell Syd when her article was late— "Sorry, I'm horny"?

Fifteen assaults on homeless people reported this year, all investigated, no arrests. She added a quote from the director of Denver's homeless shelter criticizing the police department and countered it with a quote from Chief Irving about the difficulties of holding anyone accountable when the victims refused to press charges and couldn't be relied upon to testify.

That wasn't a kiss, but this is.

Good lord, if that was his idea of a kiss . . . ! She felt a flutter deep in her belly.

She'd meant to tell him to stop, to shove him away, but the moment his lips had touched her skin, her brain had shut down and her ovaries had taken over. Clearly, her eggs hadn't gotten the memo about how much she hated him. They liked him just fine. In fact, they liked him more than they'd liked any man she'd met so far.

Not even Scott—the man she'd thought she'd loved, the one man she'd had sex with—had made her feel like this. In fact, the gap between what she'd felt when Scott had kissed her and what she'd felt when Julian had kissed her was so wide there was no way to bridge it. Scott had been pleasant sunshine. Julian was fire.

It's called sexual attraction.

She didn't care what it was called. She wasn't interested. She'd worked hard to build a decent life for herself. She'd scrimped and saved for every college credit, studied hard, worked long hours. She'd done all she could to learn manners, to learn how to dress and how to speak. She'd put poverty and shame behind her. She wasn't going to risk her happiness to satisfy some hormonal urge. She wanted a man who would cherish her, be a reliable and loving father to her children, and encourage her in her career. She couldn't imagine Julian doing any of those things. More than likely he'd forget her name five minutes after they'd had sex.

He did come to your rescue, girl. If Syko and Flaco had gone loco, you'd have been grateful to see him.

That was her eggs talking again. She ignored them.

Homeless teens. Homeless teens were much more likely than any other group of teens to be exposed to drugs, violence, and sexual abuse. Some were so desperate they traded sex for food and shelter, making them easy prey for traffickers and child pornographers. Others sought refuge in gangs, whose members took them in and gave them a sense of family—for a price.

Tessa shuffled through her notes, found the horrifying statistics and a quote from an expert on homeless youth, which she followed with a concerned quote from Chief Irving.

Had she actually wrapped her arms around Julian's neck? Yes, she had. But that wasn't the worst of it. She'd also pressed herself into his hand, parted her thighs, called his name. And this time she couldn't blame it on adrenaline. She'd enjoyed it—all of it.

His mouth on hers. His fingers teasing her nipples. His hand pressing expertly between her thighs. His erection hard and huge against her belly. Julian had brought her more pleasure than she'd ever found with a man—and they'd both been fully clothed.

If you try to tell me next time I see you that you haven't been thinking about fucking me, I'm going to call you a liar.

"Oh, shut up!" It was only when she'd heard her own voice that Tessa realized she'd spoken aloud. Slowly, she looked over her shoulder to find the other members of the I-Team staring at her.

JULIAN SURVEYED WHAT was left of Tobias Ronald Grant, age twenty-five. Most of his head was gone. "My guess is a forty-four Mag in the face at point-blank range."

Nothing less than the bastard deserved.

The ME nodded. "That's my assessment, as well. When I examined him, he'd been dead for less than twenty-four hours, placing the time of the murder last Friday evening."

Julian had been in the middle of interrogating a member of the city planning board about his illicit interest in teenage girls when he'd gotten a call from Chief Irving telling him that fingerprints taken off a body they'd pulled out of a trash bin in Commerce City Saturday afternoon were a match for prints taken from inside the basement apartment.

Here was María Ruiz's killer, the man who'd pulled the trigger.

So Burien had taken the botched shooting poorly, just as Julian had anticipated. He'd probably shot Tobias in a fit of temper, and then gone about his business, leaving his surviving minions to clean up the mess. It was execution, Burien-style.

"Any other evidence at the site?"

"A fine set of rims, but that's it. Nothing on the body. *Nada*."

"DNA results?"

"We're running him against the samples from the apartment, as well as the samples found in María Ruiz's body. We ought to know if there's a match by the end of the week. I don't think we've ever tested so much semen at once in the history of the department. It's pretty disgusting, really."

"Disgusting is the least of it." Julian zipped the bag, pushed the gurney back into the locker, shut the steel door. This was good police work, and he intended to give Irving's men their props. "Thanks. Keep me posted."

"Will do."

Julian walked out of the morgue, down the hall, and out to his truck, an uncomfortable stirring in his gut. Of the three murders he'd predicted in the aftermath of the Ruiz shooting, the first was now confirmed. That left old Mr. Simms, who, fortunately, had left the state. And Tessa.

TESSA DROVE EAST on I-70 through to the police department's shooting range on the edge of town. She'd taken time to go home and change into jeans and a T-shirt and had gotten stuck in rush-hour traffic. Fifteen minutes late, she sat in the parking lot, looking at the concrete building, feeling strangely afraid.

She'd never actually fired a gun before, and she didn't want to. Somehow the idea of actually learning to defend herself with a firearm made the violence of that night seem all the more real. She didn't want to admit that she might truly be in danger. She didn't want to think that she might have to pull the trigger one day. Aiming her pistol at Julian when she'd still thought him a murderer had been terrifying, and she didn't feel like reliving it, even in the safety of the shooting range.

A part of her wanted to call Chief Irving to cancel, but she remembered how Julian had disarmed her and how stupid she'd felt standing in the alley with a dozen armed gang members afraid to draw her own gun. If she was going to carry it, she had to learn to use it. Besides, whoever Chief Irving had assigned to give her lessons was no doubt already here waiting for her. It would be impolite in the extreme to stand him or her up.

She took a deep breath and forced her butterflies aside. Then she grabbed her purse, got out of the car, and walked up to the front entrance. Not surprisingly, it was well guarded, signs on the walls spelling out rules and regulations. She'd just started reading through them when she heard his voice.

"You're late."

She whirled to find Julian standing behind her. His leather jacket was gone, a white T-shirt stretched across his chest, a leather cord with a dark turquoise stone hanging from his neck. An ominous-looking handgun sat in a black holster strapped to his left shoulder.

If you try to tell me next time I see you that you haven't been thinking about fucking me, I'm going to call you a liar.

She felt her cheeks burn, and the words were out before she could stop them. "Oh, no way! No, not you!"

He raised an eyebrow. "Shall we get started?"

Julian led her down a hallway, past vending machines offering soda and junk food, around a corner and toward a set of heavy double doors. She tried not to notice how scrumptious his ass looked in blue jeans or how slim his hips were compared to his shoulders or the way his body moved like a cat's. And for a moment she forgot the reason she was here.

He stopped at a counter to the left of the double doors, signed in on a clipboard.

"Darcangelo." An older man behind the counter acknowledged Julian with a nod. "You'll be in fifteen today. What you firing?"

Tessa realized the man was talking to her. She sat her purse on the counter, pulled out the .22, her butterflies returning full force. "This."

"Did you bring your own rounds?" the man asked.

She hadn't thought of that. "Just what's in the cylinder."

Julian frowned. "Give me a hundred. Put it on my account."

Tessa reached in her purse for money. "No, I'll pay for—"

The man slid a box of bullets across the counter to Julian. "There you go."

Before she could object, Julian was walking through the double doors.

The room was a dimly lit cavern with long lanes like a bowling alley. On the far end hung paper targets that looked like the outlines of men. On the other were a series of tall dividers like stalls above which hung numbers. The air smelled strange—gunpowder? Apart from the low thrum of a ventilation system, the room was quiet.

Julian led her to stall fifteen, took the revolver and the ammunition from her, and set the ammunition down on a nearby counter. Then he removed the bullets she had carefully loaded and set them aside, too. "So tell me what you know."

"About guns?" Tessa asked, feeling oddly disoriented. She draped her jacket over a nearby chair and set her purse on the floor.

He handed her back the pistol. "That's what we're here for."

Feeling both embarrassed and edgy, she went through the basic parts of the revolver—the safety, the cylinder, the barrel, the hammer, the handle, the trigger.

He turned her hand over and dropped six bullets into her palm. "Let's see you load it."

She'd have done it more quickly and smoothly had he not been watching, but she didn't tell him that. Something about him standing there, watching her through those dark blue eyes, turned her fingers into thumbs. Careful not to point it at anyone, she slipped the bullets in one by one, then snapped the cylinder into place.

"Good enough," he said. Then he took a couple pairs of safety goggles and what looked like earphones off a nearby shelf. "Put these on."

She set the loaded pistol down on the counter and did as he asked, her pulse picking up. Any second now he was going to ask her to fire the gun, and the thought terrified her.

Knock it off, Tessa. You're stronger than this!

He was giving her instructions. She forced herself to focus on the sound of his voice—deep and warm—and not the rapid beating of her heart. "Keep your eye on the front sight. Never try to hit someone in the head. It makes too small a target.

Aim for center mass—the middle of the torso. A few rounds in the chest and belly will stop anyone."

Tessa took aim, shut her left eye, focused on aligning the front sight with the upper body of the target beyond.

"Don't lock your right elbow. Support your right arm by—"

Bambam! Bambam!

Tessa gasped, her heart exploding in her chest, her knees buckling. The tile floor tilted, sucked her down, even as the pistol slipped from her hands.

¡Ayúdeme! ¡Me van a matar!

Julian heard a .45 fire double taps a few stalls down, saw Tessa's entire body jerk. The blood disappeared from her face, and she sank toward the floor.

"Easy, Tessa." He took the pistol, which was about to fall from her hands, caught her around the waist and guided her into a chair.

Bambam! Bambam!

Her body jerked again, and she gave a little cry, her hands fisting in his T-shirt. Her heart was beating so hard Julian could see it against the cloth of her pink shirt.

He pulled off her goggles and ear protection. "It's okay, Tessa. It's just—"

Bambam! Bambam!

She jerked, gasped, her pupils dilated, her eyes almost glazed.

"Damn it!" He pulled her against him, wondering how many rounds the shooter had left. "Cease fir—!"

Bambam! Bambam!

There was no way the shooter was going to hear him.

"Ah, hell!" Julian scooped her up, carried her past the other stalls, and out the exit to the staff lounge, which was mercifully vacant. He kicked the door shut behind him, set her down on an old orange sofa, and sat beside her.

She was shaking violently from head to toe, her breath coming in shallow gasps, her face buried against his throat.

He understood what had happened—she'd heard the shots, and her mind and body had reacted with the fear she'd felt at the moment of the murder. It was posttraumatic stress. He'd seen it claim its share of trained agents over the years. But what the hell was he supposed to do about it? He'd been trained to stalk and kill bad guys, not comfort damsels in distress.

"It's all right, Tessa. Slow your breathing." Feeling awkward, he pulled her into his arms and held her, stroking the silken strands of her hair, curls wrapping themselves around his fingers. She smelled like heaven and felt soft and small in his arms. "That's it. Slowly. In and out. In and out."

Black rage flared in his gut. This was Burien's doing— another woman terrified and traumatized.

Her breathing gradually steadied and with it her pulse. Still shaking, she lifted her head. "I-I'm s-sorry! I'm so, so sorry!" She released his T-shirt and looked up at him, as if surprised to find herself pressed against him. "I . . . Oh, God! Oh, Julian! What . . . ? D-did I shoot?"

Julian shook his head. "Not a shot."

She buried her face in her trembling hands. "I-I'm so embarrassed!"

"Don't be. Let me get you something to drink. Coke or Pepsi?" Julian rose and walked to the staff vending machine.

"O-okay."

He slipped a few quarters into the machine, punched the Pepsi button. A can rattled out of the machine. He grabbed it, popped the top, carried it over to her, and knelt down in front of her. She was still trembling so hard that he had to close his hands over hers and lift the drink to her lips. "Take a sip. There you go. And another."

She swallowed, her face much as he'd seen it that first night—pale and filled with both shock and horror. "Thanks."

"You're welcome."

She met his gaze, looked away. "You must think I'm a complete wimp."

"No." He lifted a silky curl off her cheek, tucked it behind her ear. "I don't."

Watch it, Darcangelo. You're treading dangerous ground.

He'd already kicked himself in the ass a dozen times for kissing her in the stairwell. He didn't need to make matters worse.

"I-I keep seeing her face, hearing her voice. Every night I dream . . . and there's so much blood!" Tears pooled in her eyes. She dashed them away. "Damn!"

He sat beside her, stroked her hair. "It's not a crime to cry, you know."

"I-I'll bet you don't cry."

He didn't. He hadn't cried since he was five and his father had backhanded him and called him a pussy. "I cry all the time—sad movies, Hallmark commercials, the opera."

She looked over at him, blinked—and smiled. "Nice try, but I don't believe you."

He shrugged and ran his knuckles over the soft curve of her cheek. "Why don't you let me take you home? I think you've had enough of the shooting range for one day."

She sat up straighter, shook her head, her long golden curls bouncing. "I can't."

For a moment he thought it was the ride home she was refusing, and he knew he had only himself to blame. He'd practically mauled her in the stairwell today. Could he blame her for wanting to stay away from him?

"I have to do this, Julian. I have to try. If I don't face this, I'll never have the strength to come here again, and I might as well not even carry a gun."

More than a little surprised that she'd even consider another attempt, he tried to gauge her frame of mind. "Are you sure?"

"Yeah."

"I'll say one thing for you, Goldilocks. You have guts."

Ten minutes later, they headed back into the range, Julian having arranged for fifteen minutes of private use. He talked her through her stance once more, drew the target in a little closer so she'd have a reasonable chance of hitting it, and gave her the go-ahead to fire.

"The gun is going to jump in your hand. Don't let that intimidate you."

A determined look on her pale face, knuckles white where she gripped the gun, she squeezed the trigger.

Pop!

The gun jerked, and he could see the surprise on her face. He started to say something reassuring, but her focus was entirely on the target. Her eyes narrowed, and she fired five times in quick succession.

Pop! Pop! Pop! Pop! Pop!

Six holes appeared in the target—all of them centered in the chest area.

Amazed, Julian looked down at her.

She put the gun down on the counter, gave him a shaky smile. "How'd I do?"

"Honey, remind me never to sneak up on you in a dark alley again."

JULIAN DIALED DYSON'S number and shoved a frozen burrito in the microwave.

He'd given Tessa his secured cell phone number in case of an emergency, followed her home, and made certain she'd gotten inside safely. Then he'd driven home, trying to sort out the irritating knot of feelings in his chest.

Lust he understood. It was a simple emotion and resolved with a good fuck—most of the time. But Tessa inspired it in him like no other woman he'd known. He'd kissed her this morning, and he'd lost control—there was no other way to describe it. Even so, lust he could deal with.

The protectiveness he'd felt at the shooting range even made sense. Even though he'd been trained to take on the bad guys and not comfort victims, the purpose of his work was to protect people, to put himself between everyday folks and the killers who roamed the streets. She'd needed his help, and he'd responded. Nothing strange about that.

But the tenderness he felt for her confused him. He'd held her, and he'd wanted to keep holding her, not for sex but to comfort her. He'd stroked her hair, and he'd wanted to go on stroking her hair just to feel the silk of it against his hand. He'd wanted to kiss her tears away, to see her smile, to drive off the demons that haunted her.

Hell, he was probably just really horny and needed to get

inside her so he could get her out of his system. And yet a part of him was grateful that someone had interrupted them and kept him from fucking her mindlessly in the stairwell. What the hell was that about?

She deserves better. That's what that's about.

He needed to stay away from her, for her sake as well as his own. If Burien was after her, that meant he was probably watching her. If he was watching her and saw Julian with her . . .

Not a good plan.

As far as Julian knew, Burien didn't know he existed, much less what he looked like. Julian would live longer if he kept it that way. The last thing he needed was to be recognized at Pasha's or on the street. Burien's answer to FBI agents was as simple as it was messy—a bullet to the brain.

"Dyson here."

"Got an ID on the killer. Tobias Ronald Grant, age twenty-five." Julian pulled the salsa out of the fridge. "His prints match several taken from the basement apartment. He's done time—sexual assault, robbery. Head blown off with a forty-four. We should have an answer on DNA by the end of the week."

"I'll see what else I can dig up on him—associates, known addresses, that sort of thing. Margaux's finishing up in Longmont. Turns out her lead was solid."

"Burien?"

"She can't prove it. She found a so-called massage parlor where the women—all South American—were being forced to turn tricks. Whoever was running the place was long gone by the time she got there. She's sorting through the leads she got from the victims, but the language gap is slowing her down."

"I can help out if you'd like."

"Ah, hell, Julian. You know how territorial Margaux can be."

He knew, but he didn't care. "This isn't a competition. She can deal with her grudge against me on her own time."

"No argument here. How's it going with your interrogations?"

"I've brought in fifteen johns so far. Most of them spilled their guts the moment they saw the photographs I took of them outside the crib, but they're not telling me much I don't already know. We're getting search warrants for their home and work computers and waiting for DNA tests before deciding on charges. If any one of them shows up inside María Ruiz, we'll push for rape."

"Anything else?"

"We should ask the local cops both here and in Omaha to put a watch on the two witnesses, Mr. Simms and Ms. Novak. If Burien stays true to form, it won't be long—"

"Simms is dead. His brother found him yesterday morning, but it's not what you think. The ME in Omaha has ruled it a heart attack."

CHAPTER 10

TESSA DROPPED HER overflowing basket of dirty clothes onto the folding table and began to sort it into piles. She'd come home from the shooting range wanting macaroni and cheese, a hot bath, and a good night's sleep only to realize she hadn't done laundry in more than a week. Not wanting to go to work without panties, she'd eaten supper and then lugged her laundry stuff down the hallway to the laundry room she shared with everyone else on her floor.

A load of towels. A load of colors. A load of delicates. A load of whites.

Fortunately, three machines were available. It was, after all, Tuesday night—not prime washing time.

It was then she realized it had been exactly one week since the shooting. Whoever that girl had been, she'd been dead now for a week. And without meaning to, Tessa found herself mulling over the facts of the case.

A teenage girl gunned down in public in a drive-by. One witness who remembered the girl coming to the gas station with three other young Latinas every Sunday afternoon to buy candy under the watchful gaze of an older woman. No smiling, no talking. Two other witnesses who'd seen the four girls coming and going from the now-empty basement apartment three blocks away from the gas station. Police tape around the apartment entrance on the night of the shooting.

Tessa had assumed it was gang related, and perhaps it was. But her new homeless boyfriend, Arthur, had raised other possibilities. Could the girl have been a prostitute fleeing her pimp? A drug mule fleeing a dealer? The victim of a predator who'd pulled her off the street? The autopsy might shed some light on those possibilities, but Tessa didn't have the autopsy report. She'd have to do something about that.

She stuffed the load of towels and washcloths into one machine, put four quarters in the slot, and added a capful of detergent.

Out of the corner of her eye, she thought she saw someone move. She glanced up, expecting to see one of her neighbors walking down the hallway.

No one was there.

Prickles ran down the back of her neck.

You're just jittery from the shooting range, girl.

She stood for a moment, watching the hall. Then, feeling silly, she loaded her darks in another machine, her mind drifting back to the case.

She still considered it strange that four teenage girls would buy candy in grim silence. Were they quiet because they were shy and didn't speak English, or were they quiet because they were unhappy and afraid? Why would they be afraid with the older woman there to watch over them? Unless . . .

What if they were afraid of the older woman? What if she wasn't there to watch over them—but to control them?

The idea slid into Tessa's mind like a puzzle piece snapping into place.

She dropped her third load into the last remaining washer, fed it quarters, and poured in soap, mulling over the implications.

There was Chief Irving's words to consider, as well—and those of a certain extremely handsome and irritating undercover cop. Both had repeatedly warned her this was a dangerous case and seemed to have some notion of who the killer was.

Be damned glad the three bears aren't home, Goldilocks.

Had Julian meant there were three suspects and that they had lived in that apartment?

A man's shadow fell across the gray tile floor.

Tessa's head snapped up.

No one.

Ice slid down her spine.

Certain someone had been there, she walked to the laundry room door, stuck her head out, and looked down the long hallway, but saw no one.

"You're imagining things," she told herself.

Feeling uneasy, she put the load of delicates back into her laundry basket, together with the detergent and the remaining quarters, and carried it quickly down the hallway to her apartment, glancing over her shoulder a time or two, her pulse racing. She fished out her keys, let herself in, and locked the door behind her.

She took a deep breath, leaned against the door.

Get a grip, Tessa.

She decided to use the time waiting for the wash cycle to finish to do a little housework. It wasn't the restful evening she'd planned, but at least the work would be done. She dusted and watered her plants, sorting through the facts of the shooting and asking herself questions until her brain was tied in knots. Then she plugged in the vacuum, ran it over her carpet—and nearly jumped out of her skin when the phone rang.

A telemarketer.

Tessa was less polite than usual, refusing to listen to their pitch and hanging up.

Sure the machines were finished washing her clothes, she grabbed her keys and the dwindling roll of quarters, opened her door, and peeked into the hallway. It was empty, fluorescent light shining brightly down on familiar white walls and gray carpeting.

You're just creeping yourself out thinking about this stuff.

Without admitting to herself that she was hurrying, she walked back to the laundry room, moved her laundry from the three washers to two big dryers and fed them quarters. Then she almost ran back to her apartment, ignoring the prickles on her neck and refusing to look over her shoulder.

What is wrong with you, Tess?

What she needed was some relaxation and sleep. She filled her tub with hot water and lavender bath salts, got out a fluffy white towel, and let her jeans and T-shirt fall to the floor. By the time the water was cool, her laundry would be dry, and she'd be ready for bed.

She slipped into the tub, sighed. The heat felt heavenly, the soft lavender scent easing the tension from her muscles and the worries from her mind. She forced herself to let go—and found her thoughts taking a completely different turn.

Yesterday she'd hated Julian Darcangelo. Okay, so maybe she hadn't *hated* him, but she'd been very, very angry with him. He'd interfered with her job, and he'd implied her work on this investigation was nothing more than vanity journalism. But today . . .

Today he'd kissed her. It had been more than a kiss, of course. It had been foreplay, full blown and erotic. He'd made her knees go weak, made her forget she was standing in a public place, made her want do anything she had to do to get him inside her. He'd made her wonder if sex with a man could really be all it was played up to be.

If you try to tell me next time I see you that you haven't been thinking about fucking me, I'm going to call you a liar.

She didn't particularly like the language he'd used, but she had to admit that's precisely what she'd been thinking about most of the afternoon. Even remembering it made her belly clench and her nipples tighten. She'd never had a man kiss her with that kind of intensity before. If that was how he kissed, what would it be like to have sex with him? She would probably catch on fire, burn down the building, or maybe the whole city.

But had he kissed her just to prove a point or because he'd really wanted to kiss her?

Certainly, he had wanted to prove something. But she remembered the deep sound of his groan, the way he'd nipped her throat as if he'd wanted to eat her whole, the feel of his erection, huge and hard, against her belly. Though she couldn't claim to understand men—really, who could?—he'd seemed to be just as carried away as she was.

Of course, that didn't mean he cared about her. All it meant was that he wanted to have sex with her—which made him a lot like the men she'd avoided since college. And yet he was nothing like them.

Maybe you're hoping I'll kiss you again.

God, he was arrogant. But although she'd found his arrogance infuriating, tonight it made her smile. And it wasn't hard to figure out why.

He'd been there for her. When the blast of the other gun had sent her into shock, he'd been there for her. He'd kept her from falling onto the floor. He'd taken the gun from her hands. He'd held her against his chest. He'd even lifted her up and carried her, for goodness sake! Then he'd done his best to comfort her.

No man had ever been there like that for her before.

She closed her eyes, remembered the feel of his hands on her hair, the concern in his blue eyes, the soothing sound of his voice.

It's all right, Tessa. Slow your breathing. That's it.

She must have dozed off, for she found herself dreaming that she heard a click and the sound of someone breathing.

Then a cold, rough hand squeezed her breast.

She gasped, and her eyes flew open—just as the bathroom went dark.

Tessa screamed, terror shooting like liquid ice through her veins. She jumped to her feet in the water, shrank back against the cold tile wall. And over the thunder of her own heartbeat, she heard her front door slam.

Barely able to think, breathless with panic, she flew from the tub to her bedroom, unsure where her purse was, unsure where the gun was. She saw her cell phone, grabbed it from its charger with shaking hands, and pushed the call button. The little screen lit up, and she saw that the number it had dialed was the last one she'd programmed in—Julian's.

* * *

JULIAN DIDN'T BELIEVE it. No matter what the autopsy report said, something told him there was more to Mr. Simms's death than had met the ME's eye. There wasn't a shred of hard evidence to back up his feeling, nothing beyond the niggling in his gut.

He was midway through his aikido routine, wrestling with his doubts, when his encrypted cell rang. He saw the number on the LCD display.

He answered. "Tessa?"

"Th-there was a m-man! In my a-apartment. H-he came in wh-when I was a-asleep in the tub. H-he touched me. H-he . . . Oh, God, Julian, I-I'm so afraid!"

Julian took the stairs from his basement two at a time. "Is he still there?"

"I d-don't know. I-I screamed. I think h-he ran." Her breath broke in a sob.

"Hang up, and dial nine-one-one! Lock your door, and don't let anyone inside unless they show you a badge. Grab your gun, and do whatever you have to do to protect yourself. Do you hear me, Tessa? If it moves, and it isn't a cop, shoot it! I'm on my way."

The seconds seemed like hours as he grabbed his shirt, his shoes, his harness, his Sauer, and his keys. He punched in his security code, hit the controls to the garage door, and vaulted into the front seat of his pickup. Tires shrieking, he backed out of the garage, down the driveway, and into the street.

He took Speer, then tore through an empty parking lot, over a sidewalk, and up a one-way street to get onto Fourteenth, somehow managing to get into his harness with one hand on the wheel. Then he called in over his radio, forgetting his Denver ten codes and resorting to profanity instead.

"I'm en route to a possible sexual assault in progress. That's a ten-whatever-the-hell—and send backup, goddamn it!"

She'd said he'd touched her. Had he raped her?

Either way, he was dead meat if Julian got hold of him.

Denver's darkened streets seemed to stretch on forever. He

pushed the truck up to sixty, managed to squeak through a yellow light at Curtis, then drove the wrong way up another one-way street. Yet no matter how fast he drove, he knew he couldn't get to her in time if the son of a bitch was still there. Rape took only minutes, murder far less.

He tore around the corner, screeched to a stop in front of her building, and ran up the sidewalk. The front entrance to her building was secured—a glass door with a deadbolt—so he used the FBI master key, shattering the pane with the handle of his Sauer and reaching inside to force the handle. Then he took the stairs, sprinting up seven flights, weapon ready, to find the hallway outside her apartment in blackness.

His breathing slowed, his pulse dropped.

And he listened.

Silence.

Whoever the attacker was, he'd probably turned out the lights to cover his escape.

Julian made his way quickly and carefully down the hallway to her door, his senses trained on the darkness. "Tessa, honey, it's me, Julian."

He heard the bolt tumble, and a shaft of light spilled across him from inside her apartment. Then she was there, alive and clinging to him.

"Julian!" She was wearing only a white towel, tears on her face, a look of horror in her eyes, the ends of her long curls damp.

He would have liked to clear the apartment, to make certain the bastard was gone, but having a nearly naked woman in his arms made that difficult. He tucked the Sauer away, shut and locked the door behind him, held her trembling body close, relief flowing thick in his blood. "It's all right. I'm here. Let's get you warm."

By the time the first two cops arrived, weapons drawn, Julian had wrapped her in a blanket and gotten the full story. Then, rage a boiling black venom inside him, he stood behind her and listened to her tell it again to detectives, while officers combed through the apartment and the hallway outside, checking for fingerprints and signs of forced entry.

Feeling shaky and nauseated, Tessa tried to answer the lead detective's questions, Julian's presence bolstering her.

"Was your front door locked?" The officer sat on her coffee table, scribbled with a pen, looking strangely calm.

"I-I think so, sir. I always lock it. But I'd been going in and out, and I was really tired. M-maybe it wasn't locked." She struggled to remember.

"Did you actually see anyone?"

She shook her head, huddled more deeply in the blanket. "The lights went out."

"Is it possible what you experienced was just a dream?"

She felt tears prick her eyes, squeezed them shut. Her stomach rolled. "N-no, sir. He left . . . He left bruises. I-I saw them. Oh, I think I'm going to be sick!"

"Breathe, Tessa." Julian's voice was deep and soothing, his lips against her ear, his hands resting reassuringly on her shoulders. "Just breathe."

She drew a deep breath and another and another.

The wave of nausea passed.

She heard a voice from the bathroom say they'd found two distinct sets of prints on the switch plate and the doorknob.

Uniforms. The flash of a digital camera. Lights flashing red and blue in the street below. It was just like the night of the shooting. Only she was alive—unlike María.

Whoever he was, he hadn't killed her. Which surely meant he was probably just some random pervert who'd crossed paths with her completely by coincidence and had no connection to the shooting.

If he'd wanted to kill her, she'd be dead.

She shuddered.

"Do you feel you need to go to the hospital, have a doctor look you over, check those marks? If there are bruises—"

"No." Tessa couldn't do that, bruises or no bruises. "I'm not hurt."

"Is there anyone we can call for you—family, a close friend?"

They'd asked her the same question a week ago. "I'll call someone myself, thank you."

Kara and Reece would take her in, but they'd already done so much for her. Lissy was pregnant, but she and Will would surely welcome her, as would Holly and Sophie and even Kat. But Tessa didn't want to trouble any of them.

"Then I guess that about wraps things up." The officer put away his notepad and pen and pulled out his business card. "Call me if you think of anything else."

And then the police were gone.

Julian sat beside her and pulled her against him. He felt warm and steady, something sure in a world gone insane. "Tell me what I can do, Tessa."

She wanted a shower. She wanted to sleep. She wanted to forget.

She looked up at him, touched by the concern in his voice. "Would you mind staying while I take a shower? I don't think I can go into the bathroom again tonight if I'm alone."

He nodded. "If you want, I'll stay the night on your couch."

She stared up at him. "You would do that?"

"Just try and stop me."

Tessa sat on her couch, huddled in the blanket, while Julian cleaned black fingerprinting powder off the switch plate in the bathroom and drained her bathwater. She felt like a bit of a baby watching him do things that she could have done. Hadn't she always taken care of herself? Yes, she had—even when she was a little girl.

Still she was grateful that he'd offered. She really didn't want to see her bathroom as a crime scene. How had he understood that?

Perhaps the same way he understood that she needed a shower in the first place. After all, she'd just had a bath. But this wasn't about being grubby; it was about feeling clean again. She needed to scrub the feel of the man's hand from her body, wash away the aftertaste of horror, rinse the night from her skin.

It felt strange to have him in her apartment. As always, he seemed to fill the space with his presence, dominating the room just by being in it. But it didn't feel threatening to her. Instead, it made her feel safe.

After about five minutes, he walked out of the bathroom, drying his hands on a towel. "It's all ready for you."

He'd taken off his leather jacket, but he was still wearing his shoulder harness, gun and all. She got the feeling he didn't often go without it. What must that be like—to always be ready to fight and kill?

"Thank you." She stood, drew the blanket securely around her, feeling his gaze upon her as she walked past him to the bathroom door.

She stopped, looked at the tub, her feet strangely reluctant to enter the bathroom, the echo of her own screams playing through her mind.

He came up behind her, rested his hands on her shoulders. "No one is going to bother you, Tessa. Anyone who tries will have to get through me first."

She looked over her shoulder at him, managed a smile. Then she stepped into the bathroom and shut the door behind her.

JULIAN RUMMAGED THROUGH her cupboards, listening to the sound of running water. He hoped soap and water would be enough to wash away the sense of violation she must be feeling. He was just grateful the bastard hadn't done more.

Oh, how he wished they'd caught the son of a bitch.

Baking soda. Vanilla. Chocolate chips. Spices. Cooking oil.

The memory of her, half naked and in tears, made his jaw clench. Someone had watched her, had followed her into her apartment, had crept up on her while she'd lain, vulnerable and naked, dozing in her bath. The perpetrator had gotten close enough to do whatever he'd wanted to do with her—beat her, rape her, kill her—and what he'd done was squeeze her breast.

It didn't sound like Burien. One of his thugs would likely have kidnapped her, raped her at his leisure over a period of hours or even days, shared her with friends, then shot her and thrown her body in a ditch. Julian wouldn't have known she

was dead until she'd been bagged and tagged. The thought—
and the unwanted images it conjured—sickened him.

No, this wasn't like Burien at all. Perhaps one of Tessa's
readers had taken an unhealthy interest in her. Perhaps some
college kid who lived in her building had decided to major in
rape along with accounting and was working his way up.
Maybe some junkie had hoped to rob her but had gotten distracted by the sight of her.

And yet could it be coincidence that within a week of
watching a murder committed by Burien's goons, one witness
was dead and the other had just been attacked in her home?

Hell, no.

That's what his gut said. His gut was rarely wrong.

He wondered if and when he should tell Tessa about Mr.
Simms. Certainly not tonight. She'd been through enough
already.

Dinner plates, saucers, and bowls. Crystal wineglasses.
Coffee mugs.

Her apartment was small but tidy, with little touches that
reflected her personality—tasteful and feminine. Pots of flowers. Framed Monet prints on the walls. Puffy lavender pillows
on an overstuffed sage-green sofa. A solid oak bookshelf overflowing with classics, volumes of poetry, and romance novels.

No one stepping into this apartment would imagine that
Tessa had grown up as the illegitimate daughter of a dirt-poor
teenager. There was nothing of struggle and deprivation in the
place. Tessa had remade herself and left her past behind.

Julian respected that. He understood it. But he had made
a very different choice, embracing his past with a literal
vengeance.

Oatmeal. Peanut butter. Tuna fish. Cans of soup.

He heard her turn off the water in the shower, and a few
moments later the bathroom door opened and her bedroom
door closed. He tried not to think about her drying off, rubbing lotion into her skin, getting dressed.

He finally found what he was looking for—a bottle of
booze—and poured two shots of rum in a coffee mug. Then
he set about heating water. It was a recipe he'd picked up

from Juanita, the prostitute who'd become his father's de facto girlfriend and who'd probably been the closest thing to a mother Julian had known. She'd made this for him when he'd been nine or ten and sick with a cough. It hadn't done a thing to clear his chest or bring down his fever, but it had knocked him out.

By the time Tessa emerged from her bedroom, he had the drink ready for her.

He looked up, and the sight of her sent raw current arcing through his gut. Her hair hung in long, wet tendrils, her skin dewy and translucent. She was wearing a fluffy white bathrobe, her ankles and feet bare. Light pink polish glistened on her toenails, made her little toes look like candy.

He wanted to kiss her, to untie her bathrobe, watch it fall to the floor, and kiss every inch of soft woman it revealed, including her toes. He wanted to bury himself inside her and feel her melt around his cock as he made her come again and again. But there were dark circles beneath her eyes, and he could tell she'd been crying. Between the assault and her time at the shooting range, she'd had one hell of a day. He was an ass for even thinking about sex.

Her gaze fell on the mug in his hands. "Coffee?"

Julian searched his mouth, found his tongue. "It's past midnight. You don't need caffeine, honey, you need sleep."

She gave him a sad smile. "I've given up sleeping."

"Drink that. I guarantee you'll sleep tonight."

She looked doubtfully at the clear liquid, took the mug, sniffed. "It smells like . . ."

"There's rum in it. Go have a seat on the sofa, and drink it down." He leaned against the wall and watched as she carried the mug into the living room, sat, took a ladylike sip, and shuddered.

She glared at him. "This isn't going to make me sleep. It's going to make me choke."

"Drink it all at once."

Her gaze on his, she brought the mug to her lips, drank, made a pinched face. "Blech!"

He crossed the room and sat down beside her. "Feeling sleepy yet?"

"Oh, please!" She looked up at him as if he were being ridiculous and set the empty mug on the coffee table. "Do you think what happened tonight had anything to do with the murder?"

"I don't know. We took some prints. We'll have to see what we get."

She sank slowly into him, her words slightly slurred as his potion kicked in. "Maybe he was just a random boob grabber, just some creep. He really scared me."

"I know." Julian settled her against his chest, found himself wishing he could take away her fear. "Don't think about that now."

But she didn't seem to be thinking at all, her body boneless, her eyes closed.

For a few minutes, he held her, stroked her damp hair, unsettled by the emotion building in his chest and yet reluctant to let her go. When it seemed she was truly asleep, he scooped her up, carried her to her bed, laid her down on the sheets, and pulled the covers over her, bathrobe and all. Then he stood, looking down at her. "Sleep tight, Goldilocks."

He was about to turn away, when she spoke, her voice soft and drowsy. "Julian?"

"Mmm-hmm?"

"You're not so bad."

But he was. Oh, yes, he was.

CHAPTER 11

TESSA SLEPT DEEPLY through the night. Because she'd forgotten to set her alarm, she slept through the I-Team meeting, as well. She had no idea that Julian had peeked into the room twice to check on her. Or that Tom had left a message on her cell phone demanding to know where she was. Or that Sophie had called worried about her. When she finally awoke and saw that it was ten-thirty, she felt rested and refreshed—and thought it was the weekend.

She stretched and saw that she'd slept in her bathrobe.

That was strange. Why had she done that?

She must have—

She sat up with a gasp, as the events of last night crashed in on her. She remembered doing her laundry, thinking someone was watching her. She remembered dozing off in the tub. She remembered hearing someone breathe, thinking she was dreaming—and then feeling a hand close over her breast.

Sudden darkness, the icy horror, her own screams.

How distant it all seemed with bright sunlight pressing against her closed curtains and a night's rest behind her—like the echo of a nightmare. But it hadn't been a dream. It had been terrifyingly real.

She shuddered.

She remembered other things, as well. Julian's voice on the other side of her door. Julian holding her, wrapping her in a warm blanket, comforting her. Julian offering to stay the night on her couch and—

She gaped at her closed bedroom door.

Good lord! Was he here?

She slipped out of bed, crossed the room, opened her door, and stepped into the hallway to find him sitting on her couch, reading the paper, a cup of hot tea in his hand. His long hair was loose, hanging to his shoulders, and he wore no shoes and no shirt.

He looked so blatantly . . . *male*.

He saw her and stood. "Morning. How are you feeling?"

"Um," she said, stupidly, her mind suddenly blank, "I slept."

He grinned. "Thought you might."

The leather thong with the turquoise stone still hung around his neck. His nipples were a dark wine red against smooth olive skin, his shoulders broad and powerful, his arms lean and muscular. Dark curls were sprinkled across a well-built chest, tapering to a vee that traveled down the center of a six-pack and disappeared beneath the low-slung waistband of his jeans. Muscles she'd never seen on anything but marble statues curved around his sides just above his hip bones and dipped toward his groin.

Tessa felt her belly draw tight, heat flooding her cheeks.

She was staring at him, blatantly ogling him.

It's called sexual attraction.

She jerked her gaze up to his face, saw that he'd been looking at the kitchen clock.

"I hope you don't mind that I helped myself to some tea," he said.

"No! No, of course not." She realized she must look pretty awful standing there in her bathrobe with messy hair and no makeup. "Are you hungry?"

"I don't want to put you to any trouble." He grabbed his shirt, slipped it over his head, all those muscles shifting as he moved. "I can grab something later."

"It's no trouble, truly." And then it dawned on her. "Oh, God, I'm so sorry! Here you offered to stay here as a kindness to me, and I didn't even get you a pillow or blanket!"

"Relax." He tucked his shirt into his jeans. "I wasn't expecting to you play hostess. Good article, by the way—balanced, informative without being sensational."

"Considering your low opinion of reporters, I'll take that as high praise." She turned toward the kitchen, wondering if she had enough eggs to make them each an omelet. That's when it hit her. "It's Wednesday! I'm late for work! Damn, damn, damn!"

Julian watched as she rushed to the phone and dialed what he assumed was the newspaper. Her hair was a mass of tangled curls that his fingers itched to touch. Her face was fresh from sleep. Her bathrobe was wrinkled and had slipped to reveal one slender shoulder. In short, she looked sexy as hell.

Back off, buddy. No picket fences, remember?

"Hi, Tom, it's Tessa . . . I overslept. My apartment was broken into last night, and . . . Yes, sir, I know. I was up late with the police . . . In about an hour. I have an interview at one and was planning on writing a follow-up to today's story focusing on the exploitation of homeless teenagers—probably twenty inches if I can get it."

Whoever Tom was—her boss?—Julian instantly loathed the guy. It seemed to him that someone who'd been through what Tessa'd been through over the past week ought to be entitled to a little sympathy, if not a few days off. Yet it was obvious the guy was grilling her.

At the same time Julian was relieved to hear she intended to go to work. If she was at the newspaper, at least she'd be surrounded by other people and behind secured doors. The last thing he wanted was for her to be home alone. He had a job to do and couldn't stay with her all day. He was taking a big risk being with her at all.

He intended to ask Irving to assign someone to watch her twenty-four-seven, but it would probably take a day to make those arrangements. He would have to fill in the gaps in the meantime.

"I realize that, sir. It wasn't intentional." She hung up the phone, looking upset and frustrated, her gaze on the clock.

"I've got an idea," Julian said, picking up the elastic band he'd left on the table and tying back his hair. "How about you get ready for work, and I'll make breakfast."

While she took a shower and dressed, he threw together some huevos rancheros, popped toast in the toaster, and poured them each a glass of OJ. He'd just set a jar of salsa on the table when she emerged from her bedroom, wearing a sleek periwinkle-blue dress that made her blue eyes seem even bluer and her curves curvier. Her hair hung down her back in perfect spirals. Those same little pearls he'd found so tasty yesterday once more adorned her earlobes. Her feet were bare apart from her pantyhose, frosty pink polish just visible through the tan-colored nylon.

"Wow!" she said staring at the table. "You really did make breakfast."

"Save your astonishment for something more complicated than eggs, honey, or I'm likely to take it as an insult."

She sat, picked up her fork. "The only other man I've ever seen cook anything is my friend Kara's husband."

"The senator." Julian sat, picked up his toast, took a bite.

Her eyes narrowed. "I'm not going to ask how you know that."

"And I'm not going to tell you."

While they ate, Julian talked her through what would be happening that day. The cops would be running a check on the prints they'd lifted and ought to know before the end of the day if anything turned up. In the meantime, he was going to ask Irving to assign someone to watch her building around the clock.

"Are you sure that's really necessary?" She sipped her orange juice. "I hate to pull some cop off the street. For all we know, last night was just some random thing."

He could tell she was trying to be brave, and he had to admire her for the attempt. But he knew last night had scared the hell out of her. It had scared the hell out of him.

"Could be." Then he told her what he'd kept to himself. There was no easy way of saying it, so he simply said it.

"Mr. Simms, the other witness, is dead. His brother found him two days ago in their house in Omaha."

The color drained from her face, and her gaze collided with his, her eyes wide.

"The coroner ruled it a heart attack, but I'm not buying it."

"Wh-why not?"

"As a reporter, do you ever go on instinct, Tessa?"

She nodded, and he could tell she understood.

"I'd like you to meet me at six at the shooting range. We can take up where we left off."

"I thought you said I had great aim."

"There's a hell of a lot more to shooting a gun than aim."

"Okay." Then she closed her eyes. "I wish I were tougher. I really am trying to be strong about all of this, but inside I feel so afraid."

He reached across the table, took her hand, felt the current that always seemed to pass between them. "From where I'm sitting, honey, you're doing just fine."

Her small fingers laced through his, and he saw her pulse leap against her throat. "In case you're wondering, I no longer despise you. I have almost completely forgiven you for arresting me and blowing my interview."

He wanted to kiss her, to pull her into his lap, to lift that dress and put a really big run in her pantyhose. But this wasn't the time, and he wasn't the right man. "You're welcome."

Five minutes later, they stepped out of the elevator into the lobby, where the front door Julian had shattered with his Sauer was boarded up and awaiting replacement. His hand on her back, he felt Tessa shiver.

"He did this, didn't he?" she said as they opened what was left of the door and stepped into the fall sunshine.

"No. I did."

TESSA WAS NOT in the mood for Tom's crap. She had too much on her mind. Briefcase in hand, she tried to slip past his office unnoticed, but failed.

"Novak!"

Her colleagues looked up from their work, casting her sympathetic looks.

She turned back and marched into his office. "You bellowed?"

He glared at her from under bushy white brows. "Take a seat, and shut the door."

She refused to do either. "Why? They'll be able to hear you anyway."

"I hope you aren't planning on taking this morning as paid time off. Our policy—"

"I'm sorry if I failed to live up to your high standards this morning." She heard her voice quaver, but this time it was with anger, not tears. It was all she could do not to shout. "Last night a man who might be connected to the murder I witnessed last week broke into my home and groped me while I was asleep. Most employers would offer some sympathy or perhaps suggest some time off when one of their staff has been assaulted. But all you care about is what we can put in the paper. Are we reporters people in your eyes, Tom, or is the justice you talk about only for nonemployees?"

His cheeks turned mottled, and she could tell he was pissed. "Our policy—"

"Oh, for God's sake, Tom! Screw your policy!" Lily McMillan, Kara's petite and feisty mother, sat in a chair to the left of Tom's desk wearing a navy blue leotard, a batik broomstick skirt of orange and gold, and a rosary. Tessa had been so upset with Tom, she hadn't noticed her. "I'm so sorry, Tessa, sweetie. Kara told me about the shooting—and now this. Is there anything I can do? I know a medicine man who does cleansing ceremonies."

Tessa almost smiled. "Thanks, Lily. I appreciate the offer."

"I'm sorry you were attacked, Novak." A muscle jumped in Tom's jaw. "The paper will, of course, be happy to accommodate your every whim."

"You've got to bear with him, dear," Lily said, as if speaking of a child. "He's learning."

Tessa tried not to laugh. "Thank you, Tom."

The Lily McMillan Fund, indeed.

She turned to find the rest of the I-Team standing behind her and felt a rush of warmth. They'd been ready to back her up. They walked with her back to their desks, each of them showing her in his or her own way that they cared.

Kat gave her arm a squeeze. "A ceremony isn't a bad idea. Let me know if I can help."

Matt offered to fetch her a latte. "Nine shots or ten?"

Sophie walked with her to her desk, gave her a tight hug. "God, Tess, I was so worried! I'm so glad you weren't hurt! Do you want to talk about it?"

But Tessa didn't think she *could* talk about it—not here, not now, not if she wanted to hold it together and get through the afternoon. "Thanks. I appreciate it, but I . . . I just can't."

Sophie seemed to understand. She changed the subject, started back toward her own desk. "Your article has spawned a media feeding frenzy on gangs. All the stations picked up on it. Gangs are all they're talking about."

"Copycats." Tessa sat at her desk, sorted through press releases and e-mails, then screened her messages.

A long rambling message from someone who felt the Denver police had confiscated his ganja plants unfairly. A message from the director of the Denver Rescue Mission praising today's article. An irate message from a woman who lived near Curtis Park complaining that Tessa's article was going to make it impossible for her to sell her house.

Her finger was still on the delete key when the next message began to play.

"Hi, Tessa. It's your mama. You sound so professional in your message. I thought you might want to know your grandpa died. His liver finally gave. I left Rosebud after the funeral—saved all the money you sent and got a job waiting tables at a Denny's here in Aurora. It's a good job—nice people. Anyway, I don't want to bother you none. I know you're busy. I been keeping track all these years, reading your articles over the Internet at the library. I'm real proud of you. I wanted you to know that. I hope I can see you now and again. My number is . . ."

But Tessa didn't hear. Numb with shock, she sat, frozen,

until the message ended and the voice-mail program prompted her into action. She hit replay and had listened to the message three times before she managed to get the number down.

Her grandpa was dead, and her mother had moved to Colorado.

For her grandfather, Tessa felt nothing. He'd been a drunk, and an angry drunk. She'd spent her childhood doing all she could to avoid him, only feeling safe when he'd lain passed out next to an empty bottle. The world was a better place without him.

But her mother . . .

Tessa had cherished her when she was little. Then Tessa had grown up, and she'd learned to feel shame.

Tessa's mama is her sister—and her mama. That's what my mama says.

Tessa didn't have time for a family reunion. Her world was already in chaos. She'd witnessed a murder. She was in the middle of an investigation. Some crazy man had followed her into her home and groped her. And she might be well on her way to becoming infatuated with a man who was interested in her only for sex. The last thing she needed was her mother—or any part of Rosebud, Texas—back in her hard-won life.

She saved the message, tucked the piece of paper with her mother's phone number into her desk drawer, and picked up her files. She had an interview in half an hour, and she needed to prepare.

ALEXI LOOKED AT the photograph of the young woman reclining in her bath. She was quite pretty. Her long, curly blond hair trailed in the water, clung to her skin. Her breasts were full, her nipples ripe and rosy. She looked like she was sleeping—or newly dead.

"So this is the reporter." Alexi lifted his gaze to the man he'd ordered to watch her. "Did you kill her, too?"

The man—Alexi thought his name was Johnny—shook his head fiercely, sweat beading on his upper lip. "No! You told me to watch her, so that's what I'm doing. I'm doing exactly what you said."

"This I am glad to hear. It saves me the trouble of shooting you as I did your friend." Alexi looked again at the photo. The girl would look better tied to his bed. "You must have gotten very close to take this picture, yes? Did she see you?"

Johnny—if that was his name—shook his head and grinned, a smile that revealed crooked teeth. "I'm more careful than that. She was sound asleep."

There was a gleam in the boy's eyes Alexi recognized. "You want her, I think."

Johnny licked his lower lip. "I was thinking there might be other ways of getting her out of the way besides killing her."

Alexi laughed, feeling a new respect for the man who not long ago had been on his knees in a pool of his own piss. "If I tell you to kill her, you can do whatever you want with her before you pull the trigger. But I do not yet know what to do."

So far the girl hadn't proved to be a problem. She'd written the eyewitness account, true, but since then she'd been pursuing gangs. This was not a bad thing. The more the police and media focused on gangs, the easier it was for Alexi to conduct business unseen.

Besides, Alexi had bigger problems. Zoryo was missing. The man who'd been his friend since they were boys selling drugs on the frigid streets of Gzel had vanished from the face of the earth. No one had seen him for a week.

It was possible he'd been arrested, but Alexi would have heard something by now. He had moles in the police department and a puppet to keep him informed of the goings-on at the FBI. He knew, for example, that the idiot he'd shot last week had been found and identified and that his fingerprints had been linked by the tireless Julian Darcangelo to the basement apartment and, thus, the shooting. He knew the old man's death had been ruled a heart attack as planned. He knew that one of his operations in Longmont had been shut down—small potatoes, as Americans liked to say, but unfortunate.

But none of his sources had heard a thing about Zoryo. And that frightened Alexi all the more. Was it possible Zoryo had double-crossed him? If so, Alexi would take care of him, old friend or not.

He tucked the photo into his pocket. "Go keep an eye on your princess, but do not become so infatuated with her that you find it hard to pull the trigger if that time comes. If you need pussy, you know where to find it."

CHAPTER 12

JULIAN LEANED LAZILY against the wall of the interrogation room and let his prey sweat. The man stared down at photographs of himself approaching and leaving the basement apartment, his face pale, perspiration beading along his receding hairline.

Harold Norfolk was a prominent obstetrician who delivered lots of babies, served as a deacon in his church, donated generously to charity—and had a taste for teenage girls. He had a lot to lose. And a lot to answer for.

Norfolk sat back in his chair, his gaze not quite meeting Julian's, his lips drawn back in an arrogant grin. "You showed me these before. They prove nothing. I probably had a patient in the neighborhood, went to the wrong address."

"Just paying a house call?" Julian allowed himself a slow, predatory smile. "You are a veritable saint, Dr. Norfolk. I didn't think doctors paid house calls these days. Did your visit by any chance include fucking any one of four underage girls held captive in the house?"

The good doctor's nostrils flared, and his eyes widened almost imperceptibly. An adrenaline surge. "I-I demand to speak with my attorney. I won't say another word—"

Before Norfolk could finish, Julian lifted him out of his

seat by his expensive silk necktie and leaned down until their noses almost touched.

"If you think calling some high-priced lawyer is going to get you out of this, doc, you're sadly fucking mistaken." Julian let the loathing he felt drip from his voice like venom. "Some of the fingerprints taken from a case of birth control pills found in the apartment match those you so generously left on these photos last time you were here. That means your next house call could be to a cell in Supermax."

Norfolk was shaking now, his voice high pitched, his eyes wide. "Th-this is harassment and assault! I asked for an attorney! You can't continue this interrogation! You can't touch me! I know my rights!"

Julian tightened his grip, drew him closer still, lowered his voice, using every bit of menace he could summon to its fullest advantage. "I've got a murdered teenage girl and three others who are trapped in a living hell out there somewhere! Either you cooperate fully with this investigation, or you'll find out just how little I care about your rights!"

He released Norfolk, stepped back from the table, watched fear work its icy claws into the bastard's chest. He knew he was pushing it, stretching the law to the breaking point. But this wasn't about getting a confession that would be admissible in court. It was about extracting information that might save lives—including Tessa's. If he didn't get the information before Norfolk spoke with his attorney, he would probably never get it.

Norfolk buried his face in his hands. "My wife . . . my career . . . This will ruin my life!"

"Pardon me if I don't give a shit. What about the lives of those girls?"

"What do you want me to say? That I'm sorry?" He jerked his head up, and he seemed to vacillate between defensiveness and hysteria. "Okay, I'm sorry. I shouldn't have given in to lust and sought out the services of prostitutes, but I'm not the only man to fall into sin."

"Save the repentance for Jesus, doc. It might fool him, but it doesn't work on me. They weren't prostitutes, and you knew it. They were teenage girls forced to work as prostitutes. Girls forced to have sex with dozens of men each day. Girls you put on the pill so they wouldn't inconveniently get pregnant. That's not just sin, doc, that's *industrial-scale rape!*" Julian articulated every syllable, lingered on the words.

"How was I supposed to know how old they were? Some girls look like—"

"I doubt a jury will believe a trained ob-gyn can't tell a sixteen-year-old girl forced to have sex from a willing adult woman." Julian leaned across the table, resting his weight on his palms. "Either you tell me everything I want to know and help me save the other girls' lives in exchange for leniency, or today starts your one-way trip to hell."

Norfolk swallowed convulsively.

Over the next hour, Julian hammered him with questions. What were the names of the men who'd controlled the operation? How had he learned about the crib? Where were Denver's other illicit cribs? When had he begun supplying syringes and birth control pills? Was he currently providing medical supplies to any similar operations?

He'd just asked Norfolk how he communicated with the various pimps running these cribs when someone knocked on the door.

Keeping one eye on Norfolk, Julian opened it, saw Irving. He stepped into the hallway and shut the door to the interrogation room behind him, leaving Norfolk to stew.

Irving handed him a file folder. "Got word on the fingerprints taken from Ms. Novak's bathroom."

Julian opened the folder and scanned quickly through the pages.

"They're an exact match for one of two sets of prints that dominate the basement apartment. There's no doubt the attack on Ms. Novak is tied to the shooting and to Burien."

"God*damn!*" A sick, slick feeling in the pit of his stomach, Julian looked down at the face of the man who'd stalked and assaulted Tessa. Shaggy brown hair. Wide face. Eyes far apart and proportionately small. Long nose. Thin lips.

The punk's name was John Richard Wyatt, age twenty-two,

and he had a list of priors that went on for three pages—vandalism, cruelty to animals, felony theft, burglary, assault, possession with intent to sell. Add to that kidnapping, human trafficking, false imprisonment, and a host of sex crimes, and Wyatt was headed for eternity in prison.

Julian recognized him. He'd seen him enter and leave the basement apartment a few times during his hours of surveillance. He hadn't known for certain whether he was a horny repeat john or one of Burien's thugs. Now there was no doubt.

The bastard had already gotten close enough to Tessa to kill her. What had stopped him? Why had Wyatt grabbed her breast when he could have taken everything—including her life?

The question burned in Julian's mind, leaving him angry and on edge.

"We'll get a warrant, put out an APB." Irving ran a hand over his bristly hair.

"Don't." Julian handed the folder back, resisting the irrational urge to rip it into pieces. "We handle him the way we handled Zoryo. The moment Burien knows we've identified him, he'll pop John-Boy here and toss him out with the rest of the garbage."

And that wouldn't do—not when Julian wanted a crack at him first.

"Then we'd better bring him in fast. I want your plan within the hour." Irving glanced at his watch. "In the meantime, I've got to prep for a goddamned press conference. The city is in a gang hysteria. The damned TV stations took Ms. Novak's story and ran away with it. The mayor has called twice."

"Have you notified her?" Julian knew the news would shake her up. The thought of fear returning to those big blue eyes made him want to hit something.

"About the prints? No." Irving gave Julian a look through narrowed eyes. "I thought I'd leave that to you. In the meantime, I'm doing my best to hack through red tape and see if I can't offer her witness protection. The city bean counters know the feds are calling the shots on this investigation and think you boys should pay for it."

Julian shook his head. If Burien had eyes inside the FBI,

federal protection would be like no protection at all. "I don't trust—"

"I know." Irving pointed toward the interrogation room door with a jerk of his head. "How's it going with Dr. Family Values?"

"He's given me some solid leads—a couple places to check out, some names. He mentioned Pasha's, as well. We'll need a warrant for his home computer."

"He's given you all that without requesting counsel?"

"He's asked for his lawyer a couple of times. I only man-handled him once."

Irving poked Julian in the chest. "The *next* time he asks to call his attorney, make sure you comply. The DPD goes by the book."

Despite his rage, Julian couldn't help but grin. "Yes, sir. *Next* time."

It just so happened the next time came the moment Julian opened the door.

Dr. Norfolk, apparently having rediscovered his bravado while Julian was out of the room, greeted him with shouts. "I want to call my attorney! I demand to see my attorney!"

Julian raised an eyebrow. "Why didn't you just say so?"

TESSA LISTENED THROUGH her telephone headset, heart aching, as the girl told her story.

Nicki had run away from an abusive home at the age of fourteen only to end up selling crack on the streets with gang members, who'd taken her in. Actually, they'd "beaten" her in, giving her the honor of walking a gauntlet of other female gang members who'd assaulted her as a rite of initiation.

"I had a broken rib and was pretty bloodied up, but I was used to that. Besides, they were trying to be my friends. I was proud that I'd been beaten in instead of sleepin' with someone."

Tessa realized her teenage self, if given that choice, would have done the same thing. "Did the gang members give you a place to stay?"

"I sold crack, hooked up with one of the boys, stayed

mostly in his mama's place in the projects. I carried his pistol sometimes when the cops came round. They'd usually stop and search him if they saw him, but they left me alone."

By the time Tessa got off the phone, a sad picture had formed in her mind, a picture of poverty, hopelessness, violence, and an urban jungle in which unlucky teens were left to survive as best they could with little help from anyone.

It was *Lord of the Flies* on the streets of Denver.

Nicki had eventually been rescued from the streets by a sympathetic pastor. The rest of her gang mates hadn't been so lucky. The kid who'd been her boyfriend had been shot and killed when a drug deal he was working went bad. The rest of them were still on the streets, selling drugs, watching one another's backs, scrambling to stay alive.

Tessa had almost finished writing her article when her cell phone rang. For a moment she didn't answer, thinking it might be her mother. She wasn't ready to deal with that, not yet, not with everything else that was going on in her life. Then she remembered her mother didn't have the number to her cell phone.

She picked up the phone on the fourth ring, answered. "Tessa Novak."

"Are you at the paper?" It was Julian.

"Yes."

"Good. Stay there. Don't even go out for a cup of coffee. We got the results on the fingerprints. They're a perfect match for one of the sets we found in the basement apartment. The man who attacked you was one of the girl's killers."

He was saying something about Chief Irving working on witness protection for her, something about a police escort, but she could scarcely hear him over the buzzing in her ears.

The man who'd come into her apartment, the man who'd followed her, the man who'd crept up on her and squeezed her breast *had been one of the girl's killers*.

"Tessa, can you hear me? Are you all right?"

"Y-yes." It was a blatant lie. "Why didn't he kill me?"

Pull it together, girl!

"We'll talk about that later," he said. "Just don't leave the building alone. My guess is he's waiting out there for you. An officer will come for you at five and escort you to the shooting range. See you there."

She hung up, forced her trembling fingers back to her keyboard, and returned to writing her article, determined to do Nicki's story justice no matter what was going on in her own life. And as she'd worked, she found herself taking strength from Nicki's survival spirit. Still a child, Nicki had seen and endured things most adults could scarcely fathom. She had prevailed.

So would Tessa.

After all, the worst thing that had happened to Tessa was that some killer had snuck into her apartment and chosen to grab her breast over shooting her. It wasn't nice, but it could have been a whole lot worse. She'd been lucky.

This wasn't about her anyway. It was about a girl who had been running for her life and had been ruthlessly murdered. The killers were only interested in Tessa because she stood as a witness to that original violent act. But they were picking on the wrong person.

Tessa was done being afraid. She was an investigative journalist, damn it! It was her job to find the bastards and nail them to the wall. And that's what she was going to do.

THE SUN WAS setting over the Rockies when Tessa took the exit and turned into the shooting range parking lot, the black-and-white police cruiser behind her. She waited in her car until Officer Petersen met her at her door, then walked beside him into the shooting range, her heart rate picking up, a few irritatingly persistent butterflies flapping in her stomach.

She'd promised herself she wouldn't freak out again, and she knew she wouldn't. But now that she was here she couldn't stop herself from feeling nervous. Nor could she stop the sense of anticipation she felt at the thought of seeing Julian again.

It hadn't been easy keeping her mind off him. Okay, it had been next to impossible. It wasn't just the sight of him without a shirt that she kept remembering—though that fine image kept popping into her head at the most inopportune moments—but other things, as well. He'd broken glass to get to her, smashing through the front door of her apartment building as if he couldn't reach her fast enough.

She didn't know what to think about that, but she liked it.

Tessa thanked Officer Petersen for the escort, then walked through the hallway back toward the range itself. She found Julian standing at the counter talking with the same man who'd checked them in yesterday. Dressed in low-slung jeans, a black cotton T-shirt stretched across his broad shoulders, his harness in place, he seemed to radiate raw masculinity.

If her mind didn't understand it, her body certainly did. Just seeing him left her insides feeling warm and liquid.

He glanced over his shoulder and turned to face her, his gaze sliding over her. Then he frowned. She realized he was looking at her clothes. She was still wearing her dress and heels—not very practical attire for a shooting range, she supposed.

"I didn't bring anything to change into," she said, feeling silly.

"That's fine. I just don't want you to twist an ankle. Did you bring extra rounds?"

"Yes." She wasn't stupid enough to make that mistake twice.

"Let's go." Julian turned and led her through the double doors.

She followed him to what should have been the center stall. But where there ought to have been dividers, there was now only a wide-open space. Two thick panels of vinyl hung from the ceiling, each about two feet wide. Downrange stood six targets, outlines in the shapes of men, each mounted on some kind of frame that seemed to rest on a spring or track.

"We're going to do something different today. Clearly you can hit a stationary target when you've got time to use that front sight and aim. But most of the time, bad guys don't stand still, and you don't want to be standing still, either. We're going to practice shooting at moving targets under conditions more similar to what you'd encounter in a real firefight."

"So it's a shoot-out at the O.K. Corral." Those few butterflies flapped their wings harder.

His blue eyes dark with an emotion she didn't understand, he looked down at her, brushed his thumb down her cheek. "I know all of this has been hard on you, Tessa. I'm going to do my best to catch these guys. But just in case I don't or they get me first, I'm going to teach you how to stay alive and how to kick ass."

Touched, Tessa reached up, took his hand, and, without thinking, kissed his palm, his skin soft and hot against her lips. "If anything happens to you, Darcangelo, I'll kick *your* ass."

He grinned, his smile making her breath catch. "I'd like to see you try."

First they reviewed what they'd done last time. Next, he told her what to do in case of a misfire or a "squib load."

"In a revolver, the cylinder will usually advance to the next round, and you'll be able to discard the misfired round when you reload. If it's a squib load, meaning that the charge wasn't strong enough to force the bullet out of the barrel, the cylinder might jam. You won't be able to fire again until the round is removed—something only a gunsmith can do. If the bullet lodges in the barrel and you fire again, the barrel is likely to explode. Squib loads are rare, but if they do happen, a revolver is useless."

"What do you do then? Drop the gun and run like hell?"

He chuckled. "No, you hold on to the gun and run like hell. They don't know the gun is useless. Point it at them, and they're likely to duck for cover. And if they catch you, you can always beat the crap out of them with it. Steel is steel."

Then he showed her what she'd be doing. The vinyl panels were intended to simulate cover of some kind—the edge of a wall, a tree, furniture. The targets were the other shooters. Scattered across the room, each would move in its turn and in random order. Her job was to remain safely behind cover while hitting each target in the chest region when it moved. The targets were positioned in such a way that she'd have to turn back and forth to fire, making use of both panels.

"Like this." Julian turned and waved to a man in a control booth Tessa hadn't noticed before. Then he stood with his back to one of the vinyl panels, pretending to hold a gun in his hands.

The first sprang up, lurching forward by about a foot.

Julian pivoted, pointed his fingers, and "fired" in one smooth motion. "Bam!" he said, reminding her of a little boy playing cops and robbers.

But this was anything but a game.

Then the second moved. Then the third. Then the fourth, fifth, and sixth.

"Bam! Bam! Bam! Bam! Bam! Like that. Try to hit center mass."

It didn't look too hard.

Julian suppressed a grin as Tessa, revolver in hand and pointed at the floor, reached down and slipped off her heels then carried them to the nearby bench. She was being practical—a good thing. Why it should amuse him so damned much, he didn't know. Perhaps it was the sight of her, all feminine curls and curves, with heels in one hand and revolver in the other. He'd seen lots of women packing guns over the years—special agents, cops, killers—but none of them could match Tessa for sheer girliness.

Given what he'd told her this afternoon, she was doing remarkably well. He hadn't been sure what to expect, and he'd been prepared for the possibility that she'd be too overwhelmed and afraid to fire a single shot. But if she was afraid—and he was certain she must be—she wasn't showing it. He hoped her nerves would hold. She had a rough couple of days ahead of her, and that was if everything went according to plan.

He would tell her about that later. Right now he wanted her to concentrate.

Looking determined and focused, she took position as he'd shown her behind one of the panels, the pistol pointed at the ceiling, its barrel pointed a little too much toward her.

He walked over, adjusted the angle. "Forget what you've seen on TV shows. The only people who hold guns like that are people who want to shoot their own noses off."

"Oh." Pink spots appeared on her cheeks.

"Ready?"

She nodded.

He gave the signal.

The first target moved. She spun toward it, and he saw one of her eyes close as she fixed her gaze on the front sight and fired. By then the second target had already moved. Before she could turn to face it, the third had moved. Still, she took aim and shot at each one, hitting three of the six.

When she was done, she glanced at the targets, a look of satisfaction on her face. "Well, I hit half of them. Not bad for a first try."

Julian hated to burst her bubble. "If this were real life, that guy," he pointed to the second target, "would have shot you while you were distracted and aiming at the first guy. You were using your front sight. Remember, you can't do that. Just aim and fire. And keep under cover. It's more important *not* to get shot than it is to hit your target. Okay, reload."

The targets clicked back into place as she slipped six fresh rounds into the revolver and snapped the cylinder shut.

"Ready?"

She nodded. "Lock and load."

Julian gave the signal.

Pop! Pop! Pop! Pop! Pop! Pop!

This time none of the rounds she fired hit anything.

She frowned. "I think those ended up in Kansas."

"That's okay. You're not supposed to know how to do this. That's why we're here."

For the next hour he repeated the drill, giving her pointers, correcting her, until her cheeks were pink from the exertion and frustration. They'd gone through more than a hundred rounds, and she'd hit her target only eleven times—fairly typical for a new shooter.

"Damn it!" She looked adorably pissed off. "This is impossible! I keep getting shot, and I can't hit the target if I can't use the sight!"

Julian crossed his arms over his chest, fought back the smile that kept creeping onto his face. "Sure you can. It just takes practice."

She glared up at him. "And I suppose you can hit them all."

He nodded. "Easily."

"Well, Mr. Armed and Dangerous, let's see it." She pressed her pistol into his chest.

He pushed her hand away, drew out his Sauer. "This is a three-fifty-seven SIG Sauer. It conceals easily, is fairly light-weight, and packs a mean punch. The magazine I carry holds twice as many rounds as your revolver, and I can reload quickly by popping in a new magazine. If it jams, I can have it operational again in seconds by tapping the butt against a hard surface to make sure the magazine is in place and then racking the slide."

He demonstrated as he spoke, releasing and reloading the magazine, tapping the butt and drawing back on the slide. Then he looked up to see a dejected expression on her pretty face.

"Your gun is better than mine."

He couldn't resist. "And bigger."

Her gaze collided with his, and she blushed. Then her eyes narrowed. "Shut up, and shoot."

"Yes, ma'am." Julian took position, shifted his mind from Tessa to the task at hand, nodded to Hal in the control booth.

As soon as the first target moved, his response became automatic. He registered only sound, motion, and the hard kick of the Sauer in his hands. He fired the sixth round, replaced the half-full magazine with a full one, and slipped the Sauer into its holster.

When he looked up, she was glaring at him.

"Show-off."

He allowed himself one smirk, more to irritate her than because he truly felt smug about his target shooting. "You shouldn't compare yourself to me, Tessa. I was trained by the best and have been practicing almost daily for fifteen years. You've done this once."

"That won't matter next time that guy comes around and decides to blow my head off." Her gaze dropped to the floor, the fear he'd known she must be feeling finally coming to the surface.

He closed the space between them, tucked a finger beneath her chin, and lifted her face, forcing her to meet his gaze. "I'm going to do everything I can to make sure there isn't a next time."

"Why didn't he kill me, Julian?"

"Let's talk about it over dinner."

CHAPTER 13

JULIAN FOLLOWED TESSA home, hanging far enough behind her to keep an eye out for Wyatt. There was no sign of the bastard. Perhaps the police escort she'd had to the shooting range had scared him off for the moment. Or perhaps Burien had already rearranged his anatomy for last night's screwup—if what he'd done last night had, indeed, been a screwup.

Julian watched from a half block away as she turned into her parking lot and parked in her assigned place. He spotted the unmarked police car in a visitor's space nearby, where plainclothes officers had been keeping her building under surveillance all afternoon. The night shift would be relieving them soon—two undercover vice cops handpicked by Julian and strapped to play rough.

If Wyatt came skulking around tonight, he was going to find himself facing more than a soft, terrified woman.

Julian had asked Tessa to let him sleep on her couch tonight. She'd seemed relieved to know he'd be there, but she'd made him promise not to knock her out again. "No more Molotov cocktails, or whatever that was," she'd said. "I don't even remember getting into bed."

Julian had thought it best not to tell her that he'd carried her. Instead, he'd gone over the procedure with her.

As planned, Tessa walked into the building first, the plainclothes unit keeping a careful eye on her as she strolled up the
walk, let herself in through the newly repaired door, and
checked her mailbox. Julian waited until she'd been inside for
several minutes, then followed her, using the duplicate he'd
made of her key to get inside the lobby.

Ten minutes later he stood in her kitchen trying his best to
answer questions.

"The truth is," he said, uncorking a bottle of red wine, "I
don't know."

He poured the burgundy liquid into a crystal glass, set it
down before her, then put the bottle aside. He didn't drink unless his cover demanded it.

She sat at the table, looking up at him, hands clasped nervously in her lap. She'd changed into jeans and a blue V-neck
shirt that drew his gaze to her breasts despite his best inten-
tions. He forced himself to look at her face, forbidding his
eyeballs from seeking anything farther south than her chin.

You're a pig, Darcangelo.

She looked at the wine without really seeming to see it,
then picked up the glass and took a sip. "Maybe my scream
scared him away."

Julian had tried to logic his way through this all afternoon.
There were two possibilities: either Wyatt had been acting on
Burien's orders when he'd assaulted Tessa, or he hadn't. Because Julian couldn't fathom what Burien stood to gain by
having one of his thugs manhandle her, Julian was inclined
to believe it was the latter. Perhaps Wyatt hadn't yet been ordered to make the hit and had gotten carried away while
watching her. Or perhaps he'd been ordered to kill her and had
lost his nerve. If it were the latter, he'd be dead in no time.

"I doubt it," Julian said at last. "These guys are ruthless.
They enjoy hearing women scream. I'm guessing he did something he wasn't supposed to do and lit out of here before you
could see him. Either that or he was supposed to kill you and
couldn't do it."

Tessa studied him, and he could almost hear the wheels in
her sharp mind turning. "You know who he is."

Julian had been trying to decide all afternoon what he should tell her. Her life was in danger in ways she couldn't possibly imagine, and letting her in on the truth, or part of it, might make a difference. But she was also a reporter, and there was no way to know for certain that she wouldn't print everything he told her. And although she hadn't yet printed anything she knew about him—his name, for example—he wasn't sure she'd be able to resist writing an article about Burien if Julian gave her the big picture. Besides, he hadn't been authorized to tell her anything. She shouldn't even know who he was.

"This is strictly on a need-to-know basis and off the record, got it? If you print anything I tell you, you'll be aiding and abetting murderers."

"Got it." She set the wineglass back on the table. "Off the record."

"His name is John Richard Wyatt, age twenty-two." Julian took Wyatt's mug shot out of his pocket, put it on the table. "He's got a long list of priors, and it's getting longer. He was involved with the shooting you witnessed, probably as an accomplice.

"The man I believe pulled the trigger is already dead, face blown off point-blank with a forty-four Magnum, no doubt as punishment for leaving witnesses. We found his body last weekend, together with a set of rims, and linked the body through prints to the basement apartment. He was still wearing that leather jacket."

He saw her eyes widen—a reaction she quickly suppressed—and he wondered if he should tone it down. He didn't suppose journalists talked about crime in the same casual, gory detail that law enforcement professionals did. Or did they?

Her gaze dropped to the mug shot. Her arms crossed over her chest as if she were hugging herself—an unconscious, defensive gesture that wrenched something in his chest.

"He looks like a kid."

"The 'kid' is a sociopath."

She pushed the mug shot away as if she suddenly couldn't stand to look at it. "Any chance you're going to tell me exactly what this is all about? What was going on in that apartment? Why did they—whoever 'they' are—murder her?"

Julian picked up the mug shot, tucked it out of sight. "Isn't what I've told you enough, Tessa? Do you need to hear more to understand that your life is in grave danger?"

"Can't you even tell me her name?" A sheen of tears glittered in her eyes.

He knelt face-to-face beside her, caught a tear with his thumb. "You're trying to make sense out of something senseless, Tessa. Knowing her name won't make this any easier. Take my word for it."

"I-I watched her die, Julian. I can't explain . . ." She squeezed her eyes shut, as if to force back her tears, turned her face away from him.

"María Conchita Ruiz. She was sixteen."

María Conchita Ruiz.

Tessa ran the girl's name through her mind again and again, her brain screaming that sixteen was far too young to die. And she realized Julian was right. Knowing the girl's name only sharpened the edge of her regret.

"*¡Por favor, señor, ayúdeme! ¡Ayúdeme! ¡Me van a matar!*"

Someone knocked on Tessa's door, making her gasp, sending her to her feet. "That can't be the pizza. I would have to buzz them in."

"Easy, Tessa." Julian ran a hand down the length of her arm, pulled his gun from his shoulder harness. "Someone was probably coming in at the same time and let them in. People in Denver are naive and sloppy about security. I'll get it. You stay out of sight."

Heart thudding, she grabbed her purse, fished out her .22, and backed deeper into the kitchen, watching as Julian looked out the peephole.

She told herself she was safe and remembered how quickly and smoothly he had taken out the targets at the shooting range. She'd never seen anyone move that fast or with such precision. If Wyatt came around tonight it would be he, not Tessa, who was in danger. She forced her fear aside, but couldn't stop her relieved sigh when Julian holstered his gun, shot her a grin, and opened the door.

"It's twenty-fifty-three," a young man's voice said. "We take checks with ID."

She saw Julian pull his wallet from his back jeans pocket and pull out a few bills.

"Thanks," the kid said. "Dude, is that, like, a real gun?"

Julian answered, his deep voice tinged with humor. "Yeah, dude, it is."

They ate their pizza at the table, Tessa insisting on using real dishes, even if they were eating fast food. Julian seemed to be trying to keep the conversation light, asking her questions about her job, about other investigations she'd worked on, about Tom.

"From what I could tell this morning, the guy is a jerk," he said, refilling her wineglass.

"Tom, a jerk?" Tessa, feeling more relaxed, couldn't help but laugh. "He just takes the responsibility of journalism very seriously—but, yes, he is a *total* jerk."

By the time their plates were in the sink and they'd moved to the living room, Tessa was feeling more peaceful than she had in days. The wine had spread like a summer sunset through her veins, leaving her feeling tranquil and lazy.

"Why'd you decide to go into journalism?" Julian asked her. He'd removed his harness, draped it over a nearby chair, and sat on the floor beside the couch, his weight resting on one arm, one knee bent, his black T-shirt stretching distractingly across his chest. His dark blue eyes watched her, his gaze warming her as much as the wine.

She stretched her legs, reclining against a pile of pillows on the couch. "No more questions about me. You know everything about me. You know things about me no one else knows, stuff I wish you didn't know. You can probably answer that question yourself."

His eyes narrowed slightly, as if he were measuring her. "I'd say it has to do with a need to fight for the underdog, to stand up for people who can't stand up for themselves. With your background you naturally identify with the underdog. And I think you need the acknowledgment, the public recognition. It proves to you that you escaped, that you're no longer Tessa Bates."

Tessa felt her face flush. "I do not need—!"

He raised a dark eyebrow. "Did I cut too close to the bone?"

In fact, he had. But she wouldn't give him the satisfaction of knowing that. "Enough about me. You've asked your twenty questions. Now it's my turn."

"Fair enough."

"How old are you?"

"Thirty-two."

"Are you married, divorced, sing—?"

"Never married. Never will be."

"Aha." His answer didn't surprise her, but for some reason it did take her mood down a notch. "Kids?"

"Not as far as I know."

"What is 'Darcangelo'?"

"My last name." He was biting back a grin.

"No! I mean what ethnicity." She grabbed a pillow off the couch, hit him with it.

He fended off her attack with his forearm. "I'm half Italian."

"Which half?" The words were out before Tessa could stop them.

Was she flirting with him? She *never* flirted with men.

His lips curved in a slow, sexy smile that made her heart trip. "From the waist down."

She felt her breath catch, felt her face burn, found herself chasing her own scattered thoughts. "Why did you become a cop?"

He reached up, brushed a strand of hair from her cheek, the split second of contact like a static burst against her skin. "I like busting bad guys."

Coming from anyone else, this might have seemed a wisecrack. But Tessa could tell he meant it. "That's what matters to you—patrolling Gotham and getting bad guys off the streets?"

"Something like that."

He was too close, his body seeming to radiate heat. He hadn't really touched her, but she was already at the melting point, her body thrumming with blatant, undeniable longing. She'd never felt this way, not even when Scott, spouting poetry he hadn't really meant, had peeled off her clothes and taken her virginity in his dorm room.

Tessa picked up her wineglass, took a sip, tried to remember what they were talking about. His job. "That sounds dangerous to me—and lonely."

"Speaking of lonely, why isn't there a man in your life? A beautiful, smart woman like you with a successful career—I would have imagined you'd be married by now."

She almost choked, suddenly wishing they were talking about the weather. But then, why not come right out with it? He already knew so much about her.

She set her wine aside. "The women in my family don't have much luck with men. My grandma married my grandpa—really bad luck for her. My mom . . . Well, you know about my mother."

"She had a baby at fourteen. Yeah, I know. It must have been tough for both of you."

Tessa had been trying not to think about it, but their conversation made that impossible. "She called today. Bless her heart! I haven't spoken with her since I left, and then she calls out of the blue, tells me she's working at the Denny's in Aurora."

"Are you going to get together with her?"

Tessa shook her head, shrugged. "I don't know. It's complicated."

He gave a slight frown. "She's your mother."

"That's the problem." Tessa's words sounded cold, even to her own ears. "Do you stay in touch with your mother?"

"I never knew my mother." His voice and his face were expressionless.

She stared at him, astonished. "You never knew your mother? Did she give you up for adoption or die when you were born?"

"No."

For a moment they sat in silence.

"I'm sorry," she said at last. "That was rude of me."

He acted like he hadn't heard her. "So your mother made a mistake, and you're ashamed of her. What does that have to do with your reason for avoiding men?"

"Now who's being rude?" Tessa glared at him. "I don't *avoid* men. I'm just careful. The last thing I want is to end up like her or like my grandmother—alone with a baby or married to an abusive drunk. Besides, the *idea* of having sex with a man is *loads* better than the reality."

He came face-to-face with her in one smooth motion. "Sure about that, are you?"

Pulse racing, Tessa found herself looking at his mouth, wondering if he would kiss her, wishing he would kiss her, hoping to God he would kiss her. "Pretty sure."

One of his hands slid into her hair, cradling the back of her skull, angling her head so that her mouth was aligned with his. "I'll take that as a challenge."

And then he *did* kiss her.

Slowly.

He brushed his lips over hers once, twice, three times, sending shudders through her. Then with a low groan, he slipped his other arm around her and drew her against his hard chest. But still he didn't kiss her full on, tasting first her upper lip, then her lower lip, then the corners of her mouth again and again, until her lips tingled and ached and she was shaking with need.

She shouldn't be doing this. She didn't want to be used, didn't want to be a notch in yet another man's bedpost. She didn't want to make another stupid, heartbreaking mistake. She'd been careful all these years not to fall into bed with men who wanted nothing but sex, men like Julian. But then she'd never really met a man like Julian, and it had been so long since she'd let a man touch her, so long since she'd allowed herself to *feel*.

He pulled back and looked down at her, his lips wet, his brow furrowed, his eyes dark. "How am I doing so far, honey?"

He didn't give her time to answer, but kissed her—hard.

Oh, God, yes!

He thrust deep with his tongue, plundered her mouth with stunning thoroughness, finding her most sensitive places, sucking and nibbling her lips, tilting her head to take the kiss deeper, cutting off her breath, consuming her. She moaned, kissed him back, her fingers clenching in his hair, her body deliciously aware, liquid heat pooling between her thighs.

He fisted his hand in her hair, forced her head back, and kissed the exposed skin of her throat, nipping the sensitive spot just beneath her ear, sucking on her earlobe, pressing his lips against her pulse. The stubble of his beard grazed her skin, the slight pain a source of pleasure.

"More?" He whispered the word against her throat, his voice rough, his breathing every bit as ragged as hers.

"Oh, God, Julian!"

Julian took that as a yes, ignoring the voice in his mind that told him this was wrong, listening instead to her little whimpers and moans, to the response of her body and the answering tension in his own. He didn't want to think about who wanted picket fences and who didn't. He didn't want to think about his damned job. He didn't want to think about Burien.

The only thing he wanted to think about was Tessa.

With a groan, he drew her off the sofa and pulled her to the carpet beneath him, kissing her harder, his brain buzzing with raw, urgent lust. She arched against him, the soft, feminine feel of her making every muscle in his body tense, his cock already straining hard as steel against his jeans. He'd meant to take it slow and easy, but he wasn't taking it slow now.

Still kissing her, he reached with one hand, pushed her shirt up, and jerked her bra down, baring two of the most beautiful breasts he'd ever seen—full and creamy white, their light pink nipples puckered with arousal.

"Jesus!" He ducked down, greeted each rosy peak with an impatient flick of his tongue, then closed his lips over her right nipple and tasted her.

She gasped, then moaned, a sensuous, feminine sound,

her fingers sliding up his neck to fist in his hair. "Oh, Julian, yes!"

Driven by her pleas and moans and his own blistering need, he tugged on her nipple with his lips, flicked it, sucked it, cupping her other breast greedily, his thumb tracing circles on the petal-soft tip.

God, she was sensitive! She reacted to each stroke of his tongue, each tug of his lips, as if his mouth were caressing her entire body, her breath coming in gasps and shudders, her hips lifting off the carpet, the musky scent of her response driving him damned close to the edge.

He shifted his mouth to her other nipple and sucked hard, his hand skimming down the silky, hot skin of her belly. He made fast work of her zipper, then slid his hand beneath her panties, his fingers threading through her damp curls. He didn't waste time, but parted her puffy lips and thrust first one finger, then two into her slippery heat, taking care to graze her clitoris as he drove deep and then withdrew.

She cried out, her fingers digging into his shoulders, her thighs parting to give him better access. "Oh! Oh, God, Julian!"

"You're on the brink. I can feel it." He brushed his lips over a tight, wet nipple, his hand busy stroking her inside and out. "After you come, I'm going to rip those jeans off your body, wrap your legs around my waist, and fuck you the way you've wanted me to since we met."

"You . . . arrogant . . . oh!" she panted, her head turning from side to side, her eyes squeezed shut, her skin glowing pink. "Oh, oh, God, yes!"

Then her breath broke, and she came, arching off the floor, her inner muscles clenching tightly, making him nearly explode at the thought of his cock replacing his fingers.

He rode through it with her, kept his rhythm steady, his mouth on her breasts, her throat, her lips, as the quaking inside her slowly subsided—and the fire inside him flared.

Suddenly her hands were tugging at his T-shirt, pulling it out of his jeans, her hands sliding hungrily over the skin of his belly and chest. "I need to touch you! I want to touch you!"

"Jesus, honey, fine by me." He pulled his shirt over his

head, tossed it aside, then reached down to help her with his zipper, hunger for her raging in his veins.

Almost painfully hard, his cock sprang free.

Then a voice crackled over his radio. "Suspect sighted. Code Black."

CHAPTER 14

STILL SHAKEN BY the force of her climax, Tessa found her-self being hauled to her feet, her mind reeling from pleasure to alarm in the span of a single heartbeat. "Wh-what—?"

"Quiet!" Julian zipped his jeans, pulled on his shirt, and strapped on his harness, his hair hanging loose around his shoulders. Then he held the radio to his mouth. "Copy that. Welcome wagon ready. Over. Where's your gun, Tessa?"

She pointed toward the kitchen, tugging her bra and shirt back into place over her still-aching breasts. And then she heard it—the sound of someone moving outside her door.

Her mouth went dry, adrenaline kicking her already-racing pulse up a couple notches.

Julian hurried into the kitchen, moving almost silently, re-turning in a blink with her revolver. "Get to your room, lock the door behind you, and take cover behind the bed. Don't come out till I tell you to, understood?"

She nodded and took the revolver from him, suddenly sickly afraid not for herself, but for him. She touched a hand to his arm. "Be safe!"

His gaze met hers, something like surprise in his eyes. Then the look vanished, and he motioned with a jerk of his head. "Go!"

She hurried into her bedroom, shut and locked the door, then ran to the other side of her bed and knelt down, trying to listen over the hammering of her own heart.

She heard her door open, heard Julian swear, heard the thud of footfalls racing down the hallway. Then a door slammed, and she knew someone had reached the stairs. From the stairwell—or was it from outside?—she heard more shouting, men's angry voices. A few minutes later there came the approach of sirens, distant wails that grew louder until it came to a stop just outside.

And then . . . nothing.

She waited in the dark of her bedroom for what seemed an eternity, listening. Had Julian chased him down the back stairs and caught up with him outside? Was Julian cuffing him and putting him in a squad car? Had the creep run off down the street? Was Julian safe? Was it all finally over? God, she hoped it was over!

The silence grew unendurable, her apprehension overwhelming. She stood, tiptoed over to her door, opened it a crack, and saw nothing but the cheery light from her living room. She stepped into the hallway, gripping the revolver tightly in her sweaty hand, her senses heightened. Pressing herself up against the wall, she glanced round the corner. Her front door stood slightly ajar, but she was alone.

She hurried to the door and looked out to find the hallway empty. Then her gaze fell on a flyer that someone had stuck to her door—and her stomach dropped to the floor.

It was a printout of a photograph. Of her. Asleep and naked in the bathtub.

"What the hell are you doing out here?"

She whirled about to find Julian striding toward her, an angry expression on his face. Then she saw his hands. They were stained with blood.

"I KNOW HOW it happened. Wyatt got the drop on Taylor and fired a round into his gut from a trey-eight equipped with a silencer. But I want to know *how* it happened. Goddamn it! We had him—*we had him*—and somehow he escaped!"

Tessa sat on her couch, hugging a pillow to her chest, while Julian shouted at Chief Irving over his cell phone. Anger rolled off him in dark waves, but she knew he blamed himself.

While he'd been getting dressed, one of his men had been shot in the stomach by a .38 round that had penetrated Kevlar. Wyatt had apparently used a silencer, and no one had known anything was wrong until Julian had literally tripped over the officer's unconscious and bleeding body at the bottom of the back stairs. Julian had stopped to save the officer's life, and Wyatt had gotten away.

It sickened Tessa to think a police officer lay in the hospital, almost killed for trying to keep her safe. It sickened her almost as much to think the bullet they'd pried from his intestines could just as easily have been fired at Julian. By comparison, the naked photograph of her seemed insignificant, harmless. And, yet, in some ways it was what shocked her the most.

While she had lain asleep in the tub, this freak, John Wyatt, had crept up on her and taken her picture. He'd done more than that, of course, but it hadn't been until she'd seen the printout that she'd remembered hearing the *click*. In fact, it was probably the click that had awoken her enough to notice his breathing in the first place.

When Julian had finished yelling at her for being in the hallway, he'd taken the printout, sealed it in a plastic bag, and sent it off as evidence with one of the responding officers.

"This is his own doing," he'd said more to himself than to her, bloodstains on his jeans and T-shirt. "He was sent to watch you, but my guess is he's become obsessed. He's stalking you like a predator, trying to terrorize you before he moves in. He wants you to know he's coming. He wants you to be afraid."

"Well," Tessa had said, feeling nauseated. "He should be happy. He succeeded."

Who were these guys? What was this really about?

Julian had spoken of Wyatt as if he worked for someone else.
He was sent to watch you.

He'd spoken of the man he'd thought was María Ruiz's killer in the same way.

The man I believe pulled the trigger is already dead, face blown off point-blank with a forty-four Magnum, no doubt as punishment for leaving witnesses.

Were Wyatt and the dead killer nothing but hired guns? Why would anyone hire killers to take out a sixteen-year-old girl? What sort of criminal would be heartless enough—and have enough money—to hire people for such violent crimes? A drug kingpin? An arms dealer? A crime boss? Was there really any chance that the shooting had been gang related as she'd initially thought?

There's worse things than gangbangers on these streets.

Who or what had Syko been thinking of when he'd told her this?

In the kitchen, Julian was still arguing with Chief Irving. "I know he attacked one of your men, but if you put out a warrant, he'll be dead. He's now my best and surest path for closing this investigation quickly. If I can catch him, get what he knows from him . . . Fine. Do it your way. It will be my job to try to reach him before anyone else."

Tessa's mind absorbed these words, puzzled through them, stuck on one phrase.

I know he attacked one of your men.

One of *your* men.

Not one of *our* men or one of *the* men or one of *my* men. One of *your* men.

What was going on here? It sounded to her like Julian was talking about bending the rules, playing light with Wyatt's civil liberties. Why were they keeping this case so tightly under wraps? They still hadn't even released María Ruiz's autopsy. And who was Julian Darcangelo, this mysterious man who had stepped out of the shadows to help her?

It seemed almost unbelievable to her that a couple of hours ago the two of them had come within moments of having sex on her floor. Even though they hadn't finished the act, it was still the most amazing sexual experience she'd ever had. He'd made her feel like the center of a blazing universe, as if he'd been aware only of her, as if he'd felt what she'd felt, as if her pleasure had mattered more to him in that moment than anything else. And when the first sultry shock of climax had washed through her, she'd felt a surge of emotion that had been as undeniable as it was terrifying.

She was falling in love with him.

This was *not* part of the plan. She didn't want to fall in love with him. Or if she did, she wanted it to happen *after* he'd fallen in love with her—and shouted his feelings from the rooftops, bought the ring, and gotten down on one knee. She didn't want to be used again. She didn't want to take the risk only to find herself as alone as her mother had been.

"She's shaken but safe for the moment," she heard Julian say. "We need to get her into witness protection sooner rather than later. I've got other things I need to be doing. I'm not a damned babysitter!"

His words hit her in the stomach, and something inside her shattered like glass. Her body went cold, a sensation very much like pain settling behind her breastbone.

She'd thought he'd stayed on her couch because he'd at least cared about what happened to her. He'd seemed so concerned. She hadn't realized he'd seen it as a burden. And what about the intimacy they'd shared earlier? Did that have anything to do with real feelings and desires, or had he just been trying to prove something again?

"I'll take that as a challenge," he'd said.

And she'd melted like butter.

You have only yourself to blame, Tessa.

Perilously close to tears, Tessa met him when he stepped out of the kitchen and handed him his leather jacket. "I'd like to thank you for all you've done to ensure my safety. You've risked your life for mine, and I won't forget that. But I'd like to ask you to leave now. I don't want or need a babysitter."

Julian drove through Denver's darkened streets on his way to LoDo, the events of the night playing through his mind, his body tense. He glanced at the clock on his dash. Four a.m.

The whole thing was his fucking fault. If he hadn't been distracted, he'd have been able to respond the moment he'd gotten the call. Instead, he'd lost precious minutes stuffing his dick back into his pants, retrieving Tessa's gun from the last place she'd misplaced it, and getting her out of harm's way. By the time he'd been armed and in position, Wyatt, who'd already shot Taylor and knew the cops were there, had stuck the picture to the door and fled. Julian had opened the door in time to see the bastard vanish down the stairwell and had chased after him, only to find Taylor lying half dead in a pool of his own blood. Bad fucking luck the bullet had gone through Taylor's vest. It happened.

If Julian had opened the door sooner, if he'd gotten to Wyatt right away . . .

Taylor would still be in the hospital with his belly ripped open and a tube in his nose, but Wyatt would be sitting in interrogation spilling his guts, perhaps even giving Julian that key bit of information he so desperately needed to close this case: where Burien was hiding.

Damn it! Damn it to hell!

Julian slammed his fist onto the steering wheel. He was furious with himself for letting Wyatt get away. He was angry Taylor had nearly been killed. And he was annoyed that Irving had gone official and gotten a warrant. It was as good as writing Wyatt's epitaph, and Julian wouldn't be able to use him once he was dead.

But this wasn't about Wyatt. Not really.

This was about Tessa. It was about five foot five of soft woman who'd come apart in his arms—and then tossed him out of her apartment. She'd overheard the "babysitting" comment he'd made to Irving, and she'd decided to take it the wrong way.

How was she supposed to take it, you imbecile?

Already on edge, Julian had ignored the hurt he'd seen in her eyes. "You want me to go? What happens if Wyatt or one of his buddies shows up, Goldilocks? Will you take him on with the revolver you never keep at hand?"

"My safety is no longer your problem," she'd said, her chin high, her voice tight.

"You've survived on pride in the past, Tessa, but this time it might get you killed."

A part of him had wanted to explain. He'd been trying to

make Irving understand that she needed more protection than he could give her, that he needed to be out on the streets doing what he did best. But his mouth and temper had gotten ahead of his brain, and the words hadn't come out right. Instead of clarifying what he'd meant, he'd thrust his arms into his sleeves and told Tessa she was being stupid.

"No, stupid was earlier tonight," she'd said, her voice ice. "But I do learn from my mistakes. Yes, I do learn."

Then she'd shut the door in his face.

Furious with her and with himself, Julian had walked away, leaving her alone in her apartment under the watch of a fresh plainclothes unit.

All night as he'd trolled alleys, streets, and strip clubs looking for any sign of Wyatt, he'd told himself this little misunderstanding was for the best. He'd come terribly close to doing something tonight that he knew he shouldn't do. Another thirty seconds and he'd have been deep inside her. It would have been the most incredible fuck of his life, and he'd have come hard and fast. But then he'd have seen an even worse look of hurt in her eyes than the one he'd seen tonight, and he'd have had to live for the rest of his life knowing he'd caused it.

He and Tessa might have compatible biochemistry—okay, *combustible* biochemistry—but they were as different as two people could be. She was classy, educated, sophisticated; he'd gotten his education on the street, capping it off with a GED and FBI training. She knew about books and art; he knew about guns and killing. She'd smoothed the edges off her rough childhood; he'd sharpened his and turned them into a weapon.

He didn't have to ask to know she wanted marriage, a home, a few kids, while he wanted . . . what?

To bust Burien? To spend the rest of his life in seedy hotel rooms, illegal massage parlors, and dark alleys, wondering who would fire the round that would finally bring him down? To spend his free time mingling body fluids with women for whom he felt nothing and who felt nothing for him?

Hell of a life, Darcangelo.

He turned onto Wynkoop heading toward Union Station, aggravation grinding at his gut.

What was wrong with him? He'd never questioned his relationships with women before. Sex by itself had always been enough, the casual booty call a much better fit for his lifestyle than having a woman at home waiting for him, expecting things from him that he didn't know how to give. But now that life seemed somehow cold, empty, the thought of kissing some random woman, of tasting and stroking her, of putting himself inside her felt strangely . . . unappealing.

This was insane. He just wanted Tessa so badly because he hadn't had her. That was all. She'd come, and he hadn't. It was just unfinished lust. Blue balls. Hormones. Nothing more.

No, it was the scent of her that lingered on his skin beneath the reek of cigarettes and blood and strippers' cheap perfume. It was the sound she'd made when he'd first kissed her—a sexy, feminine sound somewhere between a gasp and a whimper. It was the look on her sweet face when she'd come—a look of surprise mixed with excruciating pleasure.

He'd felt a savage sort of satisfaction at that moment, knowing she'd believed she wouldn't enjoy it, knowing without a doubt that she had. Whoever her previous lovers had been—and judging from her response there couldn't have been many—they couldn't have been worth much in bed. If Tessa hadn't enjoyed sex with them it certainly hadn't been her fault. She was one of the most responsive women Julian had ever met.

His groin grew tight, and he felt himself getting hard.

Who the hell do you think you're fooling?

He wanted Tessa. Not just a woman. Tessa.

Which was precisely why he was going to stay far away from her. He wouldn't touch her again. He would keep his pants zipped and his hands to himself.

He slid his truck into an alley a few blocks away from the train station. Then he checked his weapon, tried to block Tessa from his mind, and stepped out into the cool night.

ALEXI STARED AT the jail report, rage making his head explode and his vision spotty. "Get out! Get out—all of you!"

He heard footsteps and closing doors, but his mind barely registered them.

Zoryo was dead. The Tiger was gone. He'd killed himself, strangled himself to keep his secrets. He'd proved his loyalty with his death.

Alexi crumpled the paper in his hand, slammed his closed fist down on his desk, an animal sound forcing itself way out of his throat. He stood, kicked his chair over, and tore his office apart, smashing glass, breaking wood, knocking books to the floor.

But it wasn't enough. He wanted Darcangelo's blood, wanted to feel it run over his hands, wanted to taste and smell it. He wanted to hurt him, to make him suffer until he begged to be shot. He wanted to laugh in his face and stretch the unbearable torment into long, endless hours. He wanted to destroy him.

Out of breath, his vision nearly gone, Alexi sat and felt in his top desk drawer for drugs that would make the migraine go away. He fumbled with the foil wrapping, popped a pill onto his tongue, and let it melt, the pain already excruciating.

How had this happened? Darcangelo wasn't playing by the rules. Somehow he'd tracked Zoryo down, locked him up, and questioned him without anyone in Alexi's organization knowing. Zoryo had been dead for a week, and Alexi hadn't heard a thing. There'd been no warrant, no APB, no arrest report to alert him. Nor was there an autopsy report to tell him what had happened to his childhood friend. There was only this internal record from the jail, a detailed account written by the jail captain and buried among hundreds of others.

He would miss his old friend terribly. No one could drink vodka like Zoryo. They'd known each other since the beginning, had come to America together. Though Alexi would be able to replace Zoryo in his organization—there were always men looking for the kind of opportunities Alexi offered—his friend was gone.

If Darcangelo could pull off something like this with one of Alexi's key people, he was more of a threat than Alexi had realized.

Alexi pressed a hand to his shattering skull, squeezed his eyes shut against the fluorescent light, and realized his fingers had gone numb. He stood, stumbled through the wreckage of his office to the light switch, flicked it off, then sank down on the sofa.

Zoryo's death wasn't the only bad news Alexi had gotten tonight. That stupid fool, Johnny, had shot a cop and was now being hunted. The fool had stumbled into a stakeout Darcangelo had set up, shot his way free, and was now on the run. Alexi would have to get rid of him. He could not leave any loose threads for Darcangelo to pull.

But what about Darcangelo? The bastard had no family, no friends to torment. His ties with his own agency were weak and frayed. The man lived alone, cared about nothing but his latest assignment. He hadn't taken a lover in three years.

Then Alexi laughed. It seemed so simple.

He squinted, turned his head, and picked up the photograph of the journalist that Johnny had given him. He couldn't see her through the sliver that remained of his vision, but that didn't matter. There'd been a reason he'd let her live, even if he hadn't known it himself at the time. He would plan carefully, make certain he did nothing to endanger himself. With Tessa Novak's help, he would destroy Julian Darcangelo, starting with the only thing the man cared about: his work. Then, when he had suffered enough, Burien would have him killed.

CHAPTER 15

TESSA'S LIFE NO longer felt real. It didn't feel real as she lay awake all night, her thoughts veering from kisses to killers and back again. It didn't feel real as she drove a rental car to work sandwiched between two patrol cars. It didn't feel real when she arrived at the paper to find television news crews waiting in the lobby to interview her about last night's attack and Denver's supposed gang crisis.

"Ms. Novak, do you believe this is in any way connected with your coverage of Denver's street gangs?"

As if drifting through a made-for-TV movie, Tessa deflected their questions by expressing her gratitude to the Denver Police Department and her concern for Officer Taylor, then let Sophie bustle her into the nearest elevator.

"My God, Tessa, you look exhausted," Sophie said, looking more than a little worried. "I can't believe you came to work today."

"Can you do me a favor?" Tessa reached into her purse, pulled out a five. "Can you get me a quadruple-shot vanilla latte?"

"Sure." Sophie took the money. "But you are going to have to sleep eventually."

"Tell that to the guys with the guns."

Tessa found a half dozen messages on her voice mail, including another from her mother.

"I saw on the news what happened, Tessa, and I'm awful scared for you. If you're in some kind of trouble, I want to help. If you need a place to hide out or some money, let me know. Please call just to let me know you're all right. You can reach me at—"

Hide here! Hurry, Tessa Marie! Grandpa's drunk, and he's awful mad at you for spilling your cereal. I'll come get you when it's safe.

The memory of crawling into the darkness beneath their mobile home, skinning her knees in the dirt, shot through her memory. Tessa had been five, her mother nineteen. It had been almost a ritual—hiding in the spidery dark, waiting for Mama to tell her it was safe. Her mother had stood between her and her grandfather, kept the old man from beating her, taking the blows herself.

So your mother made a mistake, and you're ashamed of her.

Yes, Tessa was ashamed of her.

And for the first time in her life that bothered her.

She deleted the message, her fingers hovering in indecision above the keypad for a moment before she dialed Chief Irving's direct line.

She couldn't deal with her mother. Not yet. Not today.

She'd spent the hours before sunrise running the details of the case through her mind again and again, trying to separate assumptions from facts. Then she'd worked the facts onto a spreadsheet and come up with a plan of action. Getting her hands on María Ruiz's autopsy report was at the top of the list.

She got Chief Irving's voice mail, started to demand the autopsy, but found herself apologizing for what had happened to Officer Taylor instead. Only when she was about to hang up did she remember why she had called. She quickly tacked a request for the autopsy onto the end of her message.

"If we don't receive the document today, I'll be filing a formal request under the Colorado Open Records Act," she said as Sophie walked toward her, a steaming-fresh latte in hand. "Thank you, sir. I'll be waiting to hear from you."

She hung up, picked up the cup, sipped, groaned. "At least there's one constant in the universe—caffeine. Thanks, Sophie."

Sophie sat. "If you think you're going to get away with not telling me what's going on, you're flat-out wrong."

And Tessa saw she meant it.

They met in a quiet corner of the cafeteria downstairs—Tessa, Sophie, Holly, and Lissy. Kat had been in the middle of an interview and too busy to join them. Sipping her latte, Tessa told them what she hadn't been able to tell them yesterday, leaving out any mention of Julian—the way he'd broken glass to get to her, the way he'd comforted her, the way he'd driven her over the brink with his mouth and hands. The way he'd let slip his lack of true feelings.

Instead, she stuck to the events pertaining to the case, hoping they'd forget about the man in the black leather jacket. After all, that's what she needed to do—forget Julian.

By the time she'd reached the part where she'd found the nude photo of herself, they were staring openmouthed.

"Apparently, he'd shot Officer Taylor on the way in, realized Taylor's presence meant the cops were there, and stayed only long enough to decorate my door before sprinting off." Tessa shrugged, feeling a strange sort of numbness about it all. "I made a spreadsheet last night—well, this morning. I need to get the girl's autopsy, and then I need to talk to those gang members again. They were trying to tell me—"

"You made a spreadsheet? God, Tessa, you're as crazy as Kara!" Holly looked angry. "Neither of you know when to call it quits. If I were you, I'd catch the next flight to Madagascar and hang with the lemurs until Chief Irving told me the bad guys were behind bars."

"You should come stay with me and Will," Lissy offered. "He's got a big, old shotgun, and I know he wouldn't hesitate to use it. He cares about you, Tessa. He's mad as hell about what you've been going through. You shouldn't be alone."

Tessa hadn't been alone, but she didn't say that. "I can't, Lissy. What if it had been Will who'd gone after Wyatt and had gotten shot? I'm not putting any of you in danger. Besides, I think they're moving me to witness protection this weekend."

Holly gave a wry laugh. "Wait till Kara and Reece find out. Reece will show up armed like the Marines and drag you—"

"Except you, Holly. I wouldn't mind risking your life. Can I stay at your place?" Tessa almost laughed at the look on Holly's face.

"Yes, I'd mind! Are you kidding? I don't want crazy, boob-grabbing killers coming around my place. Sorry, Tessa, but friendship has its limits."

"Nice, Holly." Lissy glared at her. "Tessa, you can stay with us."

Then Sophie, who'd been quiet, looked at Tessa through narrowed eyes. "You're not actually thinking of going back out on the streets to search for those gangbangers, are you?"

"Of course not!" Tessa lied. She glanced at her watch. "I-Team meeting."

Five minutes later, she found herself telling the story again, this time in the conference room in front of the entire I-Team plus Tom and Syd. She was glad she'd gone through it once already, because she was even more numb the second time around. No tears, not even a break in her voice.

She told them about Chief Irving's plans to transfer her into a witness protection program over the weekend and explained she'd probably be telecommuting for the next few weeks starting Monday. She'd expected Tom to argue with her about this, but he merely nodded.

"Irving has been in contact with me," he said. "IT will have a computer ready by the time you leave on Friday."

She put herself down for a twenty-inch story about last night's shooting. As a follow-up to her original piece, it would also be a first-person account, a personal look at the aftermath of being a murder witness. She knew she'd have to walk a fine line to tell the story without revealing anything Julian had told her off the record, but she was confident she could do it.

"I also have an interview in half an hour with a woman in Boulder who runs a program for homeless teens. I'm not sure what it's about, but I'll check in afterward. I might be able to squeeze some inches out of that."

Tom, who seemed to be in a strangely good mood, actually smiled. "Good work, Novak. Glad you're safe."

"He's getting laid again," Joaquin whispered as they left the meeting. "Kara's mother took him back."

"THE WAY I see it," Julian told Wyatt, "you owe me your worthless life."

Wyatt glared at him from behind a black eye and a handful of stitches but said nothing.

Julian had spotted him at six in the morning, trying to hop a train for Vegas. When Wyatt had realized Julian was after him, he'd reached for his .38 despite a crowd of early commuters. Julian had taken him down with a kick to the face.

They'd been at it for four hours now, Wyatt refusing to speak and Julian suppressing the urge to break the bastard's neck. Here was the son of a bitch who'd assaulted Tessa, who'd photographed her, who'd surely intended to kill her. Here was the piece of shit who'd shot Taylor. Here was the scum who'd kept María Ruiz prisoner, sold her, and helped murder her.

"Do you really think Burien intends to let you live? That's why you were skipping town, isn't it? You knew he'd come after you. Were you there when he lit up Toby Grant?"

Wyatt's glare lost some of its anger and his skin went pale.

"Blew his head off with a forty-four Mag, didn't he? What a damned mess! We had to ID him with fingerprints. No head." Julian looked Wyatt in the eyes. "Burien's got a round chambered for you right now, Wyatt. Every cop out there wants a piece of you for what you did to Officer Taylor. Truth is, I'm the best damned friend you've got. You can either cooperate with me, or I'll put you in minimum security, where you can sit and wonder when—and how—Burien's going to finish you."

Julian let the silence stretch, let fear do its job. It seemed like he'd spent the bulk of his hours interrogating people lately, playing the intimidation game. Hadn't it been just a week ago that he'd had Zoryo in this same room?

He leaned down, drew Wyatt's gaze to his, held it. "Tell me about Pasha's."

Wyatt's body jerked, and his pupils dilated, but he remained silent.

So Zoryo hadn't been lying. Pasha's *was* tied to Burien.

Julian sank into a chair, crossed his arms over his chest. "Why do you want to die for that bastard? Why are you going to make your future—which sucks, by the way—harder than it needs to be? Don't you see that you're a throwaway in his eyes? They tossed Toby's corpse in a trash bin to rot. Symbolic, don't you think?"

Wyatt looked down at the floor, looking suddenly less like a tough guy and more like a kid, his body shaking. "You really think you can keep him off me?"

Julian leaned in, lowered his voice. "I know I can."

And Wyatt broke.

For the next hour Julian grilled him relentlessly, doling out rewards of bathroom breaks, coffee and doughnuts, adding a dash of make-believe sympathy and even praise.

"You had no idea what you were getting into, did you, Johnny? You had no idea what he'd expect you to do. You didn't want to hurt those girls. I can see that. Once you got in with him, he called the shots. But he never controlled you, did he? You fooled him—you fooled Burien. That journalist—he only told you to follow her. You came up with the rest on your own, didn't you?"

Wyatt nodded, a serious look on his face. "She's a hot little piece. He told me I could have her, do whatever I wanted to her when it came time to pop her. But I didn't want to kill her. I was going to find a way to make him think she was dead and keep her."

Julian stood and turned his back to Wyatt, almost unable to control his rage, an image of Tessa's frightened blue eyes in his mind. "He'd never have figured it out. You'd have won."

"And she'd have been grateful and happy to do whatever I wanted, 'cause she'd always know I could have killed her instead."

If you so much as think *of touching her, Wyatt, I'll make you eat your own balls.*

Julian changed the subject, not sure how long he could keep from killing Wyatt otherwise. "How can I find him, Johnny? How can I find the man who wants to kill you?"

Wyatt seemed to hesitate at this final betrayal. "He always met us at an empty warehouse in Commerce City. It's on Brighton Road not far from the old refinery. That's where he popped Toby. Shit, he's going to pop me, too!"

"I'm not going to let him." Julian motioned to the guys on the other side of the one-way mirror to get Wyatt out of his face. "We're going to put you in protective isolation and under guard, and I'm going to have one of my own men bring you whatever you want from the commissary."

"I'd like a pack of smokes."

"You know they don't allow cigarettes in jail, Johnny." Julian stepped back as two officers entered and got Wyatt to his feet. "But if what you told me checks out and I catch that son of a bitch, I'll smuggle you in a whole goddamn carton."

He watched the guards lead Wyatt away, heard Irving come up behind him.

"That was top-notch work, Darcangelo. I ought to save this as a training tape."

"Let's get that warehouse under surveillance."

"Done. If Burien shows up again, we'll be waiting for him." Irving paused. "You should know that Ms. Novak called this morning to request the autopsy report of one María Conchita Ruiz. I don't know how she got the name, but—"

Julian almost laughed. He'd told her the victim's name off the record in an attempt to comfort her, but she'd lost no time using it to her advantage. As long as she didn't publish it, he supposed she was keeping her side of the deal. "She got it from me."

Irving raised a bushy eyebrow. "Want to tell me how that happened?"

"Not really. Got any fresh coffee in this place?"

* * *

TESSA WAS IN the middle of writing when Kara walked up to her desk looking worried and holding out a latte. "Coffee break, Tess."

Tessa told her story for the third time, only this time it wasn't so easy. Perhaps because she knew Kara had been through something even worse, Tessa found it difficult to hide her feelings.

"It all feels surreal—like I'm living someone else's life," she said, trying to put into words how she'd felt all day.

"Well, let's see." Kara counted on her fingers. "In the past nine days, you've witnessed a murder, had the man you thought was the killer pull you into a closet and kiss you, been arrested, been groped by one of the real killers, had a cop shot outside your home, found a naked photo of yourself the killer stuck to your apartment door. I can see how a person might find that unsettling. The bottom line is you've been through hell, and you need sleep."

"That's easier said than done." Tessa wanted to tell Kara about Julian, to make sense of her own feelings by sharing them, to ask Kara's advice. But she knew talking about her emotions would force her to *feel* them, and she was doing such a good job of not feeling now. It was better to say nothing and to stay numb than to open herself to the hurt she knew was there.

"Reece and I want you to stay with us until this blows over."

Tessa shook her head. "As much as I'd love to take you up on it, how do you think I'd feel if something happened to Reece or you or one of the kids? I can't, Kara. But thanks. It means a lot to me that you care enough to take that chance."

Kara whipped out her cell phone. "Hi, hon. Yeah, she's being stubborn."

Then Kara handed the phone to Tessa.

Reece's deep voice sounded in her ear. "You're going to stay at our place tonight if I have to carry you, got it?"

"Okay." For the first time all day, Tessa felt herself near tears. "But if you guys end up dead, don't hold it against me."

* * *

"A LOT OF homeless teens end up as victims of trafficking." Colleen Kenley, the director of a nonprofit that aided street teens, sat in the conference room with Tessa, having been kind enough to drive down to Denver from her office in Boulder. With shoulder-length blond hair and a model's face, she didn't look old enough to head an international organization.

Tessa looked up from her notes. "Trafficked? You mean sold?"

Ms. Kenley nodded. "Or transported against their will. Forced or coerced to have what we call survival sex—sex for food, shelter, protection. We've worked with teens whose experiences have run the gamut from trading sex for food or drugs to being forced into full-time prostitution."

"How terrible!" Tessa didn't realize she'd quit taking notes until the pencil fell from her hand. She leaned down, picked it up. "Don't the johns realize these kids are underage?"

Ms. Kenley's face was grave. "I think that's the point."

Tessa's stomach turned.

Then Ms. Kenley told how she'd worked with a fourteen-year-old from Utah whose parents had thrown her out of the house after she'd told them she was a lesbian. The girl had been picked up during her first week on the street and brought to a trailer somewhere in town, where she and another teen had been forced to work as prostitutes, enduring sex with as many as thirty men a night.

"They gave her heroin and beat her, rewarding her with occasional trips to a local convenience store where they let her buy candy. She could have asked for help or tried to escape, but she was too afraid to try, sure they would kill her."

Ms. Kenley was still speaking but Tessa scarcely heard her.

There were four of them, girls about the same age. They'd come in, buy gum, candy, maybe shampoo or lip gloss, then they'd go again. Never smiled. Never said a word.

She remembered what Mr. Simms had told her, and her heart seemed to skip a beat. "I-I'm sorry, Ms. Kenley, I hate to interrupt. Can we go back? I have a couple of questions."

By the time the interview was over, Tessa was certain the girl she'd seen murdered was like the girl Ms. Kenley had described—a teenager forced into prostitution. She'd been murdered for trying to flee. Tessa had no proof—not yet—but all the pieces fit.

This had nothing to do with gangs at all.

It was a case of sex trafficking.

Chills shivered down her spine.

Then, out of nowhere, Julian's words came back to her.

I know things about kidnapping and sexual assault that are beyond your worst nightmares.

She punched Chief Irving's direct line into her keypad. She groaned when she got his voice mail again. "Chief Irving, this is Tessa Novak calling to let you know I am hereby filing a request for María Conchita Ruiz's autopsy report under the Colorado Open Records Act. Expect a written version of the request via facsimile within ten minutes. Further, I wish to request an interview with you regarding Ms. Ruiz's murder and the crimes of human trafficking and forced prostitution."

The words came out in a rush, and when she hung up the phone she felt the same surge of adrenaline she always felt when she closed in on a big story.

She stood and hurried toward Tom's office, hoping she could get at least ten inches for this story—front page, above the fold. If they didn't have room, they would have to make room.

"No me he olvidado de ti, María," she whispered.

I haven't forgotten you.

"I CAN'T COMMENT on an ongoing investigation, Ms. Novak."

Julian leaned against the door, listened to Tessa's voice over the speaker as she interviewed Chief Irving, anger warring with admiration. He had to hand it to her. She'd put the pieces together damned fast, making the leap from gangs to trafficking far quicker than he had imagined she would.

"Can you at least confirm that you're pursuing a possible

sex-trafficking angle on this homicide?" She sounded exhausted but also confident. She had good instincts and clearly knew she was onto something.

"That would be commenting, and I just told you I can't do that."

"Was there evidence on the body of sexual assault, sexual abuse, or drug abuse?"

"I believe I'll let the medical examiner's notes speak to those points. You should have the autopsy report by now."

There was a moment of silence, and Julian could almost feel her frustration.

"Can we go off the record?" she asked.

"I trust you, Ms. Novak. Off the record, then."

"I have read the autopsy report, and it indicates to me that this is a case of sex trafficking. María Ruiz was fleeing her captors when they shot her down. They kept her in that basement apartment with other three girls, forced her to have sex with dozens of men, and shot her up with heroin. John Wyatt was one of her captors. The man who pulled the trigger and was later killed was another. The person you and Mr. Darcangelo are hunting for—the man who wants me dead—is the man who pulled their strings."

Irving hit mute. "I told you she was good. How the hell did she put that together?"

"Ask her."

Irving hit the button again. "What makes you leap to this conclusion, Ms. Novak?"

"I just interviewed a woman who runs a program for street teens. Some of the trafficking scenarios she describes are almost identical to observations that the medical examiner, Mr. Simms, and neighbors made about María. Unhappy candy-buying sprees. Always under supervision. Lots of cars pulling up to the house. Her age. The way she was dressed. Evidence of multiple sex partners. Needle tracks. Bruises. There's not a piece that doesn't fit, sir."

Julian stepped forward and leaned down toward the mic. "You win the prize, Tessa. I'm impressed. But what do you propose to do with this information—write a front-page article that will send these bastards deeper underground and make it tougher for us to catch them?"

"Why, it's Batman!" she said, obviously still hurt and angry with him. "I knew you had to be lurking there somewhere. I want to see these bastards behind bars as much as you do, and you know it! I want to expose them, make it impossible for them to hide! I want to wake the public up so that we can stop this terrible crime!"

He could hear the emotion in her voice, knew she meant every word. But although he admired her brains and her courage, his experience told him the real world didn't work that way. "Have you ever caught a criminal with ink?"

"I haven't personally, but I know people who have. Used in the right way, it's every bit as deadly as one of your big, fat bullets."

"Why don't you ask Officer Taylor about that?"

She seemed to hesitate. "So to summarize your quotes, 'No comment.' Is that correct, Chief Irving?"

And Julian knew she was ignoring him. He started to speak.

Chief Irving held up a hand to silence him. "I wish you'd hold this story, Ms. Novak."

"I can't do that. You know that. I have a job to do."

"I understand."

"Thank you, sir."

The line went dead.

Irving hung up the phone, leaned back in his chair. "That young lady is too damned smart for her own good. We need to end this bureaucratic bickering and finalize these papers for witness protection before she gets herself killed."

Julian said nothing, the coffee in his stomach turning to lead.

CHAPTER 16

"SLOW IT DOWN, and watch here." Julian aimed the red laser pointer at the upper-right corner of the television screen, hoping to get through this briefing as quickly as possible. He hated meetings—lots of talk, no action. "The minivan stops. Five girls climb out and use the gas-station restroom. The two cars you see entering from the left—recognize them from the bottom of the screen? They just pulled out of Pasha's. Now they roll into the gas station. Two of the girls get into one car, and three get into the other. Watch the driver of the minivan. As they drive away, he heads into Pasha's."

Irving was the first to speak. "So you're thinking they're using the strip club as some kind of distribution center?"

"You nailed it. There's plenty of traffic. The gas station lends a sort of anonymity—lots of people getting in and out of cars, lots of women using the restrooms. And using the gas-station parking lot makes the strip club less suspect. In the hours of tape I've viewed so far, this scenario plays itself out three times—different cars, but the same minivan."

Julian rewound the tape, then let the men take another look. He'd spent the evening and much of the night sifting through endless hours of videotape on fast-forward. He'd seen John Wyatt enter the club once, the showy rims stripped off his shiny black Cadillac, but he'd almost missed the minivan. Barely in the picture, it was one of thousands of vehicles that had pulled up into the neighboring gas-station parking lot. Only after he'd noticed the driver walking over to Pasha's had it caught his attention. He'd gone through the tapes again, keeping an eye on the gas station this time, and discovered a pattern. Then he'd caught a few hours' sleep, trying not to think of Tessa.

He'd been relieved to hear she'd gone home with the senator. Irving had said the guy was smart and knew how to use a gun and that his house was equipped with an alarm system. Well, that was something. Julian felt an irrational need to keep watch on her himself, but he knew where that would lead. Once they were done arguing over her hurt feelings, they'd fuck each other's brains out—and she'd be hurt all over again. Besides, if he wanted to keep her safe, he needed to find Burien.

"You think it's enough to get a no-knock warrant?" Petersen asked, his gaze still on the screen. "For all we know, it's some girls' school car pool headed by a guy who loves tits."

The men laughed.

"I'll get the warrant, but not yet. Burien isn't at Pasha's, and he's the one we want. Once he's down, his whole house of cards will be easy to topple. If we take out a few of his key locations, he'll just move someplace else like he did three years ago."

"So what do you propose?" Irving rubbed coffee cake crumbs off his shirt where they'd caught on his protruding belly.

"Keep up surveillance. Work the club. Try to find out who the major players are inside and hopefully follow them to Burien."

"What about the warehouse?" Irving turned to Sergeant Gary King, who'd been out at the warehouse most of the night.

"We've got the place under tight surveillance. We did a quick search this morning, scanned it with a blue light, found large bloodstains. We'll have building plans and a detailed map ready by the end of shift today. The place is up for sale and has been for most of a year. There's some kind of EPA trouble, so the owner, who lives in Japan, hasn't been able to sell it."

"Burien's probably using it without the owner's knowledge, doing his dirty work on someone else's turf," Julian explained. "He knows by now that we have Wyatt. I doubt he'll be back. I want someone to look into all industrial properties for sale in the greater Denver area and tag those with vacant buildings."

"God, this bastard is slippery!" Sergeant Wu shook his head. "Are we sure he exists?"

"Oh, yeah, he exists." Julian met the middle-aged cop's gaze. "And we're closer to bringing him down than we have been for three long years."

"Remember, this murdering son of a bitch supposedly has cops on his payroll." Chief Irving met each man's gaze. "The information from this briefing is not to be shared with anyone— no hints, no gossip, don't even tell yourself what you know. Wu, you head up the real-estate angle. Let's get to work. And don't forget to sign Taylor's get-well card. They're moving him out of ICU today."

Julian popped the videotape out of the VCR. He'd made copies, which he'd already placed in his vault at home. This would go into the safe in the evidence room.

He heard the door shut, looked up to find himself alone with Irving, who held up a copy of the *Denver Independent*. "You read this?"

Julian shook his head. "Did she burn us?"

"No." Irving handed him the paper. "Everything you told her off the record is still off the record. But this article sure as hell will catch Burien's attention."

TESSA AWOKE TO find herself looking into two pairs of curious brown eyes—one belonging to a boy, the other a dog.

"Mama says I'm supposed to be quiet so I don't wake you up," Connor whispered. "Did I wake you up?"

"No, sugar," Tessa whispered back. "My eyes popped open all on their own."

Connor smiled, hurried from the room and shouted. "She's awake, Mama!"

Tessa heard Kara's voice coming from upstairs. "Connor, I told you to leave Auntie Tessa alone! Come finish your breakfast. You're going to be late for school!"

Connor looked back at Tessa, gave a guilty shrug.

Tessa smiled at him, blew him a kiss, watched his cheeks flush pink.

He gave her a shy smile and ran out of the room, Jakey following behind him.

Tessa sat up, reached for her watch, and saw that it was seven-thirty. She barely remembered getting into bed last night. Her sleep had been interrupted by nightmares, and she felt almost as tired as she had when she'd fallen into bed.

Adrenaline poisoning.

She crawled out of bed, shuffled into the guest bathroom, the weight of the past couple weeks heavy on her as she stepped into a hot shower. She shampooed her hair, reality working its way through her mind like a splinter.

She'd finished her trafficking article late last night, forcing production to hold two full pages of Section A. Tom had packaged it on the front page with her recollections of being stalked and attacked—a one-two punch she hoped would hit the killer in the guts. She'd taken extra pains not to let anything slip that wasn't on the record, while taking full advantage of everything that was, the autopsy report most of all.

It had been one of the most horrific autopsy reports she'd ever read, the story of María's suffering revealed in flesh and blood. Bruises all over her body. Rope burns on her wrists. Heroin in her bloodstream. Semen from *seven* different men inside her. A broken rib that had partly healed. Signs of chronic pelvic infection. Nine mortal bullet wounds.

And yet it had been the intimate details of the report that had gotten to Tessa—the mole on María's right thigh, the tearstains on her face, the cavities in her teeth. María had been an ordinary girl with her own hopes and dreams. But her life had been stolen.

Tessa had felt so drained by he time she'd reached Reece

and Kara's that she'd barely been able to make conversation. She'd gratefully eaten the dinner they'd saved for her—something delicious and Italian that Reece had made—then wished them a good night and collapsed into bed.

Slowly waking up, she rinsed the shampoo from her hair, worked conditioner through to the ends, then reached for her razor and lathered her legs, giving the conditioner time to sink in.

Chief Irving would be taking her into witness protection after work today. Had she remembered to pack extra razor cartridges? Either way, she supposed it wouldn't matter. She'd be stuck indoors with no one but cops for company for the next few weeks. Who cared if she had razor stubble? It wasn't as if Julian—or anyone—would be coming to visit her.

You win the prize, Tessa. I'm impressed.

He'd been so angry with her yesterday, his voice dripping with sarcasm. He didn't seem to understand that she had a job to do, whether she wanted to do it or not. He acted as if her pursuit of María's killers was vain and frivolous, nothing more than an attempt to get her byline on the front page. Clearly, he didn't understand the power of the press and considered it nothing more than a nuisance.

She felt a spike of irritation, welcomed it. Anger was so much easier to deal with than the other feelings he dredged up inside her. Despite the way he'd hurt and humiliated her with the "babysitter" comment, she couldn't forget how it had felt to have almost-sex with him. All that man, all that heat, focused on her. She'd had the most stunning climax of her life—and that had just been foreplay. What would it have been like to have that enormous erection of his moving inside her?

A tight fluttering in her belly was contradicted by the nagging voice in her head.

You'd feel used, and you know it.

Yes, she knew it. Or at least her mind knew it. Her body had other ideas, her nipples puckered, her skin unusually sensitive, a wetness between her thighs that had nothing to do with her shower.

Mind over matter, Tess.

Julian probably hadn't thought twice about what had happened between them. He was focusing on his job, and that's exactly what she needed to do. She rinsed the shaving cream from her legs and forced her mind back onto the investigation.

She hoped to do a follow-up to her trafficking article today. Ms. Kenley had given her a number of sources and directed her to a mountain of documents, including an FBI report that indicated Denver was a crossroads for human traffickers, particularly those smuggling people in from Mexico. Tessa wanted to read through the report and see what other sources might be able to tell her. There had to be a way to get at this story— reviewing arrest records of prostitutes, talking with Mexican authorities at the consulate, interviewing prostitutes on the street.

What she really wanted to do was talk with Syko again, but she wouldn't be able to do that accompanied by cops. She doubted Syko and his homies would accept an invitation to come visit her in the newsroom, nor did she know how to contact them apart from asking for them on the street. She doubted she'd find them listed under Crips in the yellow pages. The only way she was going to be able to talk with them was to head into the projects of Aurora. It was about as stupid an idea as she'd ever had, given her current situation. But if she could find a way out of the building and take a cab, she could elude not only the cops, but also the killers, who wouldn't be expecting her to head off on her own. And if she covered her hair . . .

By the time she'd finished her shower, put on her makeup, and gotten dressed, she had it all worked out. She packed her things together and rolled her suitcase to the door, then followed the sound of Kara's voice to the kitchen. Kara was washing applesauce off Caitlyn's face, despite Caitlyn's squeals and squirms of protest.

"I think she likes having a messy face." Tessa couldn't help but smile.

"She's a mess machine." Kara released her daughter, who toddled off toward a pile of blocks on the floor. "I had delusions about getting her potty trained before the next one came along, but that's not going to happen."

It took Tessa a moment to realize what Kara was telling her. "You're . . . you're pregnant? Oh, my God, Kara, that's wonderful! Congratulations! Does Reece know?"

"Thanks. Yes, he knows. I'm eleven weeks along and have been throwing up every day for a month. He's been coming home from the capitol at lunchtime so I can take naps."

"I told you he was a keeper." Tessa felt a surge of happiness for her friend, tried to ignore the way the brightness of the moment revealed the shadows in her own life. Would she ever know what it was like to be pregnant, to be pampered by her baby's father, to share the joy of watching her children grow?

When Kara reached for the coffeepot, Tessa stopped her. "Sit down, for goodness sakes! I'll make my own breakfast."

While Tessa nuked a bowl of instant oatmeal, they talked about the kids, about Reece's bills for the next legislative session, about the trials of working for Tom, Caitlyn babbling happily to herself and playing on the floor. It was Kara who finally brought it up.

"I read your articles," she said. "It makes me absolutely sick—what they did to that poor girl, what they do to all of those kids, what they're trying to do to you. God, Tessa, I had to keep telling myself that you were safe, that you were downstairs asleep and safe. I thought Reece was going to explode when he read the paper."

"I have to do something about it, Kara. An hour hasn't passed since the murder when I haven't heard her voice. I have to help her however I can."

Tessa shared her ideas about how to pursue the investigation, listened to Kara's suggestions, all the while wishing she could tell her about Julian. But too soon it was time to go.

"Listen to Chief Irving. Do what he says," Kara said.

Tessa gave a snort. "Like you did?"

Kara frowned. "Exactly *not* like I did."

"Thanks for everything."

Tessa arrived at the office to find news crews from CNN and Fox parked in the parking lot. She prayed they'd come to do an exposé about Tom's temper—"Editors and Their Egos"—and tried to slip unseen into the parking lot. This proved to be impossible while accompanied by two black-and-white police cars.

She hurried through the parking lot and entered through a side door, then took the stairs up to the newsroom. She found the I-Team gathered around a bank of television sets, watching plastic Nell Parker give her morning news broadcast from Channel 12.

Matt glanced over his shoulder, grinned. "Your trafficking story has made national news. Way to go, Novak."

But Tessa barely heard him. Her gaze had fallen on the cover letter attached to a pile of documents she'd found in her in-box. Printed on plain paper and unsigned, the letter alleged that Denver police were covering up an incident in which a suspect had been detained and interrogated—and had died after interrogation while in police custody.

The attached documents prove that the officer to blame for this cover-up is an FBI special agent whose unethical methods resulted in the deaths of two fellow agents three years ago. The agent's name is Julian Darcangelo.

Tessa felt blood surge to her head and sank into her chair. Then, heart pounding, she turned the page and read.

JULIAN WAS WORKING on his computer, trying to get a read on the minivan's license plate, when Irving barged into his office and slammed the door behind him.

"This investigation is turning into a cluster fuck, Darcangelo." Looking furious, Irving tossed a stack of papers across the desk at him. "Ms. Novak just filed the biggest damned open-records request this department has ever seen, and you're at the center of it."

Julian glanced through the documents, starting with the anonymous cover letter and ending with the internal report detailing the circumstances of Zoryo's suicide, cold rage churning in his gut. When he finished, he stood and walked to the window.

Outside, the sky was turning gray, a bank of thick clouds rolling in over the mountains.

"There's no doubt about it—you have a leak."

"Is that all you have to say? What about Ms. Novak and her pending exposé on police brutality at the Denver jail?"

"Tessa Novak is the least of our worries." He turned to face Irving. "Someone wants to out me, and he's using Tessa to do it."

Irving's bushy eyebrows rose. "Why do you say that?"

"That's the only reason anyone would send this information to a reporter. They know she's interested in the story, and, worse, they know who I am, know I'm on the case."

"Then it must be an FBI leak. Not many of my people know where you came from or why you're really here."

Julian shook his head. "This is a combination of DPD and FBI records. Whoever it is has access to classified documents from both agencies. No Denver cop could possibly get his fingers on these old FBI records. And I doubt very much that an agent could walk into the jail past armed guards and checkpoints to dig into your incident reports."

"Maybe they're working together."

Julian had already thought of this. "It's a possibility. But there's something else to consider. If the guys who leaked this know who I am, Burien probably does, too."

It was a possibility he didn't want to consider, but one he couldn't ignore.

Irving gave a low whistle, his weathered face grave. "Sounds like it's time for your higher-ups to consider taking you off this case altogether."

Julian would shave his head, get a boob job, and go undercover wearing high heels and a dress before he'd give up this case. Burien was his. But he didn't say this.

Instead he nodded. "Could be."

"So, Special Agent Darcangelo, how do you propose we deal with Ms. Novak? Zoryo was your call. We played it your way, and now my department has its ass in the fire."

"It's obvious Burien has gotten the news about Zoryo, so there's no more cause for secrecy." Julian punched the combination on his safe, pulled out a file, handed it to Irving. "You'll tell her the truth. The warrant is there, along with the rest of the paperwork. Offer to show her this file off the record and explain that this anonymous source is manipulating her and likely working for the man who wants to kill her. Then ask her to withdraw her request."

"That covers my department." Irving tucked the file under his arm. "What about the information she wants on you? Should I let the feds handle that?"

And then it hit Julian.

Son of a bitch!

Tessa had probably filed the same request with the FBI. It wasn't the records themselves that concerned him. He'd had to live every day with the truth of what he'd done three years ago. It didn't matter what she knew or didn't know, as long as she didn't print it. But at any moment, he was going to be getting a pissed-off call from Dyson—or worse, Margaux—demanding to know why he'd kept them in the dark. And what fun that would be.

DYSON DIDN'T CALL until nearly four o'clock. He'd been every bit as furious as Julian had expected him to be. He'd threatened to yank Julian off the case, questioned his objectivity, and twisted the knife by reminding Julian of the times he'd gone to the mat for him. Then he'd gotten down to business and demanded a full briefing on Zoryo.

Julian had filled him in, omitting any mention of Pasha's, then brought him up-to-date on Wyatt's arrest and the discovery of the warehouse—two bits of information he was certain Burien already had. He hated keeping Dyson in the dark, hated deceiving the man who'd been his mentor, but he couldn't share information with Dyson without sharing it with everyone in Dyson's chain of command. And someone in that chain was the broken link.

Julian had just hung up when his cell phone rang again.

"I told Dyson not to put you on this case! I told him I thought you were in it for your own damned reasons!"

"What a delight to year your voice, Margaux, and what a surprise." He didn't blame her for being angry. Burien had shot her, killed two of her friends. She was very likely the only person in the world who hated Burien more than he did.

"Cut the crap. What the hell do you think you're doing?"

"I'm trying to stop a killer."

"Goddamn it, Julian! You think you want him more than I do? You weren't there when he and his goons killed half my team and put a bullet in my leg. If you blow this—"

"You've been chasing him for three years, and what have you accomplished? You've linked a bunch of websites together, tracked some of his accounts, watched his money come and go. And still he's one step ahead. There's a leak in the bureau, Margaux."

"Of course there's a leak! I know it. Dyson knows it. We stood with you when you asked for an internal investi . . ." Her words trickled to a halt. "Oh, God! Do you think it's Dyson? That's why you're keeping secrets. Or maybe you think it's me."

"I don't know who it is. I just know Burien's not getting any info from me."

"Go to hell! You're off this investigation. I want you off. Your cover's blown. Burien obviously knows who you are, and so does that little slut of a journalist!"

Julian felt his temper surge. "I wouldn't throw the term 'slut' around if I were you."

Margaux laughed. "You said you'd take care of her, and you did, didn't you? Dyson tells me you've been playing bodyguard. Is she that good in bed?"

"I wouldn't know. I haven't slept with her."

"Don't tell me you've gotten honorable in the past few—"

Someone knocked on the door to Julian's office, and Petersen shuffled in, a confused look on his face.

"It's been great catching up, sweetheart. Later." Julian hung up, cutting Margaux off in mid-sentence. "What is it?"

"Irving said to let you know a guy named Psycho called dispatch to tell Dark Angel that Blondie is back and asking questions. Does that make any sense to—?"

"Son of a bitch!" Julian was on his feet in a heartbeat, shoving a stunned-looking Petersen out of his office and locking the door behind him. "Tell Irving to alert the cops in Aurora. I think Tessa Novak is hangin' in the 'hood again."

CHAPTER 17

TESSA FOUND SYKO and Flaco much faster this time—or rather they found her. She'd asked for them in the same neighborhood where she'd run into them before and had just gotten the cold shoulder from a group of teenage girls when a gleaming royal-blue Cadillac Coupe Deville pulled up behind her, throbbing with bass.

The door opened. A kid with a face she recognized from last time climbed out, gesturing with the gun in his hand. "Yo, Blondie, get in."

Heart beating faster, Tessa ducked down and slid into the backseat, the kid pushing in after her, squeezing her in between him and another man. Only when the car pulled away from the curb did she realize Syko and Flaco weren't in the car.

"Where are—?"

The front-seat passenger turned his head, looked back at her through mirrored sunglasses. "Syko say we ain't supposed to answer no questions, so you sit quiet."

She shut her mouth, sat quiet, watching Aurora roll by outside the tinted windows, the throbbing rhythm of hip-hop bumping against her eardrums. A storm was rolling in over the mountains, pushing a cold wind ahead of it. Even though it wasn't yet sunset, the sky had gone dark, streetlights automatically coming on. Maybe it would finally snow.

It hadn't been hard to get out of the newspaper. She'd waited for the right moment, then had taken her purse and notepad and, tucking her hair beneath the scarf she'd hidden in her purse, she'd headed down the back stairs and out the rear exit into the alley. Within a few minutes she'd stood near the 16th Street Mall, hailing a cab.

No one had seen her go.

Certainly, this wasn't the smartest thing she'd ever done. But she needed to finish the interview she'd started last week before they shipped her off tonight. She wouldn't be able to interview anyone on the streets after tonight. She needed to ask Syko what he'd meant when he'd told her there were worse dangers than gangs on Denver's streets. Had he been thinking of sex traffickers? What did he know about them? Where did they operate?

She knew instinctively that Syko and none of his gang would hurt her. They had too much respect for Julian—or "Dark Angel"—to harm her. But, as Syko had pointed out, they weren't the only ones on the streets.

The kid to her right rolled down his window, whistled at some passing girls, who glanced up, smiled, their arms full of school books.

"Mmm, she likes me," he said before howling like a coyote.

The driver gave a snort. "She don't want nothin' to do with no gangsta, cuzz. She goin' to college."

"Maybe I'll go with her."

They laughed.

Tessa's thoughts drifted to the anonymous letter. She had no trouble believing Julian was a special agent and not a cop. His loner attitude, the authority he seemed to carry even with Chief Irving, his access to information—it all made sense. But she hoped the allegations in the letter were false. She didn't even want to consider the possibility that he might have illegally detained a suspect, interrogated him, and then covered up his death.

Yet hadn't she overheard him trying to do something similar with Wyatt? Hadn't he urged Irving *not* to get a warrant?

Yes, he had.

She'd already put in an open-records request, and Chief Irving had immediately denied the allegations, throwing his considerable weight behind Julian.

"You're being manipulated by someone who wants to cause trouble," he'd told her, agreeing to an interview on Monday. "The inmate in question was taken into custody quite legally, interrogated according to procedure, and then committed suicide despite every effort to prevent just that. Julian Darcangelo is not crooked."

She hoped with all her heart that what Irving had said was true.

And if it wasn't?

She was a journalist. She would do her job.

The car turned into the parking lot of a sprawling brown apartment complex and made its way in a horseshoe around to the other side. Tessa found herself being hurried through a door covered with skeletons and jack-o'-lanterns into a crowded apartment that smelled heavily of marijuana and cigarettes.

Syko sat in a recliner, surrounded by more than a dozen members of his gang, who watched her, their expressions ranging from hard-edged indifference to curiosity. She knew they saw her as just a rich white chick with a fancy education and a job. In truth, she had more in common with them than she did her friends and coworkers.

Syko took a slow drag on a joint, passed it to the kid next to him. He held the hit, pointed at one of the younger gang members sitting on a battered couch, and motioned for him to move.

The kid stood, moved aside, freeing up a place for Tessa.

Tessa pulled off her scarf and sat, feeling the heat of fifteen pairs of eyes upon her. She met Syko's gaze, tried not to show her fear or to let on that she felt their hostility, her heart beating hard in her chest. "Thanks for meeting with me."

"You didn't give me much choice, showin' up on the streets and askin' for us." He looked at her through eyes that should have belonged to a much older man. "You're either crazy, or you're braver than any chick I know."

Tessa took the bait. "Why do you say that?"

"Hell, girl. Since you been running those articles about Denver gangs, you made it hard for everyone on the streets. We got folks watchin' what we do, cops crawling up our ass."

"Maybe you all should stop selling crack and go back to school or get a job." She willed herself not to break eye contact.

The entire room seemed to hold its breath.

Then Syko laughed. "I can see why Dark Angel likes you. And he's right—you do get yourself into trouble."

Julian didn't like her, but Tessa didn't think this was a good time to clear up that particular misunderstanding.

"Know why we brought you here instead of meetin' with you on the streets?" Syko asked. "To keep you from gettin' popped. Word on the street is Slobs put a hit on you to pay you back for their boys gettin' busted."

The Bloods had a contract on her? This sounded so absurd she almost laughed. "They want to kill me? They're going to have to get in line."

He grinned. "So why you want to talk with us?"

"Last time we spoke you told me there were worse things than gangs on the streets. I wondered what or who you were thinking of when you said that."

Flaco spoke in Spanish, apparently unaware she understood. *"Se trata de esa muchacha, la que fue asesinada."* It's about that girl, the one who was murdered.

Tessa switched to Spanish, satisfied by the startled looks on their faces. *"Creo que los hombres que la mataron son traficantes—hombres que intercambian y venden a mujeres y a niños y los obligan a la prostitución."* I think the men who killed her are traffickers—men who trade and sell women and children and force them into prostitution.

For a moment, Syko seemed to weigh his words. Then he spoke in English. "When I try to sell you some rock, I don't make you buy it. I don't make you use. I give you the opportunity, but you decide. Some people ain't like that. They don't give you no choice."

"Where do they operate? Where can I find them?"

He gave a snort, but there was no humor in it. "You don't want to find them, Blondie. We're talking hard core—international players, syndicate types. They don't give a damn about nothin' but money. But don't ask me for names, 'cause I don't know, and even if I did—"

"Please!" Tessa interrupted him. "I've put my life on the line for this! All I want is to bring that girl some justice. She was only sixteen. Please tell me what you can, and I promise I won't bother you again."

Syko sat in silence for a moment. "Everyone out."

The other gang members got up and reluctantly shuffled out, including a voluptuous girl with aqua eyes and dark cornrows who'd been standing behind Syko's chair.

"Not you, sugar." Syko reached out an arm and drew her onto his lap.

The girl giggled and ground her butt into him.

Tessa sat in silence, waited for him to speak.

"Like I said, these are international players. You gotta quit thinkin' 'bout gangbangers and start thinkin' more like *The Godfather*."

And she understood. "They're Mafia."

"Yeah, but what color Mafia? That's the question you—"

A boy of about ten years old ran through the front door, rushed up to Syko, and whispered in his ear. The rest of the gang followed him through the door, looking back over their shoulders.

Syko nodded, clapped the boy on the back, then looked over at Tessa. "Someone's been looking for you."

As she got to her feet, the door flew open.

Julian.

Dressed in his black leather jacket and black leather pants, his eyes hidden behind dark sunglasses, his face shadowed with stubble, he stepped into the room like menace come to life. He glanced at her, and a muscle in his jaw clenched. Even though she couldn't see his eyes, she felt the anger in his gaze.

How had he known she was here?

"I owe you." He tossed something to Syko—a bundle of

bills—then looked at her and motioned toward the door with a jerk of his head. "Come on."

She turned toward Syko, smiled. "Thanks, cuzz."

He laughed. "Time to jet, Blondie. A-town ain't safe for you."

She had a feeling he wasn't just talking about traffickers.

Not wanting to overstay her welcome—or provoke Julian's temper—she swept past Julian and out the door.

JULIAN WATCHED TESSA hurry down the sidewalk ahead of him, chin high, purse slung over her shoulder, a dark scarf over her long curls. Wearing a gray woolen dress coat over a short black skirt and a lacy, white blouse, little pearls on her ears, heels clicking against the concrete, she couldn't look more out of place if she tried.

Had she really just called one of the most dangerous gang-bangers in Denver "cuzz"? A part of him wanted to laugh out loud. The rest of him wanted to strangle her.

He'd hauled ass to Aurora, breaking more than a few traffic laws along the way, hoping he'd find her before anyone else did, trying to decide what he'd do with her when he did. When he'd seen her sitting on Syko's couch, surrounded by pot smoke and gangbangers, he'd wanted to toss her over his shoulder like a sack of potatoes and carry her off—or bend her over his knee. How could she be so completely oblivious toward the rage she'd engendered among the town's gangs? She'd brought the cops down on their heads, and, if it hadn't been for Syko's gang, she'd likely already be lying bloody in an alley.

Trying to rein in his temper, he fell in beside her, his gaze searching for danger on the storm-darkened street. He took her arm in his, guided her toward his truck. "This way, Goldilocks."

She jerked her arm free. "No, thank you, Special Agent Darcangelo. I can take a cab. You have important things to do, remember? Like conducting illegal interrogations and covering up deaths at the jail."

"You don't know what you're talking about!" He grasped

her arm firmly this time, pulled her along with him, his fury boiling over. "Do you have any idea how stupid it was for you to come here?"

"Slow down! I can't walk as fast as you!" She pulled back on her arm, and he realized she was all but running beside him, her smaller gait made tricky by her fancy shoes. "Believe it or not, I know this wasn't the smartest thing I've ever done, but I needed to finish the interview you interrupted before Irving sent me into exile!"

"What you needed to do was drop this damned story!" He reached in his pocket for his keys, opened the driver's side door of his truck. "For Christ's sake, Tessa, you have at least some idea of what you're dealing with. Do you really think anyone who kidnaps and sells human beings is going to think twice about killing you or worse? Get in!"

She turned to face him, looked up at him through those big blue eyes of hers, her emotions as plain to see as clouds in a clear blue sky—anger, fear, grief. "What kind of reporter would I be if I didn't do everything I could to get to the bottom of this? Do you think Christiane Amanpour hides when her investigations get rough?"

He had just started to say he didn't give a shit about Christiane Amanpour when he saw it—the red dot of a laser sight quavering against the white of her blouse.

With time to do nothing but react, he stepped into the line of fire and pinned Tessa against his truck with his body, pulling her head tightly against his chest just as hell broke loose.

Bam! Bam! Bam! Bam! Bam!

Shattering pain drove the breath from his lungs as five rounds slammed into his back. In a haze of agony, he heard Tessa scream. Was she hurt? Had a stray round hit her? Had one of the bullets passed through him and gone into her?

The squeal of tires.

A siren.

Unable to tell how badly he was hurt, he thrust Tessa through the open driver's side door and across the seat, pressing her head down. Then using the door for cover, he drew his .38 and dropped—or fell—to one knee. He fired three shots at the assailant's vehicle, one of which punctured a tire. The car crashed into a parked truck.

"Julian! Oh, my God, Julian!" Tessa surrounded him with surprisingly strong arms and tried to pull him backward into the truck. He could tell by her voice she was in tears.

He had to get her out of here. He thrust his keys into her hands, then stood and staggered around the hood to the passenger side, keeping one eye on the scattering passengers from the shooter's vehicle.

Gangbangers. Not Burien's men.

He slid into the seat, slammed the door, and forced air into his lungs, nearly blinded by the pain of breathing. "Drive!"

"I need to call an ambulance!" She started to crank the wheel as if making a U-turn. "Let me at least try to stop the bleeding."

He grabbed the wheel, fighting to keep himself upright and conscious, spots dancing before his eyes. He didn't have the strength to explain. "Not safe! Get to Speer!"

She gaped at him as if he were crazy, but did as he asked, turning her head to glance at him every few seconds, her eyes wide and worried, her face streaked with tears.

"Eyes on the road!" he shouted when she came close to running a stop sign.

A call came over his radio, but he ignored it, focused instead on breathing. In. Out. In. Out. In. Out. Goddamn, it hurt!

The drive seemed to take forever, though he knew she was going as fast as she could. She was actually a skilled driver, weaving through traffic like a pro, clearly an experienced speeder. He imagined she'd put that skill to use quite often as a journalist.

They crossed the bridge onto Speer as the first fat flakes of snow began to fall.

"Left at Eleventh . . ." He forced in another breath. "And left onto Mariposa."

She followed his directions, tearing around the corner onto Mariposa, then slamming on the brakes to keep from hitting a FedEx truck that sat parked in the middle of the lane.

He bit back a groan, took another painful breath, and pointed to his house. "Slow down . . . almost there."

He pressed the button on his dash, saw his garage door roll up, warm, yellow light spilling out into the dusk.

"Th-this isn't a hospital or a clinic!" She turned into the driveway, slid the truck into the garage. "Where are we?"

He punched the button to close the door behind them, shutting out wind and snow. "The Batcave."

BLOOD STILL SPIKED with adrenaline, Tessa watched Julian punch a code into a keypad and unlock the door leading from his garage to what must be his home. He leaned heavily against the door frame as he worked, his forehead pressed against the wall, and she knew he was in pain. She could tell from the lines on his face, from his unsteady breathing, from the way his fist clenched white-knuckled around his keys. He pushed the door open, sagging against the wall for a moment as she stepped past him and into an unfurnished kitchen.

This was her fault. It was *her* fault.

Her stomach twisted until she felt almost sick.

She'd left the paper when she ought to have stayed put. Julian had come looking for her, setting aside his other responsibilities to keep her safe. Then he'd put himself in the line of fire, deliberately taking rounds meant for her. She'd felt the bullets hit him, felt his body jerk with the terrible impact, and she'd thought for sure he would die.

He had to be wearing Kevlar. That was the only explanation. There were five holes torn in the back of his jacket, but no blood. He ought to be dead or dying, but he was strong enough to walk and clearheaded enough to give her directions.

He walked over to a dark leather sofa and sat, his brow furrowed. "Help me . . . get it off."

Tessa dropped her purse, let her coat fall to the floor, and hurried to kneel before him. She peeled off his jacket, tossed it over the arm of the sofa, then unfastened his harness and draped it with his .357 carefully on top of the jacket. Then she tugged his T-shirt free of his jeans and helped him get it over his head.

He *was* wearing Kevlar.

Not certain what to do, she pulled on the Velcro straps, unaware she was crying until his thumb wiped a tear from her cheek. She looked up to find him watching her intently, his eyes strangely dark. Then his hands closed over hers to guide her as she unfastened the vest and lifted it from his shoulders. He moaned as if in relief and instantly seemed to breathe easier.

She'd just stood to hang it over the arm of the sofa—it was far heavier than she'd imagined—when she saw his back.

Huge, black bruises.

Each the size of her open palm, five swollen bruises marred the skin of his back. In the center of each was a clear sign of impact, each like a crimson bull's eye. No wonder it hurt him to breathe. The damage surely went deep into his muscles.

The bullets had hit him full-on. They just hadn't penetrated.

She thought of Officer Taylor and knew that if Julian's vest had failed he would, without a doubt, be lying dead on the street.

And all at once the shock of what had happened hit her.

She sank down on the sofa beside him and ran her hand over the muscular planes of his back, wanting to soothe, afraid of hurting him. "Oh, Julian! God, I'm so sorry! It's my fault! You could have been—"

Then, no longer able to speak through her tears, she did the first thing that came to her.

She leaned down and kissed one of the bruises.

His body stiffened, and she saw that his eyes were squeezed shut.

Kicking off her shoes, she ducked down again and kissed a trail across his skin from bruise to bruise, wishing she could heal them, wishing she could take away whatever pain he was feeling. She was the cause of this, and she wanted somehow to fix it.

How it happened she didn't know, but she found herself brushing her lips slowly over the hard curve of his shoulder, nibbling his earlobe, kissing the stubble-rough line of his jaw. He smelled of leather and soap and man, his skin hot against her lips. He felt so wonderfully warm and alive. They were both miraculously alive.

Then a strong arm encircled her waist and held her fast. He looked at her, a confused expression on his face. "Are you crying for me?"

And in his eyes she saw not a hardened undercover cop, but a vulnerable man who had never known his mother's love.

She answered in the only way she could, taking his mouth with hers. For a moment, he let her have control, allowing her to shape the kiss, yielding to her rhythm, his lips soft, warm, compliant. But touching him like this only made her want him more, and she slipped her tongue inside his mouth to taste him, flicking the velvet of his tongue tentatively with hers.

The contact seemed to ignite him. He groaned, fisted a hand in her hair, and thrust his tongue deep, taking over with a ferocity that bordered on violence.

Oh, yes!

This is what she wanted—to feel him alive and strong, his mouth ravishing hers, his body hard against her. For so long she'd denied herself, afraid to fall again. But she knew it was too late. She had already fallen for Julian—and fallen hard. In the aftermath of near death, life pumping thick and insistent through her veins, she wanted him more than she wanted to breathe, her need for him so urgent that it staggered her.

She twined her fingers in his hair, met his intensity with her own demanding hunger. It was just a kiss, just lips and teeth and tongues, and yet it carried her to the edge, the heat between her legs turning to cream, her nipples tight and aching against the lace of her bra.

And then his mouth left hers, and he spoke in a rough, breathless voice, his blue eyes as dark as midnight. "No interruptions this time, honey. You're mine."

CHAPTER 18

HIS CONTROL ALREADY shattered, Julian forced her down onto the sofa, the pain of bruised muscles all but forgotten in a rush of pumping blood and blind need. He ripped off her hose and panties as he went, catching her surprised gasp with a deep kiss. She was soft and warm and tasted sweet, her heart pounding hard against his chest.

He needed to be inside her. He *had* to be inside her.

She arched against him, whimpered into his mouth, her hands sliding out of his hair to run impatiently over his bare pecs, her fingers threading through his chest hair, spreading fire over his skin. Balancing his weight on one arm, he jerked her skirt up to her hips, forced her legs apart with his own, freed his aching cock, and guided it to her cleft.

Raining kisses on her face, he pushed his hips forward, nudged the tip of his cock into her slick heat. She was impossibly tight, her inner muscles resisting his invasion, almost as if—

The possibility hit him like a fist.

A virgin? She couldn't be!

She made a little sound, something between a squeak and a moan, and he saw she was biting her lower lip. Was he hurting her?

"Oh, no, honey, no! Please tell me you've done this before!" Even as he asked, he thrust himself deeper inside her, his body only too eager to take what his mind rejected.

"Once."

Once?

Holy fuck!

Fighting for the restraint he'd already lost, he pressed his lips against her temple and slowly withdrew. "Easy, Tessa."

He spread her legs further apart, wrapped one silky calf around his waist, lifted the other to rest on the back of the couch, positioning her to ease penetration. Then he entered her again, and again withdrew. Again and again he pushed into her and pulled back, stretching her a bit more each time, until his body shook with the need to be completely inside her.

Her eyes were closed, her breathing ragged, the leg around his waist drawing him closer, urging him on.

Unable to hold back any longer, he buried himself to the hilt, felt her contract around him like a fist. Wet. Tight. Perfect. "Jesus Christ!"

She moaned, a sound of raw sexual pleasure, her nails digging into his shoulders, her hips lifting to meet him.

And then he was moving, thrusting in and out of her, the snug, slippery friction driving him dangerously close to the brink. Determined to hold off as long as he could, he fought to relax, tried to fall into an easy rhythm, but she felt too damned good. He felt his balls draw tight and knew he was going to come—and far too soon. He couldn't hold back.

But then he saw her beautiful face, her eyes half closed, her skin flushed pink, her lips parted, and he knew he *could* hold back. For her. For Tessa.

"Oh, Julian! I never thought it could be . . . oh!"

Tessa couldn't believe what she was feeling—the delicious fullness, the sweet stretch, the silky stroke as Julian moved over her, against her, deep inside her. He felt huge and thick and hard as steel, each thrust making her ache for the next. This was the sex of her daydreams, the sex her friends raved about, the sex she'd read about in novels.

Was this really happening?

She forced her eyes open, found him looking down at her through blue eyes that seemed to burn, a look of brutal intensity on his face. His dark hair hung loose around his shoulders, his chest beaded with sweat, his muscles shifting as he drove himself into her, the whole of him fixed on one purpose—making love with her.

At the sight of him, her inner muscles clenched—hard. "Julian!"

His lips curved in a lopsided grin. Then he thrust deep, held himself inside her, ground himself against her aching clitoris, making pleasure draw tight in her belly. "I want to feel you come! Come around my cock!"

And just like that, she did.

Orgasm surged through her like a tide of molten gold, bright and blazing, the hot shock of it forcing the breath from her lungs in a ragged cry, her muscles clenching greedily around him, the fullness piercingly sweet.

She heard him whisper her name, felt his pace shift, and knew his control was gone. His hips a piston, he drove himself into her fast and hard, his quick, sure strokes carrying her headlong toward an impossible second climax. Then she felt his body shudder, his groan mingling with her cries, as he let himself go and pleasure drenched them both.

FOR A WHILE they lay together in silence, Julian still kissing her, still half hard, still inside her. In truth, he couldn't stop touching her. Or he didn't want to stop. That fact by itself astonished him. What blew his mind even more was the warm knot of emotions in his chest—tenderness, protectiveness . . . and something else he didn't want to name.

She'd only had sex once before. It both surprised him and made perfect sense. He hadn't forgotten what she'd said the night he'd almost made love to her on the floor of her apartment.

The idea of having sex with a man is loads better than the reality.

Some klutz dick had taken her virginity, perhaps even

roughly, and had given her nothing in return. Julian hoped the bastard's balls had since fallen off.

"Am I too heavy?" He brushed his lips over hers, slowly flexed his hips.

Her breath caught. "No."

He hadn't meant to have sex with her. In fact, after the other night, he'd resolved not to touch her again. But he'd never stood a chance against her soft touch, her feminine sweetness, the genuine concern in her eyes. She'd broken him in a matter of minutes—and she'd done it with tears.

He couldn't remember a woman ever crying for him before.

But sex was a one-way bridge. They had crossed over, and they could never go back. He'd brought her here, but it would only mean having to leave her standing alone one day. He would hate himself for hurting her, but he would do it anyway. In the end, he'd be no better than the last man who'd left tire tracks on her.

Except that he had, at least, given her pleasure.

Oh, Julian! I never thought it could be . . . !

He couldn't deny he'd felt a swell of masculine pride at her words. He wasn't the first man to have sex with her, but he was the first to make her come, the first to show her how good sex could be. He couldn't deny that pleased him. Of course, there was still so much to show her where sex was concerned . . .

Preferring to concentrate on that idea and not his unsettled emotions, he ducked down, slipped his tongue into her mouth, tasted her again. She was a living, breathing aphrodisiac, and he felt his cock begin to stretch and fill inside her. She felt it, too, her eyes fluttering open in apparent surprise.

He lifted his head, chuckled, then flexed his hips again, gratified by the uncontrolled tightening of her muscles. She was hypersensitive the way women often were after they came—hypersensitive and oh-so-wet, his ejaculate mingled with the hot honey of her orgasm.

And that was another thing. He *never* had unprotected sex. When was the last time he'd had sex without a condom? He couldn't remember—not at the moment anyway.

He began to grind his hips, but slowly. "Unbutton your blouse."

Her eyes widened, but she reached down between their bodies and unfastened one pearly white button at a time, until her blouse lay open, revealing her white, lacy bra and the swells of her breasts. He rewarded her with a sudden deep thrust that brought him to her cervix.

She gasped, and her body arched against him.

"Now unhook your bra." His voice sounded rough, even to his own ears.

Her hands visibly trembling, she reached between her breasts and undid the clasp. The cloth sprang back, leaving her gorgeous breasts bare. They were swollen, her translucent skin glowing pink, the rosy velvet of her nipples already tight and puckered.

He rewarded her with another deep thrust and was satisfied by her aroused moan. "Now touch yourself."

She stared up at him, clearly surprised by the idea, but she did as he asked, a look of uncertainty on her face. Her hands cupped her breasts, shaping and kneading them, her gaze fixed on his face. Then her lips curved in a slow, seductive smile, and she caught the tips of her nipples—and tugged them to hard points.

Something inside Julian roared—or maybe he growled out loud. He lowered his head, nudged her hands aside, and captured one succulent bud in his mouth.

Her response was immediate. Her breath broke, and her eyes drifted shut, a look of sheer bliss on her face. Her thighs jerked tight against him as he sucked, her back arching off the sofa, lifting her breasts toward his hungry mouth.

He couldn't remember another woman whose breasts were so responsive, and he knew without a doubt he could make her come just by suckling her. If he weren't already inside her, he might try to do that now. But he *was* inside her, and no way in hell was he going anywhere until they were both satiated.

He flicked his tongue back and forth over one taut peak,

nipped it with his lips, then shifted his attention to the other, letting his fingers have their way with the one he'd made wet.

A gasp. A throaty moan. The pull of fingers in his hair. "Oh, God!"

He kept the motion of his hips slow, wanting to draw out their pleasure. It wasn't easy, especially when he scraped her with his teeth and she began to lift her hips and thrust against him, almost riding him from beneath. He knew what she wanted, but he wasn't going to give it to her—not yet.

Tessa couldn't take any more. He was using his body as an instrument of torture, his mouth relentless and hot on her nipples, his cock moving with agonizing slowness inside her, inch by excruciating inch. She bucked helplessly against him, trying to make him go faster, trying to drive him deeper, but he only chuckled and pulled back.

"Lie still."

She groaned in sexual frustration. "I-I can't!"

"Yes, you can." He blew across her wet, throbbing nipples.

She gasped, the shivery sensation sending sparks straight from her breasts to her belly. Her hips curled reflexively, reaching for fulfillment.

This time he withdrew completely, the tip of his cock just nudging her. "Hold still!"

She tried to do as he asked, her breath coming in panting gasps as he eased himself slowly inside her once again, his tongue circling fire over her nipples, the burn heightened by his teeth—sharp, biting edges that nipped her sensitive tips, then traveled to nibble at the undersides of her breasts. "Oh! Oh, God, Julian!"

But the closer she got to her climax, the slower he went, prolonging her anguish, leaving her suspended in some kind of sexual purgatory, perched on the edge of an orgasm that hovered just beyond her reach. Every nerve in her body was on fire, the touch of skin against sizzling skin, the scorching flick of his tongue, the steel-hot slide of his cock all but unbearable.

But when her peak finally came, she wasn't ready for it, excruciating pleasure surging inside her like a wave, swelling and growing stronger as it rolled through her, tossing her along its shimmering crest. Her surprised gasp became a low moan and then a throaty cry as she felt herself being carried helplessly higher and higher. "Julian, Julian, Julian!"

She arched into him, her fists clenched in his sweat-damp hair, her legs wrapped tightly around his waist as she tried to ride it out, his slow thrusts prolonging her climax until she sobbed with the intensity of it. And then he was pounding into her, his deep strokes sending her over the edge once more, his body shaking with the force of his own release until he sagged against her, both of them sweaty and spent.

For a moment she drifted, almost asleep, her body floating.

Then Julian lifted his head, pressed a kiss to her forehead. "I need to check in."

"Check in?"

"A lot of people out there are worried about you."

TESSA WRAPPED ICE in a clean dish towel to make an ice pack for Julian. She'd seen the way he'd gritted his teeth as he'd raised himself off her and walked toward one of the bedrooms, cell phone in one hand and gun in the other, presumably to call Chief Irving and tell him what an idiot she'd been. The least she could do was try to ease some of his pain and swelling.

But his kitchen lacked more than a table and chairs. The granite countertops were bare, and most of the cupboards were empty, one holding a few glasses, some plates and bowls and another holding a box of oatmeal, several cans of soup, and an unopened jar of salsa. The fridge contained none of the items she associated with single men—ketchup, mustard, and beer—but only milk and bottled water. She'd been surprised to find ice in the ice maker.

Wishing she had a rubber band or plastic bag, she bound the ice in the towel as best she could, then carried it back into the almost empty living room, amazed that she could still walk. Her legs, having spent the past thirty minutes wrapped around Julian's waist, felt like taffy. Her body was full of sunlight, warm and glowing. And yet . . .

She had no idea how she was supposed to act, no idea how to feel. Julian had just made incredible love to her, but he wasn't *in love* with her. He'd stamped himself forever on her—body, heart, and soul—but a year from now he probably wouldn't remember who she was. He'd rocked her world, and yet he was only temporarily a part of it.

What was a woman supposed to say? "Thanks, stud"?

Regrets don't put supper on the table, Tessa Marie.

Her mother's voice rang clear as a bell through her mind. She'd been in third grade and had gotten caught stealing a book from her teacher. The teacher, a severe older woman named Mrs. March, had ripped the book from her hands and pinched Tessa's arm with fingernails stained yellow from smoking.

"Get your grubby little hands off the pages!" Mrs. March had bellowed in her face, her breath reeking of cigarettes. "White trash!"

Tessa had spent the better part of the afternoon crying in the principal's office before her mother had come from her job to pick her up and take her home. She'd expected her mother to yell at her, maybe even spank her. Instead, her mother had made her take a nap, telling Grandpa that she'd had to come home from school because she had a fever.

Strange that Tessa should think of that now. Or perhaps not so strange. That had been the first time in her life that she'd felt regret—the biting torment of wishing she'd made a different choice. Did she feel that way now?

No.

The answer came instantly and straight from her heart. There's nothing she would trade for the bliss she'd experienced with Julian. Nothing at all. Tessa wasn't even sure she'd really had a choice. The moment he'd touched her, she'd been lost.

But she *did* have a choice now. She could either feel depressed that Julian didn't love her and would soon leave her life, or she could give and take what she could, savor it, and leave the future to deal with itself.

And what if you end up pregnant because of tonight?

Well, then, she'd have Julian's baby. She was in a much better position to deal with a baby than her fourteen-year-old mother had been. Hadn't Kara raised Connor by herself until she'd met Reece?

One of the bedroom doors opened, and Julian stepped out, looking angry. He hadn't yet put his shirt back on, his dark hair hanging loose around his shoulders. The waistband of his pants was still unbuttoned, giving her a glimpse of dark hair but nothing below it. And she realized that, although he'd been inside her, she hadn't yet seen that part of him.

Her pulse tripped.

She fought to keep her voice steady and her words light. "So this is the Batcave."

The interior of his house looked new—oak cabinetry, fresh paint, polished oak floors. It also looked as if the owner had yet to move in. The living room held only the leather sofa and a plasma TV on a stand. There were no bookshelves, no house-plants, no photographs.

He stopped to adjust the thermostat. Somewhere in the house, the furnace kicked on.

"What were you expecting?" There was a note of humor in his voice.

She shrugged. "Guns. Furniture."

"The guns are here, honey. I just don't leave them lying around." He glanced at the bundle in her hands. "What's that?"

"It's time you had some ice on those bruises. Find a comfortable place and lie down."

He met her gaze, a grin tugging at his sexy lips. "Yes, ma'am."

JULIAN LAY FACEDOWN on his bed, ice pack cold on his back, Tessa's small hand resting against one of his shoulders. He'd never had anyone fuss over him like this, and he wasn't sure what to think of it. He felt mesmerized and irritable at the same time, wanting her care and attention and being angry with himself for wanting it.

He'd never brought another living soul into this house, and it felt more than a little strange to have Tessa here. But it also felt right. He'd had time to reconsider his decision, had weighed the pros and cons. She was a journalist, and he was a special agent. Revealing the location of his home wasn't in the manual. There were things in this house—evidence, documents, the contents of his computer—that she could never be allowed to see. Then again, he'd already thrown out the manual where Tessa was concerned.

Having her here meant taking a risk, but it was better than risking her life. And as he'd thought about it, he'd realized that his house was the safest place for her. Only two people knew where he lived—Dyson and Irving. The place was more secure than most safe houses. And he was in charge, meaning he didn't have to depend on anyone else to do his job correctly.

"Does this hurt?"

Like a sonofabitch. "No."

"Liar." She moved the ice pack to a different bruise. "I think you should see a doctor."

So did Irving. The old man had ripped his head off, not only for bringing Tessa home with him, but for failing to respond or check in. "Eyewitnesses said you took several rounds in the back! I was starting to think I'd find both of you dead in a ditch somewhere! Goddamn it, Darcangelo, you're not a free agent!"

Julian had apologized, then explained that he'd had the wind knocked out of him and had been unable to respond. It made for a better excuse than, "We were fucking one another's brains out and couldn't get to a phone."

Irving had ordered him to see the department's doctor first thing tomorrow and had placed him on medical leave until he was deemed fit for action. Dyson had insisted on the same and had then chewed Julian's ass off for wasting time protecting a journalist.

"She's not your job, Darcangelo. You're thinking with your dick. Did you see her article in today's paper? If she wants to become collateral damage, don't get in her way. Margaux thinks you're passing this woman information, by the way."

It had taken all of Julian's self-control not to react, his disappointment in Dyson cutting deep. Of course, he hadn't told Dyson that Tessa was now staying with him . . .

"It's just bruised muscles." Julian tried to ignore the painful pressure of the ice pack and the shock of the cold as it touched new skin. He focused instead on her touch, on the scent of sex that lingered around her, on the heat that seemed to leap between them. "The doctor won't be able to do anything besides give me narcotics and muscle relaxers, and I won't take those."

"A tough guy, huh?" She shifted, her thigh pressing against his hip.

"Drugs fog the brain, slow the reflexes. I can get as much relief from ice and heat and stretching." That wasn't strictly true, of course, but he couldn't risk being zoned out on painkillers while on assignment.

"I . . . I'm really sorry, Julian." She sounded truly ashamed. "You were almost killed—"

"No, Tessa, *you* were almost killed." The anger he'd felt earlier when he'd gotten the message from Syko reignited in his gut. "They weren't after me."

"Who were they?" Her voice was soft and held just a hint of fear.

"Irving said they were gangbangers from one of the smaller gangs allied with the Bloods. The DPD picked up two of them. The rest got away, but not for long. Syko's probably on the prowl for them right now."

"You paid Syko. He called you about me, didn't he?"

So she'd figured that part out. "Yes."

"I'll pay you back. Whatever it was, I'll pay you—"

"Forget about it." For some reason her offer, as polite and reasonable as it was, pissed him off. It was the best grand he'd ever spent. He didn't want it back.

"How did you know? How did you know they were going to shoot just then?" She asked the question casually, as if she were asking about the weather, but he could tell her calm facade was crumbling.

"I saw the red dot from a laser sight on your blouse. They'd have hit you dead in the heart, blown your chest wide open with the first shot. I doubt you'd have felt much pain."

He felt her stiffen, heard the breath leave her lungs, and

knew she finally understood just how close she'd come to dying today. It had been a matter of seconds.

"God, I . . . It won't happen again." She shifted the ice pack, her hands trembling now.

Pain and anger turned his voice gruff. "Damned straight it won't! You're staying with me now, Goldilocks. You're on *my* turf. You follow *my* rules."

CHAPTER 19

TESSA FELT EMOTIONALLY overloaded, shorted out. So much had happened in so short a time, and she could barely keep up. Julian had driven all of it away when he'd made love to her, the power of his touch making her forget murder and bullets and terror. But the reprieve had been temporary, and the reality of her situation had come rushing back, leaving her almost numb. It took her a moment to understand what Julian meant.

"Staying with you? Here?" she asked, dumbly. "But Chief Irving is taking me to—"

"The safe house isn't safe enough. I want you where I can keep an eye on you, where you won't be able get yourself into trouble, where no one else is in charge."

A little voice inside her wanted to object to the authoritarian tone in his voice, to this sudden change in plans. She couldn't stay with him. It would be too distracting, not to mention a complete conflict of interest. But she couldn't summon the words. She was tired. So tired.

He must have noticed her silence. The next thing she knew, he was sitting up, the soggy ice pack lying forgotten on the gray quilt that covered his big four-poster bed. He cupped her cheek in one big palm. "Tessa?"

She met his gaze. "I-I think I need a nap."

He frowned. "When's the last time you slept?"

She had to think. "The night you knocked me out."

"Why don't you hop in the shower, while I try to figure out what's for dinner?" He pulled her to her feet. "The bathroom's through there."

A shower suddenly sounded wonderful. "I don't have my things. They're in my suitcase in the trunk of my rental car."

"You can use my stuff for tonight. The towels are under the sink. Yell if you need anything." He turned and left the bedroom, closing the door behind him.

It took Tessa a moment to get her bearings. She undressed, draping her clothes across his bed, then walked into the sparkling-clean bathroom—a man's bathroom. It was the one room, together with his bedroom, that looked lived in. It smelled like him, like his soap, his aftershave, his skin. His toothbrush sat in a cup on one side of the sink next to a tube of mint-flavored toothpaste. A comb sat on the other. There was soap in the soap dish and shampoo and shaving cream in the shower. A razor was perched on top of a shaving mirror stuck to the white tile wall.

Feeling oddly comforted by these everyday things, she turned on the water as hot as she could stand it, stepped under the spray, and drew the transparent shower curtain into place.

The showerhead was one of the detachable massaging kinds she'd had in her last apartment. She turned it to her favorite setting and let the current pummel her. The hot water loosened her tense muscles, but it also loosened her emotions, and she found herself shaking from head to toe, until the hell of the past two weeks came spilling out of her in sobs.

Gunshots. Blood. A hard, groping hand. The photo of her naked in the tub. An officer shot. Kids living and killing on the streets. Girls kidnapped and sold like slaves. Needle tracks. Rape. Murder.

¡Ayúdeme! ¡Me van a matar!

Tessa wasn't sure how long she'd stood there crying in the pulsing spray, when she heard him enter. He stood there, wearing only his leather pants, a look of concern on his hand-some face, gun in hand. "Tessa? Are you all right, honey?"

And she knew what she wanted. Him.

She drew back the shower curtain and reached for him. "Please, Julian!"

He answered her by setting his gun aside, unzipping his pants and shoving them down his thighs to the floor. Then he stepped into the shower with her and closed the shower curtain with a jerk, his gaze raking over her as intimately as a caress.

He seemed to tower over her, filling the tiny space with his broad shoulders. But she wasn't staring at his shoulders. His erection was huge and dark, rising from a thatch of black hair to stand thick and full against his abdomen, the tip just touching his navel, his testicles hanging dark and heavy beneath.

It was the first time she'd seen him fully nude, and she wanted to touch him, to feel that satiny hardness, to taste the engorged head. But Julian didn't give her time. He crushed her to him, his mouth closing over hers in a probing, hot kiss.

One sensation collided with another. The velvet glide of his tongue. The sweetness of skin against naked, wet skin. The rasp of chest hair against sensitive nipples. The insistent press of his erection against her belly. Water pulsing against nerve endings. Moans mingling in the thickening steam.

The kiss seemed to go on forever, drawing out the minutes, heating her blood by degrees until she burned. Then he ducked down to suck her nipples. She cried out, arched into the heat of his mouth, clinging to him, her fingers twined in his wet hair. He seemed to make a feast of her breasts, tugging on her nipples with his lips, nipping her with his teeth, suckling her, flicking her with his rough tongue, every touch making the fire between her legs burn brighter.

Abruptly, he withdrew his mouth, turned her to face the wall, and stretched her arms out on either side of her head, his hands shackling her wrists, forcing her palms against the wall. Then he nudged her feet wide apart and entered her from be-hind with a single, perfect thrust, his lips nipping at the skin beneath her ear. "God, Tessa, honey, you are incredible!"

Tessa thought he was the incredible one, but she couldn't say so, not with words. He felt so good moving inside her, each stroke so deep, so right. She moaned at the wonder of it, ground her bottom into him, arched to take every bit of him she could, desperate for completion, her tortured nipples brushing against the chilly tile.

She caught just a glimpse of the two of them in the shaving mirror—her lips swollen from his kisses, his chest pressed into her shoulders as he drove himself into her. It was one glimpse, but it made her breath catch. They looked primitive—male and female caught in the primal act of mating.

Then he released her wrists, one hand spreading across her rib cage to hold her steady, the other reaching for the showerhead. She realized what he meant to do a moment before he did it.

When the pulsating spray hit her clitoris, she cried out in shock. It was too much—the pulsating water, the power of his relentless, forceful thrusts, the feel of his left hand as it worked over her throbbing nipples. She whimpered, her breath coming in ragged pants, her hands bunched into fists, her cheek pressed into the tile wall.

The tension inside her drew into a tight, shimmering ball— and then shattered. Pleasure surged through her in a great gush, swamping her in delight almost too intense to bear. But no sooner had the first wave begun to recede, when another crashed through her. And another.

Again and again she came, each peak drawn out by the slide of his cock inside her and the pulsing spray. Her body trembled, her legs no longer strong enough to hold her. She heard a woman's keening cries, then a man's deep groans as the next wave caught him, too, and carried them both into sweet oblivion.

She was vaguely aware of it when Julian turned off the water, her head resting against his strong shoulder. She knew when he wrapped her in a warm towel, his embrace keeping her on her feet. She felt him lift her out of the shower and into his arms.

"You're safe here, honey," he muttered against her cheek as

he lowered her onto soft sheets and covered her with the quilt.
"Sleep."

And she did.

JULIAN SAT IN the dark on the edge of his bed and watched
Tessa sleep, the sight of her alive and breathing making him
grateful for the throbbing pain in his back. Her hair lay in
damp, curling ropes across her pillow, one shoulder exposed,
the curve of her hips outlined gently by the quilt. There were
dark circles beneath her eyes, a faint gray beneath her dark
lashes. She'd been on the brink of exhaustion, he realized, her
emotions worn threadbare.

He'd been in the kitchen trying to decide whether to cook
the can of chicken noodle soup or to run down the street for
some carryout Vietnamese when he'd heard her crying. He'd
told himself she needed her privacy, that she'd get it out of her
system and be fine. But the wrenching sound of her sobs had
been like a razor to his gut, and unable to leave her alone with
her anguish, he'd gone to her.

He'd taken one look at her, tears in her blue eyes, her wet
hair clinging to her breasts, water sluicing over the satin of her
skin, and he'd completely forgotten his decision not to have
unprotected sex with her again. He'd forgotten everything but
the need to hold her, to comfort her, to drive away her tears.

He'd tried to convince himself that what had happened between them was only sex—nothing more than mind-blowing,
adrenaline-charged fucking. But he knew better. He'd never
wanted a woman the way he wanted Tessa. Never. It wasn't
just that she was beautiful. It wasn't just her charming combination of grit and girliness. It wasn't only her intelligence or
her quiet resolve or the vulnerability that lurked behind those
big blue eyes. It was all of that together—and much more.

Something about her opened up something inside him.

And he wasn't sure he liked it.

He'd never been generous with his soul. Too much of it
had been lost growing up under his father's roof, watching the
old man kill himself with tequila, seeing the bastard abuse

every woman who walked into their lives, being left to fend
for himself on the street. He'd buried what remained of himself, kept it to himself in an effort to stay sane, tried to seal it
off from the horrors of his job—both what he saw and what he
had to do. Not even Margaux had been able to touch that part
of him.

But Tessa had.

Almost from the moment he'd met her, she'd cut to the
heart of him, dredging up feelings he'd hoped not to feel
again—fear, helplessness, affection. She'd gotten beneath his
radar, worked her way inside him, made him care.

God, he wished things were different. He'd give anything
right now, including that little bit of hoarded soul, to be a normal man with a normal job, a man capable of caring for a wife
and children. But he wasn't normal. His father's cruelty lived
inside him. He'd tried to stamp it out by going after men like
his father and putting them behind bars, using the violence
he'd grown up with to fight violence. As a result, his life was
nothing but wall-to-wall ugly.

Tessa thought she needed him, but the truth was he needed
her. He needed her softness, her tenderness, her touch. He
needed it more than he could have imagined needing anything.
And that's why he would take everything she offered, knowing he couldn't stay, knowing he didn't deserve her, knowing
she would hate him in the end.

She stirred in her sleep, a sound like a sigh escaping her.

He'd intended to sleep on the couch, but the pull she ex-
uded was too strong. Nearing exhaustion, his body aching,
tired of his own thoughts, he slipped into bed beside her,
pulled her into his arms, and allowed himself to drift.

ALEXI MULLED OVER the news, letting his gaze travel over
the picture of the reporter lying naked in the bathtub.

Darcangelo had taken bullets meant for her and had then
disappeared with her.

Why would any man do that? There could only be one
reason.

"So Julian Darcangelo is not as heartless as he seems," Alexi said to himself, feeling almost euphoric. "He has fallen for a woman."

If Darcangelo cared for this Tessa Novak, then Alexi had what he needed to destroy him. Alexi simply needed to get his hands on Tessa.

It was time to eliminate the reporter anyway. Her last articles had hit too close to the mark for Alexi's comfort. He couldn't risk allowing her to continue. But where was she? And what would he do with her once he had her?

He reached beneath his black satin sheets, wrapped his hand around his cock, and stroked it to hardness, ideas racing through his mind, each more arousing than the last.

He could sell Tessa Novak in South America or Turkey and e-mail Darcangelo photographs of her travels. He could launch her film career and send Darcangelo free DVDs. He could turn her over to his men, let them commit every act known to the depraved male mind, capturing her agonized screams and her eventual death on video—though in her case that would be a sad waste of merchandise.

Alexi gazed at the reporter's breasts, her pretty face, her long, golden hair, so curly and sweet. Where had Darcangelo hidden her?

Dyson would know.

Alexi also needed to find out who'd tried to shoot her and kill them. He did not want other people hunting his ducks. Though he supposed it would be simpler to let others do the work and take the risk for him, he needed her alive if he was going to use her against Darcangelo.

After all, he didn't intend merely to kill dear Julian. That would be dull and unsatisfying. No, he wanted to break him. He wanted to take everything from him. Then, when Darcangelo could suffer no more, Alexi would kill him—and Zoryo would be avenged.

Now fully erect, he turned to the woman who lay asleep beside him and pushed her over onto her belly. Then he forced her thighs apart and shoved himself into her from behind, ignoring her drunken protests. Grasping her hips, he pounded

into her and let himself imagine that she was Tessa Novak—
and that Julian Darcangelo was bound and watching.

TESSA WOKE TO the sound of Julian in the shower, a depres-
sion in his pillow where he'd slept beside her. She ran her
hand over that indentation, felt his body heat still in the sheets.
She'd woken in the middle of the night to find herself snug-
gled against his chest, his arms around her, his heart beating
just beneath her ear. Then she'd drifted back to sleep, feeling
wrapped in contentment, utterly and completely safe.

Had she ever felt that way before? No, not like that. Nothing like that.

She inhaled his scent, let it fill her, then climbed out of bed,
feeling sore in places she'd never felt sore before, her heart
light despite the voice that warned her she'd have to deal with
a host of unpleasant realities sooner or later. Hoping for later,
she slipped into a pair of his boxer briefs and one of his
T-shirts and walked to the kitchen. Then she started a pot of
oatmeal, her stomach growling with hunger, her mind filled
with memories of last night.

Never had she imagined sex could be so satisfying. Or that
she was capable of multiple orgasms. Or that an orgasm with
a man deep inside her would feel so much more intense than
one without. Or that a man's touch could become her entire
world.

"Okay, Holly, you're right," she said, pouring oats into boiling water, unable to hold back a smile. "Sex rocks."

But it wasn't just sex. It was sex with Julian.

Despite her limited experience, she knew what they'd
shared last night wasn't common. It had been more than just
interconnecting body parts, more than mutually satisfying orgasms, more than a man and woman taking advantage of biol-
ogy for a few thrills. Tessa had felt transformed, carried to a
place she'd never been before. And although she knew he
viewed sex merely as a casual diversion, one that generated no
emotional ties, his touch had sent a different message.

The intense way he'd kissed her. The way he'd seemed to

notice her every breath, breathing with her. The way he'd plied her with all the erotic pleasure her body was capable of feeling. The way he'd come apart inside her, his entire body shaking with the force of it.

His touch told her she was the only woman in his world. His touch told her he needed her as badly as she needed him. His touch told her he cared about her.

But if she'd expected him to show any sign that last night meant anything to him, she was wrong. He came out of the bedroom wearing jeans, a navy-blue turtleneck and a scowl, lines of fatigue and pain on his face. Then he wolfed down his oatmeal without so much as a "good morning."

"What's wrong?" he barked when the act of sitting made her wince.

"Nothing," she lied, trying to hide the far greater pain caused by his apparent indifference. "I'm fine."

His scowl deepened.

As soon as they'd finished with breakfast, he gave her a tour of the house. But it wasn't a "make yourself at home" kind of tour. He showed her the closed door of the second bedroom, which was his office and was strictly off-limits. He showed her his basement gym with its weights, punching bag, and treadmill, which he invited her to use. He showed her the walk-in closet downstairs where he kept his guns, knives, ammo, night-vision goggles, and other hard-core gear.

"Now I know you're not a cop," she said, trying to match his indifference with sarcasm. "No one could afford this kind of stuff on a cop's salary. Got any spare rocket-launcher parts in there? Mine's broken."

He didn't so much as smile.

On the way back upstairs, he laid down the law, rattling off his rules as if they were her Miranda rights, his voice cold and hard.

"Rule number one: don't reveal to anyone—not your friend and her senator husband, not your coworkers, not your asshole boss, not even Jesus Christ—your whereabouts or the location of this house. Our lives depend on secrecy.

"Rule number two: stay out of my office. I'll have a lock

on it by the end of the day. In the meantime, don't open the door. If you do, you'll regret it in ways you can't possibly imagine. Don't even touch the doorknob.

"Rule number three: don't set even the tip of one pretty toe outside this house. Opening any door or window will trigger the alarm, and I, along with FBI-Denver, will know.

"Rule number four: don't tell anyone my name or repeat anything I tell you. Whatever I say in this house is strictly off the record. No playing reporter with me.

"Rule number five: do everything I tell you to do without argument.

"If you break any one of these rules, you will be very sorry. Understand?"

"Yes," she answered, acting bored and fighting to keep the hurt from her voice.

"I'm meeting Irving to get your stuff and to run a few errands, and I won't be back until early afternoon. You know how to reach me."

She stopped and stared after him, feeling suddenly afraid. Surely he wasn't leaving her completely alone. "Will there be officers parked outside?"

"No. Apart from Irving, no one at the DPD knows where I live. Not every cop is clean, Tessa. Someone is working for the other side. That's why you're safer here."

"Oh." She had wondered.

He strapped on his holster, his motions stiff, his jaw clenched in obvious pain. Then he grabbed his leather jacket from the sofa and looked over at her, his gaze softening.

"There are motion sensors and hidden cameras outside. No one can come near the house without triggering the alarm. If the power goes out, the generator takes over. The security code is encrypted. The windows and walls are bulletproof, and the doors and door frames are reinforced steel. The bad guys can't reach you here, Tessa."

"Thank you, Julian." She searched for the right words. "I know bringing me here wasn't part of your plan."

"No, it wasn't." He turned to go, then looked back at her. "Is there anything you need?"

"A skinny vanilla latte would be nice."

He raised a single dark eyebrow. "Right."

Then he turned and disappeared into the garage, closing the door behind him.

She heard the door latch, then a tiny beep, and she knew she was locked in. There was the roar of a truck engine. Then the grinding sound of a garage door sliding up and down its tracks. And then he was gone.

For a moment she stood in the middle of the kitchen, feeling strangely lost. Then she walked slowly over to the window and looked out onto his snowy backyard. The storm had left at least six inches so far. The wind had blown itself out, and chubby flakes drifted lazily to the ground. But she barely noticed the beauty of it.

What a tangled mess this was. She was a virtual prisoner in Julian's home. They were working on the same case, at odds with one another. She'd almost gotten them both killed. She was investigating him. And she was in love with him, while he apparently felt very little for her.

Unpleasant realities, indeed.

"You walked into this with your eyes wide open, girl," she told herself.

As if knowing that was supposed to make it easier.

CHAPTER 20

DETERMINED TO PUT herself together, Tessa watched the Saturday morning news, then returned the dozen or so messages her friends had left on her voice mail to let them know she was safe and give them the number to her new encrypted cell phone. She told them what had happened—how she'd left the paper through the rear exit wearing a scarf over her head; how Syko's gang had picked her up off the street; how a certain unnamed undercover cop had found her at Syko's place, dragged her to his truck, and saved her life by taking bullets intended for her. Then she listened as they each, in turn, ripped her head off for having left the safety of the newspaper.

Kara was furious, Reece even more so. Lissy got teary with relief. Kat casually told her to stay put before she got someone killed. Holly wanted details about the undercover cop. It was Sophie who seemed the most upset.

"You lied to me," she said. "I asked you point-blank if you were going to try to find those gang members again, and you said no."

"I'm sorry." Tessa didn't know what else to say.

But Sophie wasn't finished. "I realized you were gone maybe ten minutes after you left. I tried the bathroom, the cafeteria. I looked everywhere. I tried calling your cell, but you didn't answer. When Tom called us into a meeting an hour later and told us there'd been another shooting, I thought for sure you were dead!"

"I'm really sorry, Sophie. I know it was stupid, but I picked up a valuable lead from—"

"I don't care about leads! No story is worth your life!" Sophie seemed truly angry now.

"You wouldn't say that if this were your investigation." Because Tessa truly regretted alarming her friend, she kept her voice calm. "You'd do everything you could to get to the bottom of it."

It was the truth, and they both knew it.

"And your point is?" A touch of humor had returned to Sophie's voice. "Now tell me about this man who got shot for you. Is he the same one who kissed you at the hospital and who threw your butt in jail?"

"Yes. He's meeting Chief Irving to get my suitcases from the rental car. I'm investigating him, Sophie. And I'm in love with him." The words were away before Tessa could catch them.

Tessa found herself telling Sophie everything that had happened between her and Julian since her arrest, taking pains not to reveal his name and skipping intimate anatomical details, despite Sophie's subtle or not-so-subtle inquiries.

"I know he doesn't love me. He was very clear that he isn't interested in a relationship." It hurt to say the words out loud, to hear herself say them. "But when he touches me, it feels like he means it. I guess I'm just an idiot."

"No, you're not. If some gorgeous man were to save my life and give me multiple orgasms, I'd fall in love, too. Besides, I think he must like you a lot to have done all he's done for you. Guys don't just jump in front of bullets, Tessa, not even special agents."

"Promise me you won't tell anyone I slept with him. I don't want this to become newsroom gossip, and I don't want to sit through a lecture from Tom."

"You know I would never share anything you told me in confidence, Tess."

There was a moment of silence.

"Oh, God, you're going to tell everyone!"

"Well, not Tom."

They both burst into laughter, the first good laugh Tessa'd had since the night of the murder, and the ache in her heart lessened.

"By the way, you had a visitor this afternoon," Sophie said when their laughter had ebbed. "After word went out about the shooting on the five-o'clock news, a woman stopped by the paper. She seemed really upset. She said she was your mother. At first I thought she was just a crazy woman, but she looks just like you. I didn't know your mother lived here."

JULIAN PULLED INTO the newspaper parking lot and parked his truck beside the old olive-green Lincoln, snow crunching under his tires. By the time he'd gotten out of his truck, Irving was waiting for him by the tailgate. "This is bullshit, and you know it."

Irving met his fury with a steady gaze. "The doc says you've got ruptured muscles. It must hurt like a sonofabitch."

It did. The pain and stiffness were worse this morning. But Julian wasn't going to admit that. "It's nothing I can't handle. I don't need a week's medical leave."

"Most cops would be grateful for a paid week off."

"I'm not most cops. I have a job to do."

Irving nodded, grinned. "Exactly."

Completely surprised, Julian stood rooted to the spot while Irving popped the trunk on the Lincoln and lifted out a laptop computer and a box of file folders. Some of his black mood dissipated. "So this was intentional?"

"Where do you want this stuff?" Irving walked toward the passenger-side door of Julian's truck, arms loaded. "Of course it was intentional. With your cover likely blown and leaks around every damned corner, I figured you could use a little time away. If everyone thinks you're out of commission, so much the better."

Julian followed Irving, unlocked the door, cast a covert glance at the little Toyota four-door parked nearby, memorizing the license plate number. They were trying very hard not to look like they were watching him—and failing. He'd noticed them the moment he'd pulled into the lot. They probably thought they were being clever.

"Is Dyson in on this?"

"No. There wouldn't be much point to it if he were, would there?" Irving set the laptop and the box on the seat. "That's her rental over there."

Julian grabbed his window scraper and considered the possibilities as he walked with Irving over to the snowy mound that was a blue Honda Civic. With no obligations to the police department, he'd be free to work any angle he wanted without anyone at the FBI or DPD knowing what he was doing—and he'd could keep an eye on Tessa.

Irving was giving him the freedom he needed to close this case.

He glanced at the Toyota—they were still watching—and began to wipe the snow from the rental car's windshield. "I'll need you to keep me up-to-date, let me know what the team uncovers."

"Easy enough." Irving brushed snow off the trunk with his sleeve. "And I'll need you to make Ms. Novak's safety your top priority."

So that's what this was about. "Five rounds to the vest says I'm already doing that."

Irving nodded, walking around to the other side of the car, brushing snow aside as he went. "True enough. But I'm not talking about your vest. I'm talking about your dick. Don't think I don't know what's going on."

Julian brushed snow off the roof, fighting to keep his temper in check. "I'm pretty sure Ms. Novak is past the age of consent."

"She's also the victim of a series of violent crimes and more than a little vulnerable—not to mention utterly dependent on you. Don't take advantage of her, Darcangelo, or you'll have to answer to me."

It was a mark of how much Julian respected Irving that he kept his mouth shut. He fished in his pocket for Tessa's keys and opened the trunk.

Irving grabbed one of the suitcases, lifted it with a grunt. "Looks like we have spectators."

"I noticed." Julian took the other, his breath catching as the muscles in his back screamed in protest.

"So it *does* hurt." Irving chuckled. "I was beginning to think you were tougher than the rest of us."

"Happy now?"

They walked back to Julian's truck and slid the suitcases into the cab behind the seats. Then Julian shut the door and handed Irving the keys to the rental car.

"Do you think your coziness with Ms. Novak means she'll back off investigating you and the whole Zoryo mess?"

Julian met Irving's gaze. "Not a chance."

"Didn't think so."

The Toyota was still sitting there, its occupants watching him intently.

"Any idea who they are?" Julian pointed to the Toyota with a jerk of his head.

"The one in the passenger seat looks like Kara McMillan."

"The senator's wife." He ought to have known. "You got a ride back?"

"Got a black-and-white set to meet me in twenty at the rental place."

"Good enough." Julian rounded his vehicle, opened the driver's-side door. "Keep me posted. I'll be in touch."

Irving nodded and started back toward the rental. Then he turned to face Julian again. "Hey, Darcangelo. I'm damned glad neither of you got killed. Good work."

Julian acknowledged Irving's words with a nod, then slipped behind the wheel, keeping an eye on the rearview mirror and the little Toyota.

So Tessa's friends wanted a look at him. He would oblige them.

He waited for Irving to leave the lot, then kicked his truck into reverse and backed up until the he was bumper to bumper with the little car, trapping it. He climbed out of his truck and walked up to the driver's window.

With a buzz, the window lowered to reveal four pretty

women, one clearly pregnant. They looked guiltily at him, all except for the knockout blonde. Her gaze slid over him in blatant sexual appraisal, a little smile on her face.

And Julian knew.

Tessa had told her friends she'd had sex with him.

His anger at being watched temporarily overcome by an odd surge of male pride, he unzipped his jacket, let his holster show. Then he leaned down and pulled off his shades. "You ladies seen enough?"

Four heads nodded.

The strawberry blonde behind the wheel spoke. "We didn't mean to—"

"Sure you did. But don't worry. I won't hold *you* responsible."

"It's not Tessa's fault. She has no idea we're here." The woman who spoke had long, dark hair and sat in the front passenger seat. The senator's wife. "You won't take this out on her, will you?"

"Yes, Ms. McMillan, you better believe I will."

Then he turned and walked back to his truck, grinning.

TESSA HAD PLANNED to wait until she was good and ready to call her mother. But nothing was going as she'd planned, and Tessa knew she couldn't put it off any longer. Her mother's last message—and Sophie's news—made Tessa realize how truly frightened her mother was. It wasn't right to leave her hanging.

Tessa dialed her mother's phone number and paced the living room, a tight feeling in her stomach. What was she supposed to say to her mother after ten years of silence?

The phone rang once. Twice. Three times. She was about to hang up and call it an honest try when her mother answered.

"Hello?"

She hesitated. "Hi, Mom. It's Tessa."

"Oh! Oh, bless your heart, Tessa Marie! You're safe! Oh, thank God!" Her mother's voice grew tight, then moved away from the phone. "She's safe! This is her on the phone!"

Tessa could hear voices in the background. "Who's with you?"

"Just some friends from Denny's come over to cheer me up. We been watchin' the news, waitin' to see if they had anything new about you. I been worried sick to death!"

"You shouldn't worry, Mom. I'm fine. I'm safe."

"Where are you? Can I come—?"

"No, you can't, and I can't leave." The words came out quickly, sounding like a rejection, even to Tessa. She tried to explain. "It's not that I don't want to see you. It's that I can't. I'm in protective custody in a police safe house. I have to stay here until this is all over. The location is secret, so I can't have visitors."

"Oh. Oh, I see." Her mother tried to hide her disappointment, but Tessa heard it anyway. Then her mother raised her voice again, speaking to her friends across the room. "They got her in protective custody—that's what they call it when they put you in a secret police safe house."

"How long have you been living in Colorado?"

Tessa's new cell phone beeped, and she saw Kara was calling. Not wanting to be rude to her mother, she let the call go to voice mail.

"About three months. I wanted to get settled before I called you, didn't want to be a burden. I'm makin' pretty good money now your grandpa ain't drinkin' it." She gave a little laugh. "I got a nice apartment here in Aurora and a good job waitin' tables."

Tessa learned her mother also had a boyfriend, that she'd given up smoking, and was taking classes to prepare for her GED.

"You been an example to me, Tessa Marie. But I don't want to waste another second talkin' about me. I want to hear about you."

Then her mother peppered her with one question after the next until Tessa began to feel claustrophobic. Had someone really fired a gun at her? Wasn't she afraid? Did she like her job? Did they pay her well? Did she have good friends? Did she like Colorado? What did she think of the mountains? Had she learned to ski?

Tessa did her best to answer, an old and unwelcome feeling of annoyance welling up inside her. She bit back cutting responses, unnecessary words that would have hurt, fighting that part of her that wanted to lash out. Her mother wasn't doing anything wrong. There was no reason for Tessa to be short-tempered with her.

At the same time, Tessa would have been a liar if she'd said there wasn't a part of her that welcomed her mother's attention, even hungered for it. The sound of her mother's voice. Her soft Texas twang. Her good-natured cheerfulness. Her unmistakable pride in Tessa's accomplishments.

The conflicting emotions left Tessa feeling itchy in her own skin.

"You're such a pretty girl, Tessa. I saw your picture on the paper's website. I can't imagine men aren't beatin' down your door. You got someone special?"

I'm in love with a man who doesn't love me.

"No," Tessa said, unwilling and unable to discuss Julian with her mother. "No one. I don't really have time for dating."

"Well, I hope you can find time. There's more to life than earnin' a paycheck."

If her mother had said this before she'd met Julian, Tessa would have said something about how careers were a much better investment of one's time than any man. But now, faced with the cold inevitability of a life without Julian, she thought she understood what her mother meant.

JULIAN PULLED INTO his garage, feeling an odd mix of anticipation and irritability. He'd spent the past couple of hours shopping and thinking of ways to make Tessa pay for giving his whereabouts away to her friends—each more arousing than the next. The back of his truck was now full of groceries and household supplies, the sort of stuff he never kept on hand. And he was randy as a goat.

It looked like he'd bought the whole grocery store. He had taken up three carts, tipping a couple of store employees to help him push them along. Chicken, salmon, shrimp, spices, cooking oil, flour, sugar, pasta, eggs, butter, fresh fruits and vegetables, canned stuff, and God knew what else. He'd gotten a few practical things from the hardware store—a lock for his office door, tools to install it. But the fact that chocolate and a plant with pink flowers on it had made into his truck only proved that he was more in need of that medical leave than he'd like to admit. One of those bullets must have lodged in his brain.

And then there was the espresso machine.

He'd stopped to get her a vanilla latte, when he'd seen it sitting on display in the coffee shop. A few inquiries and helpful suggestions from the baristas, and he'd found himself purchasing the machine, together with fresh-ground coffee and several bottles of vanilla syrup.

He wasn't playing house, he told himself. This wasn't romance. He had no interest in the concerns of home and family. He didn't want to be someone's provider. He was just trying to make her stay more comfortable. After all, she had to eat.

The kitchen table and chairs would arrive later.

Okay, so perhaps some part of him wanted to make up for having been a jerk this morning. He'd come out of the bedroom, angry with himself for having lost control of the situation, and he'd taken it out on her. He'd gotten angrier when he realized he'd made her sore, angrier still when she lied about it, and even angrier when she'd tried to hide her hurt feelings behind a smart mouth. In the end, he'd managed to wipe the happiness off her face completely—which was no doubt exactly what some part of him had been trying to do.

He parked, carried a couple of sacks of groceries to the door, and punched in the access code. He had expected to find Tessa waiting nervously for him, sure she'd been tipped off by her friends that she was in big trouble. Instead she was in his bedroom having what sounded like a serious conversation on her new phone.

He carried in her computer and her box of files, then the

potted plant, then the espresso machine, and last the groceries, catching snatches of conversation.

"I'm glad you're settled, Mom. It sounds like you've made good friends."

Her mother?

Definitely a serious conversation.

He slipped out of his jacket, removed his harness, and set about putting the groceries away, unable to keep himself from overhearing. Or was he eavesdropping?

At one point in his life he'd have given anything to have a mother. Starved for a mother's love, he'd taken affection from any woman who would give it, picking flowers for his father's whores, defending them from his father's temper, even taking a blow or two that hadn't been intended for him. He wasn't sure when he'd realized they didn't care about him, that he was nothing more to them than the brat of the man who controlled their lives.

Was a similar scenario playing itself out here? Was that why he'd come home with flowers? Was that little boy still inside him starving for a woman's kindness?

You're a pathetic son of a bitch, Darcangelo.

"I need to go, Mom," he heard Tessa say, her words jerking him back to the moment. "I'll be in touch."

She stayed in the bedroom for a while, and he imagined she was crying. Then he heard her gasp and turned to find her staring into the kitchen, a look of amazement on her pretty face.

"Double coupons," he said, feeling at once stupid and intensely gratified.

"I was wondering what you were going to eat. That can of chicken noodle soup was mine." She smiled, then frowned. "Why are you putting the cereal with the lightbulbs?"

In short order, she'd taken over the entire procedure, emptying the bags into cupboards, explaining to him how a kitchen should be organized. He leaned against the refrigerator, crossed his arms over his chest, and watched as she bustled about, her delicious ass doing things for his underwear that Calvin Klein couldn't possibly have envisioned.

"I always put spices together with salt, pepper, and baking

goods and keep that near the stove," she said. Then she grabbed the dish soap from where he'd stowed it next to the salad dressing. "You definitely don't want to put cleaning products with . . . Oh, Julian! Azaleas!"

She'd discovered the plant.

She sniffed the blossoms. "Is this for me?"

"Guns and weights make for great decorating, but I thought you might appreciate something a little more feminine."

She looked up at him through those big blue eyes. "Thank you."

She set it on the windowsill, picked at the leaves, gave it a little drink of water, the attention she lavished on it making him smile. Then, when she seemed satisfied, she went back to putting groceries away, chattering about how canned goods should go together, apparently unaware that Julian didn't give a damn about green beans right now, but was biding his time until she got to the right bag.

But she found the espresso maker first. It made her squeal and earned him a quick kiss on the lips—nice, but not enough.

"You have no idea how addicted I am to this stuff." She held a bag of freshly ground coffee beans to her nose and inhaled with a moan. "Heaven!"

His patience snapped.

He walked across the room, fished around, and handed her a grocery bag she had yet to delve into. "Let's see if you know where to put these."

She reached in and pulled out a box of condoms. And another. And another. And another. And another.

"Extra Sensitive. Warming Sensations. Twisted Pleasures. Tropical Delight. Mint Tingles." She read off the names, then looked at him with a straight face. "I'd put them in the bedroom or the bathroom."

"That's where you're wrong." He wrapped an arm around her waist, and pulled her against him, reaching through the opening in the front of the boxer briefs she was wearing to stroke her. "They go here."

Her head fell back, and she whimpered. "I want to, but don't think I can!"

And he remembered. She was sore.

"No problem. The solution is on the tip of my tongue."

AN HOUR LATER, Tessa lay with her head on Julian's bare chest, her body still shaking from sensations that had felt almost too good to be true. He had a prehensile tongue—that was the only explanation.

"When you tell your friends about this, be sure to tell them about the swirly-sucky thing," he said, his hand stroking her hair, his voice rumbling deep in his chest. "If you're going to share details, you might as well be thorough."

"What's that supposed to mean?" She looked up at him, saw the knowing grin on his face, and knew exactly what it meant. Somehow he knew what she'd told Sophie. Heat flooded her face. "My new cell phone is bugged!"

"No. I met them all. Your friends were sitting in a little Toyota in the newspaper parking lot, watching every move I made. We had a nice little chat."

So that's why Kara had called five times.

"But how did they know where you . . . Oh! Oh, my God!" She remembered telling Sophie that Julian had gone to get her suitcases from the rental car. Sophie had clearly wasted no time in rounding up the others. "I'm so sorry! I didn't mean—"

In a blink he had her on her back, arms pinned above her head. "Rule number six: don't tell your friends where I'm going or what I'm doing. This time it was cute. Next time it might get someone killed."

CHAPTER 21

"The bottom line, Ms. Novak, is that Lonnie Zoryo wasn't just a rapist and killer. He was Darcangelo's best hope for bringing down the same ruthless trafficker who got away from him three years ago, a man who hasn't got a shred of respect for women or for human life. If we'd have allowed word of Zoryo's arrest and suicide to become public, we'd have greatly reduced his value to this investigation."

Tessa listened to Chief Irving's explanation, searching for the reassuring lines of right and wrong, for the simplicity of black and white, but finding only complicated shades of gray. "The autopsy report states that the suspect had a broken nose sustained during his arrest."

"The report also states that the suspect put a loaded 9mm semiauto to Special Agent Darcangelo's head. Zoryo's lucky he wasn't shot then and there. The information is in the report and in order, Ms. Novak."

So it seemed. And yet . . .

"You bent the rules, sir." She came right out with it. "You took public documents out of the system and hid them away, interfering with the free flow of information."

"Let me tell you what the free flow of information would have accomplished," Chief Irving said, his temper picking up a notch. "Absolutely nothing. The man we're looking for makes the average rapist/serial killer look like a choirboy. Temporarily withholding information gave us a week to follow the leads Zoryo gave us without tipping off his boss. We're trying to save more young women from suffering María Ruiz's fate, Ms. Novak."

"The end doesn't justify the means. We have laws—"

"Yes, we have laws. And so far the man who kidnapped, enslaved, and murdered María Ruiz has evaded every goddamned one of them."

"Is this standard procedure for the DPD?"

"Of course not. I think you know that." He paused for a moment. "And now I'm going to ask you to please withdraw your request for information, at least temporarily. If you want to crucify me and Special Agent Darcangelo and the entire DPD, that's fine, but wait until we've brought this bastard down."

Torn between her professional obligations and her own feelings, Tessa didn't answer right away. Tom would expect her to tell Chief Irving to stuff it and start asking questions *on* the record. If she hadn't watched María die, if she hadn't seen the brutality of it with her own eyes, she might have done just that. After all, the police department, under pressure from a federal agent, had covered up an arrest and a jail suicide.

But it wasn't as simple as that. Not by any means.

Just as this was no ordinary investigation for Tessa, it was clear to her that this wasn't a standard murder probe for the Denver police. What would she have done in Chief Irving's place? She didn't know.

"What about the deaths of his fellow agents three years ago? You must have reviewed his files if you agreed to take Special Agent Darcangelo into your department."

She'd asked the FBI spokeswoman for the same information an hour ago and had been told to go fish. State open-records statutes didn't apply to federal agencies, they'd reminded her. She'd been invited to resubmit her request under the Freedom of Information Act, but she'd already been told to expect a year's wait for a response.

"You'd best ask Darcangelo. I don't feel authorized to speak on that subject, apart from assuring you that after reviewing those events, I felt no qualms about working with him."

She drew a deep breath, took the plunge, imagining the way Tom's face would turn purple if he knew what she was about to say. "Okay, sir, I'll formally withdraw my open-records request on the condition that you honor your agreement to inform me fully once this investigation is wrapped up."

"You got it. Cop's honor."

Tessa hung up her phone, sat back in the kitchen chair, and gave a sigh of relief. If she'd have found out Julian had conducted an illegal arrest and interrogation, if she'd have discovered that he'd brutalized his suspect, if she'd found out that he was a liar . . .

Thank God she hadn't! She didn't want to know that the man who'd saved her life, the man who made such incredible love to her, the man she cherished was dirty.

She sipped her homemade latte, willed herself to relax, found she couldn't.

Reading the arrest and autopsy reports for this Zoryo jerk had given her a glimpse at what Julian did for a living, and the thought of anyone holding a loaded 9mm to his head sickened her. How could anyone cope with that kind of fear and danger every day of his life?

She guessed that explained why he was never without his gun, even in the bathroom, why he never seemed to sleep deeply, why even when he smiled there were shadows in his eyes.

She'd had sex with him a dozen times at least, had been staying with him since Friday night—three days and three nights—and yet she didn't know him that much better than she had before he'd brought her to the safety of his home.

Yes, she now knew he was a martial-arts expert, capable of killing with his bare hands. She knew he liked his salsa hot and ate peanut butter from the jar. She knew how to make his entire body jerk with a flick of her tongue. But she didn't know *him*. He never asked her for anything, never talked about himself or his life, never shared his concerns unless they related directly to her.

And yet, strangely, she felt closer to him than she'd ever felt to any man. Okay, so maybe that wasn't saying much. It could be that her feelings were nothing more than the intoxicating result of the physical intimacy they'd shared—hours of soul-shattering sex. Either way, she wished she could touch him inside, wished she could reach that part of him he kept hidden, wished she could drive the shadows away.

Sometimes when they made love, he seemed to open up, telling her with his body that he cared for her, seeming to need something from her that went beyond the physical. But no matter how passionate or expressive the sex, no matter the tone of his voice when he called her name, no matter how tightly he held her afterward, his reserve never completely slipped.

The space between them served as a constant reminder that this wasn't permanent. He would be leaving her life as soon as his assignment was completed. The distance left Tessa on the brink of a happiness she couldn't quite claim, knowing the loss that would follow. It was like standing on the edge of a sunrise.

She rose from the new kitchen table that served as her desk, walked to the back door, latte in hand, and tried to shift her thoughts back to her investigation. Outside, sunlight struck diamonds off the snow. Icicles dripped from the eaves. A crow stood in the bare branches of a small tree and croaked its opinions to the world.

She'd turned in today's article early, having had lots of time to work on it over the weekend while Julian was away. A follow-up to her last piece, it included an interview with the U.S. attorney's office, as well as State Department officials, describing the breadth of the human-trafficking problem, both in the United States and globally, and what steps the country was taking to combat it. The work had given her something to do during the long, dark hours besides wonder whether Julian was still alive.

He'd been out until the early morning hours both Saturday and Sunday nights doing God knows what. He'd come in, tense and angry, had taken a shower, and then made long, slow love to her. She'd given him everything she could, tried to ease the darkness she felt inside him, then had fallen into an exhausted sleep beside him.

And here she was thinking about him again when she should be working.

She turned back toward the table, set her latte down, and gathered up her notes from the State Department interview. Her gaze drifted to the page, and she smiled. The spokesman had used the term "Red China"—a phrase she'd thought had gone out of usage before she'd been born. How very Richard Nixon of him. Perhaps he'd been working for the feds since—

What color Mafia?

Syko's words came back to her in a rush of adrenaline.

Red Mafia.

She shuffled through documents until she pulled out Lonnie Zoryo's autopsy. Her gaze darted over the page, looking for one thing. And there it was.

"Birthplace," she read aloud. "Gzel, Russia."

She picked up her secured phone and dialed the State Department.

JULIAN PUNCHED IN his code, unlocked the door, and stepped inside, shutting out the night behind him. It felt so damned good to be home.

Home?

When had he started thinking of this place as home?

The answer slept on the couch, one small foot peeking out from under the quilt she'd taken from his bed. She'd been in the middle of reading something when she'd dozed off, the pages scattered across the floor beside her now-empty hand. Her face was relaxed, her lips parted, her lashes dark on her cheek. He'd told her more than once that she shouldn't wait up for him, but he knew she had trouble sleeping when he wasn't here.

He stood for a moment, watched her sleep, drank in the sight of her safe and sound, feeling the familiar stirring in his chest. Then he walked quietly off to the bathroom, threw his clothes into a heap on the floor, and stepped into a hot shower, his skin covered with the stink of cigarettes, cheap women's perfume, and violence.

Tonight had been productive, but it had also been hell. He'd spent the afternoon tracking down some of the leads he'd gotten from Dr. Norfolk and had located two more cribs, both of which seemed to be doing a booming business. He'd called them in to Irving, put them under surveillance, and then headed over to Pasha's. For a while he'd watched from the hotel room window down the street, where cameras were still rolling twenty-four-seven. Then, when the place looked busy, he'd walked across the parking lot and slipped into the slimy skin of Tony Corelli.

He'd watched Irena dance, bought her a couple of drinks, and was pushing her for a private invitation to the back rooms when a big brute with no neck and a thick Russian accent had come out of nowhere, grabbed Irena by the arm, and demanded she come with him.

"The lady's already occupied," Julian had said in his best Brooklyn Italian.

The bastard had snarled at him, called him a *huyesoska*—a cocksucker, if Julian remembered his Russian—then grabbed him by his leather jacket and tried to throw him out of his seat. Julian might have dropped him to the floor, but just as the bastard grabbed him, he'd caught a glimpse of the tattoo peeking out from beneath the asshole's shirt.

The Tiger.

He'd allowed himself to be flung aside, then watched as the man who was in all likelihood Zoryo's replacement dragged Irena through the crowd toward the guarded doors. The hopeless look in her eyes as she'd looked back at him had been a knife to his gut. He'd forced his feelings aside, shut his emotions down, and let her go.

The bartender, Chet, who'd become Tony's good friend, had taken pity on him, poured him a double whisky, and explained that Sergei was new and had taken a special interest in Irena. "But just between you and me, Tony, the guy's a prick!"

Julian had played pathetic, sucking down the whisky, angling for sympathy. "Man, you got all the luck. You've probably boned every dancer here, even my Irena. What's a guy gotta do to get some action?"

Chet had seemed to measure him. "I don't get you, Tony. You're young and good-looking. There's gotta be lots of women want to get in bed with you."

Julian had shaken his head, then looked guiltily up at Chet, his voice dropping to a whisper. "I like 'em young."

Ten minutes later he'd been scoping out hidden cameras and alarms as he was led behind the guarded doors to a private room in the back. Chet had set him up with a young, dark-haired girl who said her name was Luisa and who claimed to be from Florida but whose Spanish said Colombia. Julian had found himself in the situation he most dreaded—being put together with an underage victim he was expected to fuck.

So he'd acted like the part of the randy bastard, forking over the cash, running his gaze over the girl, trading filthy comments with the bouncer. Then the door had shut, leaving him alone with her in a room equipped for more horizontal entertainment than that offered out front. He'd pulled her onto the squeaky little cot, muttered reassurances in her ear, and after a few minutes of PG-rated cuddling, feigned a terminal case of limp dick. Cussing, he'd released her and pretended to be suffering the biggest humiliation of his life.

"Don't worry, baby. I ain't angry with you. Damn it! This never happens!" Feeling older than Father Time, he'd stroked her young cheek with his knuckles, watched the relief in her eyes. "Don't tell no one, okay, baby? I'd be real embarrassed. Here. This is for you—as long as you don't say nothing."

Knowing she'd keep his "secret," he'd handed her a hundred, waited a few more minutes, then strutted out into the hallway like a stallion who'd just had his favorite mare. He and Chet had spent the rest of the evening sharing dirty jokes and big grins, with Julian tipping in twenties.

"Man, if you need anything—*anything*—you come to Tony, and I'll set you up just like you did for me," he'd said.

He'd even bought Sergei a drink when the bastard reemerged an hour later, Irena nowhere in sight.

"Sorry for the misunderstanding, buddy," he'd said, giving Sergei a friendly slap on his beefy back.

Julian had left Pasha's hating himself but armed with the information he needed. The place was employing underage girls, some of them likely trafficked, and offering far more than private lap dances. It was likely also the hub of activity for Burien's Colorado empire—a distribution center, a money-laundering operation, a place where men with illegal tastes could meet their needs.

He'd called in a report to Irving, who'd started the process of obtaining a secret no-knock warrant. If Irena, Luisa, and the others could hold on, if they could just endure the night-mare a bit longer, he would get them out of there, even if he had to die to do it.

Julian scrubbed his skin, rinsed away the lather, searching for a feeling of clean that he couldn't find with soap. He turned off the water, wishing he could turn off his mind just as easily, then dried off and tied the towel around his waist.

He found her standing in the darkness outside the bath-room door, the quilt wrapped around her shoulders.

"Julian?" Tessa looked up at him, touched her palm to his cheek, her blue eyes warm with concern, as if she could see the tumult inside him.

She dropped the quilt to reveal the soft curves of her naked body. Then she pulled off his towel and knelt before him, tak-ing him into the wet heat of her mouth, the tug of her lips making him fill until he was thick and hard and burning.

He closed his eyes, buried his fingers in the silk of her hair, and accepted her offering, her hand and lips working in tan-dem, her tongue stroking him just where he was most sensi-tive. She was a fast learner. She'd taken to sex like a mermaid to water.

"Christ, Tessa!" He was lost in her, lost in what she did to him as she built the rhythm, stroke upon stroke, a strange pressure in his chest, his balls already drawn tight. He reached for the bedpost to steady himself, let her control the pace, the first glimmer of an orgasm burning inside him.

She was what he needed, what he wanted.

But not like this.

"Stop, honey! Stop!" He drew her to her feet, backed her up against the bed, following her down to the mattress in a tangle of limbs.

He kissed a path down her hot skin until she trembled, tasting her lips, sucking the tight velvet of her nipples, nipping her belly, hungry for her. She twisted and arched beneath him, her thighs parting as he nibbled and licked his way down her body. His fingers threaded a path through the dark blond curls of her muff, then he parted her lips and took her with his mouth.

Tessa clenched her fingers in Julian's hair as he made love to her with his mouth, his forearm pressed across her belly to control the bucking of her hips. His lips tugged at her. His mouth suckled her. And his tongue—God in heaven!

Nothing could possibly feel this good.

She heard him groan, heard a woman's panting cries, the sound of her own voice more animal than human. Then she felt his tongue thrust inside her—and she shattered.

"Julian!" She cried his name, her body coming apart in a liquid rush of bliss.

And then he was above her, inside her, the deep, rhythmic penetration of his cock driving her straight from one orgasm to the next, his kiss flooding her mouth with her own musky taste. She wrapped her legs around him, opened herself to him fully, took all she could from him, holding nothing back, as he spilled over the edge and, with a deep groan, poured himself into her.

CHAPTER 22

T ESSA WOKE THE next morning with Julian inside her, thrusting slowly into her from behind as she lay on her side, an orgasm already sliding through her as sweet as honey. Her gasp became a low, throaty moan.

He chuckled, pressed his lips to her hair. "You awake now?"

"Mm-hmm." She felt as lazy and contented as a kitten, her body replete.

But he wasn't through with her. He kept his pace slow, spreading kisses across her cheek, the whorl of her ear, her shoulder, his fingers twining with hers above her head. "What have you done to me, Tessa? I can't get enough of you! I can't get . . . enough!"

His breath broke on the last word as he shuddered and came.

They lay for a moment in silence, Tessa savoring the feeling of him inside her, of skin pressed against warm skin, his body hard and strong behind her. "Well," she said, at last. "I'm certainly going to expect more from an alarm clock from now on."

She took a shower and got dressed, while he headed first into his office and then downstairs for his daily workout. By the time he came upstairs, dressed in a pair of loose cotton pants that tied at the waist, his bare chest beaded with sweat, his hair hanging damp and loose around his shoulders, she had a pot of oatmeal waiting for them and had made a protein shake for him and a hot latte for herself.

"Breakfast of champions," she said, handing him the shake.

He took it from her, drank, a hint of confusion in his eyes, the same look she saw there anytime she did anything for him. Had no one ever done anything thoughtful for him before? She pressed a kiss to his breastbone, then sat and ate her breakfast.

He sat across from her, dug into his oatmeal. "So Irving tells me you withdrew your open-records request."

"For now." She stirred cinnamon and brown sugar into her oatmeal. "The FBI had nothing so say, so I'm resubmitting my request to them under federal statute."

He grinned. "The Federal Bureau of Obfuscation. We ask the questions, honey. We don't answer them."

Tessa didn't find that funny. "So you're not going to tell me?"

"Tell you what?"

"What happened three years ago?"

"Why is that important? Isn't it enough to know that whoever sent that anonymous letter is working for the bad guys?"

She swallowed the bite she'd just taken. "I feel like after everything we've been through, I have a right to know."

He gave a snort. "You think because we fuck a few times that I owe you my life story?"

His harsh words felt like a blow, the sting taking Tessa by surprise. She fought to hide her reaction. "No, I was thinking professionally—outside the bedroom. I'm holding off on the story at your request and Chief Irving's. I deserve the truth."

He rose, carried his bowl to the sink, then stood for a moment, leaning against the counter. "Okay, but this is off the record—absolutely one hundred percent. Agreed?"

"Agreed."

She watched him as he walked into the living room, sat on the sofa, angry tension rolling off him in waves. He rubbed his hands over his face, then rested his elbows on his knees.

"Three years ago, I was working under deep cover in Mexico, where I'd infiltrated an organization run by three crime bosses, one a Mexican official, the other two here in the U.S. I worked together with Mexican agents, at the same time supervising teams in two U.S. cities. It had taken five years to reach the point where I felt we were ready to take them—five years of watching these men brutalize women in every possible way, five years of pretending to be their friend, five years of pretending to like what they liked."

Tessa sensed the rage bottled inside him, saw regret in the hard lines of his face, and felt sick for him. "I can't imagine—"

"No, Goldilocks, you sure as hell can't." He gave a snort and glanced over at her, his eyes hard. Then he stood and walked over to the window, his back facing her, his bruises now purple. "We had synchronized our operations, planned to move at the exact same moment so that none of the suspects would have time to warn the others. We wanted to make a clean sweep, to bring them all down at once, shut down their entire operation."

She'd spent her career listening to people tell their secrets, listening as they laid bare their pain and shame, and she knew that whatever he was about to tell her wasn't a story he was used to sharing. She resisted the urge to comfort him, sure he would only push her away again.

Julian looked out the window, his gaze fixed on nothing in particular, black ice grinding in his gut. "Do you ever watch nature programs?"

She cleared her throat. "Nature programs?"

"I once saw a program where a lioness frightened a mother cheetah away from her cubs and then killed them. The filmmakers could have saved those cubs by firing a shot overhead to scare the lioness away, but they didn't. They sat and watched and filmed as the lioness killed the cheetah babies one by one. They did their job."

"Oh, Julian!"

He knew she'd understood the metaphor, knew there were tears in her eyes, but he kept going. She'd wanted to know the truth, after all. She was getting the truth.

"As we were getting in position, some of my suspect's men returned with three teenage girls they'd taken from a country village. I knew what was going to happen to them, and I wanted to stop it. It didn't seem right that anyone else should suffer, not when we had the hacienda surrounded and were armed like the fucking Marines. And so I notified our teams to move early."

He remembered the satisfaction of landing a slug in the chest of García's right-hand man, of smelling gunpowder instead of García's nauseating cologne, of seeing García in full restraints, gibbering in the back of a police van.

"Our operation went off without a hitch. The bad guy and his goons went to prison. The girls were rescued and sent home, terrified but untouched."

"You saved them." She stood behind him now.

He spun about to face her, shouted at her. "I did nothing! Our second team got their guy, too, but the third team wasn't so lucky. Somehow, someone got off word to L.A., giving him enough time to get away. His thugs shot three agents, one of whom was the woman I was . . . seeing at the time. Margaux survived to hate my guts. The other two didn't. I resigned the next day. It was my call, and I blew it. If I'd waited, if I hadn't lost control of my emotions—"

"Those girls would have suffered horribly." She touched a hand to his face, tears spilling down her cheeks, offering him an absolution he didn't deserve.

He was too selfish to push her away. Still, he had to drive his point home. "If I had waited, María Ruiz and so many like her might still be safe and alive. You wouldn't be going through this. Because of me, he got away, Tessa. It's that simple."

"It's not simple at all, Julian." Her fingers slid into his sweat-damp hair, pulled his face down to hers, her lips brushing softly over his.

For a moment, he let her kiss him, his chest tight, everything inside him straining toward the purification of her touch, toward the sweet forgetfulness he always found with her. But Burien was still out there, still hurting women, still killing.

And it was Julian's fault.

"Stop, Tessa." He set her away from him. "I have to go."

Then he walked off toward the shower, leaving her to her tears.

"SO HE SAYS whoever sent that 'news tip' is working for the bad guys?" Sophie asked.

"That's what he says, and I believe him. I just wish he'd tell me exactly who the bad guy is so I could splash his picture on page one." She hated the bastard—whoever he was—not only for the harm he'd done to women but also for the torment he'd laid upon Julian's shoulders.

"Well," Sophie said, her voice hinting that she had a surprise up her sleeve, "remember Chris, that guy I went out with at the *Post* who did the four-part series on the Red Mafia? I managed to talk him out of his source in Moscow. Okay, so I promised to go out with him again, but, hey, what are friends for? He wasn't that bad of a kisser."

"Oh, my God, Sophie!" Tessa felt her spirits lift. "That's incredible! Bless your heart!"

"I'm e-mailing you the number now. Just remember there's a ten-hour time difference between Denver and Moscow. Don't wake the poor guy up in the middle of the night."

"Ten-hour time difference. That means it's almost five a.m. there right now."

"Does this mean I'm forgiven?" Sophie asked. "We didn't mean to get you into hot water."

"I don't know. He wasn't happy about it. Secrecy is survival in his business."

"I hope he wasn't too angry with you."

Tessa remembered the groceries, the espresso machine, the azalea, and the hours of mind-blowing oral sex that had followed.

When you tell your friends about this, be sure to tell them about the swirly-sucky thing. If you're going to share details, you might as well be thorough.

She fought to keep the tone of her voice grave. Sophie deserved to feel some guilt, after all. "I got through it."

"Holly said she thought he would probably punish you with his tongue."

Tessa felt herself blush. "Actually, he didn't bring the four of you up until after he was finished using his tongue."

Sophie groaned. "God, Tess, if it weren't for the murder and mayhem, I'd say you were really lucky."

Tessa felt her spirits slip again. Was she lucky? Certainly, she was lucky to be alive. She was lucky to have a man like Julian protecting her. She was lucky to spend nights in his bed, to feel the shattering heat of his touch. But he didn't love her.

You think because we fuck a few times that I owe you my life story?

Some stubborn part of her wanted to believe he hadn't meant it the way it had seemed. He'd lashed out at her only because answering her question meant dragging his soul over barbed wire. Three years ago, he'd made a decision anyone with a heart would have made—he'd decided to save those girls. But he'd paid dearly for it, losing his girlfriend, two of his men, his job. He'd obviously spent every day since blaming himself, carrying the weight of the killer's crimes on his own shoulders.

Was that why he pretended not to have feelings? Was that why he was so determined not to get too involved with a woman? And who was this bitch Margaux who'd left Julian to deal with his anguish and regret alone?

Margaux couldn't have loved him, not the way Tessa loved him.

"Yeah, I am lucky," Tessa said at last.

Then Sophie recounted the entire spying-in-the-parking-lot incident, from the moment Julian had arrived in his truck to the moment they realized he'd trapped them to the smile on his face as he'd walked away. "He is the hottest guy I have *ever* seen. Holly said so, too, though I believe she used the word 'fuckable.'"

"That sounds like Horny Holly."

There was noise in the background—the harmonious sound of Tom's shouting.

"Oh, crud, I have to go. Tom just went ballistic over my headline."

"Sorry I'm not there. Good luck, and thanks so much, Sophie."

Tessa hung up, walked back to the table, set the cell phone aside, and downloaded her e-mail, wondering what time she should call this source in Moscow and what, exactly, she should ask him. Perhaps she could ask him about Lonnie Zoryo, see if he knew whether Zoryo had ties to any known criminal—

Tessa stared at the screen of her laptop, felt her stomach knot. There in her in-box was Sophie's message—together with five from an address she didn't recognize. They looked like spam, but the subject line read, "TESSA WILL SUFFER."

Her hand moving almost of its own volition, she clicked on one of the messages and felt the blood rush from her head.

JULIAN GUNNED HIS truck into the garage, the black mood he'd been in all day growing darker by the moment, his own words a knife to whatever was left of his conscience.

You think because we fuck a few times that I owe you my life story?

She'd reacted as if he'd hit her, her head snapping back, her eyes going wide. Then she'd sucked up her emotions and let it go, somehow finding it within her to shed tears for him, to touch him, to kiss him. As if he'd needed her to comfort him. As if he deserved her compassion. As if she could change what was inside him. And what had he done?

He'd pushed her away.

It only proves what you've known all along, asshole. No picket fence.

He parked, closed the garage, keyed in his code, telling himself it was stupid for him to have come home. He ought to be heading to Pasha's or looking at surveillance tape or casing out one of the empty warehouses Irving's men had identified. An apology wouldn't make a goddamned bit of difference in the long run, because he'd only hurt her again. Better to quit while he was behind.

Except that he needed to be near her.

He knew something was wrong the moment he opened the door. Tessa didn't meet him or call out a greeting. The house was dark and silent. The stove was cold. Her computer sat on the table in sleep mode, its screen dark, the ON button pulsing green.

Then he heard a choking sound.

"Tessa?" His gun was out in a heartbeat. He moved quickly down the hallway to find the door to the bathroom shut and locked. "Are you all right?"

She didn't answer. And then he understood why.

She was throwing up.

He tucked his gun back in its holster, stood there while the toilet flushed, waited for her to open the door. But she didn't. "Are you sick?"

Brilliant question, Darcangelo.

And then it struck him. Maybe she was pregnant. But it was too soon for her to be showing symptoms, wasn't it?

He did some quick math, tried to figure out how soon she would know, and realized he didn't know a damned useful thing about pregnancy or her cycle—where her eggs had been or when. The only thing he knew for certain is that he'd more than done his part to start a baby boom.

"Christ!" He waited for her to answer, wanting to rip the door off its hinges. "If you don't talk to me, I'm going to pick the lock!"

The door opened with a soft *click*.

Tessa stood there, her face white as a sheet, her eyes haunted.

He felt her forehead for fever. She was ice cold. "What's wrong, honey?"

She looked up at him, her voice almost a whisper. "There were pictures—in my e-mail."

"Son of a *bitch!*" Julian turned and strode in a hot rage down the hallway to the dining room, certain he knew exactly what kind of pictures could have upset her so much. He grabbed her mouse, woke the drowsy machine—and felt his gorge rise.

There on the screen was a digitally altered image of Tessa suffering unspeakable horror.

Five messages. Twenty images. A repertoire of cruelty.

Burien had Wyatt's photograph of Tessa in the tub and was making the most of it, dredging up some of Zoryo's finest work and doctoring Tessa's face onto the bodies of other victims. The bastard was trying to frighten her, showing her just what he hoped to do to her.

"TESSA WILL SUFFER," read the subject line.

Over my dead body, Burien.

Fighting to control his fury, Julian tossed his jacket aside, unhooked his harness, and walked back to the bedroom. He needed to call Dyson, get someone started tracing these e-mails—probably a hopeless task. But first he needed to make sure Tessa was all right.

He draped his harness over the footboard of his bed and strode over to the bathroom. She was brushing her teeth, her motions wooden. He stroked her hair until she was done, then wrapped an arm around her shoulders, led her to the bed, and drew her down onto the quilt beside him, pulling her into his arms. "Come here."

Tessa heard the steady thrum of Julian's heartbeat, felt the strength of his arms around her, and gradually the sharpest edge of her terror receded. "Those pictures—that was all real, wasn't it?"

"Yes." Julian's voice was deep, soft. "That was Zoryo's handiwork."

The man Julian had arrested. The man who'd held a gun to Julian's head. The man who'd committed suicide in prison.

"I'm glad you caught him. I'm glad he's dead." She said it, and she meant it, the rules be damned. And then she had to get it out. "That's what his boss plans to do to me."

"He's never going to have the chance." Julian kissed her hair. "He won't get near you."

She pressed herself deeper into his chest, tried to force the images from her mind, the brutality beyond anything she could have imagined. "God, I've been so stupid!"

"No, you haven't."

"I had no idea, Julian. I didn't know anyone could do anything so terrible to a woman!" She shuddered, a wave of revulsion, of sheer terror, passing through her.

He held her closer. "Try not to think about it. Just let it go."

"Those poor women!" She squeezed her eyes shut. "I can't get the images out of my head! How do I make them go away?"

And then it hit her.

She sat up, stared at him. "My God, Julian, you're exposed to this every day! How do you—?"

He pressed a finger against her lips. "It's my job, Tessa."

Something about the way he said it—the quiet strength, the resignation, the hint of buried despair—closed around her heart like a fist. "It hurts you."

He sat up, rested his weight on one hand. "Somebody has to do it, and I'm better suited to it than most men."

She ran a hand up his arm. "You're as human as any man, Julian. You have the same right to feel as everyone else."

"Don't try to figure me out, Tessa." He pushed off the bed, pulling away from her, a dark scowl on his face, an edge to his voice. "It's a waste of your time."

She hopped off the bed, cut him off at the door, her hand pressed against his chest to stop him. "Don't try to push me away! It's my time to waste."

"Tessa!" One word, her name—a low growl of warning.

A muscle clenched in his jaw, his heart pounding against her palm.

She held her ground. "There's nothing inside you that scares me, Julian."

She saw in his eyes the moment his control snapped. In a heartbeat, she found herself pinned beneath him on the floor, her arms stretched over her head, her wrists cuffed by one big hand. He glared down at her, an almost feral look on his face, his thighs forcing hers apart. "You really want to know what's inside me?"

Then his mouth closed over hers in a brutal, punishing kiss.

CHAPTER 23

TESSA DIDN'T OBJECT. Not when he forced his tongue roughly into her mouth. Not when he used his free hand to rip open her blouse, scattering buttons across the floor. Not when he ground his pelvis against hers, thrusting in crude imitation of sex.

He meant to frighten her, she knew. He wanted to show her how violent he could be, how badly he could hurt her. And yet it was himself he was hurting.

Tears slipped from the corner of her eyes down her temples as she yielded her body to his rage, her heart aching for him. Somehow he'd gotten her pants off and was now yanking his zipper down over the bulge of his erection. Then he buried himself inside her, pounded his fury and desperation into her without finesse or gentleness.

It was over quickly.

He groaned, shuddered, then sank against her, his face buried in the crook of her neck, his breath coming fast and heavy. For a moment he lay against her. "Jesus God!"

It was a cry of remorse. He released her wrists, started to pull away, but she held him fast, kissing his hair, her tears falling freely now.

"I'm okay, Julian," she said, wanting to reassure him. "It's all right."

"I'm so sorry! Christ!" He raised his head, looked down at her, the anguish in his blue eyes like a knife through her chest. He wiped the tears from her cheek, then lifted himself from her, zipped his jeans, and dropped back against the footboard, his eyes squeezed shut.

His voice when he finally spoke was that of a stranger. "My father was a pimp."

Tessa sat up slowly, tried to take in what he'd just told her, waited for him to say more, covering herself with what was left of her blouse.

"He took me from my mother when she divorced him and hightailed it across the border. I was two." He gave a cruel laugh. "It's not that he wanted me with him—far from it. He just wanted to hurt her. I didn't know that at the time, of course.

"I'm not sure how my father got into the flesh trade. I guess being on the lam he didn't have a lot of career options. We moved from barrio to barrio—him, me, and his ever-changing stable of *putas*. He dumped me in their laps, left them to raise me while he drank himself slowly to death and gambled the pesos they earned for him.

"Some felt sorry for me—poor little American boy with a real *cabrón* for a father. Others hated me because they hated him. What an idiot I must have seemed to them—bringing them flowers, drawing pictures for them, offering them seashells and other stupid gifts."

Tessa gulped back a sob. Whatever she had expected him to tell her, it hadn't been anything like this. It was no wonder he held himself back. He'd grown up unloved and utterly alone. Who had cared for him when he was sick? Who had comforted him at night when he'd had bad dreams? Who had made sure he got a bath and clean clothes?

At least she'd had her mother.

"Sometimes I went to school. Sometimes I didn't. As I got older, I spent more time on the streets. I learned to speak Mexican Spanish like a native, and I learned to fight dirty. My old man and I got into more than a few scrapes, usually over him roughing up one of his girls. He kicked the shit out of me more than once, but by the time I was fifteen, I was more than able to return the favor."

Julian had never told a soul the details of his childhood, not Margaux, not even Dyson. He had no idea why he was telling Tessa now, except that he owed her the truth. Hell, after what he'd just done to her, he owed her his balls on a platter.

God! Christ! Son of a bitch!

"I grew up thinking it was normal to have a dozen women hanging around the house half dressed, to wake up and find my father hung over with two women in his bed. But listen to me—I'm talking about it as if growing up with a house full of whores was a *bad* thing. It wasn't, not always. I got laid *a lot*. I learned what a good blow job was when I was fourteen. By the time I was sixteen, I'd had more lessons in female anatomy than the average gynecologist."

"Oh, Julian!"

He could tell from her voice that she was in tears, but he couldn't look at her face. He couldn't bear to see the truth of what he'd just done to her written there.

"The first woman I had a crush on was one of my father's girls. Only after I'd found her in his bed did it dawn on me that she wasn't free to live her life the way she wanted. It was then I finally understood the reality of what my father did for a living. He owned women, controlled them, exploited them sexually for his own profit. I hated him from that moment forward."

Julian told her how he'd begun to spend more time on the streets, looking for a piece of the action to call his own, venting his rage on the world, eventually getting into a fight with a man over a girl he'd met in a cantina. He'd slammed his fist into the man's face, accidentally killing him and landing a thirty-year prison sentence. He'd resigned himself to living and dying behind bars, when he'd gotten an offer from the FBI he couldn't refuse.

"They pulled me out, shipped me stateside, and gave me a new life. I got my GED, mastered aikido, learned how to shoot. And I learned the truth about my mother. They showed me the crime files, the newspaper articles, nurturing my hatred for my father and all men like him. By the time they sent me back to Mexico two years later, I was a weapon, loaded and ready to go off. I might have gone after my old man, tried to bring him down, but he'd taken the easy way out and drunk himself to death. I spat on his grave."

He heard Tessa sniff, then clear her throat. "What about your mother? You found her, didn't you? Working for the FBI—"

"Yeah. I found her. She died in car accident six years after I was taken. Nice Irish girl. The FBI had a thick file on the case. She never quit looking for me." Julian felt strangely naked and spent, lost in memories he wished to God weren't his. "My father always told me she was a whore. Turns out the only thing she did wrong in her entire life was fall in love with him."

Deeply weary, Julian closed his eyes, and they sat for a moment in silence.

He heard her shift, felt her breath shiver across his cheek. "I'm so sorry, Julian!"

Then her lips brushed over his, as soft as the touch of a butterfly's wings, her hands resting on his shoulders for balance as she straddled him. But he didn't deserve this—her gentleness, her tears, her forgiveness.

"Tessa, don't!" He turned his head away.

"Why not? Because you don't want me to touch you? I know that's not true." She slid a hand down his chest, pressed her palm against his thudding heart.

He opened his eyes, grabbed her shoulders, gave her a little shake, pressure building in his chest. "Didn't you hear a goddamned thing I just said? I'm a convicted killer! I've fucked more whores than you have pairs of shoes! I've spent my life keeping company with the worst of the worst—rapists, traffickers, stone-cold killers!"

She touched a soft hand to his cheek, tears streaming down her sweet face. "Maybe so, but that's not who you are. You held me when I was afraid, stayed with me. You took bullets for me. You make me feel things no man has ever made me feel. You're not a monster!"

The pressure in his chest almost beyond bearing, Julian could scarcely speak. "You can say that—after what I just did to you?"

She gave him a shaky smile. "And what do you think you did? Do you think you raped me? You big idiot! You didn't take anything from me I wasn't willing to give. I love you, Julian."

Her words shocked him, drove the breath from his lungs. For a moment he could do nothing but stare at her. Then he gritted his teeth, forced out the words. "I am *not* worth this!"

"God, for a special agent you sure are a fraidy cat." Then she leaned into his chest, wrapped her arms around him, and kissed him.

With a groan, Julian felt the torrent inside him rise up black and venomous—and break like a wave against her gentle strength.

He opened his mouth to her, gave in to her touch, accepted her passion. Her lips never left his as her hand slid up his thigh, fought with his zipper, stroked him to readiness. Then she lowered herself onto him, taking him with her heat, filling the bleak emptiness inside him, penetrating his darkness.

Musk and salt. Mingled cries. Shattering pleasure.

A baptism of tears, of fire, of light.

Redemption.

She collapsed against him, her head resting on his shoulder, her breath coming in shudders. Julian held her, kissed her hair, felt his own heartbeat slow. And for the first time in as long as he could remember, he felt clean.

THEY ATE A quiet dinner of sushi, sharing a single plate. Then they took a shower and crawled back into bed, where Julian made long, slow love to Tessa, showing her all the finesse and gentleness he'd denied her in his rage, giving back everything he had taken.

Now Tessa lay sleepless in the dark, her head on Julian's chest, his heartbeat strong, his breathing deep and even as he slept. She'd never known him to sleep so deeply and realized he must be exhausted. He'd revealed things he'd never told another human being, baring his soul to her out of a mistaken sense of guilt. And what he'd told her had broken her heart.

She imagined a tiny boy torn from his mother's arms, doomed to grow up without love amid squalor, depravity, and violence. She imagined the terror and grief of a young mother, doomed never to see the child she loved again, not even knowing if her son were still alive. The unbearable sadness of it all welled up inside her.

"I love him," she whispered to the darkness, not realizing she'd spoken until she heard her own voice. "I'll watch over him."

Something in the darkness seemed to ease.

Then, at last, she, too, fell asleep.

TESSA SIPPED HER latte and sorted through documents on her computer, reading the criminal histories of the nearly 100 known Red Mafia leaders suspected to be operating in the United States. She'd already eliminated those who dealt only in drugs or weapons, but that still left more than 60 men, all of whom had some alleged involvement in prostitution or pornography.

"What a bunch of losers," she muttered to herself.

She heard a "humph" and glanced up to find Julian standing at the other end of the table, arms crossed over his bare chest, a frown on his face—his surliness surely proof that she was on the right track. He'd been hovering nearby from the moment he'd heard her on the phone with Moscow this morning.

Still, she couldn't feel irritated with him. It was just his way of protecting her—one of the many ways he'd showed her today that he cared for her. He'd gotten up early and had already forwarded the threatening e-mails to his own computer and purged them from hers by the time she'd opened her eyes. Then he'd woken her up with a kiss and a homemade latte. While she'd made breakfast, he'd rigged her e-mail account so that it would reject all e-mail from unknown addresses, ensuring she wouldn't get any more unwelcome surprises over the Internet.

Even so, it wasn't easy to sit down at her computer and look at the screen. She'd found herself wondering if Kara's mother knew any weird New Age cleansing ceremonies for laptops.

She glanced up at Julian. "You know, instead of glowering at me, you could just tell me who the bad guy is."

His scowl deepened. "Not a chance. If you write an article about him, you'll only send him into hiding, and I'll have to start from square one."

"What if we published every known fact about him—his picture, his mother's maiden name, his favorite color, his hometown? Wouldn't that make it impossible for him to hide?"

He gave a snort. "You think underground crime lords eat at Burger King and stroll down Main Street? These guys keep to the shadows, Tessa. Most of their men don't even know what they look like. You can't flush them out with bad publicity."

She wasn't convinced. "Do you know what he looks like?"

He hesitated. "Yes."

Then a sound she'd never heard before interrupted them— a high-pitched metallic whine.

The alarm!

In an instant, Julian was on his feet and reaching for his gun. "Get downstairs! Arm yourself, and hide!"

Heart thumping, Tessa made a dash for the stairs. She'd made it halfway down, when she heard Julian cut loose with a stream of profanity.

The alarm went silent.

"What the fuck are you doing here?" He sounded furious.

A woman answered. "Thanks for the welcome. Dyson sent me. He said you'd had some e-mail trouble."

Tessa walked back up the stairs in time to see a tall, gorgeous redhead walk through the front door—and kiss Julian full on the mouth.

So THIS WAS Margaux. Dressed in tight jeans, cowboy boots, and a red leather jacket, she was almost as tall as Julian, her body slender and athletic. With high cheekbones, a slim nose, and full lips, she looked like a runway model—except for the gun she carried in a hip holster.

Tessa couldn't stand her.

It wasn't just that Margaux had kissed Julian or that she'd once been his lover or that she'd hurt him or that she was sexy and beautiful. It was all of those things together—and something more.

Green isn't your color, girl.

Tessa tried to force aside her irrational jealousy. After all, it was obvious that Margaux and Julian wanted nothing to do with one another. They were barely able to be civil to one another. Then again, what woman wouldn't be jealous? Margaux was an Amazon. She radiated sophistication and sexuality. Men probably flocked to her like ants to apple butter.

Margaux had shaken her hand, given her a warm smile. "You must be the little reporter. And you are little, aren't you?"

Tessa had put on her sweetest smile. "I imagine that even most men seem short to a big woman like you."

Margaux had glanced pointedly at Julian. "Most men come up short one way or another, that's for sure."

Tessa had wanted to smack her. "Maybe it's not the men. Maybe it's the company. Certainly, Julian has never failed to rise to the occasion."

Margaux had shot her a look of pure venom, then she'd gone off with Julian to his office, where the two of them now sat behind the closed door, presumably trying to trace the e-mails. This was Margaux's area of expertise, and according to Margaux at least, she was very good at it. Tessa thought she was probably very good at other things, too.

With no small amount of discipline, Tessa turned her mind back to her work, reading one by one through the criminal CVs of guys with names like Vladimir, Anatoli, Aleksander, and Pavel, looking for any possible tie to Colorado, human trafficking, or a deceased creep known as Lonnie Zoryo. She'd already tried searching for those terms and had turned up nothing. So much for taking shortcuts.

Some guy named Yuri with a bad cocaine habit. One Todor

who was only nineteen. The thousandth Aleksander. One Ilya who was nearing seventy. An Alexi.

She scrolled through the document, about to move on, when she saw it: Gzel, Russia.

For a moment she sat, frozen. Then she grabbed for her file on Zoryo, flipped through the pages searching for the autopsy report and quickly scanned it, her adrenaline humming.

"Birthplace: Gzel, Russia."

Could it be a coincidence? She glanced back at her computer screen, checked birth dates—1952 and 1949. They were almost the same age, Zoryo a few years older. Could they have known each other? And then she found the clincher.

Both had been arrested during a police raid in Moscow on May 14, 1982.

Heart pounding, she looked at her watch and saw that it was midnight in Moscow. Certain her source must be asleep, she picked up her phone and called the newsroom instead. "Sophie, I think I found him. I think the man I'm looking for is named Alexi Burien."

"WHOEVER DID THIS knows exactly what they're doing. Burien must have one hell of a tech expert. This is going to take an eternity to unravel—if it's even possible."

Julian leaned back against the door, arms crossed over his chest, fighting his growing irritation as he watched Margaux work. Why in the hell had Dyson sent her? They'd both agreed that Julian would forward the e-mails to whichever expert Dyson assigned to track them. Perhaps Dyson was checking up on him, making sure he was keeping out of trouble. Or perhaps Margaux had talked Dyson into giving her his address in order to make sure he wasn't holding out on her again as he had with Zoryo.

Thank goodness he had his files on Pasha's encrypted under another username.

He decided to come right out with it. "Why are you here?"

Margaux slipped a CD into his computer, dragged the

e-mails onto it, and clicked BURN. "Unhappy to see me?"

"Cut out the games. Did Dyson send you, or was this your idea?"

She shrugged. "It was my idea. I have to admit I was curious to meet this reporter of yours. She is, after all, the first woman you've hooked up with since I dumped you."

His irritation grew into real anger. "So you managed to talk Dyson out of my location and came out here just to check out Tessa?"

She popped the finished CD from his computer, slid it into a crystal case, and dropped it into her purse. "I would never have imagined you'd get involved with a woman like her—girly, unsophisticated, inexperienced. She's probably a great breeder, though."

So Margaux was jealous. She'd always felt uncomfortable about her height. "You mean 'feminine, genuine, and relatively innocent'? Leave her alone, Margaux."

"Oooh, listen to you! Mr. Protective. You really have gone over the edge." Margaux stood and walked to the door. "Don't worry. I'll keep my claws off your little toy."

Julian followed Margaux down the hallway, wondering how he could ever have thought her attractive. What he'd once found stunning now seemed vulgar, tawdry, even cheap. There was nothing soft or tender about her, not a warm, caring impulse in her body. She lived for the thrill of the hunt, for the adrenaline of the bust, for the kick of a hard orgasm.

Which pretty much describes you, too, Darcangelo.

No, not anymore.

Tessa glanced up at him, talking to someone on the phone, a nervous look on her face.

"I need to go, Sophie. Thanks. I'll call you tomorrow." She set the phone aside. "Were you able to trace it?"

Julian shook his head. "I'm not sure we ever will."

"We'll get to work on it, but it's not like it's a huge priority." Margaux glanced at her watch, then over at Tessa. "It's just a few threatening e-mails. Compared to most of the shit we see, it's nothing. But then, I suppose to a sheltered debutante like you—"

"Margaux." Julian cut her off.

"It's okay, Julian." Tessa laid her hand on his arm. "It's obvious that although Margaux might know a great deal about computers and violence, she doesn't know anything about good manners. Nor does she know a thing about me. For that reason alone, her attempts to insult me only make her look pathetic and desperate."

Margaux laughed, but her face flushed an angry red. "Your kitten's got claws."

"Let me see you out." Julian strode to the front door, opened it.

Margaux took the hint and followed. "Good to see you again, babe."

Julian caught her wrist before she could grab his crotch. "Give Dyson my regards."

CHAPTER 24

"YOU KNOW HOW most of the time you plumb a man's depths and find yourself stranded at the bottom of a Dixie cup?"

Tessa couldn't help but laugh at her mother's folksy but descriptive metaphor. She'd never realized what a funny sense of humor her mother had. "Yes, I know that feeling."

"Well, Frank ain't like that. He's always got somethin' important to say. He's real respectful to women, sweet as sugar to me. But I don't know—gettin' married at my age?"

"You're only forty-two, Mom. That's not exactly old." Tessa fluffed up the pillow she'd propped behind her back and switched the phone to her other hand. She felt decadently lazy, still lounging naked in bed when it was almost noon on a workday. "Do you love him?"

"Yeah, I guess I do. But I spent my whole life takin' care of other people, and I don't want to saddle myself—" Her mother's voice trailed away. "Oh, Tessa, I didn't mean you! I never felt burdened by you!"

Tessa couldn't fathom how that could be true, and she felt touched somehow that her mother still loved her enough to try to spare her feelings—as if Tessa didn't already know that her existence had been a terrible mistake. "You were talking about Grandpa."

"That's right. I just set out on my own, after all. I'm afraid to get tied down too soon. I'm afraid of makin' a mistake."

Tessa understood that feeling, too. "Is Frank willing to give you some time?"

Julian opened the bathroom door and walked out, a damp towel around his waist, his hair hanging wet around his shoulders. He walked over to his closet and dropped the towel on the floor. The rounded muscles of his tight ass shifted as he walked into the closet and pulled a pair of jeans off a hanger. Then he bent down and stepped into them, giving her a quick glimpse of his heavy testicles before the faded denim concealed him from view.

"Are you there, Tessa?"

"Oh, yes, Mom. Sorry. I got distracted for a moment."

Julian glanced at her over his shoulder, a smug grin on his face.

She stuck her tongue out at him—which only made his grin wider.

He turned around and slowly unzipped his fly in a mini striptease, leaving his cock to hang free, thick and veined. Then he turned around and slowly pushed the jeans down his hips, baring his delicious ass again with a naughty bump-and-grind motion.

Tessa's mind went blank. She mumbled something to her mother. "Uh-huh."

He leaned down, dug her foot out from beneath a tangle of sheets and blankets, and began to kiss and nibble her toes. Shivers ran up her leg, leaving goose bumps on her skin.

"Frank's takin' me to a Halloween party tonight. Everyone from Denny's is gettin' together at the bowlin' alley."

"That sounds fun." Tessa watched as he kissed and licked his way up her calf to her knee, felt herself grow wet. "Are you going to wear costumes?"

"One of the girls is pregnant, and she's comin' as a nun. I don't know about the rest of us. I'm just too old for that stuff."

Julian's lips, so hot and smooth, reached her inner thigh. He kissed her skin, nipped her with his teeth, soothed her with his tongue.

"N-no, you're not, Mom." It was hard to think, hard to breathe. "I'm sorry, Mom. I have to go. No, everything's fine. I'll call you again tomorrow."

Tessa dropped the phone, met his gaze, saw the heat in his eyes. Desire licked hot through her belly. "Now!"

He chuckled, rose up, his cock now fully erect. His hands closed around her ankles, and he dragged her slowly toward him across the bed, forcing her legs wide apart. Then he sank down and tasted a path up her other leg until his breath was hot between her thighs.

She buried her fingers in his wet hair, whimpered. "Please, oh, please, Julian!"

He parted her lips with his fingers and took her with his mouth, flicking her with his tongue, tugging on her clitoris with his lips, tasting her wetness. And then he did it—the sucky-swirly thing—and slid a finger deep inside her.

She came hard and fast, exploding against his mouth, the rush of pleasure almost too intense to bear, as he kept up the rhythm, drawing out her climax, making it last.

For a moment she lay there, floating. Then she heard Julian swear and opened her eyes to see him fighting to get a condom over his erection. And then he was inside her, driving into her with strong, sure strokes, his lips closing over hers, carrying her musky taste into her mouth.

She moaned, met him thrust for thrust, wrapping her legs around him, her hunger building to a second peak with such speed and ferocity that it astonished her. But this time he went over the edge, too, soaring into the void with her.

They lay there for a moment, panting.

"So," he said at last, "how about for Halloween, you dress up as a naked woman?"

"Only if you go as my muff warmer."

He raised himself onto his elbows, gave her a grin. "Honey, you've got yourself a deal."

JULIAN'S GOOD MOOD lasted until he got into the kitchen. He'd just grabbed a bottle of water out of the fridge and was about to slip into his harness when he saw it. Stuck to a manila folder was a small to-do list on a yellow Post-it note. At the top of the list was written "Get crim. hist. on A. Burien."

Get criminal history on Alexi Burien?

"What the . . . ?"

He set the water aside, opened the folder, and began to read through it, his temper building. Inside were dozens of pages listing some of the most notorious criminals to come out of the former Soviet Union, some of whom he'd helped put away, some of whom were still at large. He'd known she'd called Moscow to talk with some expert about the Red Mafia. He'd had no idea how far that conversation had taken her. There on top was a document with Alexi Burien's name circled in red.

"What are you doing?" She stood there wearing one of his T-shirts, her hair a sexy, tangled mass, a look of confused irritation on her face.

He fought to keep his voice calm. "Who tipped you off to him?"

She lifted her chin, frowned. "I figured it out for myself."

Then she told him how Syko has given her the tip that had led to her investigating the Red Mafia, how another I-Team reporter had hooked her up with the Moscow source, and how she'd gotten this list from him.

"From there, it wasn't that hard. I looked for someone who had ties to Lonnie Zoryo. They're from the same town, are about the same age, and were busted on the same day in Moscow for running a prostitution ring."

Julian stared at her, his anger at war with admiration. "Irving is right. You are too smart for your own good. What exactly were you planning on doing with this information, and when were you planning to tell me?"

"I didn't know I had to keep you apprised of—"

"Damn it, Tessa!" He threw the file down onto the table. "This is not like any other investigation you've done before! Burien is a predator! He hurts women for fun! You just can't publish this without risking lives, starting with your own! At the very least, you owed it to me to tell me what you'd discovered!"

Her face flushed pink. "The same way you owed it to me to tell me who was trying to kill me?"

Julian took a step toward her. "You're missing the point! I can't do my job if—"

"No, you're missing the point!" She poked him in the chest. "If people knew this kind of thing happened around them, don't you think they'd keep their eyes open? Don't you think María's neighbors would've called the police if they'd realized what all those male visitors might mean? Light is the only thing that truly burns away the shadows, Julian!"

"It also sends the roaches scurrying for cover."

She threw up her hands, shook her head. Then a look of sadness came over her face, and her gaze dropped to the floor. "I'm not your enemy, you know. I wasn't planning on writing anything—yet. I have an interview today with Chief Irving. You'd have found out."

Feeling like an ass, Julian drew her into his arms and tried to explain. "I can't let Burien get away, Tessa. Not this time."

"I want you to get him, too, Julian, not only for what he did to María and the hundreds of other women he's hurt over the years but also because of what he's done to you." Her voice was soft with concern.

He kissed her forehead, then released her and finished clipping into his harness. "Should I pick up anything from the store? Milk? More coffee? Woman stuff?"

From the look in her eyes, he knew she'd seen through him. "I won't know if I'm pregnant till next week at the earliest. And don't worry. I know the last thing you want is a baby. I won't ask anything of you."

As Julian backed his truck into the slushy street a moment later, he tried to figure out why her words—which ought to have been music to his ears—had felt like a smack in the face.

CHIEF IRVING REACTED pretty much the way Tessa had expected him to react. "Jesus H. Christ on a frigging crutch! Who gave you his name?"

Tessa explained how she'd identified Alexi Burien as the suspect, at which point Chief Irving began swearing again.

"I hope to God you're not running with this in tomorrow's paper," he said.

"No, sir, I'm not."

Tessa had just endured a long, uncomfortable conversation with Tom on this very subject. Tom had wanted to go page one, above the fold, hammer headline. But Tessa had insisted they wait.

"Who are you working for, Novak? The cops—or me?" he'd shouted. "Your job is to gather facts and present them to the public, not to protect the interests of the goddamned police department!"

Tessa had calmly explained her reasons for wanting to hold the story. No other paper was going to get the story from them, because the rest of Denver's media were still out chasing crack dealers and gangbangers. And while it was her job to print the truth, she wouldn't be doing the community any favors if she enabled a murderous trafficker to escape.

In the end Tom had relented, but he'd been less than pleased with her.

Chief Irving, on the other hand, sounded immensely relieved. "I'm really happy to hear that, Ms. Novak. I promise you, I'll give you access to everything we have on this bastard down to the lint between his toes once he's brought in. For now, I have to say, 'No comment.' "

The two words every journalist hated most.

"Can't I ask the questions first?"

"Just saving us both time."

Tessa hung up, frustrated, and spent the rest of the afternoon trying to dig up information on Alexi Burien. She'd been on the phone with Moscow twice and had managed to get his entire criminal record faxed over, only to discover that she couldn't read a word.

"Russians keep their records in Russian?" she teased herself. "Imagine that."

She couldn't call her source again; it was three in the

morning where he was. She sent an e-mail to him instead, asking him if he would be willing to translate the documents for her over the phone tomorrow.

Fighting a latent feeling of sadness, she ran a mile on the treadmill, then did a bit of housework and took a long shower. She slid soap over her skin, her hands resting for a moment on the naked curve of her belly. How ironic it would be if she were accidentally pregnant. Wasn't that the one thing she swore would never happen to her? Wasn't motherhood a part of her life that she'd intended to plan carefully? Hadn't she spent her life feeling ashamed because there was no father listed on her birth certificate?

And here she was, waiting and wondering, much as her mother must have done.

She'd told Julian she wouldn't expect anything from him, half hoping he would object or express concern. Instead, he'd listened, glanced down at the floor for a moment, and then walked off without a word.

Did you expect him to propose, girl?

His apparent indifference had left her feeling far more desolate than she would have imagined. She'd spent the afternoon trying not to think about it, focusing on her job. But here in the steam with only her own thoughts to distract her, she couldn't avoid a growing sense of loneliness and even grief.

Get used to it, Novak.

This investigation couldn't go on forever. When this Burien bastard was behind bars, Julian would be free—free to move on with his life, free to put the past behind him, free to forgive himself. And she desperately wanted that for him, even though she knew it would also leave him free to forget her.

She had just dried her hair and was in the middle of zipping her jeans when someone knocked on the door.

Her heart shot into her throat. She stood rooted to the floor, aware only that something was terribly wrong. And then she knew.

The alarm. It hadn't gone off.

Had Julian forgotten to arm it? Surely not. He never forgot things like that.

The knock came again.

Mind racing, she grabbed a T-shirt, slipped it on, then looked frantically about for her secured cell phone. She would call Julian, dial 911. Then she remembered that she'd left the phone out on the table by her computer.

"Damn! Damn! Damn!"

The .22.

She dashed around the bed, grabbed it out of the top drawer of Julian's nightstand. Taking a few seconds to make sure it was loaded, she clicked the cylinder back into place and walked slowly down the hallway, pointing it at the floor, her breath coming in shallow gasps, her palms sticky with sweat.

More knocking—or was that her heart?

Then someone shouted her name.

Tessa peeked around the corner.

It was Margaux. She stood before the front window, holding up a shining silver CD, a sheepish smile on her face.

"Sorry!" she mouthed.

Tessa let out a relieved sigh, her heart still hammering. She slipped the .22 surreptitiously into the waistband of her jeans and covered it with her T-shirt, hoping Margaux hadn't seen it. The hag would probably laugh at her for overreacting.

She walked to the front door, then hesitated, tempted to let Margaux wait until Julian had come home. She had no desire for a rematch of yesterday's verbal battle, no desire to even speak with Margaux. Then again, Margaux was trying to help.

Tessa unlocked the door.

"Not in a hurry to let me in, were you?" Margaux said, brushing past her in a tight pair of black jeans and the same red leather jacket.

"I was in the shower and had to get dressed." Tessa had just started to shut the door when she heard the unmistakable tromp of heavy feet running on the porch. "Oh, God!"

Fueled by adrenaline, she threw herself into the door, tried to slam it, but they were faster and much stronger. She found herself hurled backward as two men forced their way inside. She hit the wall, felt the bite of steel against her hip.

The gun.

It all happened in a heartbeat.

The pistol in her hand. The squeeze of the trigger. The recoil. *Pop! Pop!*

A grunt. A spray of blood. A man down.

Then pain exploded against her stomach, doubling her over, driving the breath from her lungs. She clutched at her belly, the little revolver falling to the floor. For a moment she thought she'd been shot. Then with a sense of astonishment, she realized Margaux had kicked her.

And the pieces slid into place. Margaux had led the men here. Margaux had betrayed her. Margaux had betrayed Julian. *Margaux was the leak.*

"Fucking stupid bitch!" Margaux kicked her again, her boot connecting painfully with Tessa's ribs, splaying Tessa across the floor.

"Oh, Eddie!" a man's voice shouted. "She popped Eddie!"

"Forget about him, and worry about your own ass!" Margaux snapped. "Make it quick!"

And Tessa knew she was dead.

She heard the unmistakable *click-click* of someone sliding the rack of a semiautomatic, felt rough hands grab her by the hair, felt the hard kiss of steel against her temple. "Stupid whore! You killed Eddie!"

Tessa coughed, drew in a shaky breath, expecting it to be her last.

But it wasn't fear she felt. It was regret.

Regret for the years she'd lost with her mother. Regret that she would never see Julian again. Regret for the grief her death would cause them both.

Tears pricked her eyes, and she sent her thoughts skyward. *Find happiness, Mama. And please, Julian, don't blame yourself for this!*

"Quit fucking around!" Margaux bent down, picked up Tessa's pistol, slipped it into her pocket. "She's already made enough noise to draw in the neighbors."

Tessa coughed again, croaked out the words, "Julian . . . will kill . . . !"

Margaux laughed. "No, Julian will die."

Tessa expected a bullet, but instead she found herself being held down, the man's knee in her back, his iron grip around her arm. Out of the corner of her eye, she saw a syringe.

They were going to drug her.

"N-no!" She tried to pull her arm away, twisted, arched, kicked.

But he was too heavy. With his dead weight thrown over her, she couldn't budge. She felt a sharp poke and a rush of warmth in her vein.

"Not too much!" Margaux hurried across the room, unplugged Tessa's laptop and grabbed her files. "If she dies before she gets to Burien, he'll make you eat your balls."

They were taking her to Alexi Burien.

How could she have been so stupid? How could she have opened the door? If only she'd waited for Julian.

Julian!

Tessa wanted to fight back, wanted to leave some kind of clever clue for Julian. She wanted to warn him about Margaux. But a strange euphoria had muddled her mind, dulling her pain and fear, leaving her to drift in confusion.

CHAPTER 25

JULIAN SAT AT the bar at Pasha's, locked in the personality of Tony Corelli, while one of the three teenagers he'd pretended to screw this past week danced onstage. "She's really something! Ain't she something?"

Chet nodded, grinned, poured him another shot. "Great ass."

Julian smacked a ten onto the counter, saw Irena watching him from a nearby table where she sat topless on Sergei's lap, the misery in her eyes an indictment. He'd seen the bruises on her face, seen through the heavy layer of makeup to the signs of violence beneath. And although the bruises were proof of Sergei's brutality, Julian knew it was the emotional wounds that hurt Irena most.

Staying in character, he winked, blew her a kiss, smiled.

It was almost seven p.m., early in the evening for a place like this. The room reeked of booze and testosterone, alcohol putting a disorderly edge on the pervasive horniness. Up front, a group of college kids had just gotten started celebrating some guy's twenty-first birthday by doing body shots off one of the girls. The sullen forty-something in the southeast corner had been warned not to jerk off by the bouncer. Two guys who looked like they hadn't had a hard-on in twenty years watched the stage longingly.

Julian felt itchy. He wanted to get out of this hellhole and go home to Tessa. He wanted to try to clean up the mess he'd made with her. What did she mean she didn't expect anything from him? Did she really think he'd leave her to face an un-planned pregnancy alone? Did she think he cared so little for her that he'd knock her up and run?

Have you ever given her reason to think anything else, Darcangelo?

No, he hadn't. Well, that was going to change. He might not be able to marry her, but if she was pregnant he'd make damn good and sure she had everything she needed.

But he couldn't go home to her—not yet. His night here was only beginning. He'd made good use of his time behind the guarded doors this week to scope out cameras, alarms, ex-its. He knew there was a stairway near the rear exit that led down to a basement and that the stairway was always guarded. He knew eight men were usually on guard duty, armed dis-creetly with high-caliber pistols. Before he left tonight, he wanted to get another crack at that basement.

He'd passed all of this on to Irving, whose most trusted men were gradually infiltrating the neighborhood around Pasha's. One had gotten a job at the gas station. A team was always on watch in the upstairs hotel room, where tape was still rolling. Plainclothes officers now watched the parking lot twenty-four-seven, prepared to tag the white minivan with a GPS monitor the next time it showed up. Hopefully the device would give them the most important bit of information—where Burien was hiding.

The pieces were sliding into place.

"So you think she'll be free for a bit of nookie after her number?" Julian pointed to the dancer with a jerk of his head.

"Could be." Chet gave him a knowing grin. "Want me to check?"

Julian grinned, licked his lower lip. "Oh, yeah."

He hated doing this, hated himself for doing it, but she was his backstage pass. Unless he was a paying customer, the only way to get behind the guarded door was to start shooting, and it wasn't yet time for that. He'd just raised the shot glass to his lips when his cell rang. He pulled it from his pocket, glanced at the number.

It was Irving.

Julian answered with Tony Corelli's accent. "Yeah, I'm kinda tied up now."

"Get home now, Darcangelo."

Julian felt a hitch of fear in his stomach. "Tessa?"

"Go now! I'll meet you there." Irving hung up.

Phone still in hand, Julian pushed blindly through the tables, past the bouncers, and toward the front door.

"Hey, Tony, what about—?"

"I gotta go!" he shouted back, forcing his way out the door.

Then he was running, oblivious to surprised stares, to oncoming traffic, to the slamming of his own heart. Through the parking lot. Down the street. Around the block. Up to his truck.

If Burien had her . . . If he'd killed her . . .

Oh, Christ!

Fear, cold and sharp, twisted in his gut.

He unlocked his truck, jumped behind the wheel, and tore off down the street, swerving to avoid a car backing out of its parking spot, just making the yellow light.

If Burien had hurt Tessa . . . If he had her . . .

His police scanner spat static—and a request for crime-scene cleanup at his address.

Jesus God, no!

He gunned the engine, his blood slick with adrenaline, the seconds measured in heartbeats as he burned through the streets, the chaos in his mind fusing into a semblance of a prayer. "God, let her be alive! Let her be safe!"

Left onto Eleventh. Left onto Mariposa.

Squad cars. Red-blue-red-blue-red. An ambulance.

Let her be alive!

He burned rubber into the driveway and had just leapt from the driver's seat when he saw the EMTs step outside guiding a gurney. On it lay a body zipped in thick black plastic.

Dead?

Julian's heart burst inside his chest, knocked the air from his lungs, his throat constricting as if squeezed by invisible claws. Somehow he stayed on his feet, carried forward on wooden legs. "Tessa?" he whispered.

His hand reached out of its own accord, tugged at the zipper. The plastic fell open to reveal a man's face.

Not Tessa. Not Tessa. Not Tessa.

Breath filled his lungs, and his thoughts coalesced into a single burning question.

Where was she?

He shoved his way through his own front door, shouted for her. "Tessa!"

"She's not here." Irving stood beside a pool of blood, talking with a detective.

And Julian knew.

Burien had her.

"Goddamn it!" Julian slammed his fist into the wall. "When?"

"Neighbors heard a couple shots, called it in. I'd say it's been about thirty minutes."

More than enough time for rape, for brutality, for torture. More than enough time to put her on a private plane headed for Mexico, Turkey, Serbia, or any one of a thousand places where men would be willing to pay for a pretty young blonde. More than enough time to pull a trigger.

Julian fought to control his regret, his rage, his fear. He needed to think clearly if he was going to find her.

You're a special agent, Darcangelo. Act like one.

He took in the scene at a glance, forced his mind to focus on the details—the intact door and lock, the disarmed alarm, the single pool of blood on the floor, Tessa's missing computer and files.

"Looks like an inside job to me," Irving said, echoing Julian's thoughts. "No sign of a break-in. The alarm didn't sound."

"Who's the DB?"

"I was hoping you could make him. Looks like she lit him up with her little twenty-two—a couple slugs to the chest. The son of a bitch didn't make it three steps inside the house before she popped him."

A vicious sense of satisfaction surged through Julian.

Good for you, Tess.

But the feeling was quickly washed away by his certainty that Tessa had been terrified when she'd pulled that trigger. She'd been fighting for her life and had killed a man—and he hadn't been here.

"The question is, how'd he get in?" Irving walked to the back door, checked the lock, then turned to face Julian. "Either she let them in, or they had a key."

"She wouldn't have unlocked the door—not unless it was someone she felt certain she could trust." Julian forced his mind to think through it. "The guy in the bag is proof that she didn't trust them. She doesn't usually carry the pistol. She would have had to run and get it. She must have known something was wrong before they got in."

That probably meant they'd had a key.

Two people knew where he lived, but only one of them had a key to the house.

Dyson.

The realization left him feeling hollow, sick, utterly betrayed. He had known it had to be someone close to Dyson, but he'd hoped to God it wasn't Dyson himself.

That's when Julian saw it—a small silver disk sitting in the middle of the table. It looked like the disk from a high-end digital camera. Dread knotted in his gut, the images from the e-mail Burien had sent Tessa flashing through his mind.

"That doesn't belong to you?" Irving asked.

Julian shook his head, held out his hand for a pair of nitrile gloves.

Irving slapped the gloves into his palm. "You don't have to look at it."

"Yeah, I do." Julian pulled on the gloves, picked up the disk by its edges, and carried it back to his office, surprised to see it that the door was still closed and intact. He unlocked it, saw that his files were still there, his computer untouched. Clearly, they'd come for Tessa and weren't concerned about his evidence. Or perhaps the shots Tessa had fired had made them jumpy, forced them to hurry.

Almost unable to breathe, he booted up his computer, placed the disk in a plastic adapter case, and loaded it, watching as his multimedia program launched, the seconds ticking by like hours.

A blurry image opened on his screen. Tessa her head down, golden curls hiding her face, her hair swaying back and forth as if she were walking or being carried. And then a man's voice.

"A bit of Mexican tar, and there's no fight left in her."

Heroin.

They'd drugged her.

Julian felt his teeth grind.

The camera pulled back enough to show Tessa being led toward the front door, a man's arms beneath hers, holding her up. She looked dangerously close to a fatal overdose, her body almost limp, her head nodding as if she were barely conscious.

But she was alive. At least she was alive.

"No!" She gave a weak cry, made a helpless effort to twist away.

Julian's gut burned with helpless rage.

Then the man's hand grabbed Tessa's hair and jerked her head back.

"Say hi to the camera! Say hi to Darcangelo!"

"Julian?" She searched for him as if she expected to find him standing there, hope slowly fading from her eyes, tears spilling onto her cheeks. Then she seemed to focus on the camera, her words slurred. "The camera crew . . . let the lion kill . . . the cheetah cubs. That's okay. They did . . . their job."

Pain ripped through Julian's chest as he realized what she was trying to say.

Despite the drug, despite her fear, she was trying to send him a message. She was trying to tell him to stick to his assignment—*even if it meant letting Burien brutalize and kill her.*

Julian swallowed the rock in his throat, forced himself to keep watching.

"Whatever, sweetheart." The man who held her up laughed, clearly mistaking her words for drug-induced babble. "Take a good look, Darcangelo, because we're going to make a star out of her. Next time you see her, she'll be on DVD!"

Not a fucking chance, asshole!

Beneath the man's words, Tessa's voice had taken on the tone of a child singing a nursery rhyme, except that the words to this rhyme made no sense.

Then the clip ended.

Julian clicked PLAY, watched it again and again until every second of it was burned into his brain—the hopelessness in Tessa's tear-filled eyes when she realized he wasn't there, the raw courage beneath her slurred message, the cruelty in the voice of the man whose fist was bunched in her hair, her nonsensical little rhyme as she drifted away in a heroin haze.

It was clear that Burien intended to brutalize her on camera and send Julian the recordings. That fit Burien's sadistic M.O., his warped sense of fun. On the one hand it meant he didn't intend to kill her right away. On the other . . .

There were so many ways to destroy a woman.

Three years ago Julian had let his emotions interfere with the job, and Burien had escaped. God only knew how many women Burien had hurt since then, how many lives he had ruined. Every one of them was Julian's responsibility.

And now the bastard had the woman he loved.

The words came to his mind so naturally that it was a moment before he realized what he'd just admitted to himself.

He was in love with Tessa.

God, yes, he loved her. He'd loved her since the night she'd taken his rage inside her and answered it with tenderness. He'd loved her since she'd peeled off his Kevlar and kissed his bruised muscles, her concern for him spilling out in tears. Hell, he'd loved her since she'd melted against him in that hospital linen closet.

Not that it did her one damned bit of good. He had tried to protect her from Burien, but he had failed. With leaks in the police department and a leak in the FBI, would he have been able to keep her safe anywhere?

Yes. He could have taken off with her, gone underground, hidden her someplace even Dyson couldn't find her. He could have stuck to her twenty-four-seven. He could have been here.

Instead, he'd stayed with his assignment. He'd done what a federal agent was supposed to do. He'd done his job.

And it was a job he was going to finish—tonight.

But it wasn't Tessa who was going to die. It was Burien.

Julian was about to hit QUIT, his gaze lingering on Tessa as she drifted off, singing the words of her nonsensical rhyme—and it hit him.

The words weren't nonsense. They were Spanish.

Darcangelo, you idiot!

He turned up the volume, scrolled back, and listened.

"HOW MUCH DID you give her?"

"No more than two hundred migs, I swear. Must've been really pure shit."

"Her pulse is really slow, Alexi. If you want to keep her alive, you'd better hit her with naloxone or have someone watch over her and make sure she doesn't stop breathing."

Tessa heard voices—two men and a woman. She knew they were talking about her, knew she needed to wake up, knew something was wrong. A vague sense of urgency prodded her, strands of memory knitting together—only to unravel.

And then she was drifting again.

JULIAN DREW THE straps of his new Kevlar vest tight, slipped into his double harness, then secured a pair of loaded .357 semiautos into the holsters. He already had two spare magazines tucked into his jacket and a seven-inch Ka-Bar blade in an ankle rig.

If all of this wasn't enough, he'd just kick the shit out of them.

He pulled on his leather jacket, stuffed a pair of black gloves in one pocket and a black ski mask in the other, and took the stairs two at a time. The house was now dark and empty, Irving and crime-scene cleanup having left about twenty minutes ago.

Irving had pulled him off the case, officially listing him as off duty. It didn't make a damned bit of difference to Julian. Sanctioned or on his own, he was going after Burien.

He'd just gotten behind the wheel of his pickup when his cell phone rang. He glanced at the number. It was Margaux.

"Dyson told me what happened," she said. "Don't get me wrong—I didn't like her. She seemed like a common bimbo to me—kind of helpless and stupid. Not your type at all. Still, I wouldn't wish Burien on my worst enemy."

"What do you want?" He opened the garage door, backed down the driveway and into the street. "Somehow I don't believe you're just calling to express your heartfelt concern."

"Give me a little credit here. You and I were lovers once, remember?"

"Not if I can help it."

She seemed to ignore the insult. "It was obvious when I saw you together yesterday how much you care about her. Dyson said you had some new evidence, and I thought maybe you could use my help."

"Didn't you say it would be a cold day in hell before you'd work with me directly on anything again?" He slipped into traffic, headed toward Speer and the crime lab.

"Well, then I guess the devil is wearing long johns. What you got?"

"A disk." He told her about the recording, told her how he thought Tessa was trying to tell him something at the end. "At first I thought it was just the drug, but then I realized she was speaking Spanish. I need to use the equipment at the lab to enhance her voice and get rid of the bastard who's talking over her."

For a moment Margaux said nothing. "Dyson didn't mention anything about a disk."

"I didn't tell him. I think he's the leak, Margaux."

"God, I just can't believe that! You're fucking kidding me. Dyson?"

"The evidence is pointing in one direction. If I can decipher what Tessa is trying to tell me on this recording, I might be able to prove it." He pulled up to a stop sign, where a group of college kids in Halloween costumes bounced and laughed their way across the intersection, probably on their way to a party.

"I'm a lot better with computers than you are. How about we call a temporary truce and I meet you at the lab? I want to get to the bottom of this as badly as you do. I owe Burien a bullet, remember?"

"Okay, a temporary truce. What's your ETA?"

"Twenty minutes."

"See you there."

CHAPTER 26

JULIAN GOT THERE first. He punched in his clearance code and took the stairs up to the darkened computer lab. Without turning on the lights, he booted up one of the computers and got it ready, launching the programs he'd need. He slipped on a pair of gloves and took the disk out of the paper envelope in which he'd sealed it, then popped it into the computer, turned up the volume, and let it play.

He heard the elevator open with a metallic ding, heard the click of her boot heels against the tile floor, heard the lab door open.

He glanced up, saw Margaux enter, red leather jacket screaming even in the darkness. He gave her a nod, shifted his gaze back to the computer screen. He'd taken a segment of sound and was working to break it down.

"All right, let's see it." Margaux flipped on the lights, set her handbag aside, and looked over his shoulder at the screen, the odor of her perfume loud and repellent.

Julian clicked the back arrow and let the recording play from the beginning.

A bit of Mexican tar, and there's no fight left in her.
No!
Say hi to the camera! Say hi to Darcangelo!

Julian?

While Margaux watched the screen, Julian watched Margaux. She seemed nervous. Her pulse beat hard against her throat, and there were little beads of perspiration along her hairline.

The camera crew . . . let the lion kill . . . the cheetah cubs. That's okay. They did . . . their job.

Whatever, sweetheart. Take a good look, Darcangelo, because we're going to make a star out of her. Next time you see her, she'll be on DVD!

"Do you hear that?" Julian asked as Tessa began singing her little rhyme. "She's saying something in Spanish. If I could enhance it, get this stupid bastard's words out of the way, I'm sure she's trying to tell me something. She already gave me one hidden message—that bit about the lion and the cheetah cubs."

Margaux shot him a disbelieving glance. "That sounded like heroin talking to me."

"That's because you don't know her, and you're not really listening. She was telling me to do my job—to catch Burien even if it means letting her die."

"She's a brave little cookie, isn't she? I bet she's not feeling quite so tough now."

Julian ignored Margaux's attempt to provoke him—and the bolt of ice-cold fear that shot through his gut. "She's also incredibly smart. Do you know she pegged Burien on her own with no help from me? She looked for someone with ties to Zoryo and had a contact in Moscow fax her Burien's entire criminal record."

"Really?" Margaux sounded genuinely surprised.

The recording ended.

Julian scrolled back to the moment Tessa started singing. "So how do I capture just her voice and enhance it? She's spelling something in Spanish, but I can't quite make it out."

His pulse dropped. His breathing slowed. His senses grew sharp.

"Well, first you need to save it as its own file." Margaux described the steps, but he was listening to something else.

The tight creak of leather. A hand sliding into a pocket. The almost soundless tick of a finger coming to rest on a trigger.

Julian dropped Margaux to the floor with two blows, the violence over in a heartbeat. She lay there, twisting in pain, her .45 skidding to a stop beneath the desk.

Julian retrieved it, unloaded it, slipped it into his pocket. "That was really stupid, Margaux. Security records would show you were the last person through the door. Your prints are on the light switch. They'd have pegged you right away."

She groaned, rolled from her back to her side, her arms clutched around her middle.

"Don't feel bad." He knelt down, forced her onto her belly, wrenched her arms behind her back, and cuffed her. "I'm sure you'd have taken me if I hadn't been expecting it."

He patted her down, taking her extra magazine and the snub-nosed revolver she kept in a pocket holster. And then he found it—Tessa's .22. He held the little revolver in his hand—hard evidence of Margaux's betrayal.

It took everything Julian had in that moment not to rip her to pieces.

Margaux looked at him over her shoulder. "You can't save her, Julian. It's too late."

"For your sake, that better not be true." Julian stood, jerked Margaux to her feet, and slammed her into a nearby chair, staying out of range of her lethally long legs. Then he pulled out one of his SIGs, flicked off the safety, and aimed it at her. "Start talking."

"How did you know?"

"Just the way I said. Tessa told me." He reached over, careful to keep an eye on Margaux, and let the recording play again. When it came to the end, he sang along with Tessa. " 'Eme-a-ere-ge.' You thought she was just high on smack, but she was spelling in Spanish—M-A-R-G."

"I should have gagged the little bitch." She shrugged, then gave what he supposed was meant to be a sexy smile. "Oh, well. You always were the more cunning linguist."

"Don't make me puke."

"We were good together—for a while."

"We were nothing—just a couple self-centered head cases getting off together." The very idea of touching Margaux sickened him now. "What happened to you? How long have you been working for that son of a bitch?"

"You really want to know?" She glanced at the SIG. "I guess you do."

Julian listened as Margaux told him how Burien's thugs had caught her a full year before Operation Liberate, how they'd beaten her and taken her to him. Instead of killing her, as she'd thought Burien would do, he'd spent the next few weeks seducing her, fascinated by the idea of a female special agent.

"I've always had a thing for powerful men," she said. "Alexi showed me what real power was. In those few days, he taught me things about pain—and pleasure—I had never imagined. Do you know how good it feels to break and to be forced to yield control?"

Julian thought of Tessa and the way her tenderness had broken through him, torn him open, forced him to yield his most inner self to her. But Tessa hadn't been trying to control him. She hadn't been trying to hurt him. She'd acted out of concern for him, out of love.

Margaux was talking about dominance of the most violent kind.

"Burien's a sadistic killer, a rapist, a sociopath! He enslaves women. How could you, as a woman, forget that?"

"I didn't forget. I just quit caring."

Julian stared at Margaux, almost unable to believe what he was hearing. He remembered that incident—at least the version of it she'd told him four years ago. They'd been lovers for about a month when she'd gone missing in L.A. Julian, who'd been in Mexico at the time, had been certain she'd been taken and would turn up dead in an alley. When Dyson had called him to say she'd escaped battered but alive, he'd been overwhelmed with relief.

"So it was all a lie—how you'd fought your way free, escaped, gotten away with invaluable information about their operation?"

"Burien let me go. I became his eyes and his ears."

If she'd gone to work with him that long ago . . .

It hit Julian with the force of a bullet. Blood rushed to his head, his pulse pounding in his ears like thunder, rage surging from his gut in a red tide.

He spoke through gritted teeth. "Burien didn't escape three years ago because I tried to save those girls and moved too early. He got away because he knew we were coming. *He got away because you helped him!*"

"I made it look real. I took a bullet for him."

Julian leaned down, shouted in her face, his hands aching to choke the life from her. "You let his goons kill two members of your own team, and you let me take the blame! Worse than that, you enabled a man who preys on women to keep killing!"

He stepped away from her, barely able to control his loathing.

It had to be Stockholm syndrome, trauma-induced psychosis, insanity. That was the only explanation for her actions. Burien must have beaten her, tortured her, twisted her mind.

"Does Dyson know?"

"That old dickhead?" She gave a snort. "He has no idea."

"So for three years, you've been charged with finding Burien—"

"And for three years, I've made sure he stays one step ahead of me." She looked up at Julian with not a trace of remorse on her face. "It's been amusing to watch you creep and crawl through the alleys, sniffing for him, always coming close but going away empty-handed."

"Why didn't he just pop me and get it over with?"

She shrugged. "I think he enjoyed watching you fail. Besides, you kept him on his toes, helped him shore up his operation, got rid of his enemies for him. You got rid of Pembroke and García. All I had to do was leak the right information, and you were on it like a Rottweiler."

Stunned, Julian ran the past three years through his mind—years of grinding guilt, years of fruitless searching, years of desperate frustration. By controlling Margaux, Burien had controlled him. But not anymore. That was the past.

Julian needed to focus on the present. "You sent Tessa the threatening e-mails, didn't you? You're the brilliant tech person working for Burien."

She smiled, obviously pleased that he'd put the pieces together. "I needed to flush you out somehow. I created the problem, and I offered the solution. Dyson believed I truly wanted to mend fences and help your new little girl toy. He didn't bat an eye when I asked for your address."

"He gave you the key."

"No! He doesn't trust anyone that much." Margaux grinned. "Tessa let me in. I held up a disk, made her think I had information for her, and she opened the door. True, she hesitated for a moment—and she had the pistol."

Julian could see it unfold in his mind. Tessa hearing a knock at the door and running for her gun. Seeing Margaux, trying to decide whether to let her in. Realizing too late that she'd been tricked, firing at one of her attackers.

If he'd been there . . .

"How'd you get past the alarm?"

She shrugged. "I turned it off from a control panel down here."

"Very clever, Margaux. But why go to all this trouble? Why not just shoot her?"

"Alexi wants to destroy you. First he plans to torment you using her, then he plans to kill you." The smirk on her face told Julian she found it funny. "Killing Zoryo was a mistake."

"Zoryo killed himself."

Margaux looked at him as if he were an idiot. "*You* put him behind bars."

Julian was done wasting time. "Where is she, Margaux?"

"Strapped spread-eagle to Alexi's bed. You want to watch? I'm sure Alexi won't mind having a captive audience."

"Tell me how to get there."

"So you can blow my head off and run after her? No deal. If you want to see her again, uncuff me. You won't get through his security without me."

"All right. We'll do it your way." Julian took the mouse in his free hand, turned off the record program, and saved the newly recorded file as an MP3. "Let me catch up on e-mail first."

"Wh-what was that?" For the first time Margaux sounded truly afraid.

"That was your little confession. I'm sending it to Dyson, to the Denver Police Department, and to Tessa's newspaper—just in case anything happens to me, and I'm not around to let everyone know what you've been doing these past few years."

"You son of a bitch! No!" She sprang from the chair, then stopped short, her gaze on Julian's weapon.

"Go ahead, Margaux!" Julian let every bit of hatred he felt for her show. "Give me an excuse! There's nothing I'd love more than to *pull this trigger!*"

She slowly sat, her face pale, her pupils dilated. "Alexi will get me out of this."

"Once he knows you've been exposed, he'll probably send someone to kill you himself. Good thing you like pain, isn't it?" Julian sent the e-mail, then stood and jerked Margaux to her feet. "Let's go. It's time for you to introduce me to your boyfriend."

He thrust her ahead of him, held the SIG to her back, and followed her out of the lab, down the hall, and toward the stairs, silently praying that he wasn't already too late.

Hang on, Tessa. I'm coming.

TESSA OPENED HER eyes, her head throbbing, her mouth dry as sand, an older man's face swimming in and out of focus.

"Finally you are coming back to us," the man said. "I am glad. I was thinking the party was over before it began."

A party? Where was she?

It was so hard to think, hard to stay awake.

Later—she couldn't tell how much later—she heard the man's voice again.

"Now I see you in the flesh I understand why Wyatt wanted you for himself. You are a very pretty girl, Tessa Novak."

Wyatt?

John Wyatt.

The man who'd stalked her. The man who'd attacked her while she'd been asleep in the tub. The man who'd been sent to kill her.

A spark of panic ignited in her belly, moved sluggishly to her brain.

She willed her eyes to open, found the man still beside her. His gray hair was cut short, his face narrow, his cheekbones high and sharp.

"Too bad for him he is in jail, no?" The man spoke with a strange accent. "But we will have more fun without him, I think."

It was a Russian accent.

Russian.

Red Mafia.

Adrenaline, potent and hot, shot through Tessa's veins, her memories of what had happened returning full force. Margaux's surprise visit. Two men rushing in. The kick of the gun in her hand as she shot a man. The shock and pain of Margaux's boot in her belly. The cold prick of a needle.

Margaux had betrayed Julian, kidnapped Tessa, and turned her over to the man Julian had torn his soul apart trying to bring to justice.

Dread slid down Tessa's spine like an icy finger. "Alexi Burien."

He watched her through eyes like frost on barbed wire, his thin lips spreading into a satisfied smile. "So Darcangelo told you about me."

Burien sat beside her on a large bed, dressed in navy blue. Behind him stood a camera on a tripod. Its lens was pointed at her.

Her mouth went dry, her fear mingling with a strange giddiness, as if only part of her were in the room and the rest were floating. The drug. Whatever they'd given her was still in her bloodstream.

"N-no." She unstuck her tongue from the roof of her mouth. "I-I figured it out myself."

He took a handful of her hair, rubbed it between his fingers as if testing its texture. "Why do I find this hard to believe?"

"Because you're a misogynist pig." It took her a moment to realize what she'd said. She gasped, then held her breath.

"Did you just call me a pig?" He looked shocked—and he pulled out a knife.

She tried to pull away from him only to find she couldn't move, her wrists and ankles bound to the bed with thick leather straps. Terror ripped through her, drove the breath from her lungs in a panicked wail. "No!"

The surprise on his face transformed to cruel arousal, and he laughed. "Are those tight enough, little one, or should I make them tighter?"

Overcome with horror, she froze, stared up at him.

Burien is a predator! He hurts women for fun!

Julian's words from this morning came back to her.

And she understood.

The more she fought Burien, the more fear she showed, the more he would enjoy hurting her, the more power he would have over her. If she didn't react, if she hid her fear, maybe she could get the better of him long enough to get word to Julian. Maybe she could endure him. Maybe she could survive.

Or maybe Burien will just kill you sooner.

She swallowed, her heart beating so hard she thought she might be sick. "W-what a small penis you must have to use a knife on women."

"You are brave, little Tessa, but you are also wrong. I do not think you will find me lacking." He took the collar of her blouse and slowly cut it open, the tip of the razor-sharp blade passing a hairsbreadth from her skin.

She fought the urge to scream. "Compared to Julian? Please!"

Burien pushed her blouse aside, slid the cold knife between her skin and the front clasp of her bra, then cut it open with a jerk. The silky cloth fell back, revealing her breasts. He scraped over her with his gaze. "Do you know what is going to happen to your Julian? He will live long enough to see what has become of you—and then I will kill him."

Despair sank icy claws into her chest as she realized she

would probably never see Julian again. All it would take was one bullet, and one or the other of them would be gone.

Julian!

She forced back her tears. "*You* won't kill him. You'll send one of your little minions. You're afraid to be anywhere near Julian Darcangelo."

Burien drew a deep breath. "You should show me a bit more respect."

"Respect? For you?" Hysterical laughter bubbled up from inside her. "You know what they say in Russia—*tough-ski shit-ski.*"

His nostrils flared. "You are trying to make me angry, but I can see you are afraid. You tremble. And see how your heart beats?"

He touched the cold tip of the blade against her breastbone.

She met his pitiless gaze, a surge of contempt taking the edge off her fear, her voice quavering with rage. "You think tying women up and hurting them means you're powerful? You're still the same pathetic bully who beat up old ladies and sold crack on the streets of Gzel!"

The blow took her by surprise, pain exploding against her cheek, leaving her dazed. She tasted blood, her head pounding.

"You know nothing about me! We will see how brave you are after—"

Someone knocked on the door. Then a voice shouted in Russian from outside the bedroom. Amid the words she didn't understand was one she did—Darcangelo.

Julian?

A look of alarm on his face, Burien answered in Russian, leaping from the bed and grabbling a large pistol from the drawer of his nightstand.

Then Tessa heard a woman's voice outside the door. "Get out of my way, idiot!"

Margaux.

Burien let loose with a string of Russian words that must have been profanity, then stepped back, pistol aimed at the door. "Come in!"

Margaux entered accompanied by one of Burien's armed goons.

Between them walked Julian.

He'd been beaten and stripped down to his jeans. Even his shoes were gone. His wrists were bound before him with duct tape, and blood trickled down his face from a cut on his temple. He looked angrier than she'd ever seen him, his jaw tight, his expression hard as stone. He glanced over at her, his gaze passing lightly over her before it fixed on Burien.

"I know you're busy, Alexi, but obviously this couldn't wait." Margaux walked over to Burien, kissed him on the cheek, then turned to Tessa. "Don't you look cute all tied up?"

But no one was listening to Margaux.

Burien and Julian stood a few feet apart, glaring at one another with unmistakable hatred, Burien's gun aimed directly at Julian's chest. If Burien pulled the trigger . . .

Tessa's heart seemed to stop.

Then Burien's face broke into a smile. "Julian Darcangelo. For so many years, you have been looking for me, and now you have found me."

CHAPTER 27

"WHAT CAN I say? Persistence pays off." Julian kept his voice neutral and forced himself to focus on Burien's face and not Tessa.

The sight of her—bound, her breasts bare, fresh bruises on her cheek—was like a dagger to his gut. She looked vulnerable, helpless, terrified. He wanted to start breaking heads, to go for Burien's throat, to fight his way over to her. But one mistake now would get them both killed, so he quashed his feelings, buried them deep, clearing his mind of everything but the moment. He couldn't let himself think about her or what she'd been through, not if he wanted to get her out of this.

At least she's alive.

He had known Margaux would try to give him away to Burien's security. If she'd betrayed him when they were lovers, she'd certainly have no qualms about doing so now. They'd gotten through the gate that guarded Burien's mountain estate and into the main building before she'd made her move. She would have failed had the elevator not opened just then and disgorged two more thugs, one of whom had leveled a Glock at Julian's head. Margaux had taken her fury out on him with a few kicks, then she'd had the men strip-search him, leaving him naked apart from the duct tape on his wrists.

"Bring back memories?" he'd asked, when he'd caught her looking at his cock.

She'd thrown his jeans in his face.

Now here he was in what looked like Burien's bedroom, disarmed, his hands tied, outnumbered three to one. Bigger than most family homes, the room held a king-sized bed, a bar, an enormous plasma TV, as well as some chairs, a sofa, and a few devices that looked like they belonged in a medieval torture chamber. A camera stood next to the bed on its tripod, the lens focused on Tessa.

Julian felt his jaw clench, then willed himself to relax, waiting for that moment when his heart rate would slow and his mind would clear. But the moment didn't come, and he knew why. This time the stakes were too high. This time, there was Tessa.

"You have interrupted me, I am afraid." Burien motioned toward Tessa. "But what kind of host would I be if I did not invite you to join me?"

"I told him you wouldn't mind an audience." Margaux walked over to the bar and poured herself a drink, ice clinking against crystal.

"This is true." Burien nodded. "In fact, having you watch while I rape your Tessa again and again has been a favorite fantasy of mine these past days."

Julian looked into Burien's soulless brown eyes, subdued his rage, kept his voice casual. "We all have hopes and dreams, don't we? Too bad most don't come true."

Burien chuckled. "We shall see. But first, before I fuck her, I want to know how you found me."

Julian pointed to Margaux with a jerk of his head. "Ask her."

Margaux told Burien how Julian had lured her into meeting him at the lab and, already tipped off by Tessa's covert message, had been ready when she'd tried to take him.

"You did not know about this message?" Burien did not look pleased.

Neither, judging from her startled expression, did Tessa. Her gaze met his, her blue eyes filled with confusion and terror—and love. If Julian hadn't already been in love with her, that would have done it.

"Shhh," he mouthed. Then he gave her a wink.

"She spelled my name in Spanish, but it sounded like gibberish to me. I don't speak Spanish." Margaux took another drink, walked over to stand at the foot of the bed. "It looks like she's all out of clever ideas now."

Burien turned to Julian again. "So you forced Margaux to bring you here?"

Julian nodded. "But only after I had recorded her confession and sent it to every law enforcement agency in the state. I know the whole story—how you turned Margaux into your pawn, how you used her to stay ahead of the law, how you escaped three years ago only because she tipped you off. I know the truth, and so do the FBI and the Denver police."

A heavy silence fell over the room as Burien turned to face Margaux.

Margaux's face drained of its color. She took a nervous sip. "I had no idea he was recording me. I thought we'd get him here, your men and I would take care of him, and that would be the end of it. I'm afraid my cover is blown, Alexi. I'm going to have to stay underground with you."

Burien glared at her with undisguised disgust. "Stay underground with me? You stupid *suka!* What use are you to me now?"

"I know I fucked up. I'm sorry. But there are still lots of things I can do for you—computer work, undercover ops, security. Besides, there's more to our relationship than—"

"You were my eyes inside the FBI." Burien raised his .45. "Now you are nothing."

Margaux's eyes flew wide. "Wait—!"

A loud blast. Tessa's scream. A spray of blood.

Margaux fell backward, landing lengthwise at the foot of the bed.

Julian started toward Tessa, hoping to use the distraction to put himself between her and Burien, but the cold jab of the Glock against his bare back stopped him.

Wait, Darcangelo. You'll get your chance.

Tessa fought back a wave of nausea, her heart slamming in her chest. Blood had sprayed across her jeans, and she could smell it.

A muscle clenched in Julian's jaw, the only sign that he felt anything. "I told Margaux the two of you were destined for a nasty breakup tonight, but she didn't listen."

How could he stay so calm and cool when someone had just been killed? How could he act so relaxed with a gun aimed at his back? How could he joke about murder?

This is what he does, girl. It's his job.

Burien whirled on him, aimed his pistol at Julian's heart. "Do you see how I have hurt you? I corrupted one of your lovers, turned her against you, used her. And in a moment I am going to make sweet Tessa wish she'd never met you. But first I would know if the police are on their way. I do not wish to get caught with my pants down."

"How can they know where I am when I didn't know where we were going? Margaux drove. We came in her car."

Burien spoke in Russian to his goon, who drove his fist into Julian's kidney.

Julian gave a grunt, sank into the man's fist, his brow furrowed, breath hissing from between his clenched teeth.

The sight of his pain made Tessa's chest hurt.

Oh, Julian!

"Don't feed me horseshit, Darcangelo! You probably brought a GSP device!"

"You mean a *GPS* transmitter?" Julian's voice was strained. "Ask Igor here. He stripped me down to my skin."

Igor?

And then Tessa felt it—something cold and hard. She looked down and watched a bloody hand lay a pistol—Julian's pistol?—on the bed and nudge it beneath her leg.

Margaux was alive?

Barely able to breathe, Tessa watched as the hand tucked the gun beneath her left leg and then began to unbuckle the leather around her left ankle with fumbling fingers. Margaux

meant to set her free. She'd given her the gun and was trying
to free her. But why?

Who cares why?

Tessa looked over at Burien, who had his back to them both,
and to Igor who's attention was riveted on Julian. If Burien
turned around, if Margaux's motions caught Igor's eye, it would
be over. But before the buckle was unfastened, Margaux's fingers went still, her hand lying limp against Tessa's foot.

No! Don't die! Don't die!

Burien was shouting in Russian again, but Tessa barely
heard him, her thoughts focused entirely on Margaux's blood-
stained fingers. They twitched, began to move again. And then
Tessa's left ankle was free.

Her pulse a deafening roar, she slowly bent her knee, guiding the pistol upward with her heel until it pressed against her
left buttock, her gaze fixed on Burien and "Igor." She tried
to pull herself close enough to her wrist to unfasten the
strap with her teeth, but with her right ankle still held fast, she
couldn't quite reach. She needed her right ankle freed.

But where was Margaux? What if she were unable to reach
Tessa's right ankle? What if she were dead?

Please don't be dead! Please don't be dead!

Teetering between hope and dread, Tessa lay still—and
waited.

"Enough fucking around!" Burien shouted. "Where is your
cell phone, Darcangelo?"

"I think Igor took it." Julian bit his lip as if trying to remember. "Or maybe I let it drop into the bushes outside your
gate to give the cops a signal to follow."

Another kidney punch.

This time Julian's knees seemed about to buckle.

Then Tessa felt the cold brush of Margaux's fingers on her
right ankle and nearly moaned with relief. But it was clear that
whatever strength Margaux had was fading. Several times her
fingers stilled or slipped away, and Tessa was certain each time
that she had died. But finally the leather slipped away, and
Tessa's right ankle was free.

One excruciating inch at a time, she pulled herself upward, praying no one would notice her movements. Closer, closer, closer. And then she was there, her teeth sinking into the thick leather that bound her right wrist, tugging, pulling until it was free.

Someone's cell phone rang, playing Bach.

Tessa froze.

Burien reached inside his pocket, drew out his phone, and shouted into it in Russian, his gun still pointed at Julian's chest. Then he tucked the phone back in his pocket, the look on his face changing from anger to panicked fury. He lifted his pistol and pointed it at Julian's face.

"There's a line of cop cars on their way up the canyon. I am told there is a SWAT team with them. I'm afraid I have to cut our conversation short. I have a helicopter to catch."

The breath left Tessa's lungs in a rush as she realized what Burien meant to do.

He was going to shoot Julian at point-blank range—and make a run for it.

Desperate, she reached beneath herself with her one free hand and grabbed the pistol.

"But what am I thinking? Ladies first, of course." Burien turned toward Tessa.

"Not this time!" She met his gaze and, heart in her throat, pulled the trigger.

What happened next was a blur.

Burien's shriek of pain. His rage as he knocked the gun from her hand. The barrel of his pistol as it hovered before her face. Julian somehow kicking Burien in the side of the head. An explosion of gunfire. Igor crumpling. Burien sinking lifeless to the floor.

And then Julian was there, unbinding her wrist, pulling her against him, wrapping her in a blanket. "Are you all right, Tessa? Talk to me, honey!"

But she could barely think, much less talk. "H-help Margaux. S-she untied—"

"I saw, honey. She's dead."

So much death, so much blood.

From somewhere nearby came a voice on a bullhorn. "Freeze! Police!"

"It's over, Tessa." He kissed her hair. "Let's get you out of here, away from this mess."

Trembling uncontrollably, Tessa burrowed into the strength of Julian's embrace, felt him lift her into his arms, the tears she'd held back finally spilling down her cheeks.

THOUGH HIS JOB was far from done, Julian stayed beside Tessa when a detective took her statement. He rode with her in the ambulance down the winding canyon into Denver, holding her hand while the EMTs examined her for shock, possible concussion, and the lingering effects of heroin overdose. He stayed with her in the emergency room while the nurse took her vitals and started an IV—and then insisted on treating the cut on his temple.

And then, finally, they were alone.

He kissed Tessa's bruised cheek, his heart full of emotion he didn't know how to express—and terrible questions he didn't know how to ask. "Whatever he did to you, Tessa, however he hurt you, I know you can get through it."

She lay in the hospital bed wearing a blue-and-white hospital gown, her long curls tumbled out across the white pillow. "He didn't . . . He didn't rape me, if that's what you're thinking. He was waiting for me to wake up."

Julian released a breath he hadn't realized he was holding. "I wouldn't have gotten there at all if you weren't so damned smart. You don't remember doing it, do you—giving me your secret message?"

She frowned. "I remember wishing I could warn you about Margaux, but then . . ."

"You did warn me." He sang the little rhyme that spelled part of Margaux's name, ran his thumb over Tessa's cheek. "If it weren't for your quick thinking, I wouldn't have found you. I wouldn't have found him. You brave, smart, beautiful woman."

Her eyes filled with tears again. "I'm not brave. I was terrified! I was afraid of what he might do to me, of what he planned to do to you. I was afraid I'd never see you again."

And then she told him how she'd heard a knock on the door and had grabbed her revolver, knowing something was wrong because the alarm hadn't gone off. How she'd let Margaux in, thinking Margaux had come with information about the e-mails. How she'd heard boots on the porch and had tried to slam the door. How the men had forced it open. How she'd shot one of them—only to find herself on the floor, the breath kicked out of her.

"I tried to fight them, tried to crawl away, but the guy who was with her held me down, grabbed my arm, and shot me up with something. I remember knowing you would blame yourself and thinking how terrible that would be. After that . . ."

"You were worried about how I'd *feel*?" Her unselfish sweetness pierced him, made it harder to control the torrent inside him. "Jesus, Tessa!"

"Of course I was worried about how you'd feel! You hold yourself responsible for everything. If I'd disappeared forever or been killed—"

"I should have been there. I should have realized Margaux was the leak."

"See what I mean?" She gave him a shaky smile, her cheeks wet with tears. "Idiot."

Then she told him how she'd awoken to find Burien beside her. How she'd been terrified to realize she was tied to his bed. How she'd tried to act like Burien didn't scare her, even insulting him, in hopes that it would allow her to get the best of him somehow.

"You insulted him?"

Amazed, Julian listened as Tessa recounted her confrontation with Burien, from her comments about the probable small size of his penis to her calling him a pathetic bully and flinging his years as a petty drug dealer in his face. It scared the hell out of him even to think of her in that situation—helpless, desperate, and mouthing off.

"Then he pulled out a knife, and I thought . . ." Her voice broke, the anguish on her sweet face making his stomach knot. "It was all I could do not to scream."

Julian held her, let her sob out her fear, her tears seeming to release some of the pent-up tension inside him, as well. He'd come so close to never finding her, so close to losing her, so close to watching her die. He felt grateful just to hold her, grateful just to be near her, grateful for whatever miracle had gotten them both to this moment alive.

"I wish I could take this away from you, Tessa. I wish somehow I could change things so that you'd never even heard of Burien. I wish you'd never had to fire a gun or watch somebody die. But I can't change it. I can't fix it."

Slowly her tears subsided, her body still shaking. She looked up at him. "W-why do you think Margaux helped me in the end?"

"Revenge against Burien. Nothing more. I think she believed he loved her."

"He was a monster. I don't regret pulling the trigger."

"And you say you're not brave?" He kissed her hair, her forehead, her salty cheeks. "God, Tessa, when I think how close he came to killing you, it scares the hell out of me."

She gave a weak laugh. "Nothing scares you."

"That's not true." He stroked her hair, savored the feel of it. "I got home just in time to see them roll a gurney with a body bag on it out of the house. I thought it was you, Tessa. I thought I'd lost you, and it seemed to me the whole world had died. And then I unzipped it and saw that man's face. And even though the relief almost knocked me on my ass, I was still terrified, because I knew Burien had you."

Tell her you love her, Darcangelo! Say it!

A knock came at the door, and the doctor stepped in.

The moment passed.

In short order, Julian was booted into the hallway to wait and to wrestle his demons while the doctor examined her. Only when the nurses wouldn't quit staring at him did he realize he still wasn't wearing a shirt. He decided to make the best of it.

He smiled. "Is there a phone I can borrow? I seem to have gotten here without my cell phone or my wallet."

"YOU'VE GOT SOME bruises, emotional trauma, and a possible mild concussion, but nothing dangerous or life threatening," the doctor said, looking up from Tessa's chart. He was a young man, not much older than she was. "There's no doubt you came close to a fatal overdose, but it's mostly out of your system now. I'd like to keep the IV going and keep you here overnight for observation."

"Is that really necessary?" Tessa felt silly being in the hospital when nothing was wrong with her. "I'm not really hurt."

"I wouldn't suggest it if I didn't think it medically prudent. We advise at least twenty-four hours of observation when it comes to possible head injuries."

"Oh." Then she asked the question she'd been burning to ask. "How soon can a test show whether a woman is pregnant?"

"Our most sensitive tests won't show a pregnancy until a few days after you miss your period. Do you think you might be pregnant?"

"I'm not due to start my period until next week. I was wondering if heroin could hurt a developing baby."

The doctor nibbled his lip for a moment, frowning. "I'm not really sure, to tell you the truth. But if you miss your period, wait a few days and get tested. I'm sure a good obstetrician will have the answer. Let me go get your friend and explain what we're doing. He's pacing the hall out here, distracting the nurses with his Tarzan attire."

Tessa didn't like the idea of a bunch of fluttery Florence Nightingales staring at Julian's chest. "Doctor, could he borrow some scrubs or something?"

The doctor grinned. "Sure."

In a few moments, Julian reappeared, wearing a green shirt and followed by the doctor, who was explaining to him why it was best for Tessa that they keep her overnight.

"It's just for observation. We'll make sure she gets a good

night's sleep and keep an eye on her. If she's still stable to-morrow morning, we'll discharge her."

"Sleep?" Tessa couldn't imagine sleeping, not with the bloody images that crowded her head. "I don't think that's going to happen, not after today, not after . . ."

But the doctor just smiled. "You want to bet on that?"

The doctor wished them both well and went off on his rounds. Tessa found herself quickly moved to a private room on the third floor with a view of the city's twinkling lights.

She gazed at the lights, feeling oddly detached. "It seems strange to me that one minute we're in the world of a crazy killer who controls the lives of so many people—and the next we're sitting here, safe and sound, among people who are oblivious to what happens out there."

"They won't be oblivious once you write your article. You'll let them know the truth. You'll be a voice for María and all the other people hurt by traffickers."

"I guess you're right." Tessa had almost forgotten about that.

Then Julian took her hand, brought it to his lips, and kissed it. "I'm sorry, Tessa. I have to go. Irving's got a squad car waiting for me. I have to finish it."

She looked up at him, startled. "But Burien's dead."

"Yes, but his empire still stands. There's a power vacuum now, and we need to move quickly, before someone fills it. With the records from his computer, we ought to be able to piece together exactly what he's been doing and bring a stop to it. There are girls out there—girls like María. I need to find them."

Tessa nodded, feeling terribly selfish for wanting him to stay. "I understand."

There was so much they needed to talk about, so much still left unresolved between them—their feelings, their relationship, the possibility of a baby. But it would have to wait. It was enough tonight that they were both still alive.

"I might be called out of the state for a while, but I'll be back as soon as I can. Is there anyone you want me to call?"

My mother.

The thought popped into her mind, but it had been too long

since she'd called her mother for anything, and she couldn't bring herself to say it. "No."

"Here we go." A smiling dark-haired nurse breezed through the door, a syringe in hand. "The doctor ordered a sedative to help you sleep."

Julian frowned. "Is that safe, given what's already in her bloodstream?"

The nurse nodded. "The doctor explained your other concerns, as well, and I checked with the pharmacy to make sure it's harmless."

Tessa knew the nurse was talking about her possible pregnancy. "Thanks."

"Do you need anything else?" the nurse asked.

Tessa met Julian's gaze, forced herself to sound untroubled. "I'm fine."

The nurse injected a clear liquid directly into Tessa's IV, and almost immediately Tessa felt herself begin to relax.

"Julian?" She held fast to his hand, managed to smile. "Rescue those girls, but please be careful! I won't be there this time to watch your back."

He chuckled, brushed his lips over hers. "Nothing's going to happen to me. Close your eyes, angel. Try to sleep."

CHAPTER 28

TESSA AWOKE FROM a deep night's sleep to see sunshine beating against the curtains of her hospital room. Looking down at her was a face she hadn't seen in ten years.

"Mama?"

Her mother took her hand, squeezed it. "You're awake."

For a moment, they just looked at each other. And then they were hugging and laughing and crying at the same time, the rush of emotion taking Tessa completely by surprise—joy, regret, relief.

After a few minutes, her mother released her, reached for a box of tissues, and grabbed one for each of them. They wiped their tears away, still laughing.

"God, I'm happy to see you, Tessa Marie. The officer who called told me some of what happened, and I been worried sick. I got here last night, but I didn't want to wake you up."

"You stayed here last night?" Something warm blossomed in Tessa's belly.

"Of course I did! Where else would I be when my girl is in the hospital? I slept in here where I could keep an eye on you."

Warmth turned to a sticky feeling of guilt.

Tessa had turned her back on her mother, abandoned her, denied her existence for ten years. And her mother had spent their first hours together again in a chair, watching over her. "That couldn't have been too comfortable."

"Oh, I was fine! The chair folds out like a little bed, and one of them nurses brought me a blanket. They been real nice."

Tessa couldn't help but smile. "You look good, Mom."

It was true. Her mother's once long hair was cut to just beneath the shoulders, her blond curls shot through with streaks of gray. There were a few wrinkles at the corners of her eyes, friendly wrinkles. But it was the look in her eyes that struck Tessa most. She looked happier than Tessa had ever seen her.

"Well, I'm gettin' older, but look at you! You're so pretty, Tessa. Like a little china doll all grown up. But listen to me chatter! Do you need anything? Can I get you anything?"

"No, I'm fine."

"Well, I don't know about 'fine.' I don't think any woman who's been through what you been through can say she's 'fine,' at least not before she's gotten it off her chest by tellin' her mama all about it."

Her mother's blatant nosiness made Tessa laugh, but she found herself telling the story from the beginning, taking care not to reveal Julian's name, but leaving out nothing else from María's murder to the moment she'd pulled the trigger and shot Burien.

Her mother sat in the chair and listened wide-eyed, her expression ranging from fear to outrage to shock. When Tessa started to tremble, memories rousing the fear she'd tried to sleep off, her mother took her hand and held it tight. That simple touch was like a lifeline. Then when her story was done, her mother stood and hugged her close.

"I'm so sorry for what you been through. I can't even imagine it. But it's all right now. That son of a bitch is in hell where he belongs, and you've got a good man watchin' over you. It was him who called me, wasn't it?"

"I think so." Somehow Julian had known what she'd needed even though she hadn't been able to admit it, even to herself. "I love him, Mama."

"I know."

A knock at the door interrupted their conversation as a

nurse arrived to check Tessa's vitals and deliver a late break-fast tray.

"I know it looks like a medical experiment," the nurse joked, "but it's actually an omelet. We try to keep the food here really terrible so patients won't mind going home."

While Tessa ate breakfast—the food was actually much bet-ter than the nurse had led her to believe—her mother shared the news from Rosebud, catching Tessa up on ten years of gos-sip in record time. Then she told Tessa more about Frank. But as her mother spoke, the food began to stick in Tessa's throat, until finally she pushed the tray aside.

"Aren't you hungry?" her mother asked.

Tessa looked into her mother's eyes. "I'm sorry, Mama. I'm sorry I left you the way I did. I'm sorry I didn't—"

"You hush about that." Her mother took her hand. "I know why you left, and I never blamed you a day for it."

"I should have called. I should have stayed in touch."

"You sent money every month, regular as clockwork."

"Money is just money. I should have called."

"You had a lot on your mind—college, gettin' a job, workin' at the paper."

Her mother was trying to let her off the hook, but Tessa's conscience would have none of it. "Was I so busy that I couldn't pick up a phone *for ten years*? All my friends think I'm from Georgia. They have no idea I grew up in Texas. I let them believe—"

Her mother patted her hand. "Let me tell you a story. It's about a fourteen-year-old girl who grew up with a mean drunk for a daddy and a boneless mama. She hated livin' at home. She hated the ugliness. She hated the smell of whisky. She hated being poor. She hated the way the other kids made fun of her. More than anything, she wanted to get out, to see the world."

Tessa was almost afraid to hear the rest of this story. "Mama, I—"

"Hush, and listen! One day when she was bussing tables at the diner, she met a tall, handsome man—a truck driver out of California. He told her stories about the road, told her she was pretty, offered to show her the country. Well, she made it as far as the next truck stop before he'd gotten what he really wanted from her. She found herself standin' in the Texas heat, ashamed, alone, and tryin' to hitch a ride back to Rosebud."

As her mother spoke, Tessa couldn't help but think of María and the others like her who'd been kidnapped or lured from home by promises of a better life, only to find themselves enslaved. And she realized that something very similar had happened to her own mother—and that she was the result.

"That truck driver thought he'd gotten the better end of that deal, but he was wrong. The girl he'd left on the highway ended up with the most beautiful blond-haired baby girl, so pretty she looked like a baby angel come to earth. And she was smart and strong and brave. And when that baby girl grew up and left town and tried to build an honest life for herself away from the shame of her childhood, her mama's hopes and dreams went with her. I wanted you to run, Tessa. I wanted you run as far and as fast as you could."

Tears ran down Tessa's face, and she saw her mother for the first time not as her mother, but as another woman. Her mother had wanted to escape as desperately as Tessa had, but she hadn't made it. Instead she'd ended up with a baby. "Why didn't you tell me?"

"I never told you because I didn't want you to feel bad, but I'm tellin' you now because you're grown up and you need to understand." Her mother's chin wobbled, tears misting her eyes. "I know you were ashamed of your grandpa, and I know you're ashamed of me."

Tessa shook her head, wanting to deny it. "No, Mama, I—"

"I know it, Tessa, and it's all right. It's all right." The look in her mother's eyes was as fierce as fire. "No matter that you didn't call, no matter that you were ashamed of me, I always thought of you and felt proud. I made a lot of mistakes in my life, but there's one thing I done right. And that's *you*."

Tessa swallowed the hard lump in her throat, tears blurring her vision. "I'm so sorry!"

Her mother wiped her tears away. "Baby, there ain't nothing

to be sorry for. It's a new day, and we're together. You're safe, and that's all that matters."

In the sweet light of her mother's forgiveness, a weight Tessa hadn't realized she was carrying lifted from her shoulders and was gone.

TESSA WAS DISCHARGED later that morning. Her mother drove her home and came inside with her. Through the door that Julian had smashed. Into the elevator. Down the long hallway where John Wyatt had watched her. In through the door where Wyatt had taped the naked photograph of her. Into the kitchen where she and Julian had eaten together.

The garbage had long since gone over, as had everything in the fridge. Her plants were dead. Everywhere she looked there were memories. Memories of Wyatt. Memories of grim-faced detectives. Memories of Julian.

I'm half Italian.
Which half?
From the waist down.

"You got yourself a nice place," her mother said, hanging up her coat. "You just go rest, while I get rid of the garbage and those plants."

"You don't need to do that, Mom. I can—"

"Don't you give me any sass!" Her mother frowned. "If a mother wants to help her daughter, I reckon she can."

The signs of rot and loss were soon cleared away, the mail brought in, and the windows thrown open to let in the fresh, cold mountain breeze. Tessa filled her lungs, the scent of sunshine, snow, and pines lifting her spirits as much as her mother's friendly chatter.

It was over. She was home.

Just after lunch, the entire I-Team came over to check on her, together with Holly and Lissy. They crowded through her door, their smiles not quite masking the worry in their eyes— or their curiosity as they looked at her mother.

Tessa could tell her mother felt out of place, though she

greeted them all with a ready smile. Why had Tessa been ashamed of her—this woman who'd survived so much so young, who'd worked so hard, who'd kept even her obligations to her drunk loser of a father?

Done with deception and shame, Tessa gave her mother's arm a reassuring squeeze. "I'd like you all to meet my mother, Linda Bates. She moved to Denver a few months ago from Rosebud, Texas, where I grew up."

"Texas?" Holly looked at her confused. "I thought you were from Georgia."

"That's what everyone thinks," her mother said. "She lived there so long she picked up the accent, bless her heart."

And without words the message was sent from daughter to mother and back again.

You're my mother, and I'm welcoming you into my life.

You're my daughter, and I'm standing by you.

"We all pitched in and got you this," said Sophie, holding out a extra-large latte. "Three shots of Mexican organic, one extra pump of vanilla—just the way you like it."

"Oh, God!" Tessa took the cup, raised it to her lips as if it were a silver chalice, certain she was in heaven. "You all are the greatest!"

They settled in the living room, Kara helping Tessa's mother to bring them cups of tea and glasses of water while the rest of them brought her up to speed on events in the newsroom. Tom and Chief Irving had been fighting every day, most of it having to do with Tessa. Some drunk had walked into the lobby and taken a piss in a potted plant. A guy from Lakewood was threatening to sue because Joaquin had photographed his dog without his permission.

Then Holly brought the conversation to a screeching halt. "So, are you going to tell us what happened, or do we have to wait to read it in the paper?"

"Holly!" Kara scolded. "I thought we agreed—"

"It's okay." Tessa had known they would ask. They were investigative reporters, after all. They were hardwired to stick their noses into other people's business. "I don't mind."

Leaving out Julian's name, she told them what they didn't

already know, from her discovery of Burien's identity to the moment when Burien at last lay dead on the floor. Somehow it was easier to tell the story this time, perhaps because she was surrounded by friends, perhaps because she'd told it before, or perhaps because her mother stood in the background watching with sympathetic eyes.

When she finished, there was silence.

Kara stood, hugged her tight, her voice breaking. "God, Tessa, I am so grateful you're alive!"

Matt nodded. "Way to go, Novak."

Sophie was too busy dabbing her eyes to speak.

"Where I come from, we'd slaughter a mutton and hold a feast." Kat smiled. "Tessa Novak, warrior woman."

That made everyone laugh and broke the tension.

"This is why I write for the fashion section." Lissy rubbed her pregnant tummy. "No one threatens to kill you for writing about handbags and wedding dresses. I don't know how you did it, Tessa, but you deserve to have your picture on the cover of *Newsweek*."

Holly smiled. "I want to hear more about Mr. Secret Agent Man. When are you going to see him again? And when do we get to know his name?"

"I don't know."

And just like that Tessa's spirits dropped a notch.

They dropped even further when her mother had to go work the three-to-eleven shift, reluctantly leaving her alone in her apartment. They dropped further still when a squad car arrived late that afternoon with her suitcases, retrieved from Julian's house, and her computer and files, which had been found intact in Burien's office. Amid the boxes the officers had carried up was one that held the espresso machine Julian had bought her.

She had expected her clothes and files. But the espresso machine?

Of course he sent the espresso machine. He bought it as a gift for you, and he's moving your stuff out.

She set it on the kitchen counter and went into her bedroom to unpack her clothes, a melancholy ache settling in her chest. Why it hurt so much Tessa couldn't say. They hadn't really been living together, after all. He'd taken her to his house only to keep her safe. It made perfect sense for him to send everything that belonged to her over to her apartment now that Burien was dead. And yet . . .

Some part of her had hoped. She'd seen the look in his eyes in the emergency room. She'd felt his tenderness when he'd held her. She'd tasted his fear for her. And she'd dared to hope that she meant more to him.

Hadn't he all but said as much? Yes, he had.

I thought I'd lost you, and it seemed to me the whole world had died.

It wasn't the same thing as saying he loved her, but wasn't it close?

Then again, he'd sat in this living room less than two weeks ago and told her he never planned on getting married.

Remember that part, Tess?

She hung up her bathrobe, found an unopened condom in the pocket, held it.

Warming Sensations.

If she were pregnant, would a baby change his mind? Would she want a baby to change his mind? Would she want him in her life knowing he hadn't stayed for her?

The answer scared the hell out of her.

She loved him. She wanted him nearby no matter what.

The phone rang, interrupting her thoughts.

She hurried out of the bedroom, hoping it was Julian.

It was Tom. "Glad it's over, Novak. When will you be back at work?"

DRESSED IN FULL body armor, Julian got into position, adjusted the weight of the HK MP5 submachine gun in his hands, and glanced at his watch. Two-twenty-eight a.m. After God knew how many years and how many lives and how much suffering, it would all come down to the next few minutes.

It had taken a team of FBI computer experts more than forty-eight hours of nonstop work to sort through Burien's files and uncover the locations of his cribs, stash houses, and strip joints. It had taken another forty-eight hours to mobilize, putting each location under surveillance and pulling together local cops, county sheriffs, state patrol, federal agents, and U.S. marshals for what was one of the biggest law enforcement actions in the history of the country.

It had been Julian's job to coordinate strategy. Involving eight states—Texas, Colorado, Utah, Arizona, New Mexico, Nevada, California, and Washington—Operation Abolish was synchronized down to the last second. In two minutes, law enforcement officers in more than a hundred cities would make their move, neutralizing anyone who resisted and setting victims of modern-day slavery free.

There had never been any doubt in Julian's mind where he would be when the action came down. Not only did he want to stay as close to Tessa as possible, he had unfinished business at Pasha's. He'd taken a position near the strip joint's heavily guarded rear exit, his biggest goal the safety of the girls inside.

He adjusted his earpiece, checked his weapon one last time, and waited for the clock to run out. As he listened to the final countdown, he felt like he'd been waiting for this moment all of his life. His pulse slowed. His senses sharpened.

Three . . . Two . . . One . . .

"Freeze! Police! Drop your weapons!"

It was over in less than two minutes. Overwhelmed both in numbers and firepower, Burien's thugs threw down their guns and whined like dogs. All except Sergei, who grabbed an AK—and got a round through the shoulder for his efforts.

"Chet, is that you?" Julian bending over a prostrate form on his way to the basement. "You look like you could use a drink."

"Tony? Tony Corelli?" Chet lifted his head. "You bastard! You played me!"

"Yeah, I'm a shitty friend. What can I say?" Julian moved on, shouting back over his shoulder. "And my name's not Tony."

One by one the suspects were searched, placed in full restraints, and marched to the police wagon that would take them to the Denver jail. Ambulances and victims' advocates stood nearby, waiting to take the girls to the hospital for evaluation and to help them get started down the long road to recovery—and home.

As Julian suspected, Irena and the other girls were in the basement, where they'd obviously been living. He found them huddled together, in tears and terrified, hiding behind an old, battered sofa. He approached them slowly, not wanting to frighten them further.

"It's all right. It's over. You're safe now." He said it first in English and then in Spanish, knowing that it would take time for his words to sink in. "No one is going to hurt you."

Irena met his gaze above the back of the sofa, pale and trembling, then gaped at him in amazement. "Tony Corelli?"

He heard gasps, whispers.

Five more heads slowly lifted, five sets of eyes staring at him in astonishment.

"My name is Julian. I'm a federal agent, and I came to get you out of here."

Shock turned to relieved tears and smiles.

Then, wearing only a T-shirt and panties, Irena stood, walked over to him—and planted a kiss on his cheek. "I knew you weren't like the other men. You never touched me."

The girls were soon wrapped snuggly in blankets, hope restored to their young faces, EMTs and advocates escorting them up the stairs and into freedom.

And as Julian stood there, at last wearing his own skin, it hit him.

It really *was* over.

CHAPTER 29

TESSA SLID HER key into the lock and let herself into her apartment, shaking her head at the masked trick-or-treaters who stood by her door expecting candy. "Sorry, kids."

Careful to lock the door behind her, she flicked on the lights, set aside her briefcase, and slipped off her shoes. Then she walked into the bedroom to change, wanting soft pajamas, fuzzy slippers, and mindless late-night television.

It had been a long, long day. She'd have been home hours ago if she hadn't joined the rest of the I-Team for dinner and drinks. They'd put the trafficking package to bed this evening, and everyone had been in the mood to celebrate—everyone except Tessa. Unwilling to drag her friends down, she'd joined them anyway and had done her best to have a good time.

There was so much to celebrate. She was alive and unhurt. She knew from her interview with Chief Irving that Julian had gotten safely through this morning's raid. She and her mother were getting reacquainted and were fast growing close. She had good friends, colleagues who cared for her and who'd been there for her. And her investigation was done.

It was the biggest package the *Denver Independent* had ever run, eating up half of the A section and beating Kara's pollution exposé by a full twenty inches. Tessa's first-person account of being held captive by Burien, together with her article about Operation Abolish, took up the top half of the front page, set off by a sixty-point hammer headline. The articles jumped to the inside, filling all of page three and part of page four. Sophie, Matt, and Katherine had written sidebars, Matt doubling as fact-checker.

It had been more draining to write the articles, to relive the horror of it, than Tessa had imagined. She hadn't cared this time when she'd gotten teary, hadn't felt embarrassed when Sophie had come over and hugged her, hadn't cared one bit when Tom had put his hand on her shoulder. She'd known even while she'd been writing that it was her best work to date, and she'd felt a deep sense of satisfaction when she'd finally sent the last file to the copy desk.

How strange it had been to write the stories and not once mention Julian. He was the driving force behind all of it. He'd pursued Burien for so long, had hunted him relentlessly, had sacrificed years of his life to bring the bastard down, but his courage and heroism were credited to anonymous "investigators," "experts," or "sources close to the investigation." He had saved so many lives, including hers. He had stopped a killer. But no one would ever hear of him.

Tessa slipped into her softest nightgown, dropped onto her bed, and stared at the ceiling, feeling utterly miserable. She knew she was going to be dealing with ragged emotions for a while—Kara and the victim's advocate had both warned her about that. But the feelings inside her weren't all due to her ordeal. Some of her moodiness was likely just hormones. She'd started her period this morning—right on time. As relieved as she'd been to know there'd been no innocent life inside her for the heroin to harm, she'd also been deeply disappointed. Having Julian's baby would have meant always having a part of him with her.

And that's what it really came down to—having him near. In the short time they'd lived under the same roof, she'd gotten used to waking up beside him, watching him get dressed, smelling his aftershave. She'd gotten used to sending him for groceries and cooking him dinner. She'd gotten used to reaching for him at night and feeling his arms close around her.

She could get along without him, of course, but only if she had no choice.

She hadn't seen or heard from him since late Friday night in the hospital. She'd hoped to hear from him today—a phone call, an e-mail, a text message. Still, she knew he must have spent every waking moment since he'd left her side working hard. To pull off an operation involving so many law enforcement agencies across eight states . . .

She couldn't imagine the effort that had gone into it.

Perhaps he was exhausted and asleep. Perhaps he wasn't finished yet. Or maybe he'd been called out of state. Hadn't he said that might happen?

I'll be back as soon as I can.

She'd held onto those words these past few days, clung to the hope they offered. He would be back. He'd said he would be back.

"You're being ridiculous," she told herself. "You know he's busy."

But knowing it didn't make her miss him any less. It didn't take away her uncertainty. It didn't stop the ache in her chest. One way or another she needed to know. Were they a part of one another's lives, or should she start trying to hack him out of her heart?

She closed her eyes, tears trickling down her temples into her hair.

TESSA MUST HAVE fallen asleep, because the next thing she knew her cell phone was ringing. She jumped out of bed, made a crazy dash for her purse, dumped it out on the floor, and grabbed her phone. "Hello?"

"I woke you." It was Julian.

A surge of pure joy rushed through her at the sound of his voice. "That's okay."

"I need to see you."

"Where are you?"

"Standing in the hallway outside your door."

She managed not to run the few steps it took to reach it. "What are you doing out there?"

"Trying to be patient."

Her pulse quickening, she unlocked the deadbolt and opened the door to find Julian standing in his black leather jacket, dark stubble on his jaw, his face lined with exhaustion.

He stepped inside, shut the door behind him, drew her into his arms. "God, Tessa, honey, I've missed you!"

"I missed you, too!" She buried her face against his neck. "I'm so glad you're safe!"

Julian felt emotion coursing through Tessa, held her tighter. "It's all right."

For a while they stood there, Julian reluctant to let her go. It seemed forever since he'd last seen her, last held her, last touched her.

It was she who finally ended the embrace. She took his jacket, hung it in the closet, offered him a cup of hot tea. Dressed in a silky pink nightgown, her hair tousled from sleep, she looked adorably innocent and feminine. But there were still bruises on her cheek—a reminder of how close he'd come to losing her.

"What are you doing out so late? It's nearly two a.m."

"I just got in from D.C."

Julian sat at the kitchen table and, like a coward, resorted to small talk while she set water on to boil. Uneventful flights both ways. Decent weather for this time of year. Lots of paperwork. "The feds make you fill out forms in triplicate every time you wipe your ass."

"The Federal Bureau of Obfuscation." She set two cups of hot water and several kinds of tea bags down on the table, a smile on her pretty face. But her smile didn't quite reach her eyes, and he could tell she'd been crying.

He couldn't blame her. She'd been through hell.

"It really is over, Tessa." He reached out, took her hand, and held it as he told her what had happened after he'd left her side—how he'd helped the tech team to interpret what they'd found in Burien's computer, coordinating with other law enforcement agencies, making sure provisions were made to care for victims at the scene.

She listened, asked a few questions. "When I read how many cities were involved, how many places, I couldn't believe that you'd managed it in four days."

"We had to move fast, before word got out that Burien was dead. Having his computer files made all the difference. Without those, we'd have spent months tracking down leads."

"Chief Irving told me you'd found María's three friends. I'm so glad."

Julian nodded. "One of our teams found them in Englewood. Their parents are on their way here to get them."

"Chief Irving says you deserve a medal. I think he's right."

"He says that about you, too." But Julian hadn't come here to talk about his job. "How did your article turn out?"

You didn't come to talk about her job, either, dumbass.

She took a sip of tea, set her cup down. "I guess we'll see tomorrow. I think it's solid. I hope it opens people's eyes."

Julian nodded, traced the silk of her knuckles with his thumb. "It will."

"All day I've been wondering what it must be like to have your life stolen—and then suddenly to get it back again." She looked at him through eyes filled with sorrow for other people's misery. "Think of the parents who learned today that the daughter they thought was dead is still alive. Think of the girls who are going home to start their lives over. I can't imagine it will be easy for them, but at least they have a chance. You gave them that chance, Julian."

"Tessa . . ." He stood, walked the length of the small kitchen, stopped, his back to her. "Jesus, I don't know how to do this."

"Julian?"

Just do it. Just say it.

"A month ago, if you'd told me Burien would be dead and his operation shut down, I wouldn't have believed you." He turned to face her. "I'd been hunting him for so long that the chase itself became my life. When he escaped, I took the blame. I thought my poor judgment had given him a break and gotten those agents killed."

She rose, walked over to him, slipped her arms around him, offering him tenderness as she always did. "That was Margaux's doing, not yours. I suppose it will take you a while to get used to that fact."

"Yeah." He kissed her hair, stroked it. "In a way, I feel like I'm starting my life over, too. I want to do it right this time, Tessa. I want—"

She stepped back from him, a tear rolling down her cheek. "There's no baby, Julian."

It took him a moment to understand what she'd just told him, and the intensity of his own disappointment took him completely by surprise. "You're not pregnant?"

"I got my period this morning." She gave him a shaky smile, another tear following the first. "You're free to build whatever life you want, to go wherever you want."

And then he understood.

He reached for her and pulled her against him. "No, Tessa, I'm not free. There's this little problem of how much I love you."

She stared up at him, eyes wide. "Y-you . . . what?"

"You don't need a baby to keep me close." His throat grew tight, his voice strained, raw emotion pushing through him. "I love you, Tessa. God help us both, but I do."

Tessa almost couldn't believe what she was hearing. She'd steeled herself for the moment he found out she wasn't pregnant, for the moment he told her his work in Denver was done and it was time for him to move on. She hadn't been expecting this. "Julian, I—"

He held a finger to her lips. "Do you know why I went to D.C. today?"

Had he told her? She tried to remember. "To fill out paperwork in triplicate?"

"Yes." He grinned, then his expression grew grave. "And to resign—for good. Irving offered me a position heading up his vice unit, and I accepted. Being a special agent doesn't go together well with trying to keep a pretty wife safe and happy."

Tessa's heart gave a leap, nearly broke through her chest. "What are you saying?"

He drew in a breath, looked at his feet, then back at her. "I know I'm no woman's idea of the perfect husband. I'm a convict and a killer. I've got a bad temper and no real education. I swear too much. I've got no roots, no family. Hell, I don't even know what family is."

Tessa touched her hand to his cheek. "You're strong, brave, protective—"

"So is a Doberman."

She started to object, but he stilled her again.

"I never planned to get married. I never even thought about it. But you touched me, Tessa. Somehow, you broke through me. You showed me something in myself I'd never seen before. You taught me what it is to feel at home. Do you know I'd never felt at home anyplace until you?"

"Never?" She couldn't imagine that.

"Never." His knuckles grazed her cheek, the look in his midnight-blue eyes achingly tender. "You burned through my life and changed everything. I love you, and if you'll give me a chance, I'll do my best to become the man you deserve."

"Oh, Julian!" Tears of happiness spilling down her cheeks, Tessa stood on her toes and kissed him. "You already are that man."

EPILOGUE

TESSA SAT ON the front porch with Kara, the two of them sipping southern sweet tea and watching their husbands discuss Monday's special Senate committee hearing, in which Julian was to play a major role.

"I chair the committee, so I'll introduce the bill and give you about ten to fifteen minutes to address the senators," Reece explained, looking anything but senatorial in a grubby T-shirt, cutoffs, and sandals. "Then I'll open it up to questions. It's hard to say how long that part of your testimony will last—probably half an hour to an hour."

In the aftermath of Operation Abolish and in response to Tessa's investigation, Reece had forced the state legislature into special session, introducing an emergency bill that would create a statewide human-trafficking taskforce, training law enforcement at all levels to address the crime. The bill also set aside funds for programs to aid homeless youth and to rehabilitate trafficking victims. It was a bold bill, and the *Denver Independent* had thrown its editorial weight behind the measure.

"Remember to address me as Mr. Chairman and to refer your answers to me," Reece added. "The other members of the committee are referred to as 'Senator So-and-So.'"

"Got it." Julian wore an old pair of jeans and an equally

grubby T-shirt, his hair loose around his shoulders, his expression serious. He looked younger these days, happier, the hard lines of his face seeming to have softened. "Will the hearing be open to the public?"

"Yes," Reece nodded, "and you can expect a media circus."

"He isn't nervous, is he?" Kara whispered, reaching for her hungry baby, who had begun to fuss in Tessa's arms.

Tessa gave four-week-old Brendan a kiss on his downy head and reluctantly handed him back to his mother. "Are you kidding? Julian's terrified. This is completely new to him."

She looked over at the man she loved, felt something swell inside her. So much was new to Julian. In the past seven months, he'd gone from living in the shadows to owning a home, from being a loner to having a doting mother-in-law and a circle of close friends, from having no love in his life to having a wife. He'd gone from special agent to police detective, and he'd done it more smoothly than Tessa could have imagined.

That's not to say there hadn't been problems. It was taking time for Julian to get used to making decisions as two people instead of just one. He was so protective of Tessa that it sometimes got on her nerves. He still swore too much. And then there was his tendency toward secrecy. Tessa could understand encrypting information about their bank accounts and credit cards. But their gym membership?

Still, Julian never let her doubt for a moment that he cherished her, proving his love in so many ways. In the kindness he showed her mother and Frank, who were getting married in June. In the respect he demonstrated for her unfolding career. In the way he listened when she needed to talk. In his skill with the espresso machine. In the way he made delicious love to her at night—and any other time of the day, if the opportunity arose.

Tessa hadn't dreamed she'd ever feel this content, so many pieces of her life fitting perfectly together. Although it had been hard to leave the I-Team, she couldn't very well keep the cop beat when her husband was a member of the force. Like Kara, she'd opted to go the freelance route, doing investigative articles for national magazines and writing nonfiction books. Working freelance made it possible for her to be home during the day, to arrange her own schedule, and to spend more time with Julian.

She spent no small amount of that time worrying about him. His job was still too dangerous to suit her. Late-night surveillance. No-knock raids. Too much time on the streets. But it was a far cry from the sort of soul-shredding deep-cover work he'd done for the FBI, and he seemed to enjoy it. He and Chief Irving butted heads fairly often, but he seemed to enjoy that, too. The two of them had grown close, Chief Irving becoming a kind of father figure for Julian, even standing up with him at their wedding. Of course, if Reece's bill was signed into law, Julian would spend more time training other cops than working on the streets—which was just another reason Tessa wanted it to pass.

But Reece and Kara hadn't come over on their Saturday just so that Reece could coach Julian on Monday's testimony. Reece was also here to help Julian paint the trim. Lissy and Will would soon be joining them.

The historic Victorian house they'd bought had needed a fair amount of work, and painting the trim and the old picket fence was the last of it. The trim would be finished today, and Tessa hoped the fence would get done soon. It was more gray than white, the paint having chipped away to leave splinters. Some of the planks had come loose and leaned sideways like crooked teeth. It would take a lot of work to repair it—far more work than to have a landscaper install a new one—but for some reason Julian insisted on keeping and restoring it.

Maybe Tessa could ask Kara to nudge Reece into offering to help.

"Probably most of the objections you'll face will be from senators who don't believe trafficking is a big enough problem in the state to warrant legislative action," Reece said.

Julian shook his head as if unable to believe such nonsense. "I think I can handle those objections with no problem. We both agree that Tessa isn't testifying, correct?"

Reece looked over at Tessa. "Are you all right with that, Tess?"

Julian met Tessa's gaze. "You're not testifying. I don't

want you to go through that again. You've been through enough."

Tessa had been a witness at several trafficking trials, including John Wyatt's. Having to describe her ordeal in the courtroom had reawakened her nightmares and left her feeling shaky for a week. "I'll do whatever you need me to do to ensure the bill passes."

Reece stood, walked over to Kara, and kissed Brendan on his fuzzy dark hair. "I think we've got it covered."

"Shall we get started?" Julian rose, glanced at his watch.

The men walked toward the side of the house—just as Lissy and Will pulled up in front.

"Slacker!" Reece shouted to Will. "We were supposed to get started an hour ago. Where've you been?"

Will grinned, helping Lissy lift the infant seat out of their car. "William didn't want to wake up from his nap."

"Sure," said Julian, "blame the baby."

While the men got down to the business of paint and ladders, Lissy joined Kara and Tessa on the porch, looking stunning in a designer sundress, ten-week-old William wide awake and sucking on a pacifier.

Tessa scooped the baby up, kissed his pudgy cheek. "You look just like your daddy. I wonder if you'll grow up to be a football star."

"So, Tessa, I can't help but notice the way you've been fawning over babies lately. When are you and Julian going to have one of your own?" Kara asked, Brendan nursing drowsily at her breast, his hands bunched into tiny fists.

"We're waiting." Tessa adjusted William in her arms. "As much as we both want a baby, we also want a little time together first. Julian's had to adapt to so many changes in his life. I didn't want to make it harder on him by having a baby too soon. In July, we're taking that trip to Ireland to meet his mother's aunt. We plan to start trying when we get home."

While the men painted and sweated in the late-spring sunshine, Tessa and her friends chatted and started making salads and other treats for supper. They were in the middle of a discussion about the nonfiction book Tessa was writing on trafficking victims—she and Julian had flown to Mexico last month and met María Ruiz's family—when Sophie parked her Toyota out front and she and Holly strolled up the walk, each carrying a lawn chair.

"We heard the guys were painting your trim today," Sophie said.

"You came to help." Tessa opened the screen door to let them in. "Bless your hearts!"

"Oh, no! We're not here to help. Are you nuts?" Holly unfolded her chair in the middle of the lawn and sat. "We're here for the scenery."

Tessa gaped at them, not sure whether to laugh or feel irritated.

Lissy looked out the window. "Are they ogling our husbands again?"

"Let's join them," said Kara, smiling.

Julian looked down from the roof to find five pairs of sunglasses staring up at them, as if painting trim were a women's spectator sport. "Are they always like this?"

"Yes," Reece and Will said together, smiling.

Reece pulled his shirt over his head, dropped it to the ground below. "Personally, I enjoy being treated like a sex symbol—especially by my wife."

"Think of it as an investment." Will took off his shirt, as well, displaying his football-player physique. "You'll reap the benefits in the bedroom tonight."

Julian grinned. "All right then, boys—let's work it."

He pulled off his shirt, picked up his bottle of water and drank, letting it spill down his throat and over his bare chest.

From below, he thought he heard Holly groan.

By late afternoon, the work was done, the mess cleaned up, and the tools put away. Steaks were sizzling on the grill, and the women had set out a cooler of cold beer and other edibles to tide them all over till dinner.

"I guess all you have left is that old picket fence." Reece took a deep drink of his beer. "It could use some sanding, a few nails, and a couple coats of paint. I can pop by next weekend, and we can take care of that in a few hours."

"Thanks." Julian let his gaze travel the length of the worn fence. "I'll handle it."

"Are you sure? It's no problem."

"Thanks, Reece, but it's kind of my pet project. I've been saving it for last."

Dinner passed with laughter and conversation, continuing until after dark. Several times Julian got an odd feeling that he'd somehow stumbled into someone else's happy life. It was a feeling he got a lot these days. But Tessa was there beside him, her presence, her touch, the sound of her voice grounding him, making it real.

They saw their friends off together, walking them to their front gate, Tessa's fingers laced with his, her hand silky and warm. As the cars drove away, she glanced down at the fence and then up at him—and her eyes narrowed.

"Kara says you turned down Reece's help painting the fence."

Julian nodded. "It's something I want to do myself."

"What is it about you and this fence?"

Julian drew her into his arms, tried to find the words. "I guess a white picket fence stands for all the things I thought I'd never have and didn't deserve—a home, a wife, a family. Now it's a reminder to me never to take a single day for granted."

"Oh, Julian!" Tessa sniffed, her pretty eyes misting over. "And to me it was only a splintery old fence!"

"Well, it *is* a splintery old fence, but it's *our* splintery old fence."

Julian held her in the stillness, drinking in her scent, savoring the moment—the distant hum of the city, a hint of summer on the mountain breeze, a lazy quarter moon overhead.

"You know that stunt you pulled this afternoon where you let water pour down your bare chest?" Tessa slid a hand beneath his T-shirt.

"Mmm-hmm." He nuzzled her hair, his blood heating up.

Finally they were getting to the benefits Will had mentioned.

She ran her fingers through his chest hair. "It reminded me that it's been a while since we made proper use of our shower massager."

"Honey, I think you're right. It's been at least a week."

"Come." She took his hand, led him back toward the house, its windows spilling friendly golden light into the night.

And Julian knew he was home.

Turn the page for a preview of the next
paranormal romance from Emma Holly

PRINCE OF ICE
A Tale of the Demon World

Coming November 2006 from Berkley Sensation!

IT WAS A balmy end-of-summer evening. Beauty veiled the outer city in a riot of trees and flowers. Corum, who had dispensed with his usual driver, piloted himself and his father out to the semirural compound of the Purple Crane.

Corum knew his father wouldn't believe his son had truly done this unless he saw it with his own eyes. This was why Corum had allowed his father to make the arrangements with Madame Fagin and why he sat beside Corum in the aircar now.

When Corum set the vehicle down on the landing site—a quiet click signaling that the antigrav had shut off—he knew he needed to explain his limits. He could not change his father's opinion of him, whatever it was, but it could only control him if he let it.

Determined not to do so, he turned in his seat.

"Sir," he said, and Poll Midarri took his hand off the door release. "I must clarify my expectations before we go in."

"Yes?" said his father, wariness and surprise mixing in the subtle lift of his brows. The reaction struck him as curious. Though Corum was aware he had not and probably would never win his father's full approval, that hint of caution positioned him on what his fighting teacher called the power ground. Whether his father knew it or not, Poll Midarri was, in this moment, deferring to his son.

The knowledge released some of the tension tightening his spine. He chose his words carefully.

"Sir, I would prefer that you let me handle the transaction from here. I understand your wish to witness this, but anything that needs to be said to Madame Fagin or the girls can be said by me. I hope you don't take this as disrespectful, but your comments are not required."

His father stared at him, his mouth gaping slightly before he shut it. "I begin to understand why those young men call you the Prince of Ice, and why opponents twice your age fear to face you in tournaments. You claim with self-possession what others have the nerve to reach for only in anger."

"Sir—" said Corum, abruptly fighting a need to apologize.

"No, don't spoil it." Corum's father allowed him a glimpse of his curving mouth as he turned to open the door. "I rather enjoy seeing you like this. And you may rest assured I'll honor your request."

Centering himself with an effort, Corum released his flight straps and flipped his own door out and up.

The instant he stepped onto the plascrete, he felt a change in the atmosphere. Trees surrounded the landing site, and stars had begun to glint in the sky above. As a soft, warm breeze blew his business robes against his body, he realized he was excited. His skin tingled with interest, his muscles tensing for some unknown action they wished to take. With his first full breath, his nostrils flared. The air smelled delicious, a whisper of foreign spices riding its currents. Despite his reluctance to be on this errand, every receptor in his body was acting as if his life began anew tonight.

Apparently unmoved by this phenomenon, his father was already heading down the neat brick path to the main house. Corum followed with an eagerness he tried to quell even as tiny hairs stood up on his arms. When a servant opened the door, his cock twitched and swelled. By the time they'd been led down the antique-laden hall, it stood so upright the head was brushing his belly.

Luckily, his voluminous outer robes would hide this, the

erection being too rigid to betray itself by moving. Corum fought a flush nonetheless. He didn't think his penis had ever been this hard, not even during his erotic dreams. He felt as if a heated poker had lodged between his legs, and his balls were pulsing and hot. The urge to gratify the ache was distracting. To have his sluggish libido rouse itself at this particular moment was simultaneously humorous and annoying. If he were not careful, in his current state, he'd be offering to buy the Purple Crane's entire stable—and fuck them all tonight.

"The girls are ready," said the servant, glancing in silent question from father to son. "Please peruse them at your leisure. Madame Fagin will join you shortly."

Given his private agitation, Corum hoped his father would remain outside. He did not, but at least he was silent as he followed Corum through the door the servant held open.

Behind it was a pretty tea-green parlor, lit softly—and flatteringly—by old-fashioned floating globes. No bigger than his fist, the colorfully painted surfaces cast a glow upon the line of five young women. They were dressed identically in gray silk robes. Each head was lowered, each pair of hands clasped demurely before its owner.

They all looked beautiful, but Corum could hardly think for the successive waves of lust now blazing through his body. Sweat had begun to trickle down the small of his back. The air seemed thick, heavily scented with the spice he'd caught a whiff of outside. Was Madame Fagin burning some aphrodisiac perfume? If she was, it was potent. He found himself unconsciously breathing deeper to get more of it. He shook his head, hoping to clear it and concentrate, but the effect simply grew worse. He wanted to growl at someone, to throw them to the floor and ravish them—or possibly just run from the room until these uncomfortable feelings dispersed.

His feet weren't interested in escape. They were leading him down the line of beauties, past two sisters close enough to be twins, past a startling blond girl, and one so slender he winced at the thought of any man covering her. And then he reached the last, at which point his feet refused to move again.

He couldn't have said exactly what stopped him, only that

he had to. This girl was shorter than the others and interest-ingly curved. Her breasts looked as if they would be heavy, and his fingers curled into his palms with a sudden need to test if they were. For the life of him, he could think of noth-ing sensible to ask her, though he suspected he ought to. In-deed, the only action he could conceive of was crushing her in his arms.

She began to tremble as he stood there staring stupidly, struggling against his body's even stupider urges. Her breath came shallower, and he didn't think she was simply nervous. Her body heat had increased. Beneath the heavy silk of her outer robe, he saw the tightening outline of her nipples. That sight did quite enough to him by itself, but as her temples be-gan to glow with perspiration, finally he knew.

The perfume that had been maddening him was hers. Mixed with her natural scent was pepper and orange and a hint of cloves. On further reflection, he realized it probably wasn't an aphrodisiac. Madame Fagin wouldn't have allowed one of her girls this advantage and not the rest—especially since it would have meant risking her license. It was just his bad luck that he really, *really* liked the smell this girl had chosen.

Before he could stop himself, he filled his lungs. This was a mistake. With the breath, a fresh bolt of arousal stabbed up his cock. His glans actually hurt from how tight it was.

He should have left then, should have known he wasn't think-ing clearly, but his slippers might as well have been nailed in place. He was staring so hungrily his eyes teared up. Her beauty was everywhere he turned: the soft curve of her cheek, the full, red mouth that made him want to lick his own, her generous breasts and hourglass waist. He loved the little enamel flowers trembling by her ear. Her hair was wonderful, too, glossy in its elaborate braided arrangement. He wondered how it would look down, that red-kissed black like garnets dipped in ink.

The words shuddered into a memory. *Garnets dipped in ink.* He knew who that description belonged to.

Except it couldn't be. The coincidence would be too great. He dared not even want to hope such a thing.

"This is Buttercup," said Madame Fagin, adding to his

confusion. "She is our youngest student. Perhaps you'd like to consider one of the older girls."

He had not heard the madame arrive. For that matter, he had forgotten his father stood behind him. It took a moment for her suggestion to register.

"No," he said as soon as it did.

The sound startled the young woman who could not be Xishi into looking up. At once, the room was too bright. He saw her face through a blur for one heart-stopping instant before she looked down again. Was it her? His gut seemed certain, but his mind questioned. A person changed in fourteen years. Memories faded. Could he really project her childhood features into today?

"This one," he said. He suspected it was reckless to be doing this but could not stop. In clear defiance of reason, exhilaration flooded him. "I will take this one."

"Very good," said Madame Fagin, pretending his voice had not been overly emphatic. "Shall we go to my office to discuss terms?"

Corum didn't want to leave. He forced his legs to move as his father considerately remained behind, honoring his earlier request. At the door, he simply had to look back. The slimmest girl was hugging the one he'd picked, but she barely responded. Over the other's shoulder, her eyes were wide and round on him. Was it recognition he saw there, or simply astonishment? His longing to return to her was appalling, and still he was unconvinced who she was.

This is desire, he thought, awed by the knowledge. *This is the secret I was asleep to before.*

XISHI KNEW AT once it was Cor. Despite strict instructions not to raise her eyes, she'd been unable to resist stealing a look at him as he walked the line. The resemblance was unmistakable. This was the same handsome Cor Midarri she'd watched win a holovised all-city tournament through a shopwindow. She would have known him even without the distinctive silver streak in his hair.

A strange, hot jolt flashed through her body at the recognition. She assumed it was due to the awkwardness of the situation: wondering if he'd know her, what he'd think of her choices, fear he might suspect her of presumptuous thoughts. By the time he paced slowly past Amaryllis, however, she knew embarrassment was not the only cause for her warmth.

The sight of him affected her physically. It was more than his good looks. Prince Pahndir was just as handsome, but Cor possessed a grace above the common run. Every step was perfect, every muscle of his face peaceful. His black and gold robes fell from impressive shoulders in precisely the manner robes should fall. Even his aura was restrained, a muted blue-white glow around his tall outline. He seemed the embodiment of yamish serenity and style, including being unreadable.

The flaming spirit she'd known when they were children appeared extinguished, yet she found this mysterious person he'd grown into just as interesting. She longed to rub against him as if he were a particularly sleek and independent cat. The strength of the desire surprised her. Their lessons had often been exciting, but today the flesh between her legs pulsed with an intensity it had never shown before. Moisture welled and threatened to run down. She wanted to coat his sexual organ in her cream, wanted to drive his hardness in and out of it. Most of all, though, she wanted to caress that unruffled smoothness until it turned ragged.

She wanted to torment him with wanting her.

Shocked at herself, she tried to check her emotions as he approached. She mustn't let him guess the wildness of her reactions. He paused in front of Tea Rose, and she immediately wanted to throw a bag over her best friend's head. She thought she'd die if he didn't choose her, but an instant later she thought she'd die if he did.

If this was what true desire did, she had been too quick to judge Prince Pahndir as weak. He was royal, after all, and his needs would naturally be more keen.

At the thought of *Corum* going into heat, a trickle ran down her thigh.

This, of course, was when he stopped in front of her. She

began to shake and could not will the response away. He was just standing there, staring, the warmth of his body increasing hers. It took all her strength not to fidget, for even the sight of his feet in their slippers was enticing. What could he be thinking? Why didn't he speak?

Madame Fagin came over and said something, Xishi's flower name, she thought. When Cor cracked out a sharp "no," Xishi positively could not keep herself from looking up.

As she did, a white-gold flash obscured her vision, whether from his aura or hers she couldn't tell. She looked down again, ashamed of her poor control, and heard him say he was choosing her.

Madame Fagin's predictions notwithstanding, she had never been so astounded in her life. She could barely think as Cor and the proprietress moved away, could barely respond when Tea Rose wrapped her in a gentle hug.

"How nice for you," said her friend, seeming to mean it. "He's very rich, you know, and terribly elegant!"

Cor paused at the door, allowing Xishi another glimpse of him. This time no light show interrupted. He *was* elegant, as polished and perfect as a frozen pond before skaters came. Perversely stimulated by his coolness, Xishi's insides throbbed with resurgent fire.

She honestly couldn't say if this was the worst moment of her life or the best.

PAMELA CLARE began her writing career as an investigative reporter and columnist, working her way up the newsroom ladder to become the first woman editor of two different newspapers. Along the way, she and her team won numerous state and national journalism awards, including the 2000 National Journalism Award for Public Service. A single mother with two teenage sons, she lives in Colorado at the foot of the Rocky Mountains. Visit her website at www.pamelaclare.com.

Debut romantic suspense from a
rising historical star.

EXTREME EXPOSURE

PAMELA CLARE

Sparks fly when a hardboiled reporter meets a
handsome senator. But a political scandal and
attempts on her life could drive them apart.
Or maybe adversity will draw them into a bond
even more intense than their
steamy sexual embraces.

0-425-20633-5